Hunter's Vix

R. T. Leader

Copyright © R.T. Leader 2023

The right of R.T. Leader to be identified as author of this work has been asserted in accordance with the Copyright, Designs and Patents Act, 1988.

This book is a work of fiction.

Names, characters, places and incidents are either a product of the author's imagination or are used fictitiously. Any resemblance to actual people living or dead, events or locales is entirely coincidental.

You hack everything down in battle...
God of War, with your fierce wings,
you slice away the land and charge
disguised as a raging storm,
growls as a roaring hurricane,
yell like a tempest yells,
thunder, rage, roar, and drum,
expel evil winds!
Your feet are filled with anxiety!
On your lyre of moans
I hear your loud dirge scream.

Like a fiery monster you fill the land with poison.
As thunder you growl over earth,
trees and bushes collapse before you.
You are blood rushing down a mountain,
Spirit of hate, greed and anger,
dominator of earth and heaven!
Your fire wafts over our land,
riding on a beast,
with indomitable commands,
you decide all fate.
You triumph over all our rites.
Who can explain why you go on so?

Lament to the Spirit of War
(Enheduanna, c.2300 B.C.E)

Prologue – Death of a Planet

The supermassive volcano spewed rock and ash high into the atmosphere, the horizon glowing red with violence and fury. Even here, a hundred kilometres away, the booming sound echoed through the canyon, and the shaking ground created ripples in the water.

Carving a channel through the canyon, the river had distributed boulders around its banks, eroding some to shale over the centuries. Clinging to the frigid rocks, green algae spread, fed by the nutrients from the ground and the mineral-rich water. Weak sunlight shone down the canyon, casting jagged shadows, through the rough-hewn cliffs. On all the boulders beside the river, slimy tendrils spread wherever the light struck, grasping and searching for every spot of energy the sun could provide.

When the cold, white sun dipped below the horizon, a brief period of rust-coloured dusk existed; and as darkness came, uncounted points of light punctured the uninterrupted night sky. On occasion, the irregular-shaped twin moons drifted across the star field, their luminescence reflected in the river.

During the hours of night, a single point – brighter than the stars around it – often rose from the craggy horizon. This heavenly body had a white-blue hue from the sun's reflection.

The intense heat from the volcano, which spread its black clouds high into the atmosphere, gave the landscape a fiery glow.

Despite this heat from the giant mountain, only at

certain points in the planet's journey around the sun would the temperature rise enough for the water to flow, spending most of the year in icy suspension. At these times, the life that struggled to find a platform ceased all cellular activity until the warmth returned.

Given a few million years, a speck of time in the universe, the slime on the rocks would evolve a consciousness; but it was doubtful it would ever become a sentient species. Life would always struggle here. To thrive, it would need a stable planet. It would need a warmer temperature. It would need a thicker, more oxygen-rich atmosphere.

A place existed nearby where this would be far more likely. One that shone brightly as a white-blue dot.

For a moment, life on this planet hung in the balance.

Time halted.

A critical point reached.

Then – as the dawn broke – its fate was sealed.

Deep below the surface, further than the molten heat of the mantle, the rocky iron core spun white-hot. The spin created the magnetic field, extending into space, deflecting the sun's radiation, protecting the planet. Universal forces worked. The spinning core of the planet slowly ceased to rotate. The magnetic shield surrounding the globe faltered and died, thrown off by a dead core. After a few brief years, the rotating ball stilled and was no more than an over-sized rock. It had barely been a moment in time - a tiny fraction of existence.

The great volcano stopped exploding; the water stopped flowing.

The slimy rocks browned. Life that had strived – so desperately – to establish itself, suffered its extinction.

Never to return in the timescale of the cosmos.

High in the atmosphere, below the orbiting twin moons, the air leeched into the vacuum, the sun's ionising wind scratching it away like sandpaper.

On the surface below, the water evaporated, leaving dry canyons and large areas of powdered desert. Wadis and flood plains remained. They scarred the ground with the branching channels, left behind for eternity as the liquid turned to gas and escaped into space.

The volcano, piled high above the cold plains, stopped booming - its pyramid dome casting its shadow over the cold deserts.

In the thin film of atmosphere that remained, dust devils flitted across the landscape for a few seconds before disappearing, and the whipped-up sand pounded the rocks. Smoothed boulders that once travelled along riverbeds, now embedded themselves in situ - a rubble-strewn field of desolation. Meteorites fell to the ground, the craters they formed unchanging over eons.

Frozen carbon dioxide at the poles capped the planet, and over millennia the iron ore in the ground oxidised turning the once blue globe to red.

Across the short gulf of space, this planet's neighbour - its white-blue twin – continued its evolution.

Part One: Singularity

"Life and Jah are one and the same. Jah is the gift of existence. I am in some way eternal, I will never be duplicated."

Bob Marley

Chapter One – Resurrection

I

Amy Hunter drummed her fingers on the console. The panels before her lit with a flashing array of buttons, but she was concentrating on the large red one.

"Do you mean to tell me, that after a year spent designing this lab, another year excavating this cave, twelve months building the power plant, and then another eighteen months building this – after *all* that time, *all* that effort, and *all* that expense - we can't even turn it *on*?"

Through the glazing, her voice echoed around the chamber beyond as it emerged on the loudspeaker. The large window took up the whole wall in front of the console, with laminated glass two centimetres thick. Around the edges, where it met the rock wall, reinforced rubber sealed it in place. To the right of the window, a revolving steel airlock gave access to the antechamber where they kept the white clean suits to keep the room beyond sterile.

John Hunter, his large frame filling out one of the overalls, stood at the top of a ladder. Equipped with a tool belt, canvas gloves, and face covering with sight protection visor, in his hand he held a welding torch.

"I just don't understand it," he said, into the transmitter in his visor. "Everything is connected, the cables aren't loose, and the cells are fully charged. There's just no reason it shouldn't have power…"

Amy sighed and looked at the computer screen in front of her. "It is saying that the batteries are fully charged, but when I press the button – nothing."

To prove her point, she slapped the red button several times.

John flipped the shield visor down and gave the power cable another blast from the welder. Sparks burst around him and turned his white suit blue before drifting down to the ground, four metres below.

The machine stood in front of him, cables emerging from the rear and disappearing into the rocky recesses where they fed into the circuitry of the underground laboratory. Ahead of the machine, stood on the other side of the glass, he could see his wife glaring at him. She folded her arms.

"You know that there is a table full of food getting warm in the sun topside?" she said, "Plus a very expensive bottle of bubbly. An hour you said, we've been here nearly three."

John turned off the welder and tugged at the cable. It did not budge.

"Try again?" he said.

Amy pressed the button on the console once again.

"Anything?" asked John.

"Nope," replied Amy.

"Are you sure?"

Amy threw her arms up - how many different ways could she say it. She addressed him angrily, "I should've listened to my father."

"Your father was not a nice man," said John. He hung the welding torch on his belt and started to climb down the ladders.

"But I should've listened to him anyway. This was our retreat when my father wasn't working and I wasn't at school. I spent my summers here when I was little."

"I know," said John. "You've told me this tale a thousand times."

"Mother used to tell me pirate stories," she continued, ignoring him, "She told me that this cave below the house was where they used to hoard all their stolen booty."

John reached the bottom of the ladder, flipped up his visor, and took a step back to look at the machine; casting his eye over the connections, he looked for anything out of place.

"One afternoon," Amy said, even though he was not listening, "I was probably only eight or nine, I came down here - on my own - to see if the pirates had forgotten about any treasure in the cave. The staircase down the cliff was just being built, so I had to climb half the way down. I thought I could find some pieces of eight, or an eye patch. As I got to the bottom, the sea spray had made the rocks damp, and I slipped and fell inside this cave, knocking myself out and spraining my ankle."

John shook his head; he couldn't see anything out of place. It was exactly as he had intended to build it, and all the cabling looked secure. Frowning, he scratched his close-cropped hair through the fabric with the tough material of his glove. Moving in front of the base of the machine, he padded over the concrete floor. Opening the inner door to the airlock, he stepped inside, and pulled it closed behind him. It hissed as the air pressure equalised.

"How long were you down here again?" he asked, humouring her, as he removed his belt, visor, and helmet.

"Hours," said Amy. "My parents had been searching for me during that time and were terrified that I'd fallen off the cliff into the sea. They had to get a boat from town to investigate, and heard me crying me as I came round."

John stripped the rest of his clean suit to his khaki shorts and black vest underneath and opened the inner door to the control room.

Amy, sitting with her arms folded and legs crossed, in front of him, looked down at her lap, reliving her memory, her white lab coat extending down to her knees. Her caramel blonde hair, tied in a rough ponytail from the crown, bobbed as she spoke.

"My father was very angry, although I think he was more relieved I'd not fallen to my death. He told me off and told me to stop filling my head with fancy stories. He banned me from ever coming down to these caves again."

She looked John in the eye and pressed the red button several times to emphasise her point.

"I think he was right," she said.

"Your father only ever took an interest in your life when he found out that his white, privileged daughter intended to marry a lad from North London with African heritage."

"My father was a busy man who travelled the world because of his job…," said Amy.

"Your father was a bigot who packed you off to boarding school, and then university, the moment your mother died."

"We shouldn't speak ill of the dead," said Amy. She knew he was right, but did not like to dwell on the flaws of her father. "If he'd not packed me off to University, I wouldn't have met you, would I?"

John smiled a little and reached into his toolbox next to the console. Selecting a ratcheted screwdriver, he gave his wife a playful glance. He pressed the button on the hilt of the screwdriver and it snapped up.

"Your mother, on the other hand, sounded like a lovely lady," he said.

"I used to love playing pirates when we were here."

John used the screwdriver on the rear console panel, pushing the end to release the screws with a bang. After removing the four screws, the panel fell open.

"I actually could believe that this cave used to be a pirate stash," said John.

"A lot of pirate activity used to take place in St Lucia," said Amy. "Lots of little inlets and coves to flee to."

John reached inside the wiring of the console and picked out a circuit board. He then reached back to his toolbox and selected a soldering iron. A small puff of smoke later and he held the circuit board up to Amy.

"X marks the spot," he said. A silver X-shaped solder had attached the loose wire to the board. He packed up the wires inside the console and reattached the panel. Placing the screwdriver and soldering iron back in the toolbox, he turned to his wife.

"Be my guest," he said, with a smile.

Amy hesitated for a moment, and gave him a knowing, intimate, smile.

Her hand hovered over the red button, and she paused for dramatic effect.

Then, closing her fingers, she brought her fist down.

A whine reached their ears from the clean room, and the console lit up with monitoring LEDs and digital displays. Through her chair, Amy felt the vibration as the machine powered up for the first time. As it became active, the surrounding air hummed, and the concrete walls shook with the energy surging through the circuitry. In the clean room, a beast of metal and wiring roused for the first time.

"It's alive," said John.

II

The Jamaican man offered the bowl to the sunbathing tourists, with a broken-toothed smile. The bowl, shaped from the leaves of the aloe vera plant, was one of many that hung from a sling around his neck. The couple were middle-aged, wearing ill-fitting shorts and T-shirts that exaggerated their belly rolls, and exposed snippets of skin where the white residue of poorly applied sun cream had stained the fabric. They sat on the sand, sharing a large beach towel with "St Lucia" written on it in large letters and framed with palm trees. Soaking up the heat given from the sun at its zenith, their reddening faces expressed irritation at the Jamaican man's presence as he attempted to sell his wares. Persistence was the key, he found, and sometimes they gave him money just to go away and stop bothering them. Not this time though. The sunbathing man grabbed the bowl, his flushed face adding to the over-exposure they were subjecting themselves to, and threw it away in the sand. It landed a few metres away, half-buried, just above the tide line.

The Jamaican man mumbled an insult under his breath and retrieved the bowl. The couple resumed their sunbathing, the woman glaring at him as he retreated from them, still muttering to himself.

The sling around his neck seemed a lot heavier today, and the sun seemed stronger. A hot sweat had broken out on his forehead below his long locks, the droplets merging and forming rivulets down the lines of his face. He had struggled to sell any of the bowls; it was not turning out to be a good day.

The hardened soles of his feet sank into the sand as he made his way around the cove, but he found his vision swimming. The swish of the tide along with the sound of the tourist's excited cries, as they frolicked in the shallows, reverberated in his ears.

Placing his hand below his loose vest, clutching the skin on the left of his chest, he inhaled deeply. He squinted up to the sun as it beat down, and wiped his brow with his forearm.

He needed shade.

Retreating from the beach, he found the nearest palm tree and sunk to his haunches, groaning as he did so, and unhooked the sling around his neck. Placing his back on the trunk, it felt rough and hard, but his head lolled back to rest against it and he closed his eyes.

After a few moments of catching his breath, from his sling, he produced a small silver flask. Unscrewing the lid, he took a sip of the rum. It tasted sour and stung as he swallowed, but he took another sip.

With his eyes still closed and the rum calming his nerves, he descended into a micro sleep where his regressing memories appeared.

Despairing on the dockside as the fishing boat departed port, leaving him abandoned on St Lucia… A dispute regarding his payment for overtime worked, leaving the captain sprawled over the rudder wheel whilst flexing his own, smarting fist… Laughing with his crewmates as the catch exploded out of the nets across the deck, the choppy waters of the Caribbean tossing everything around… A Jamaican police constable chasing him, during his late teens, after he had grabbed a handful of costume jewellery from a shop front. The constable's red-striped cap flew off as he dodged his outstretched arm and dived into the dock… His mother holding him at night in the light and warmth of an open fire, his father sitting opposite, the odour strong as his dark, brooding face red wreathed in the glow and smoke of marijuana.

His eyes burst open, the influx of memories brought moisture to his eyes, and he swallowed hard, despite the pain in his chest.

Reality came back into focus. Tourists and locals crossed his vision as they made their way along the beach. In the distance, boats seem to be floating in mid-air as the sea matched the colour of the sky.

He needed a rest, he thought. Take the day off, head back to his shack, have a smoke, and a little sleep. Chill out and try to stop that blood pounding in his ears.

He took another swig from his flask and winced.

III

Sitting on the wall at the bottom of the garden, John looked out over the Caribbean Sea, feeling the cooling stone through the seat of his trousers. Across the bay, tourist boats clustered around the base of the extinct twin volcanoes that drew people across the globe to St Lucia. The verdant double pyramid of The Pitons dominated the coast on this side of the island, rising from the sea precipitously, shaped like shark's teeth, their tips pointing to the sky. Gros and Petit Piton, the smaller was only around fifty metres shorter than its larger sister. A white mist lay around their shoulders, clinging to the trees and undergrowth, as John sat hypnotised by their beauty.

In the bay between the mountains and his garden, the town of Soufriere bustled with visitors and locals alike. The white steeple of the church was just about visible as it poked from the town centre. Surrounded by buildings painted in bright colours, the town was a tourist hub; and from his viewpoint, he could hear the faint sound of the diesel boat engines on the cool breeze, as they moored into the quayside.

John smiled to himself as he waited for Amy to emerge from the house. He had showered and changed after they completed their morning's work, and now wore a white linen shirt, with his brown trousers. Amy had said the shirt contrasted well with his skin tone, and she liked seeing him in it, on the rare occasion he changed out of his overalls.

He turned his gaze and looked across the terrace garden, a semi-circular space that hugged the edge of the hill where it met the cliff. Angular lawn areas mixed with blooming flowerbeds, fed with automatic sprinkler systems. A narrow pathway sat between these areas, which joined a paved patio area that ran the curved length of the wall at the back of the garden. In this paved area, they had set up a large fold-table with plates laden with food for their celebration. The smell of grilled fish reached his nostrils and made his stomach growl. Spotting the champagne when he emerged from the house, John had lifted the bucket along with a pair of flutes next to the wall as he waited.

At the apex of the wall, a gap opened to the staircase that descended the hillside to sea level. Zigzagging the twenty-five-metre drop to a small jetty, a combination of sun and salt had bleached the wooden steps. At the base of the staircase, a landing led to the jetty. Opposite, a wrought iron door opened into the cliff and provided the entrance to the cave that had now become their laboratory. The rusted hinges screeched whenever they opened it, and they kept it padlocked shut for security.

Across the terrace, the house glimmered in the sun. Resembling a Roman villa, whitewashed walls reflected the brightness, while the terracotta roof tiles shone in their curvature. Pillared verandas lined the upper floors that opened from the bedrooms, where they could take in the magnificent, beautiful vista.

As he sat, he kept his eye on the French windows for Amy. They gave access to the garden through the kitchen and indoor dining area on the ground floor. The front of the house matched the rear in style, although no verandas sat on the upper floors since it was mostly in the shade of the hillside that continued to rise beyond it. A large wooden front door was so heavy that Amy had trouble opening it at times and they framed it with potted ferns, giving it a somewhat colonial feel.

John had loved the house since the day he moved in with the woman who became his wife. It was her inheritance from her father following his death, in a car accident, on assignment in Saudi Arabia. Her father had the wealth to ensure the very best architects had built this property, which he had used as a holiday home during his life; and – given the spectacular view along with the sea access - sat in a very desirable part of the island.

Emerging from the house, Amy's hair, now released, fell over her shoulders and the straps of her dress, allowing the late afternoon sun to warm the skin on her shoulders and arms. She breezed over the lawn towards her husband, the printed blooms on her long skirt rippling.

"Here's my English rose," he said as she approached. She smiled at her husband despite her lifelong trait of being uncomfortable with compliments.

John lifted the champagne from the bucket, and popped the cork, liquid fizzing over his hand. Filling two glasses, he handed one to his wife and they clinked and took a sip. Amy left a little red lipstick on the rim as the bubbles fizzed.

Placing her glass on the wall, she got into a hold with John, as though they were to foxtrot. He held her back, holding her eyes with his, before placing a kiss on her glossy lips. She responded in kind, loving his gentleness despite his physicality.

"You ready for us to start celebrating?" she asked - a note of flirtation in her voice.

"I am," said John, "But let's eat first, I'm starving."

IV

The gears on the tiny Fiat ground together as it struggled up the dirt track. On either side of the road, plantain trees grew, mixed with the palms and tangled undergrowth. Many hillsides on St Lucia were dotted with residences, properties clinging to the slopes to afford a view of the beautiful coastline. On this, only two houses stood due to the steepness of the land and the denseness of the jungle.

Forcing the gear into place, Doctor Samuel Frankland made his way up the road towards his own home, which sat a few hundred metres further than the Hunter residence. He had travelled this route from the capital Castries to his home in the south of the island almost every day for forty years, through the familiar landscape of mountains and rainforest. His old car had served him well, and not liking waste, he was determined to drive it until the day it fell apart.

Just like his vehicle, he was starting to feel his sixty-seven years. He had a mind that it was time for a younger, fresher face to be the island's Chief Medical Officer. Time for him to retire. Enjoy his dotage on his island home. Sleep in each morning. Go for a stroll on the beach, or a game of draughts in Soufriere Park. These thoughts were starting to take hold, although he found it hard to accept that he no longer had the energy to do his work. Cancer had taken his wife just the year before, and with his son building his own life in Miami, he knew that loneliness had crept up on him. Retirement, as appealing as it sounded, also meant that he would not see his colleagues each day, delaying his decision until he felt ready to accept that age was hampering his work.

He rounded the corner, the Fiat's wheels kicking up the dust, and the sea came into view. Just up ahead, the Hunter's home appeared through the palm trees. Samuel had known Amy's father – whom he had met when construction started on the house back when she was just a child. As neighbours, they had been on friendly terms, but the house remained empty for many months of the year as he travelled for his work, and his family remained in England. Samuel exchanged perfunctory greetings whenever he did holiday on the island, but he had always seemed somewhat aloof and standoffish. Since his daughter had moved into the house permanently with her new husband,

Samuel had become more convivial with them; especially with John, who was more amiable. Nevertheless, they remained private, and this was despite the huge building projects they had spent years on. Deliveries of concrete and other seeming technical items had arrived by truck and boat for several years, and the constant sound of construction had drifted around the hillside to his own home. Since Samuel spent most of his time working, their project had not been too obtrusive, although it often started early and continued well into the night.

Curious about what they were doing for so long, with so much material going into it, he had enquired, in a neighbourly way, about their building work. The house itself never seemed to change, so something else must have been going on. They had told him (after apologising profusely for the noise and disturbance) that they were scientists and were building a laboratory in the caves below their home but offered no further elaboration.

Approaching their house, he expected to hear the usual work going on. He had the window open, and over the noise of the struggling engine, he heard music instead – classical music, upbeat and celebratory. The delicious smell of barbequed fish wafted from the rear of the house.

Smiling, he parked up on their driveway, just in front of the garage door. Stepping out of his car and into the sunshine, he went to the wrought-iron side gate and passed through it. After following a short path between the house and the palms, he arrived on their rear terrace.

"Well don't you two look like you are having fun," he said.

John and Amy were waltzing together on the terrace, a

vinyl record player spinning the music. Amy had champagne in her hand, and John was wheeling her around.

"Samuel!" exclaimed John as he saw his neighbour emerge from their garden.

"Sorry if I'm crashing a party, but this music is a lot different from the drills and hammers I'm used to hearing."

"Dr. Frankland, come in, come in," said Amy.

"Don't you look – different," said Samuel.

"It's not often you seen her out of her lab coat," said John, who came over and shook Samuel's hand.

"Or you out of your overalls," said Amy. "Come in Dr. Frankland, have some food with us."

"Please Amy, I told you to call me Samuel," he said. "But this is a veritable feast you are having here. Don't mind if I do."

John beckoned him over to the table laden with food and handed him a glass of champagne. Samuel took it and raised a glass to the couple.

"So, what exactly are we celebrating?" he asked.

"We've finished!" said Amy.

"Finished?"

"Finished all the building work," said John. "The lab is up and running."

The sunset cast its amber glow over the terrace, and the pips of nocturnal creatures becoming active emitted from the undergrowth. Samuel picked up a plate from the table and helped himself to the grilled flying fish, before grabbing the salad tongs.

"What do you intend to do in your new laboratory?" he asked, "You are both scientists?"

Amy took a sip of champagne and looked out across

the sea, reluctant to talk about herself.

"It's Amy that's the scientist – she's a theoretical physicist. I'm just an engineer."

"Just an engineer?" said Amy. "You designed and built it. You're making yourself sound like you're nothing more than a mechanic."

"*We* designed it, my dear," said John, giving her a wink. "I couldn't have done anything without your specifications."

"You've lost me. What exactly have you built?" asked Samuel.

"A machine," said John. "The cave area below the house is now repurposed as our lab. And in the tallest section of the cavern, we built a clean room which houses our collider."

"What does this collider do?"

"It's a particle accelerator," said Amy. "We speed up protons and smash them together, and see what comes out."

"Ah, like that device in Switzerland?" said Samuel.

"Pretty much," said John. "Although that's the Large Hadron Collider. And large is the word - it's massive. A huge loop nearly 17 miles long. We obviously have nowhere near that space in our little cave."

"So John designed this *new* type of collider," said Amy. "One that could fit in a confined space."

"What's different about it?" asked Samuel, sitting down at the food table. Grabbing a plastic fork, he realised how hungry he was after his day at work, and began to shovel the food into his mouth.

"By coiling the pipes where the protons are fired," said John, twisting his hand in a circular motion. "From the outside, these tubes look like thick coiled springs, surrounded by superconducting magnets. By coiling them, when we accelerate the particles, they loop around the coils faster and faster. Eventually, they loop around the coils millions of times a second. And then, we open up the collision chamber, and…"

John clapped his hands together.

Samuel placed down his fork and used a napkin to wipe his mouth. "This is all fascinating. And all this is taking place in your laboratory?"

John nodded. "It's been quite the project. We have no idea whether it will work, but the build is finally finished. That alone is cause for celebration."

"Now we have some tests to run," said Amy, "Calibrations mainly – making sure that the beams are travelling correctly through the pipes."

"This must require a huge amount of power," said Samuel.

"It takes three weeks for the power cells to charge sufficiently to run the superconductors," said John. "And you are right – the St Lucian energy grid is nowhere near sufficient."

"We would pretty much take up all the wattage of the island if we hooked up to the system," said Amy. "All the lights would dim whenever we used it."

"So we've gone off-grid and tapped into the island's other power sources," said John. "We have a few solar panels here and there – but they mainly run the lab equipment. Our main power source is from geothermal energy."

"Geothermal?" asked Samuel. "You mean from the island's volcanoes?"

"It was the first thing we built," said Amy. "The Earth's internal heat is very close to the surface here. We had to excavate some of the cave to get further down to where the super-heated gases are, but we built our energy plant that serves the machine alone."

"As I say though," said John. "The plant is always running, alongside the solar panels, we have here. They constantly charge the power cells where we store the energy required. And it still takes three weeks to build enough energy to run the machine for just a single collision."

"Incredible," said Samuel, as he filled his fork again. "That must have taken a huge amount of effort and planning. What is the purpose of this machine? What do you hope to discover with it?"

"It's been the goal of theoretical physicists to come up with a Unified Theory," she said. "That's a theory of space and time, and everything in it. I'm interested in the building blocks of the universe. Understand that, and everything should fall into place – hopefully. So by smashing particles together and seeing what they release, you get an idea of the very fundamental workings of physics."

"But isn't that the same goal as the one in Geneva?" asked Samuel. "Why did you come here when I'm sure you could've joined the scientific teams there?"

Amy stayed silent, and sat on the wall, staring out across the sea, smiling. John took up the explanation.

"The main issue is that to perform experiments with the LHC, you have lots of committees and people to go through before you can even get close to using it. Running it is a big deal and costs a lot of money. Here we are free to do what we choose, whenever we want."

John paused and looked over at his wife with a mischievous expression. "Is there another reason, Amy?"

She knew what he meant, and returned his gaze with one of her own. "According to John," she said, "I don't play well with others."

Samuel laughed. "You prefer to do your science alone?"

"Frankly, having to deal with suits and scientists – well they all have their own ideas and theories – and they are usually contradictory to mine."

"And she is something of a control freak," said John.

"I just like to do things my own way," said Amy, pretending to be insulted. "Here, I have the freedom to do just that."

Samuel lifted his champagne glass to his hosts. "Well, it seems congratulations are in order."

"Cheers," said John.

Amy held her glass up, and then drained it.

"So this machine you've built, does it have a name?" asked Samuel, placing his glass flute on the table.

Amy and John exchanged glances. Samuel caught it and looked at them with eyes wide.

"We've called it Vix," said Amy.

"Vix?"

"V-I-X – Vix," said Amy.

"What does that stand for?"

"It doesn't stand for anything," said John. "Vix is a nickname for it."

"You must've got the name from somewhere?"

John reached for a napkin and spotted a pen in Samuels's jacket pocket. "May I?"

Samuel handed him the pen, and John began to draw on the napkin.

"So at the top of Vix, there are two entry points where we introduce the hydrogen gas…"

John drew a couple of circles at the top of the napkin.

"…The chamber beyond removes the electrons from the gas and creates the protons. Below each of these entry points, the pipes coil around like springs as we accelerate the particles. These are surrounded by the superconducting magnets…"

Samuel felt a little lost with the technical details, but continued to follow John's drawing. From each of the circles, he drew two coiled lines in a V-shape below them.

"…And these meet at the base of the machine. Here is a pyramid-shaped collision chamber, with the wide bit at the top, and the point at the bottom…"

He drew a triangle at the base of the V-shaped coils.

"…The sides of the pyramid are covered in sensors that detect the output of the collision, but the base of the pyramid is where all the data is collected, and fed out. This was the first part of the machine we built."

He drew a straight line at the bottom of the triangle.

"This is the design of Vix," said John and handed the drawing on the napkin to Samuel. He took it and examined the picture, frowning.

"What does that remind you of?" asked Amy, her eyes fixed on the doctor, a glint of amusement in them.

Samuel looked at the drawing once again, turning it over in his hands. "I don't understand…"

"Come on Samuel, you're a doctor," said Amy. "You are familiar with anatomy, what does that look like?"

A dawning spread over the doctor's face.

"If you are comparing this to the human body," a certain blush came to his cheeks, "Well, it's crudely drawn, but it resembles female genitalia."

"Exactly what I thought when I first saw the blueprints," said Amy. "It reminded me of those drawings we saw in biology class at school – ovaries where the hydrogen is injected, the coiled fallopian tubes where the acceleration happens, and the womb where they collide. The very base, where all the data is collected, is the part of the machine we had to build first so we could get the correct specifications for the rest of it. So, right at the start, I called this bit the cervix, and over time we used the name so often, we applied it to the whole machine and shortened it to Vix."

"Vix, I like it," said Samuel. "It seems to fit."

"We think so," said John. "And in any case, it's stuck now. It will be known as Vix whatever we do with it."

Samuel looked at the drawing, tracing a line with his finger. "So these protons come in here at the top, travel down these coils, and smash each other in this triangle."

John nods back at him.

Samuel put the napkin down on the table and sat back in his chair, looking at the darkening sky.

"So when these protons collide, do they explode?" asked Samuel.

"In a manner of speaking," said Amy. "They collide with such energy that they smash apart into even smaller sub-atomic particles. Gluons, quarks – that kind of thing."

"Okay – then I'd like you to promise me one thing," said Samuel, a half-smile playing on his face. "When you are exploding the particles, please don't also blow up my beautiful island."

V

On a bower of palm fronds, the dog settled down for the night. The moon shone through the trees, and the sound of the tide came through the undergrowth to the dog's resting spot.

The dog licked the wiry fur on his back leg where a beachfront bar owner had kicked him that afternoon as he caught him going through the food waste bags, tearing open the clear plastic to get to the scraps inside.

Scavenging was how he survived, risking the ire of humans whenever he was caught. It was a tough existence, but the dog's hunger drove him to take chances.

As the chirruping of insects grew louder from the undergrowth, the dog ceased licking and his pointed head nodded. The swish of the nearby tide made his eyes heavy.

But then, a scent.

The dog's head snapped up, snout high, catching the smell of the breeze. His tongue flicked out and over his nose.

The smell was at once foul and yet familiar. Drifting in the air, distinct in itself, alongside the usual smells of sea salt and the aromatic scent of pollen rising from the vegetation.

Any opportunity for food was too valuable to ignore, even at this late hour. No humans were around at this time, so it should be safe to investigate, and the dog raised from the bed of leaves. Padding through the undergrowth, he emerged into the silvery brightness where the moon reflected from the calm sea. His paws barely sunk into the sand as he followed the scent up the beach, leaving a trail of quad-toed footprints. Pausing briefly to sniff and then cock his leg on a plastic beach chair, he moved his nose around to get the direction of his potential meal before trotting further down the beach where the smell was stronger.

The breeze caressing over the sand carried the odour down the beach, but further, it changed direction and retreated into the thick undergrowth. Sniffing, the dog found the scent almost overpowering as he reached the line of palm trees and ferns. A faint path existed here – just a thin line trodden through the plants and into the gloom.

Leaving the dappled light, the dog descended into the darkness of the path - overcoming any caution. The trail wound its way through the undergrowth, brushing the light brown fur on his flanks, following the sickly sweet smell.

Emerging into a small clearing, ringed by trees, ferns, and wide fronds of aloe vera, stood a shack. Highlighted in moonbeams and made from corrugated iron, supported by loose wooden planks, it looked like it could collapse at any moment. The dog halted and eyed the structure, his front paw hanging in the air. The smell was overwhelming and drifted from the opening – which was no more than a thin sheet of rusted iron leaning against a gap in the wall.

This shack belonged to a human, but that other smell was making his mouth salivate. He couldn't detect any of the usual human scents, but the organic stench emerging could obscure that.

The dog's curiosity and hunger drove him toward the entrance, and he inserted his snout and paw against the sheet of iron to gain entry. After a moment, the sheet fell over, clattering against the ground. The dog shrunk away from it for a second, spooked by the noise, but then the calm of night fell once again.

The dog padded through the doorway, placing each paw softly in the concrete, poised and ready to flee at any threat.

Inside, the silver light of the moon punctuated the darkness where it found gaps between the loose-fitting walls. Panting due to the stifling heat, a few tiny insects investigated him, buzzing in a light cloud around his snout. In the dim light, shelves stacked with aloe vera bowls sat next to a large Jamaican flag. Strewn across the floor were empty cans, bottles, and cigarette butts.

With each tentative step, he sought to find the source of the smell. It was much more powerful in here and seemed to be emerging from the rear, shrouded in shadow. As he stood contemplating the darkness, he could just make out a silhouette, and he took a couple of hesitant steps toward it.

On a mattress placed on the floor, surrounded by empty glass bottles, lay the body of the Jamaican man. Death had not arrived peacefully. The eyes closed, and his head had lolled to the right side. Pale skin, streaked in dried sweat. The legs had kicked out from the mattress, with the left stuck at an awkward angle beneath the right. The vest and shorts were still damp, attracting the insects, some of whom were crawling over the exposed skin. His right hand, gripped by rigor mortis, still held the silver hip flask.

The dog stood and looked at the shape, sniffing the air for any danger. After a few moments of stillness, satisfying himself that the body posed no threat, he investigated a nearby can of beans, licking the scraps of food from inside. He placed his paw by the side of the can for purchase and flicked his tongue around the interior.

The shack became very still. The flies around the body stopped buzzing and disappeared.

The dog's head flicked up - the hairs on his neck raising. Issuing a low growl, his eyes, nose, and ears searched the room for the source of this perceived threat. It was just a sense, a feeling, and it seemed all of nature in the room had felt it too.

The bark echoed through the shack, directed at the body of the man who sat in a tableau of death. Spooked, he shoved his tail down between his back legs, and his paws scrabbled over the flooring, toward the exit.

It fled, bursting out of the entrance, and ran back through the vegetation.

In the shack, the cadaver remained sat in position, but the atmosphere around felt charged – an expectancy for the potential yet to come.

A lash twitched a fraction.

The heated, sweated firmament thick with anticipation – an invisible but voltaic latency.

Suddenly, the man's chest heaved towards the roof of the shack. It hung for a second, spine bent unnaturally, and then relaxed back down. The chin rolled onto the chest, and the eyes remained closed.

Stillness for another few seconds.

The chest heaved upwards again, followed by a huge intake of breath – wheezing and rasping into the lungs - a drowned man gulping air.

The body relaxed.

The crooked legs straightened, and the foot flexed at the ankles, toes bending downwards. His fist opened, the finger bones cracking, and the hip flask clattered on the floor.

Deeper and deeper, the chest rose and fell. The head swung from side to side, building enough momentum for it to complete a circuit of the neck and shoulders, the cracking echoing around the shack. His head stopped moving but remained erect and supported.

Taking a few deep breaths, the brown eyes opened.

After taking in the dank surroundings, he turned his gaze onto himself – inspecting his arms and moving down to his hands, watching as he made fists and released them. His legs bent at the knee and his feet went below him to support his weight. He used his hands to walk up the wall behind him, pushing himself into a standing position.

In the half-light, his face caught a moonbeam, and his irises reflected red as he continued to scan the shack, taking in the green-leaved bowls, the green and white flag, and the detritus on the floor. Wiping a hand down his bare arms, a layer of sweat grease covered it.

He took a step forward – it was hesitant, and then put another foot in front. The silver light streamed from the entrance, and he made for it, stumbling a little but maintaining his balance. Putting a supporting hand on the wall beside the entrance, he looked outside at the surrounding trees and undergrowth, light creating patterns on his face.

Escaping the hovel, his bare feet sinking into the sandy soil, he paused in the clearing. Looking up, the waxing moon shone brightly, causing him to squint as the light penetrated his irises. He heard the hush of the tide, and turned his head in the direction of the shore. Spotting the same path between the palm trees and ferns that the dog had taken, he left the shack behind. The undergrowth slapped his face.

Emerging onto the platinum sand, he did not stop, his feet propelled him until they hit the tide line and the sand became wet and sticky.

Wading into the surf, the cool water first covered his ankles and rose up his thighs as he pushed on. A wave rolled over him and submerged his lower body until the water came up to his hips. He did not gulp air before he dipped his head below the waves, his locks floating like seaweed on the surface, but he remained underwater for several seconds, a stream of bubbles coming from his nostrils, before he re-emerged, salt water streaking down his face and body.

He looked up at the moon once again.

Spreading his arms wide, he let out a low, guttural cry.

Chapter Two – Feelings

I

The town of Soufriere bustled with activity. John and Amy, hand in hand, emerged from the blue-and-white-fronted supermarket, which sat on the road opposite the quay. They dodged tourists who delved into the racks selling postcards, inflatables, and cheap plastic toys. John and Amy bought their groceries at this shop each week, and the teenage girl who ran it with her mother followed behind carrying the brown bags to their waiting car.

The harbour lay in the shadow of the Pitons, the natural bay surrounded by green-covered mountains. Azure waters lapped against white-hulled boats as they disgorged more tourists - carrying expensive cameras and pointing at the conical peaks. Further, along the front, a swathe of grass, with tree-shaded benches, where the locals sat looking out over the shored barrier of stacked rocks toward the sea.

"Thanks, Kath," said Amy as she loaded the last of the bags into the Range Rover. The girl nodded and smiled, before disappearing into the pleasant, air-conditioned coolness of her shop.

John removed his Panama before entering the driver's seat, with Amy sat on the passenger side. Before starting the car, he wiped his forehead with a pocket-handkerchief.

Turning over the engine, he cranked up the cool flow from the vents.

"It's a scorcher today," he said.

"It is," said Amy. She seemed more able to take the hot temperatures during the summer on St Lucia. Having spent a large part of her life on the island, she had built up a tolerance.

John checked for vehicles in his mirrors and waited to pull out onto the carriageway. The cars had backed up along the harbour due to the number of tourists crossing from *The Pride of the Pitons,* the sizeable, multi-decked pleasure craft that was a daily visitor. The slower pace meant that nobody ever seemed to be in a rush, and John and Amy accepted that it was part of life on the island.

Once joined, the carriageway turned into the street leading to the centre, alongside the garden area, which stood in front of the church. The locals used this area to gather news and gossip, especially after the Sunday service, and it was the focal point for the town. Amy liked to sit here by herself on occasion, whenever she needed to wind down and be by herself, and gaze up at the mountains.

John drove at low speed past the church, still sweating profusely despite the air conditioning. "I don't know if I'll ever get used to the summer here," he said. "I'll be glad to get back into the cool lab this afternoon."

"That's because you've spent most of your life in Watford," said Amy. "It doesn't often get this warm there."

"Give it a few years," he said. "With all this climate change, even the streets in Watford could be lined with palm trees."

After a short journey through the outskirts, he turned onto the road that led out of the town. A few metres later, the tarmac gave way to the dusty road that led up to their home.

"Now the chores are done, what's the plan for this afternoon?" said Amy. "We looking at the calibrations?"

"That's the plan. I suspect that the beam might be out by a few microns – we'll need to check before we do our first run."

II

Looking up at the blazing sun as it rose over the mountainous interior of the island, he spent a few moments staring at it before the overwhelming brightness turned his vision white, and he used his hand to shield the glare. It took a few moments for his vision to return.

"Mani," said a voice up ahead. A voice thick with patois. "What you doin' up here? You're usually down beachside?"

The voice came from a hut just up ahead, where the road took a sharp bend to the left. The building was no more than a shed with an awning, decorated with a colourful menu that featured pictures of soft drinks, ice creams, lollies, fruits, and water. The local who spoke to him sat on a plastic chair in front, selling his refreshments to passing drivers. He wore a baseball cap with the outline of St Lucia on it.

He continued walking, hoping to ignore the roadside seller, who looked at him and spread out his arms questioningly.

What was that name the seller had called him?

Mani?

Memories in this mind. A mother, back in Jamaica. She was the only person who called him by his given name – Herman. Everyone else, even his father, had shortened it to Mani. He'd adopted the moniker from an early age and introduced himself to everyone as such.

Very well, his name was Mani.

He walked past the roadside seller, not looking at him or acknowledging his existence. The seller noticed that Mani had taken off his vest and had slung it over his shoulder. The yellow vest looked heavy as he used it to carry several items, including a large bottle of water poking out of the top. The seller stared at him in confusion as his friend continued to ignore him.

"Hey, Mani – what's up, man? You off somewhere to sell water?"

Mani stopped and looked back at him over his shoulder. Fixed him with a stare, but said nothing. The seller stared back for a few seconds, disconcerted at this change of character. A few moments later, Mani broke the stare and continued on his way up the mountain.

"Mani, you been smokin' too much of your stash, man?" the seller shouted after him as he disappeared into the undergrowth around the corner.

III

Amy led the way down the steps that led to their laboratory, and John followed, checking the news on his smartphone. They had donned their white lab coats ready for an afternoon of tests on Vix ahead of their experiments.

The wooden staircase zigzagged down the side of the cliff face to sea level below them, fixed onto the rocks by concrete piles. When her father built them, he also added the landing stage in front of the cave, which extended out into the sea as a jetty. John and Amy now had a small inflatable motorboat moored.

As they reached the landing, John opened a news story

on his phone.

"It looks like there's a hurricane brewing over the Atlantic," he said.

"It's the start of the season, it's to be expected," said Amy. She was ahead of him and fishing out the lab keys from her pocket.

"This one's going to be a big one. At least category three."

"Is it coming anywhere near us?"

"No," said John, "It's not expected to. It seems to be tracking north-westward towards Cuba and the Gulf. Maybe reaching Louisiana or Florida, depending on conditions."

"It's rare we ever get one here, so far south," said Amy. She took out the keys, several of them for around their home, and selected the cave door padlock from the ring. "I've never known one hit full on here in my lifetime, a few tropical storms – but not a full-blown hurricane. The natural spin of the Earth means they tend to move towards the Gulf."

"The Coriolis Effect," said John.

"That's the one," said Amy, and she unlocked the padlock before pulling back the metal latch.

IV

Mani spotted a potential place for shelter from his vantage point, hidden between the dense foliage and the scattered volcanic rocks. Climbing high into the central region, he needed somewhere that would offer more protection than his shack. Amongst the scrubland, the centre of St Lucia gave way to rocky outcroppings and slopes. Just below where he stood, he could see a large boulder jutting out from the hillside, a huge rounded rock ledge – weathered and covered in moss, but at its base, it curved back inwards creating a lip over the ground below.

Mani slipped down the hill, careful not to spill the goods inside his vest carryall, to make a closer inspection. The stones and shingles fell around him in a small landslide, but he kept his footing despite the sharpness of the gravel digging into his feet as they found the gaps between his sandals.

He stopped just outside the low, narrow entrance to where the rock receded into the hillside but found it blocked by winding, thick-trunked brambles; their thorny vines twisted around themselves. He looked between the brambles into the darkness beyond, and then turned and looked out across the view of the island. The slopes ahead descended in green, rolling tides until they met the cerulean waters, where wave peaks sparkled in the sunlight. It was a decent vantage point and was far enough away from any curious eyes.

The brambles prevented him from reaching the metre-high gap between the rock and the ground. They would tear into his skin if attempted to squeeze through. Reaching into his pack, he produced a pair of gardening shears that he had used to make the aloe vera bowls - long flat blades, rusted and blunted by years of use. Placing the scissor between the woody stem of the bramble, he put what strength he had in his hands to squeeze and bear down to try and split the branch.

It barely sliced into the surface.

He placed the shears back in his pack.

Reaching out with his hand, he touched a leaf between

his thumb and forefinger, and closed his eyes. The leaf began to brown. A second later, the thick woody branches began to break down, crumbling into tiny particles. Withering to dust as the infection spread through the stem, the branches, and the trunk. As he stood, the whole plant dissolved into brown powder. The fine particles caught the breeze, and drifted away.

An expression of cold satisfaction passed his face as his way to his chosen shelter, now cleared, opened up before him.

Placing his hand on the overhanging rock, feeling its warmth as it soaked up the mid-afternoon sun, he ducked his head down to look inside the gap it left. It extended about four meters and was flat: dry, brown earth, free from any vegetation. Feeling a crawling sensation on his hand, his head snapped up and he saw a line of ants crossing over it, following a straight path from the rock. He took his hand away and wiped them off, with an expression of disgust.

Throwing his pack inside the low cave, he sunk to his knees and entered himself, on all fours.

In the gloom, he found the bare soil beneath him was cool to the touch, and little air flowed in through the gap, sheltered by the rock above his head, and the surrounding flora. The space opened out a little – just enough for him to sit upright – but his long hair skimmed the rough, rocky ceiling. Mani sat back against the rear wall and ran his hand down over his locks.

He opened his vest and removed several bottles of water, some candy bars, and some plantains he had picked from the trees during his morning journey from the coast. He laid them down next to him, as he would need their sustenance in the days to come. Next to these lay the shears and he picked them up.

Pulling his hair at the roots, he began to chop.

The hair that had been with him throughout his whole life, cultivated as part of his culture, now meant nothing to him.

The braids were just in the way.

He sliced them off aggressively, scraping his knuckles on the ceiling of his shelter, and the hair fell to the earth in clumps, before he continued with another handful. For several minutes he continued, patiently and methodically moving around his scalp.

The final braid was at the back of his head, a single tail falling down his back. He yanked on it with his left hand, and manipulated the shears with his right, practically pulling the hair out of its roots. It came free with a tug and joined the other mound of hair on the floor around him. Hastily, he brushed the hair outside of the cave to let the breeze disperse it.

Running his hand over his scalp, his cutting had not been a tidy job - his hand ran over bare skin and patches of hair. They clumped in short, misshapen bunches on his head.

No matter, he thought, his appearance wasn't important. It would do for now.

Through the gap in the cave, he looked out across the island and to the sea, his eyes reflecting red as the rays invaded the shelter. Abhorrence for this patch of land emerging from the ocean surged through him. Searching through the memories, through each synapse, brought no indication of reasoning, just an overwhelming desire to cause destruction. He felt frustration at this vague and blind hatred and wondered how much of this emotion emerged from the chemical and electrical reactions taking place in the physical connections of his brain. Regardless, his only purpose now was to stop whatever it was that was causing these feelings.

His view looked north-eastward across the deep Atlantic, and the endless blue sky. Drifting his gaze onto the far horizon, where it was lost in a haze, he perceived the curvature of the planet. Beyond his visual range, he *felt* the earth around him, and where it met the water. Above, he *felt* the atmosphere. Its movements, its thermal changes, its flux. That region was where he held his concentration – where a great and powerful natural phenomenon was occurring, just beyond the horizon.

In the cave, he laid his back down on the cool floor, propping himself up on his elbows for a moment. Then he put his head down, arms by his side, and closed his eyes.

Chapter Three – Harriet

I

John grabbed a nail from between his teeth and placed it against the wooden plank. Hammering it into the wall, the noise echoing around the property, he covered the final spot of glass on the front window. Behind the ladder, Amy retrieved another bag of sand from their parked Range Rover and entered the side path to the rear terrace. She struggled with it a little, carrying it with both arms.

John punched the wooden planks over the window with the bottom of his fist, ensuring its solidity, before stepping down from the ladder.

"You want me to help you with that?" he asked.

"I can handle it," she said, the sweat noticeable on her brow. She disappeared down the path, but not before flashing him a smile.

As he climbed down the ladder, Samuel appeared in his Fiat, driving from his property and heading towards town. He halted the car and wound down his window.

"That's good work you are doing," said Samuel, looking at John's handiwork with the planks over the windows. "Thankfully I've got wooden shutters over mine, but I've still secured them together."

John nodded a greeting and wiped his hands on his overalls, covering his eyes to see the doctor against the glare of the sun.

"Sounds good, Samuel," said John, squinting in the sunshine. "It's hard to believe what we are in for, isn't it, when we are having weather like this."

"It is," said Samuel. "I was a teenager the last time we had a full hurricane. Not a pleasant memory. They are calling this one Harriet. Seems too pretty a name for what is coming."

"You know it's serious when they give them names," said John.

Amy returned from the terrace, wiping her hands on her overalls, and nodded a greeting to their neighbour.

"It's a long time since we've had one," Samuel continued. "I hope the island is prepared."

"Such a strange set of circumstances," said Amy. "I was looking at the weather data earlier on the World Meteorology website. They were expecting Harriet to move north-westwards as usual, but a formation of several high-pressure areas in the mid-Atlantic have blocked it, forcing it south-westward in our direction."

"And they reckon that since it has spent so much more time over water, it will be at least category four, maybe even five," said John.

"We have to prepare for the worse," said Samuel.

"What are your plans?" asked Amy.

"There's a concrete shelter in the middle of the island, just north of Vieux Fort, surrounded by mountains," said Samuel. "It's normally a recreation centre, but they are shoring it up and filling it with temporary beds. Food and water are being rationed, and there's a fuel generator on site in case of power cuts. It seems the safest place to be."

John nodded. "That seems sensible, away from the coast. The mountains should offer some protection from the worst of the winds, although I suspect nowhere will be completely safe."

"Are you joining us?" asked Samuel.

"No," said John. "We've decided to try and sit it out here."

"Really," said Samuel. "I'm surprised. I would've thought you'd leave the island, and fly off somewhere else. Although the last plane left an hour ago. Are you not even going to a shelter?"

"We're concerned about Vix," said Amy. "We're hoping we can make running repairs during the storm."

"Forgive me, but I don't think you fully comprehend the power of the storm that's approaching,"

"We've never experienced a hurricane, that's true," said John. "But we've made the place secure, and we've found a spot – right at the centre of the house – which is our larder. The walls are made of concrete and stone, strong enough to withstand a battering. We've stocked enough food and water to last days, and have torches and candles should the worst happen. We've placed a mattress and bedding on the floor too."

"Even so, it seems pointless to stay and try and make repairs. You'll have no chance of doing so until the storm passes."

"We're not planning to do anything until Harriet subsides," said Amy. "But we need to make sure our lab doesn't get flooded."

"Any sea water in the lab from the storm surge would ruin all our work," said John. "We've shored it up best we can, but the lab itself is just below sea level – so any water that gets through the cave entrance will travel into it."

"If it gets into the clean room, it could contaminate Vix," said Amy.

Samuel shifted on his feet, not comfortable with what they were proposing. "You're aware how unpredictable hurricanes are."

"We're willing to take our chances," said Amy. "We've spent the best part of five years, and pretty much all of my inheritance, developing Vix and our lab. We're not about to see it go to waste in the space of a few hours."

"I'm not sure we could continue with our plans if the lab gets damaged," said John. "Plus the storm itself will approach from the East – that side of the island will see the worst of the storm surge and the winds. Fingers crossed we should be protected a little here on the leeward side."

"The power of this storm is like nothing we've ever experienced," argued Samuel.

"Thanks for your concern," said Amy, folding her arms. "But our decision has been made. We'll take our chances."

Dr. Frankland realised that he could not persuade them to the shelter. He wasn't even sure himself whether his sanctuary would hold up in the maelstrom to come, so attempting to talk them around may be leading them from danger and into danger. Best to rely on what you believe yourself to be the wisest course of action; and pray that when nature strikes with its full fury, it sends its ire away from you.

"I hope that you are right," he said. "I hope that we are all lucky and come through this on the other side."

John stepped over and shook the doctor's hand. "Stay safe, Samuel," he said.

Amy walked over and hugged him through the open window of his car. "In a few days this will all be over," she said. "We'll have a drink and shake our fists at the sky."

Samuel laughed. "I hope you're right," he said.

II

Standing on the terrace, John sipped a mug of tea, gazing across the sea to the horizon. It was late afternoon and the sun burned red, sinking through a sliver of dark grey cloud. The air seemed to be dimming in varying hues of black. Taking another sip, he looked at the growing tempest grim-faced.

He had never questioned the decision they had made to come to St Lucia. It seemed a dream come true for him, to spend his days on a paradise island with the woman he had fallen in love with, making plans to pursue their fascination with the nature of the universe. Recalling, as he stood drinking his beverage, the years of toil and expense it had taken them to realise their dream; all the time maintaining the hope they had of contributing to the work of scientific understanding.

Forces of nature were now conspiring against them and the irony was not lost on him.

Looking over the stone balustrade, he could see that the usual pure blue of the sea now reflected the dullness of the clouds, and it had become choppy. Countless ridges and troughs bobbed, and the wooden jetty had become damp with the sea spray. Further, along the coast, the waves crashed against the harbour in Soufriere; the town deserted due to the evacuation.

Feeling the breeze as it cooled the perspiration in the back of his neck, the humidity felt oppressive. He felt damp and sticky, like standing in a sauna; but a sudden gust made the palm trees hiss, and he hugged himself as he watched the wide branches sway.

He drained the mug, and Amy emerged from their boarded-up home. She said nothing and just looked at John in silent communication. Catching her stare, he cast his eye over the house, the windows covered with planks, and sandbags shoring up the doorways.

He hoped it would be enough.

III

The terracotta flooring of the larder was just large enough to fit a double mattress. They had covered it with a duvet and several pillows but found themselves lying on top of it due to the temperature, which seemed to seep through the gaps in the doors and walls. They had switched off the electricity, and instead relied on a handful of candles, sat on the food-laden shelves, to provide a flickering glow of their surroundings. They had two battery-powered torches but wanted to save their charge in case of an emergency.

Sitting upright, Amy ate a packet of crisps as she listened to the sounds from outside anxiously. John lay beside her, his arms around the back of his head, attempting to relax.

For a couple of hours, they heard the wind outside rising from a gust to a shrill whistling, growing in intensity to a noise that Amy thought akin to a jet engine at the moment of take-off. Rattling and creaking, the structure strained against the storm, the wind itself trying to uproot the house from its foundations. They heard the tell-tale crashes of roof tiles dislodging and falling to the ground. Before the storm, they had anticipated losing several tiles, but the structural design of the roof itself seemed solid. John kept a stash of replacement tiles in his tool shed, but he had a feeling he would need to order more after the storm.

In between the whine of the wind, they also heard a crackling sound. Rainfall from the storm battered against the house, and they hoped the sandbags they had stacked against the entryways would keep out the elements. Their thoughts also drifted to the laboratory – wondering what flooding the storm may be causing. They had shored the doorway at the cave entrance with a mountain of sandbags, but the door itself had little in the way of waterproofing. The corridor beyond, which ran for ten metres to the control room, was on a slight incline. Water would flow down it if it got through.

Amy finished her snack, scrunched up the bag, and disposed of it in the bin liner. Laying down next to her husband on the mattress, the candlelight transfixed her. Even here, a draught still managed to penetrate their sanctuary and cause the flames to flicker.

"Did we make a mistake?" asked Amy, taking advantage of a moment of quiet.

"You having doubts?" said John.

"Ask me when the storm's passed."

John noticed Amy staring at the candle, and moved closer to his wife. He could sense her anxiety. Her body felt tense against his, and her breathing was shallow.

"When we first met – you spoke to me about how quantum entities worked," he said, "And how they can be both waves and particles. Run that one by me again."

She knew her husband well enough to realise that he was trying to take her mind off the storm; he had a protective streak running through him that could become tiresome. She also knew that his physics education surpassed most people, and he knew all about Wave-Particle Duality.

She let him ask anyway. Any chance to show off her intelligence.

"You're talking about when we first started dating, back in Uni?" she said.

"That's the one. I still haven't got my head around how they can be both a wave…" he took his right forearm and moved it like a caterpillar, "…and a particle. Surely it must be one or another?"

"You look like you are trying to do the robot," said Amy, referring to his arm movements. "We've just spent five years creating a machine that smashes protons together, and now you want a lecture on Wave-Particle Duality? This is fairly rudimentary physics."

"Indulge me," said John.

"You have some strange indulgences dear, but okay."

Amy leaned her head on John's chest, feeling the warmth from his body and the rising and falling as he breathed. She barely noticed the noises of chaos outside their closet-sized room; instead, she gazed at the flickering candle.

"So the theory goes that each quantum entity – an electron, or a photon, or whatever - can exhibit behaviour that is both a particle and a wave," she began. "Scientists just over a century ago found that they couldn't explain the behaviour of these quantum entities in a consistent manner. Then Einstein came along and realised that there is a duality between their behaviour that can only be explained by them being both a particle – like an individual packet of energy –

and a wave – which travels in peaks and troughs and has a length. They switch *states*. Sometimes they can be explained as a particle, other times a wave. So think about the energy contained in Harriet, and her transferring this energy into the sea. This energy is making huge waves that spread out across the water. But in Duality, when those waves strike the shore, they would only hit the shore in one place as an individual entity, rather than spread out across the entire coastline in the island."

John swept his hand over his head in a gesture of bafflement. "That makes no sense," he said. "How can something physical be two different things?"

"Think of it like this. Let's say that hurricane Harriet is caused by a witch called Harriet who lives in the clouds. She aims to crash against the door that opens to our lab. So she changes her state from an individual witch on a broomstick to a wave of energy, and whips up the air and creates this storm. This energy then passes into the sea and creates waves as this energy passes through them. Then, when it hits the coastline next to our laboratory, she switches her state back to being a witch and she smashes against the door. Replete with a broomstick and warty nose."

"Okay, so what you are saying is that particles are witches that can perform magic?" said John.

Amy squeezed his side playfully. "You don't have to be so literal. Quantum physics takes a certain leap of imagination."

"Let's hope this witch called Harriet stays in the water and doesn't smash up against the door of our lab."

"I agree," said Amy, and then winced as another crashing roof tile echoed around their sanctuary. The brief interlude was over, and the gales returned. Reaching a pitch: a wild cat baring its teeth, hissing and mewing. With every gust, the mattress beneath them shook, and the tins and packets of food on the shelves rattled.

Amy took her mind elsewhere, a trick she had learned growing up as an only child with a distant father. As she rested her head on John's chest, she closed her eyes and listened to the soft thump of his heartbeat. She let her mind wander to the clouds, floating in the air, the maelstrom around her, but each thump of the heart banished the destructive winds. Like the bass of a stereo speaker, the sound waves created a barrier that the gales could not penetrate, and she floated through them, protected by their pulsing.

As her mind wandered, and the night of the storm progressed, her body relaxed and she fell into a slumber.

IV

A voice seemed to be calling her, distant at first, but growing stronger. A voice she recognised, and trusted. What was that? What was the dream she was in? No, it was gone. Lost to the vagaries of the mind.

"Amy, wake up," said John.

Amy woke, her head still resting on her husband who was trying to rouse her from sleep.

"What time is it?" asked Amy, groggily.

John checked his watch. "Just a little after four."

Amy sat up, wiping the sleep from her eyes. "I was dreaming," she said.

Looking around her, she saw the candles had melted down, and the larder had stopped shaking. She could not hear any noises from outside.

"It's quiet," she said. "Is it over? It wasn't expected to be past us until near midday, wasn't it?"

"It stopped all of a sudden," said John. "Just a few minutes ago."

"You stayed awake, while I slept?"

John nodded. "I didn't want to miss our opportunity."

"Are we in the eye then?" asked Amy.

"It sounds like it," said John.

"Should we still go ahead with it?"

"I think so. I can't rest easy until I'm sure the lab isn't flooded."

Amy yawned and rubbed her face with her hands as John grabbed a torch and handed one to her.

Leaving the larder, they entered the dark kitchen. With no electricity, and the windows blocked up, the light from their torches guided them.

"Looks like the windows are all intact," said John, with a certain amount of pride.

Crossing the kitchen, their beams swept across the dining room where Amy had stacked the chairs against the wall. Reaching the back door, John unlocked it and opened it inwards. A wall of sandbags stood in their way. He pushed them over and they collapsed onto the patio outside.

"How much time do you think we have?" said Amy.

"Depends on the wind speed," said John. "I'd say about forty-five minutes? Maybe half an hour if it's a strong one."

They stepped over the sandbags into the early dawn outside. It remained very dark, but they could see the outline of the wall at the bottom of the terrace silhouetted black against the sky beyond. Around them, palm trees outlined the curve of the hill over the roof of their home. But what took Amy's breath away was the sky in front. A broiling wall of darkness, as far as could be removed from the azure vista they were so familiar with, twisted and intertwined ahead of them in hues of black and grey. It seethed and writhed, a snake pit of updraft and downdraft currents. The inner wall of Hurricane Harriet. It was moving away from them.

They walked over the flagstones slick and littered with leaves and branches. Smashed terracotta tiles added to the detritus of the storm, the rubble crunching under their footsteps.

They reached the wall of the cliff, just next to the staircase. Down below, the sea remained choppy and crashed against the rocks. At an undiscernible point, the grey water and sky merged into a single entity.

Amy looked up. Directly over her head, she could see stars in the clear sky, the photons reaching her eyes after light years of travel, twinkling through the atmosphere. It gave her the impression of standing at the bottom of a giant vertical tube.

Holding onto the balustrade, they descended the steps. John led the way, his beam of light swaying, eager to check on any damage caused. Amy followed, steadying herself with her hand, with her other shining her torch onto the staircase. Following the zig-zag of the steps, they remained on the side fixed to the cliff; despite the calm air, they didn't trust the conditions. Hugging the rock wall, they felt a small amount of protection from anything the elements may throw at them.

As they stepped onto the wooden decking of the jetty and the landing area, it was wetter than the staircase, their shoes splashing in the puddles. Water soaked through, and squelched between their toes.

Just ahead, John breathed a sigh of relief as he noticed the doors, marking the entryway to their laboratory, remained closed despite the powerful gusts. Most of the sandbags they had piled against the entrance were also still in place, but a few had slipped.

Between them, they began to unstack the sandbag pile, resting their torches on the decking. Behind them, the sound of a churning sea.

"These will also need stacking again," he said.

Unlocking the steel doors, they opened inwards, groaning on their hinges more than usual. A dark corridor greeted them - the little light from the landing did not seem to penetrate the blackness. Illuminating the interior with their torches, they could see that the walls were dry, but as they stepped inside, their feet splashed in small puddles where the water had accumulated in the small indentations in the rocky flooring.

"Water is getting in," said John shining his torch on the ground.

His beam centred on one of the larger puddles near the landing, and he followed as several streams trickled down the corridor toward the control room. They appeared to be flowing beneath the door into the room beyond.

"I'll go look at the lab," said John. "Could you start cleaning up here?"

Amy nodded, picking up the mop and bucket that they had left a few hours earlier. With the limited light, it was tricky to make sure she was finding all the puddles, but it didn't take long for the mop fabric to become soaked. Rinsing the salt water into the bucket, she chose another spot.

John followed the corridor, his light glistening on the water trails, and reached the doors to the control room. Pushing them open, he stepped onto the tiled surface, and the doors swung closed behind him. He swept his beam across the room. No light entered at all in the underground chamber; but his beam highlighted the control panel, the two fixed chairs in front of them, and then the monitor screens on either side. Along the wall to the left of the room, heading towards the door that led down to the power plant, a bank of cabinets sat. They housed drives and servers. The water had started to pool at their base.

Shining his light on the glass window separating the control room from the clean room, the beam reflected off the glass, blinding him for a moment, and he could not see Vix beyond.

It felt stuffy and damp, and he took out his handkerchief to wipe the beads of sweat that had appeared on his forehead. With no power, the air conditioning in the room, which included an atmospheric filter and dehumidifier, was not operating. In the beam, he could see motes of moisture floating. Beneath the tiled floor, he had fitted many cables. Getting them wet would be disastrous.

A prepared, folded stack of towels sat on one of the control panel chairs. Grabbing a handful of them, John got on his hands and knees and began to soak up the dampness. Quickly rubbing them back and forth over the tiles.

In the corridor, Amy continued mopping, her arm

aching as she tried to move quickly, and she felt tiredness creep over her. Her body wasn't ready for the exertion after only a few hours of restless sleep. Making her way from the entrance, down to the laboratory, she tried to be as methodical as she could in the dimness.

Several minutes later, she reached the doorway and popped her head through. John still rubbed the floor with sodden towels, trying to dry out every last drop. She looked at her bucket and saw it was almost full.

He swept his torch around the flooring, looking for puddles. Placing the wet towels in a laundry crate, he grabbed the final dry one and spun it into a fabric spiral.

"I'll put these behind the door," said John, as Amy watched him.

Joining Amy in the corridor, he laid the towel down in the gap between the door and tiles, wedging it in the gap so he could close it.

"Are we done?" asked Amy

"I think I need to put some sandbags against these doors," said John.

Amy nodded in the torch beam, and John headed back up the corridor towards the exit.

Crash!

The steel double doors at the exit, which had been ajar, smashed against the corridor walls. Both John and Amy jumped and stopped in their tracks.

A gust of cold air blasted at them.

Looking at each other with shock, John shone his beam down the corridor at the exit. The heavy doors were rattling on their hinges.

"I think we need to get out of here," said John, his

voice quivering.

Amy nodded and dropped the mop.

Together they jogged back up the corridor, John grabbing Amy's arm. The sound of wind and crashing waves, muffled while they were underground, came through the open doorway. As they emerged cold, sodden air burst upon them, and they were drenched immediately. The choppy sea whipped up even more, and at the edge of their view, the maelstrom tugged their boat on its moorings.

John dragged the doors closed with considerable effort, and Amy began trying to stack the sandbags, her hair wild in the gale.

"Leave those," shouted John.

"But what about the water?" asked Amy.

"We need to get back inside," said John.

She continued to lift the sandbags against the door as John closed the padlock. As he did so, he grabbed Amy's arm and pulled her toward the stone staircase back up to their house, leaving most of the heavy sacks scattered on the landing. Water spray swirled around them, draining the energy from their bodies as it soaked through their clothes; the strong winds seemed to freeze their sodden skin.

The handrail felt slippery to touch, but Amy held on. John followed behind, supporting her back with his large frame as they propelled themselves up the steps. The lavender air suggested the dawn was close, with the chaotic winds swirling and whipping at their progress. They couldn't see further than a few metres from the shore, but the waves boiled and smashed against the cliff.

"How long have we been down here?" said Amy, above the howling gale.

"Not even half an hour," said John. "I thought we'd have longer. Harriet must be faster moving than we thought."

Amy stumbled on the slick surface, and John took her waist in his arms and steadied her. Reaching the first landing, they turned their back to the wind as the stairs reversed, and the force helped push them forwards as they ascended. Breathing was hard against the pressure of the air, but anxiety made their gasps more laboured.

Rounding another corner, wind in their face again, Amy looked up and was horrified at what she saw. At the top of the cliff, coming over the wall of the terrace, sheets of horizontal precipitation thrust outward. The ceiling of water glinted as it combined with the gales, along with whatever loose material the wind had picked up. A horizontal torrent flowed above them.

Amy looked back at her husband wide-eyed.

John looked back at her, grimly. "It'll be all right," he said, "Keep going. We've got to get back to the house."

Amy continued climbing, but as she neared the summit of the staircase, her steps almost halted. Placing her arms in front of her face, she entered the torrent as it lashed her body, trying to force her backward and into the void below.

John was a few steps behind her, and he struggled against the blast too – but managed to get an arm around Amy's waist and manhandled her onto the terrace.

Ahead of them, across the paved space, they could see the back door into their kitchen, along with sandbags blown across the garden. The door flapped on its hinges like a sheet on a line, straining in its frame.

"Get to the house," he shouted, but Amy barely heard

him. He shoved her forward.

Calling on her last reserves of energy, she began to pump her legs toward the doorway. Her body stood at an acute angle to the ground, her sneakers scrabbling for purchase on the paving. The entryway back into the sanctuary of their home appeared blurred to her eyes, and swam around her vision, bobbling around as she struggled. A flower bed ahead of her, with a raised stone wall, helped her and she grabbed onto the edges to pull herself along. Risking a glance behind, she saw John also struggling – his large frame fighting the pressure against it. He waved a hand towards the house, encouraging her to keep moving.

The terrace that was so familiar to her, that she had crossed a thousand times without thought, had now become the enemy.

A marathon effort with every step.

Keep pumping the legs, she thought, *get to sanctuary.*

Broken rubble, smashed into fine powder, whipped up into her face and caused her eyes to sting. She felt the need to rub her watering eyes, but didn't dare to release her handhold.

Finally, with a stretch of her arms, she grasped the door frame and dragged herself into the house. She fell inside, to a kitchen in chaos. Crockery had fallen off shelves, chairs on their sides, and the curtains flapping furiously. But the pressure of the wind abated, and it was dry.

She let out a cry of relief.

Grabbing an upturned barstool near her feet, she wedged it against the slamming kitchen door, attempting to keep it open for John.

She looked out of the back door, back into the chaos

beyond, and saw his silhouette nearing the door. He emerged out of the shadow of the storm, just a little further than arm's reach, and saw Amy standing, waiting for him. Amy stretched out her hand; ready to grab his when he got close enough.

John smiled at her gratefully.

She did not see the trunk of a palm tree until it was too late. The log smashed against the roof of the house, crunching tiles, before falling into the terrace. Caught in the hurricane winds, and without slowing, it smashed directly into him. For a brief moment, she saw the trunk, entwined in mid-air with her husband, rolling back over the terrace, and into the darkness over the edge. It disappeared from view over the wall.

Amy screamed his name, her arms reaching outward.

Chapter Four – John

I

Dr. Frankland replaced the phone receiver and leaned back, stretching his neck from the aches within. A tension headache had formed and he removed his glasses to massage the bridge of his nose, placing the frames on the desk in front of him.

Daylight streamed through the blinds of his office at the Castries Infirmary, casting its rays upon metal filing cabinets. Shelves stacked with medical literature surrounded him, their worn, leather-bound spines soaking up the heat. On his desk, a rather ancient desktop computer sat to his left, and on the right, the landline telephone.

The tropical climate was a fact of life on his island, but the heat was not conducive with his headache. Recalling the conversation he'd just had with the Governor, he reported that the hospital was critically short of bandages, painkillers, and antibiotics. Asking the Governor to trigger the emergency relief plan, where they requested international aid, was the last resort. Wealthier nations, either untroubled by natural disasters, or at least well-placed to deal with them, would send over what they were running short of. This meant the other unaffected Caribbean islands and the US, would send supplies, with a token amount delivered by Europe.

The Governor had argued him down. He didn't want St Lucia – and more importantly its tourist industry – tarnished by admitting that the island's healthcare system couldn't cope with natural events such as this once-in-a-lifetime hurricane. His concern was that their main source of income for the economy would suffer if the people planning to holiday on St Lucia were to see images of medical equipment being loaded onto freight airplanes. Despite Samuel's assertion that it would look even worse if they saw the injured and dying lacking basic medical care, the Governor argued – not without merit – that even though the islands had been in the direct path of a category five hurricane, as it had just been confirmed by meteorologists, the statistics had shown that they had suffered far fewer deaths than expected.

He had to admit, during the height of the storm, as he cowered in a hall full of frightened people, he had believed its severity would cause a huge number of deaths and injuries, but the outcome was better than he had feared. Seven fatalities confirmed and thirteen others reported as missing.

Just over a hundred had come to the hospital injured. Cases ranged from broken bones and concussions to the walking wounded with cuts and bruises that needed dressing. That morning he had seen a man who had suffered a heart attack from an undiagnosed cardiac condition and was currently in intensive care. He was just thirty-three, and Samuel did not think he would pull through.

The coastguard was sweeping the waters around the island for the missing, and rescue teams were searching around collapsed buildings for anyone trapped. Samuel wondered how many of these he would add to the overall death toll.

Many families on the island were dealing with grief or suffering through injury, but Samuel's thoughts drifted to the missing person very close to home. Soon after the hurricane lockdown had ended, and telephone coverage resumed, a call came through from Amy Hunter to say that John was missing. She was distraught, speaking to him through her sobbing. A tree had struck him when the wall of the hurricane eye returned. Once the storm had passed, a few hours later, she found no sign of him in their rear garden or down at the water's edge. She had gone out on her boat, searching for him frantically, but found no trace.

Samuel had wondered why they had ventured outside in such conditions. Considering them naïve, even foolish, for doing so considering the severity of the winds.

She had informed the authorities as soon as the storm was over, and the coastguard was searching the bays and inlets around their homes. Samuel doubted that anyone hit by the trunk of a tree travelling on hurricane-force winds, who then had fallen from the cliff into the sea, and been in the water during the worst moments of the storm, could survive.

He returned home after the storm, but only briefly, to assess the damage to his property. Like most, his roof lost several tiles and exposed some of the timber framework, and palm fronds had piled high against the walls.

When he returned to the hospital, he stopped to check on Amy, but she was either not at home, or not answering the door.

Checking his watch, he had one more round on the wards to perform to check on the injured, and then he would clock off. He was exhausted, but he should go back to see if Amy had any news, and to help her in any way possible. He could only imagine the nightmare she was going through.

II

Mani's body lay still, eyes closed, lying as if dead beneath the rock. Awareness flickered in some parts of the body, but it was elusive and fractious.

The shelter had been sufficient as the hurricane passed over. He could sense the destruction around him, not just on this island, but several around the path the storm had moved through.

Was it *done*?

Had he *stopped* it?

The answer was no. He had caused a bump in the road, nothing more. An alternative path to take, but not one with resolution.

Necrosis had begun in some of the cells, and his low energy levels prevented him from maintaining bodily functions. He needed to rely on the natural biological structure inherent in this body to allow energy to replenish. The lungs still took in air, the heart still pumped the blood, and the brain still sent and received electrical and chemical stimuli – just enough to prevent the total breakdown of cellular activity. It would be hours, possibly days, before he had received enough replenishment to resume a normal existence.

By his side, in the dank space below the boulder, sat bottles of water, candy bars, and the plantains he had picked on his way to this shelter. He had not the strength to consume any of them, but with each passing moment he absorbed the invisible forces; this would enable him, once he recharged enough, to fuel this body naturally. When he could summon movement through his muscles, and enable digestion, he would move the regulatory functions to their natural state, and then build up his reserves once more.

With these ideas sparking in the remotest parts of the brain, he switched off and returned – for a few hours – to oblivion.

III

Samuel knocked on the front door of the Hunter residence.

No reply.

Apart from a few gaps in the roof from damaged tiles, the house looked unscathed. Much of the rubble from the terracotta still lay around, and the wooden panes were still covering the windows. No doubt, Amy had either not realised, or not cared, about them. On both counts, that was not a good sign.

He knocked again, without reply. Maybe she wasn't in. Had she gone to join the search? Or maybe she had received the inevitable news?

He turned to leave, but as the breeze lessened, the sound of Amy's voice came through from inside. She seemed to be holding a conversation.

He knocked again, more tentatively, and then turned the door handle. It was not locked - home security not high on her priorities.

Stepping inside into the hallway, he glanced up the stairs, but then realised her voice was coming from the lounge area. Closing the door behind him, he was plunged into cool darkness from the boarded windows. He popped his head around the lounge doorway.

"It's Samuel. I've come to see if you're okay?"

Again, no reply to him, but the conversation seemed to go on from the lounge. Emerging through the door, he found Amy standing at the far side of the room. She was speaking on the telephone.

Slivers of light bathed the room, finding their way between the cracks in the boards. Dust motes swirled in light shafts, throwing the shaded areas of the room into deeper shadow. Scraps of food sat on dirty plates and half-drunk glasses of water littered the surfaces. The lack of ventilation gave the room a musty smell.

She didn't acknowledge Dr. Frankland entering the room, her attention on the phone call.

Replacing the handset on the wall-mounted receiver, she missed the cradle and it dropped, dangling on the cord. She ignored it and turned to face Samuel.

"They've abandoned the search," she said.

"Oh Amy, I'm so sorry," said Samuel.

She hunched her shoulders and began to sob.

III

Samuel filled the black bag with the remaining foil trays and half-eaten food, and then tied the top in a loop. He took the bag to the terrace and placed it next to the full bin.

Beneath the windows, planks lay where he had removed them from the windows, using John's crowbar; opening up her home to daylight once again might help.

Returning to the lounge, he watched as Amy drifted between the rooms, absently clearing away the plates and glasses that had accumulated over the last few days, the afternoon sun now streaming through the window.

"That looks far better," said Samuel, in a kindly voice.

"It does," said Amy. Her voice was quiet, the voice of a shy little girl. "I suppose I need to make this place spotless if I'm going to arrange the... the...," her voice trailed off, and tears streamed down her face.

She wiped them away hurriedly with the back of her hand.

"You know, he'd laugh, if he saw me like this," she said. "He always thought me the ice queen when it came to showing emotion."

"Your reaction is completely normal and understandable," said Samuel. "I'd be more concerned if you were not upset."

She took a deep breath in an attempt to regain composure.

"Let me put some coffee on for the both of us," she said.

Moving into the kitchen, a fresh breeze streamed through the open windows, and Samuel took a seat at the dining table.

Amy switched on the kettle – the St Lucian grid now back up – and grabbed the cafetiere from the cupboard below. She went over to the larder to fetch the coffee and opened the door.

The mattress was still inside.

Pausing, she took a few deep breaths and glanced at the outline of their body shapes on the bedding. The room still held his scent. Quivering, trying to suppress the grief, she entered the larder and grabbed the tin of coffee beans from the shelf. Soon the nutty, roasting smell of the beverage caught the breeze and wafted throughout the house.

"Smells delicious," said Samuel.

"It's Guatemalan," said Amy. "John's favourite…"

Samuel smiled as she brought over the coffee and two wide-bowled mugs, and sat at the table facing the doctor. She looked through the window out to the terrace and the calm, blue sea beyond.

"You'd never even know we had been through a hurricane," she said.

"I've seen a little of the island," said Samuel. "Just driving to Castries and back – to the hospital. There are a lot of damaged buildings. A lot of trees flattened. The roads are tricky - they are covered in rubble from damaged buildings and rocks blown onto them, but they are being cleared as we speak."

"I'm so sorry - I never even asked how you are after the hurricane. How your home is?"

"The roof needs fixing – just anchoring to the frame of the house. I'm surprised I still have one – another hour of that storm will have ripped it off completely."

Amy nodded before gazing out of the window. Samuel felt foolish talking about his circumstance, but after his own experience with bereavement, he knew that talking helped while working through grief.

"If John were here, he'd help you with your roof," said Amy. "He was good at fixing things."

Samuel took the initiative and poured them both a mug. It did smell delicious after the antiseptic smell at the hospital. He lifted his own to his lips and took a sip. Amy stared out to sea.

"If he were here, I'm sure I'd be asking him to help," he said.

"He would've done it without asking. That's just the way he was."

He took another sip.

"You two met at University?"

"We did," said Amy, and a smile came over her face. She picked up her mug.

"I was your studious student, totally wrapped up in my education. I didn't go in for parties – I've always preferred my own company. John saw me in the library. I didn't even notice him at the time. He said that he watched me studying, and he thought that anyone so enraptured by studying a physics book would make the perfect girlfriend."

Samuel smiled.

"I never understood why he thought that," she continued. "The first time I noticed him was leaving my residence just before a lecture. He'd found out my name on campus, through friends of friends, and decided to introduce himself. I thought he was creepy at first after he told me about the library - like some kind of stalker. To be fair to him, I wasn't the easiest person to get to know, so it was pretty much the only way to get acquainted."

"Was it love at first sight?"

"Not at all. When he asked me to go for a drink, I refused. I said no on several occasions, but I'd done a little asking around of my own and liked what I'd heard. He was a man born of Kenyan heritage, from North London, who had grown up without any of the advantages that most of the other Cambridge students enjoyed but had earned his way into University through diligence and his natural intelligence. He had bags of charisma. And charm. Truth be told, for the first time in my life, I'd fallen for someone in a big way."

Samuel smiled and took another sip of coffee. "You eventually agreed to a date?"

"I told him I was only doing it to shut him up, to get him off my back. I was convinced that as soon as he saw me for who I was – anti-social, acerbic – he'd back off and go for one of the more popular girls on campus. He took me on a picnic on a Sunday afternoon beside the river."

Her eyes shone as she relived the memory.

"The sun was out and the boats were punting down the water," she said. "We ate sandwiches and drank fizz. He made me laugh, and made me feel he wanted to be around me. It was perfect. One of those beautiful memories, although that probably sounds banal."

"Not at all," said Samuel. "You'd spent your life living in the shadow of your father. Doing everything he had wanted you to do. For the first time in your life, you were doing something for yourself – there is no shame in that."

"I knew my father wouldn't approve, but I didn't care. He made me happy. When he asked me out again, I accepted without hesitation. We dated for the rest of our time at Uni, and then, when we moved onto our post-grad course, we rented a house and moved in together."

"Sounds like a very happy time for you both."

"It was the best time. Just being together, going through student life, and not caring about anyone but ourselves. We didn't have much, my father was absent most of the time - we just had each other. And that's all we needed.

"It was nearing the end of our course when my father died, and I inherited this place. We stayed in England to complete our qualifications, but then we decided to spend a life together on this beautiful island in the sun."

Her head dropped, resting on her chest, and her shoulders heaved as the tears formed around her eyes.

"What a terrible decision," she said. "If we'd stayed in England…"

"…You can't think like that," said Samuel, interrupting her chain of thought. "We all live with the decisions we make. You don't know what fate would've been in store if you'd not moved to St Lucia."

Amy laughed mirthlessly. "All that time and expense creating Vix. I might as well sell it for scrap."

"Don't think too far into the future just yet. Just take each day as it comes. It will get a little easier, I promise you. You never forget, but the bitterness you are feeling now will pass, and only the good, happy memories will remain."

"Perhaps," said Amy, wiping the tears from her cheeks. "But I can't help thinking we've had such poor fortune since moving here."

"You were married here?"

"We were – within a month of moving in. A beach wedding with just the two of us. It was the most beautiful day of my life – marrying the man I loved."

"You are grieving right now. You should expect to feel this way for some time. But don't abandon your dreams just yet. You need time to heal from your loss"

"It's not just Vix, Samuel," said Amy. "You know why we got married?"

She looked the doctor in the eye.

"Neither of us had any religious views," she said. "We didn't need some ceremony to show our commitment to each other. We wanted to spend our lives discovering the answers to the mysteries of the universe together, that much is true. But there was another reason why we thought marriage would be a good thing."

Samuel held her gaze as her eyes shimmered in the late afternoon haze.

"What was the reason?"

"We wanted a family," said Amy.

The shimmer around her eyes turned to droplets flowing down her cheeks.

"We wanted children," she repeated. "Being married just made that whole process simpler. I took his name – Hunter – and our children would be born into that name. A loving family, living comfortably on a paradise island. That was our plan."

"I'm so sorry," said Samuel.

"We started trying as soon as we were married. After a year without falling pregnant, we had ourselves checked. Turned out John was fine, but I had an undiagnosed condition."

Samuel looked at her with sympathy. He had never pressed them as to why they had remained childless for so many years; it was not polite to enquire about such personal matters.

"Polycystic ovaries," said Amy. "I don't ovulate, never have."

"You've had that diagnosis confirmed?" asked Samuel.

She nodded. "I do have anovulation – which is why I was not diagnosed for so long. Everything appeared normal with me – with my cycle – from my early teens. It was only when I didn't fall pregnant for so long that I found out."

"That must've been devastating," he said.

She nodded and retrieved a tissue from her pocket. She dabbed her eyes.

"Did you consider adoption?"

"We did, of course, but we decided that we should first follow our dreams of becoming scientists. Then we would see if we wished to adopt. I think John wanted a child of his own though. His upbringing taught him to value family and the passing on of your knowledge to the next generation."

Samuel felt a lump rise in his own throat. This couple, who were seemingly living a dream existence, also had to deal with personal tragedy. The sense of disappointment they must have felt just after being married, to find out that the family they craved would not be possible, must have weighed them down terribly.

"So we threw ourselves into our work instead," she said, with bitterness in her voice. "I would not have blamed John for leaving me immediately, and I became somewhat difficult to live with. I snapped at him, tried to push him away. On some level, I was figuring that I wasn't good enough for him – that he needed to find someone who could give him the children he craved. He stuck around though, regardless. He never quit anything in his life. So, rather than spending the first years together raising a baby, we created Vix instead."

"You are too hard on yourself," said Samuel. "He stuck around because he loved you. He loved you through good times and bad – like any decent human being would do. Life is a flipped coin. You have good times – just like your wedding and that celebration you had when you finished your work – and you have bad, like now. What can be certain, are that good times always follow bad."

Samuel's brown eyes displayed a lot of wisdom to Amy, but she was in the midst of her grief. Any notion of good times returning felt an impossible distance to travel. Looking down into her mug, she saw the blackness of the coffee and knew her future matched.

IV

Bidding Samuel a pensive good evening, Amy closed the front door. He had left her his mobile phone number and encouraged her to ring him if she felt she needed to speak to a friendly face. Feeling grateful for such kindness, she had nodded agreement; but in truth, she wanted some time alone. She needed to process her grief, and she was exhausted from the panic and her tears.

Night had fallen, it always arrived quickly on St Lucia, and the dark house felt lifeless and empty. She spent a moment staring at nothing in particular in the unlit lounge, contemplating whether to switch on a lamp.

The telephone still hung off its hook, and she replaced it. The thought struck her that she needed to contact John's mother in London to give her the bad news, and dread crept through her. She had been ringing constantly since the news reported the island devastation, and finding out that he was missing. She would need to give her the bad news. That conversation would be the toughest of all, and she was not sure she was ready for it. Realising the time, she knew it would be the middle of the night in England, so she decided to leave it until morning.

She shook her head as her eyelids drooped. She needed sleep.

Not bothering to check the locks, she ascended her staircase to the bedroom. In the middle of the room, the double bed lay unmade, sheets piled over the mattress. Moonlight filtered through the window, but the room felt humid and her forehead shone with perspiration. Spreading open the curtains, she allowed the cooling night breeze to enter, wafting the nebulous fabric. She found the gentle sound of waves calming. She always had, ever since she was a little girl.

Kicking off her sandals, she crawled onto the mattress, bunching the pillows together to rest her head on, and pulling the sheets so they covered her lower half.

Sleep arrived quickly, but not before the thought of whether she would ever get used to sleeping alone.

V

Thud.

Amy awoke with a start. The half-light from the moon still bathed the room, and she could still hear the sound of the sea.

Had something fallen over? Maybe the night breeze had blown something off the bedside table?

She looked around sleepily. Nothing was out of place.

Who cares, she thought, closing her eyes again.

Thud.

Amy rubbed her eyes, confused. What was that noise?

She sat up in bed; still drowsy, propping herself up with her arms, looking around the room for the source. Clicking on her bedside lamp, a pool of yellow light made her blink.

Thud.

That was not coming from her room – it was

downstairs.

Was that the front door?

She got out of bed, taking a couple of steps before hesitating. She still wore the clothes from the day before.

Fear crept over her. Fear of what she might find. Fear of the unknown. Alone, she would have trusted John to investigate any strange nocturnal noises.

Thud.

Maybe it was looters trying to get in? Her house would certainly be a target.

Opening her door, she walked across the landing area to the top of the stairs, taking careful steps, trying to be soundless.

Thud.

It was definitely coming from the other side of the front door. She stared down at it, as though trying to look through the wooden panels. They had a doorbell and a knocker, but these were not used.

A step further.

Thud.

That one made her jump. Maybe it was the stress – the emotional toil of the last few days. Maybe she was being irrational. It was probably just a branch, blown loose by the hurricane, struck up against the door.

Thud.

She told herself to stop being foolish, but at the same time, she was trying to fathom what could be banging against her front door in the hours before dawn. The weather outside was calm.

Placing each foot, eyes fixed on the door as though it would burst open at any moment, she descended.

Thud.

Should she telephone someone? Samuel was five minutes away up the road. The phone was in the lounge, the room to her left. It would take a second. She would look foolish if it turned out to be nothing.

She reached the hallway and tip-toed to the front door. Looking through the peephole, she could see the road in front shone in the moonlight, but nothing seemed astray.

Was she imagining things? Was her grief playing tricks with her mind?

She put her ear to the door. She could hear something. It sounded like panting.

Thud.

She drew her head back, shocked. Something was on the other side, no doubt about it.

Taking a deep breath, she put her hand on the latch. The metal felt cold in her fingers.

With sudden resolve, she swung open the door and she yelped as a huddled body, which had been resting against the base of the door, fell inwards into the hallway. The body shook and trembled.

Amy instinctively put her hand on the shoulder of the person, who then turned their head and looked upwards at her.

Amy breathed his name.

Chapter Five – Homecoming

I

"My word, John, I am glad to see you alive," said Samuel. Dawn had not yet arrived, but Samuel had rushed over as soon as Amy called him with the news of John's return. She sat her husband down on the sofa in the lounge, piling him with a million excited questions. What had happened? Where had he been? Are you hurt?

Seemingly too exhausted to answer, John had sat staring into space but closed his eyes occasionally.

He was filthy – his clothing ripped and his arms, legs and face covered in grime. Worried that he may have injuries, Amy called Samuel.

Stethoscope in hand and ears, the doctor placed the pad over John's bare chest, moving it around, checking for any concerning sounds. Satisfied, he removed the prongs from his ears and hung them around his neck.

"Lean back for me please," said Samuel.

John looked at the doctor, not saying a word.

"Please, lean back," said Samuel, and gently manoeuvred John's body to a lying down position. John complied wordlessly.

Amy stood at the doorway, chewing her nails. The amount of relief she felt bordered on overwhelming, replaced by concern as she watched the doctor work. John had not even acknowledged her.

Inspecting the body, moving his arms up and down, Samuel did likewise with his legs. John moved them as instructed, but remained silent as he did so.

The sunrise cast peach hues as it broke, softening the light in the room, and making Samuel's investigation a little easier.

"So tell me, John, what happened during the hurricane?" asked Samuel, prodding his body and looking for a tell-tale wince of pain.

John didn't reply.

Samuel stopped and looked him in the eye. "Are you okay?"

John remained glassy-eyed, looking straight ahead.

"He hasn't said a word since he got back," said Amy, and put her thumbnail in her mouth.

"Nothing?"

"Not a word," she said.

The doctor looked at John with concern but continued his examination. Asking him to sit up, he removed the torn shirt and had a look at his back. It looked normal. From his medical bag, he retrieved his torch and shone it into John's eye. A white glint reflecting from blinded him, and Samuel blinked and wiped the end of the torch with his finger before he resumed. He shone it both eyes.

"Tongue out please," said Samuel, pressing his chin gently.

John opened his mouth and the doctor shone the small beam inside it, moving it around to check every spot, before looking at his tongue.

He turned off his torch, and dropped it into his medical bag, before snapping it closed.

"Well my friend," said Samuel, "I don't know how you've done it, how you survived, but you are in perfect health as far as I can see."

No reaction.

Samuel looked at him and frowned; Amy spotted the glance and raised her eyebrows questioningly. The doctor came over and took her by the arm and into the hallway.

"What is it?" asked Amy.

"Something's not sitting quite right with me," said Samuel.

"Do we need to be concerned – shall I get him to the hospital?"

"No, I don't think that's necessary," said Samuel. "The hospital is busy enough at the moment. And I'm not sure he needs to go as I'm more concerned with his state of mind than any physical issue."

"I was putting it down to stress and exhaustion," said Amy. "What he must've been through…"

"Yes, I think you are probably right. He's showing classic signs of shock. He's dissociative – as though he's retreated into his mind to shut out the life-threatening scare he's suffered."

"Makes sense," said Amy. "But I'm so thankful that he's back here. A couple of hours ago I was thinking how I would get through his funeral, now he's back and sitting on the sofa."

She glanced through the door at John – he sat upright, staring straight ahead.

"And he hasn't even got a scratch on him," said Amy.

"I know – it's remarkable," said Samuel. "Miraculous. I'd expect multiple injuries. Broken bones, a concussion – hell, I can't even find a bruise on him."

"He is filthy though, and smells," said Amy.

"Yes, I'm sure a bath will do him good. I'd also give

him a decent meal, he can't have eaten much, or at all, in the last few days - and make sure he gets plenty of sleep. In fact, make sure he rests as much as possible. Hopefully, in a few days, he'll emerge from this mental state, and go back to the John we all know and recognise. Try to encourage him to talk about what happened, but be gentle. The sooner he faces the stress, the sooner he can start the process of recovery."

"Thanks, Samuel, I'll do just that," said Amy, placing a grateful hand on his shoulder. "And thanks for everything you've done over the last few days. I don't know how I would've come through it without you."

Samuel smiled back at her and popped his head into the lounge – grabbing his medical bag. John remained sat bolt upright, staring into nothingness.

"I'm off John," he said. "I don't know if you are taking this in, but it is wonderful to see you alive and well. Hopefully, in a few days, we can all have a few drinks over this and get on with our lives."

John did not move.

Opening the door for Samuel, Amy squinted as the dawn light crept over the road outside. The doctor went through the door and turned back to her.

"Remember," he said, "Make sure he gets complete rest, no work whatsoever until he gets over the shock."

II

The smell of warm water and bath salts drifted through the house. Amy led John into the spare bedroom, who followed without speaking, and sat him on the bed. She laid out a large towel, along with a clean pair of his pyjamas.

He removed his tattered shirt when Samuel examined him, but he still wore the same shorts he'd had on when he disappeared.

"Come on," said Amy. "A warm bath to clean all that dirt off you, and then you need to sleep. I've put you in the spare bedroom for now so I don't disturb you – you need all the rest you can get."

John made no movement, but Amy lifted him by his hands and took hold of his waistband. She eased down his grimy shorts. He stood before her naked staring into space, with his shoulders hunched. Muck covered him – a combination of sweat and dirt from his endeavours. It was unlike the man she married, and Amy thought he looked a little pathetic.

She led him to the bathroom, where the warm bath steamed; the scent of calming essential oils filled the room with a clean aroma. Having had an interrupted sleep herself, she felt her eyelids getting heavy.

Amy held his hand as he stepped into the bath, and he didn't react when he sat down in the hot water.

For a strange moment, Amy felt a certain embarrassment at seeing her husband's nakedness. As though she was looking at a stranger. Despite seeing him unclothed daily, it felt weird to her now. She averted her gaze as she grabbed a sponge and began to wash John's torso. Dismissing her bashfulness down to his unusual behaviour, she continued to clean him. Submerging the sponge in the foaming water, she cleaned him thoroughly, visiting every inch of his familiar body. John, soapy water cascading from his broad shoulders, remained expressionless throughout.

Shaking her head, she carried on with the rest of his body, finishing with his face. He blinked as the soap drifted into his eyes.

Gently, she lifted him by his armpits and he stood up in the bath, water rolling and dripping from his body. Stepping out, Amy wrapped him with a large towel as the bath water splashed onto the floor.

After drying him, she led him back down the corridor - swaddled in Egyptian cotton. He shuffled toward the bedroom like a chastened child, shoulders bowed and head down. Sitting him on the bed, Amy pulled back the sheets and encouraged him to get in.

John looked at the mattress, and then at Amy, before complying and lying down. Amy then pulled the sheet over him.

"I'll bring you up a glass of water and a sandwich," she said. "You rest for as long as you like, and come and get me if you need anything."

She left the bedroom and, after unplugging the dirty bath water, descended the stairs, went into the kitchen, and poured some fresh water from the refrigerator into a glass. She drank the whole glass herself in a single gulp, before pouring some more for John. She then buttered some bread, put some chicken and salad inside, and sliced it in half.

Returning to the bedroom, carrying the plate and glass, she stood in the doorway, watching him lying in the darkened room, eyes closed, breathing softly. A heavy sigh emerged from her, one of relief. She may have a journey ahead in the next few days dealing with his shock, but it was good to have him home. Whatever they needed to face in the coming days and weeks, they would face it together.

She felt herself sway with her own exhaustion, putting out a hand to the wall to steady herself.

Going into the main bedroom, she drew the drapes and closed the window. She could afford a couple of hours herself while John slept. Collapsing onto the mattress, it took her seconds to fall asleep.

The morning passed, and the afternoon began to fade, and still, Amy slept – lost in an unremembered dream.

As the sun began to fall toward the horizon, her bedroom adopted a blood-red hue, and she slept on her front - her arms folded below the pillow, her breath rasping through her nasal passages.

Over the bed, John stood – naked – looking down at Amy. His face displayed no expression, but he stood still as a statue, legs planted wide, arms hanging loosely, staring at her. A chink of light made its way through a gap in the curtains and struck John's face, and his irises reflected a glowing white.

III

Amy woke with a start. A sudden realisation, while sleeping, at how long she'd been resting, as though her mind was urging her to get up.

She sat as dawn's light filtered into the room, and she looked at her bedside clock. It was a little before 6 am. She'd slept for twenty hours.

I must've been exhausted, she thought, and she felt guilty for the length of time she'd been asleep. Getting out of bed, she threw on the first pair of shorts and a T-shirt from her bedside drawers, and then made her way to the spare bedroom. The half-light, along with her grogginess, made her progress feel dream-like.

Entering the bedroom, she saw the bed was empty. The bath towel used the day before lay discarded on the floor, and the clothes she had laid out for him had gone. The plate that had the sandwich remained, but it looked like he had eaten it. Amy took that as a positive sign.

"John?" she called.

No answer.

Going over to the window, she swung open the curtains and the morning streamed in. The room overlooked the terrace, and she saw John standing at the wall, looking out at sea. Standing in the spot close to where he fell over the wall during the hurricane.

Making her way through the house, she joined him as the sun rose higher in the sky.

"Good morning. How are you feeling?"

John had his back to her but didn't move or reply. He continued looking out to sea.

Amy joined him at the wall and gazed out.

The morning was blue and cloudless, the sea calm. Not even a boat drifting by interrupted the view.

"Did you sleep okay?" she asked.

No response.

"I slept a lot. Feel much better for it too." She hoped her cheerfulness would encourage him to open up.

She looked around the terrace and saw that piles of rubble from fallen roof tiles still littered the paving and lawn; scattered leaves and palm fronds added to the untidiness and planks still sat below the windows where Samuel had left them. Not registering the state of the property at any point since the hurricane, her thoughts turned to it. John needed stability and calm while he recovered from his shock.

His hands rested on the wall, and Amy noticed a dislodged chunk from the stone next to where his fingers lay. It must've been where he fell. Looking over the edge, it was a vertiginous drop to the sea below. To avoid injury, he must have been carried a few metres to avoid the rocks at the base of the cliff.

"Do you want to talk about it?" she asked. "Do you have any memory of what happened that night?"

Again, no reaction.

"Don't worry," she said. "We're in no hurry. Take your time – I'm here when you need me and when you want to talk about it."

For the first time since he returned, Amy saw a flicker or some reaction pass across his face. His lips and mouth moved as though trying to find words. She waited for him to process the thought.

He whispered something, but Amy didn't catch it. "What was that?" she asked, gently.

"…Vix…"

John uttered his first word since his return.

"Vix?"

"Vix," said John, and looked at Amy.

She felt flustered, unsure of why he was stating that, but also delighted that he seemed to acknowledge her presence.

Progress.

"Er, Vix – yes – our machine, in the lab below?"

John resumed his gaze.

"I'll be honest," said Amy, "I've not even been down to the lab since that night. I've no idea what the damage may be."

John didn't reply.

Amy wanted to keep the conversation going. "Did you want to go down and take a look? We can go right now if you like?"

John looked at her. "Yes," he said in a monotone.

Amy nodded. "Okay, the key is in the kitchen, I'll go and get it."

She returned to the house, a spring in her step at this encouraging sign. They had after all spent years on their project, so it came as no surprise that their machine was in the forefront of his mind – although she felt a certain grievance that his first thought was not of her, and how she felt following the storm and the subsequent stressful days.

The keyring was on the kitchen table, and she grabbed it and returned.

"Okay, got the key – let's go," she said.

She led the way, and he followed behind, silent and inscrutable. Amy felt his presence behind her as she descended the steps, as though his gaze pierced the back of her skull, making her feel uncomfortable. Her curious mind examined this feeling, concluding that such disruption in their lives had led to this odd situation

As they arrived at the base of the steps, she pointed out the motorised dinghy, still moored to the wooden jetty.

"Your rope-tying skills worked," she said, nodding toward the vessel.

Strewn across the wooden platform of the landing area, in front of the cave door, the sacks of sand sat scattered. Several were missing, and Amy figured the winds had blown them into the sea. The jetty still looked damp despite several days of hot sunshine.

Moving some of the sandbags that obstructed the entrance, she paused – allowing herself a little smile – as John began to help her. With them removed, she unlocked the padlock, and they whined, as they swung open.

On her right, Amy flicked the switch that turned on the tunnel lights. After a brief flicker, they came on and illuminated the passage.

"That's promising," said Amy.

Splashing through shallow puddles, they descended the tunnel, but as they reached the inner doors, they found the mop where Amy had dropped it and the towels still in place.

They were dripping wet as Amy removed them, and she dumped them at the entrance to dry in the sun. Opening the inner doors to the control room, they entered the laboratory – John looked around with an expression of inquisitiveness. She flicked on the switch, and the strip lights hummed as they illuminated, bathing the room in white light. As she did so, she heard the hiss of the air conditioning.

"That's good," she said, "The air conditioning should filter out any remaining atmospheric contaminants. I'll leave it on for a few hours so we can get the air recycled."

John, ignoring her, took steps toward the large glass window at the front of the control room. She watched as he took one step at a time. Moving in front of the control bench and computer screens, he stood at the reinforced glass, palms resting on the surface.

The room beyond was dark, but he peered in nevertheless. Amy, wondering why he was reacting this way to the machine he built, went over to the control panel. She pressed the button to turn on the clean room floodlights.

Vix stood a few metres in front of him behind the glass wall. Standing eight metres tall, its inverted pyramid shape – supported by beams containing electrical wires, cooling tubes, and exhaust pipework – loomed over him promising potential discoveries and unknown knowledge ahead.

Amy joined him at the glass and put her hand on his shoulder.

"There she is - Vix in all her glory. She appears to have come through Hurricane Harriet unscathed."

John did not take his eyes off the machine.

"We must start work on it," he said.

"Oh no," said Amy, a smile on her face. "We are going nowhere near this thing until you are better."

"We must start work on it," he repeated.

"Did you hear me? It's good that we've come down here to make sure nothing's damaged, but you've come through a very scary ordeal. You're putting your feet up until the old John – that I know and love – is back. Doctor's orders."

John remained impassive, still staring at Vix.

Amy left his side and turned the lights off in the clean room. It seemed to break John's concentration, and he turned around to look at her.

"I think we've had enough in here for today. Come on, I'll fix us breakfast."

She turned to leave, and John stood still – as though he expected them to start work immediately. Amy reached the passageway doors and turned back at him.

"Come on, we're going back," she said, her tone firm.

John walked toward her, reluctance in his step – like a scolded puppy.

Leaving the cave, they emerged back out onto the landing area. The day promised to be warm and dry, with the blue sky stretching to the horizon. The sea looked calm and inviting.

Amy locked the outer doors and pocketed the key. As she turned, she watched John walk with plodding steps down the jetty, his feet clumping on the wooden planks. Then he stopped, fixing his gaze on the sea and horizon.

"What is it?" asked Amy.

No reply.

Again, Amy thought of the night he fell, and she looked up at the cliff. The blue sky edged the wall, and she imagined how he had fallen, winds whipping around, the trunk of a palm tree falling with him as he splashed into the violent sea. Was he remembering that night? The fall and sinking into a turbulent sea? Perhaps it would help him if he went back to the water to relive the event. It may be the catalyst he needed to spring him from his fugue.

"Hey – shall we go out in the boat? Go for a little trip?"

She pointed at the moored dinghy.

John looked at her again – it seemed some words did get through.

"I'd like that," he said.

IV

"Do you remember what you called this boat?" said Amy, steering the outboard motor, the sea spray felt fresh on her face.

John did not reply; he wasn't even looking at her.

"You called it Higgs," said Amy.

Still no reaction.

"When we took our first ride out, you joked that you were the Higgs bosun," she said.

Amy indulged herself in that little memory of his joke – his shoulders heaving as he laughed at his pun. At the time, she had rolled her eyes at him. She thought it such a terrible joke; but she realised she would give anything to hear him come up with another witticism – however awful. Now it was his turn to remain impassive.

Amy cut the engine and the hull relaxed into the sea, the gentle gurgling of the water the only sound. St Lucia receded into a grey haze, the Pitons topped with late morning sunlight.

Throughout the trip, John had stood at the prow like a sea captain in pursuit of a quarry. The spray had splashed them both, and Amy found it refreshing despite the tang of salt on her lips. At first, she thought he just wanted a quick trip into the bay so his mind could work out and process his fall; but as she steered the boat, enquiring where he wanted to go, John just pointed toward the horizon. She indulged him as she was a little curious herself, wanting to know the thought process in his brain, but as they travelled further away from the coast, enough was enough.

"How far out do you want to go, John?" asked Amy.

John didn't reply but continued gazing at the horizon.

Amy held out her arms in exasperation. "Am I going to have another one-sided conversation here? If you don't tell me why you wanted to come out so far, I'm turning the boat around."

For a few moments, all she heard was the glug of the waves lapping the hull. Then she heard John mutter something as if speaking to himself.

"What was that?"

"This is where the attack will come," said John.

"Attack? What attack?"

John offered no reply but moved his head around, eyes narrowed against the sun reflecting from the sea.

Amy shook her head, both anger and frustration rising in her.

"Are you afraid of the sea since the hurricane? Or are you just worried that a giant sea monster is going to emerge from the depths? Maybe Blackbeard's ghost ship will spring up when the full moon shines and sack the island for treasure…"

She stopped herself. "Look – I don't think this is helping, but try and process what happened that night. You were hit by a tree, and you fell down the cliff into the sea. Did you lose consciousness, or did you manage to swim to shore?"

John remained impassive.

"Even if you told me that you can't remember what happened, we can work with that. God knows I wouldn't blame you. If you have amnesia, we can sort you some treatment for it."

John turned and faced Amy.

"We must start work with Vix," he said to her. He spoke in a very firm and clear voice and looked her right in the eye.

Amy flinched as the sunlight caught his eyes, blinding her for a moment. She stared at him right back and put her hands on her hips.

"We are not going near that lab for the foreseeable

future. I want my husband back."

She throttled up the engine again and spun the boat back home.

V

The red snapper sizzled in the pan, and Amy flipped it with her spatula. Domestication was not her way, John had performed most house chores, but Amy did love to cook. It was an escape for her, a moment to concentrate on something other than her overactive thought processes.

The smell of the fish, fried along with onions and a little ginger, floated across the kitchen and dining area, and out through the open doors at the back of their home. On the counter island in the centre of the kitchen, she had prepared a large bowl of salad – lettuce, cucumber and tomatoes – dressed in orange peel and pomegranates. The grocery store in Soufriere had just had its first restock since the hurricane, and she had visited an hour earlier. The town seemed mostly undamaged from the worst ravages of the storm, situated as it was in the shelter of a bay, and with the twin mountains bolstering its southern flank.

For the moment, as she watched the fish turn golden in the oil, she thought of nothing. Not about what the future lay for her, nor about the man she loved sitting (still staring out to sea) at the table on the terrace.

Their boat trip earlier had caused her to feel anger toward him, but once she had returned, she regretted losing her temper and felt guilty. Even though he wasn't showing the slightest hint of emotion or recognition of his condition, she guessed that in some dark recess of his mind, he was struggling with demons. She had no idea how long it would take him to emerge as a functioning human but knew it was her responsibility to care for him when he needed her.

The guilt she felt was the reason she decided to make John's favourite meal – red snapper salad with oranges and pomegranates. And a bottle of the Chilean white wine that he loved. Another step in her attempt to bring some normality and familiarity to his return.

The fish was cooked, and she took the pan off the heat, and let it rest. Grabbing a couple of plates from the cupboard, she served up the salad using tongs. When she was happy with the salad arrangement, she scooped the fish up with her spatula and placed it carefully on top of the salad leaves. She paused for a second to admire her work. It looked delicious.

Outside, John sat at the table, an untouched glass of wine in front of him. Since they had returned, he had not spoken a word.

Amy appeared from the house carrying two plates; she laid them down on the table and sat opposite. John looked down at the food.

"Cheers," said Amy, lifting her glass of wine.

John considered this for a moment, before picking up his glass and looking at her with his expression blank.

Amy leaned over and clinked their glasses together before taking a gulp. The wine tasted acidic and cool. She put her glass down and picked up the knife and fork.

John didn't drink but placed the glass down before copying Amy and lifting the cutlery. As Amy began to eat, he did likewise, watching her as she consumed the food.

"Is it good?" she asked.

John chewed and swallowed the food, but then

managed a nod.

"Excellent," said Amy, as she sliced into her fish.

"When are we going to start with Vix?" asked John.

"We on this again?" said Amy, trying to keep her voice even. "Have your dinner, drink your wine, and then we can enjoy the sunset."

"Are we then going to begin work?"

Amy laughed. "Are you kidding? It'll be ten o'clock by then. We don't work at night. We'll go to bed and see how we are tomorrow."

"So we'll start work tomorrow?"

"Give it a rest, John," she said. "I'm trying to introduce a bit of normality to our lives again. When you're well, we'll start."

She kept her voice even, despite the frustration rising in her throat.

The sound of cutlery striking the plates echoed across the terrace as they ate in silence. John shovelled mouthfuls of food and did not seem to register the flavour. His wine glass remained full.

After a few moments of eating, John interrupted the silence. "What will it take for you to start working?"

Amy put down her knife and fork and wiped her mouth with the napkin. "When you're better, and thinking straight, and behaving like a regular person – then we'll talk. I want the person I recognise back. I want my husband."

"Your husband is dead," said John.

It was a simple statement, and he continued eating as though he just described the weather, but the statement struck Amy – and she sat looking at John, stunned.

"What do you mean – my husband is dead?"

"John Hunter died four nights ago."

Amy took a large glug of wine. "You could've fooled me...?"

"His skull was fractured, his back was broken and he had sea water in his lungs," said John. "He would've been unconscious when he drowned."

Amy took a large exhale of breath.

"Why are you saying this, John?"

"Because we need to start work with Vix," he said. "You said that we would not start work until your husband returned. But your husband is dead."

"Then who is this person sitting in front of me?" asked Amy.

John did not reply but continued eating his food.

"I'll ask you again," said Amy. "How can my husband be dead, if he is sitting in front of me eating a fish salad?"

But John had clammed up again, and refused to speak, concentrating on the food. She sat for a few moments as her appetite vanished, staring at John, who now seemed to be eating with gusto, filling his fork and shovelling it into his mouth.

Amy polished off her glass, tipping back her head to get every drop; before picking up John's and downing that too.

VI

"He sounded utterly convinced by it," said Amy, down the telephone line.

Samuel, at the other end of the line, sat back in his office chair and listened to her as she spoke about John.

Concerned about John's state of mind, Amy had decided to speak to Samuel again. Although he had warned her that John's mental health was struggling and that she needed patience and a calming environment for him, John's sudden proclamation had hit her hard. It was a new development, and she needed some reassurance and advice.

She endured interrupted sleep as she had woken several times due to her mind racing with concern. He had slept again in the spare bedroom, and she resisted the temptation to get out of bed and check on him, not wanting to disturb his much-needed rest. Waking in the morning to see John standing out on the terrace again, staring out to sea, she resolved to ring the doctor.

"Is he showing any emotion towards you?" asked Samuel.

"None whatsoever," said Amy. "He just stares out to sea like a zombie."

Samuel nodded. "It's classic PTSD avoidance," he said.

"Avoidance? You mentioned that before?"

"That's right. When someone goes through a traumatic experience, they try and avoid dealing with the memory of the event. They distance themselves from their emotions, and in extreme cases, conjure an alternative history that they convince themselves happened to deflect having to deal with the stress."

"But he told me that he had died?" said Amy. "Why would he say that if he's trying to avoid the memory?"

"Because he's trying to deflect it away," said Samuel. "He's inventing an alternate history where *another* John was killed in the hurricane, but he survived. It means he doesn't have to associate himself with that reality. It's the mind's protection mechanism."

"I see," said Amy. "What can be done about it?"

"I have to admit that it is concerning. I'd have hoped that he would come through it, but the post-traumatic stress seems to be taking hold. I think there are some positives though."

"Like what?"

"He's started talking to you, for one. Sometimes trauma causes patients to withdraw completely, shutting themselves off from everyone and everything. He seems to want to keep himself busy and occupied too, which is encouraging."

"So what do you recommend, Samuel?"

"Keep him talking as he needs to confront his past. Don't get angry or frustrated or he may withdraw further. Be logical and calm with him."

"Should I call out his statement that he died?"

"He thinks somebody else named John Hunter died – remember that. But yes, you need to be calm, but firm – a little tough love may push him back towards reality. Don't push too hard though, we want to keep him even."

"What if he doesn't respond?" said Amy. "Is there something we can do?"

"I can arrange for him to have cognitive behavioural sessions," said Samuel. "They are very effective for treating these maladies of the mind, and there are also certain drugs we can look at, although I'd prefer to stay off those if at all possible. They can be rather severe on the mood of a person."

"Okay, thanks again Samuel, I'll see how it goes over the next few days," she said.

VII

Clearing up the mess left by the gales felt like a welcome distraction. Around the outside of the house, rubble and vegetation still lay strewn, and Amy piled it at the side of the house, next to the pathway that led through the palm trees. She then swept the terrace with a hard-wire brush to clear the smaller particles of dirt, sweeping them through the stone wall off the edge of the cliff to the water below.

During this, John had remained sat on a dining chair at the back door, watching her. She had considered asking him to help, but she wanted to see whether he would do so of his own accord. He didn't. Whether he was sulking about Vix or stuck within the confines of his mind, she could not tell; and at that moment, she did not care. She wanted to forget herself, at least for a little while.

She finished her clear-up just before noon. The sun was overhead and she had worked up a sweat. Visiting the kitchen, she took out a bottle of lemonade from the refrigerator, unscrewed the cap and took a deep swig. Placing the bottle down on the counter, her head fell into her hands. Tears welled up, and she forced them back. She took her hands from her face, looked up to the ceiling, and wiped away the moisture around her eyes. Being level and calm was her aim – to bring some sense of serenity to their home.

She picked up the lemonade, and a couple of tumblers, and joined John. The view through the doors showed the sea merging with the horizon – the blue of the water looked indistinct from the same shade of the sky. A large cruise liner faded into the distance.

Amy poured them both a glass and sat next to him. John, without looking, raised the glass and took a drink.

"You could've helped me out this morning," said Amy, motioning to the terrace.

"You didn't ask me to help," said John.

"Should I have asked? Would you have helped if I had?"

"Yes," said John. "I'll help you in any way I can."

"Why would I need to ask, are you not able to act on your own?"

John took a swig.

A gentle breeze stirred the nearby palm trees, but it was otherwise a quiet and peaceful day. John stared straight ahead.

"Do you think we can take a walk on the beach, go to a restaurant or a bar? Like we used to when we first came here?" Amy sounded wistful.

"Those things you did with your husband," said John.

"Then who are you?"

"I don't know," he said. "This is your husband's body, but I am not he."

"Samuel explained this to me," said Amy. "You created a fantasy to avoid dealing with the memory of that night. It's best if you just confront your emotions, and talk through it – however long that may take."

"John Hunter died that night."

"Then how come John Hunter is sat here next to me?"

John paused before he replied.

"Because I *fixed* him."

"You *fixed* him?" said Amy. "Like a mechanic would fix a car? You told me last night that he had, what was it? Had a fractured skull, broken back and drowned? You fixed that, did you?"

"Yes."

"And just how did you fix these?"

"I don't know."

"Isn't it more likely that you have been affected psychologically, and are inventing a fiction to explain your survival against the odds?"

"That is not what is happening."

Amy took another sip of lemonade and turned to face John, confident in her line of questioning.

"Okay – I'll make you a deal," said Amy. "I'm a scientist. I like to have proof of things, solid evidence to prove that something is true. It is not a scientist's way to take any theories on faith or because someone has told them that it is true."

John stopped staring ahead and looked at Amy.

"So if you can *prove* to me that what you say is true," she continued, "Irrefutably and with evidence, then I'll start work on Vix immediately."

John seemed to consider this for a moment. "We'll start work on Vix if I prove to you that I am not John?"

Amy nodded and looked him in the eye.

He paused, considering what to do.

"You can't can you?" said Amy.

John stood up. Craning his neck around the terrace, his eyes glinted in the sunlight. Spotting an item in the kitchen, he left the table and entered the cooler shadows inside. Curious, Amy stood and followed.

"What do you have in mind?" she asked.

John entered the kitchen purposefully, going behind the counter in the centre of the room. Amy stood watching, her curiosity now tinged with concern, feeling as though she may have pushed him too far.

Assessing the kitchen, John went over to the cooker. Above the four hobs, a selection of knives hung from a magnetic rack, ordered by their size. Picking the left-most knife – a large meat cleaver with a hardwood handle and blade ten centimetres in width – he held it in his right hand and turned back to face Amy.

"John, what are you doing? Put the knife down," she said, trying to keep her voice calm and even despite fear growing. Suddenly she felt light-headed.

John stood in front of her with an unreadable expression on his face, holding the cleaver, his arm hanging by his side loosely. Amy stood on the other side of the island from him, her arms were outstretched and her palms forward.

"I've changed my mind," she said, "Just put it down and we'll talk some more. You don't have to prove anything."

"But you're right," said John. "You have to see the truth before we can proceed with the work."

"I don't need to see anything, put the knife down!"

Terrified at what he may be planning in his fragile mental state, she thought of telephoning the police. Certainly, she needed to speak to Samuel - he needed to be committed.

"John, please, just put the knife down and we'll talk."

He wasn't listening. He scanned the kitchen surface in front of him and noticed a wooden chopping board. He grabbed it with his free hand and placed it in front of him.

"John, what are you doing," said Amy, her voice quivering.

"Sometimes you cannot tell people the truth," he said. "They have to be shown."

"John – no…"

John placed his left hand on the chopping board, fingers splayed on the wooden surface. He raised the cleaver above his head.

"No…!" screamed Amy.

He brought it down hard. Amy heard the sound of a thud. The blade sliced through skin, flesh and bone, embedding deep in the wood of the chopping board.

Amy let out a gasp of horror, the shock forcing her off her feet, and she landed on her backside.

John's face showed no emotion and no pain. It was an impossible picture – his arm ended with the blade, and then his hand sat on the chopping board, fingers still twitching.

His biceps flexed as he lifted his arm, and the amputated stump was a flat cross-section of bone, muscle and blood vessels. It did not bleed for a short moment, as though his body was surprised at the sudden violence, but then it erupted in a crimson spray. The blood, thick and viscous flowed down his arm and onto the sleeve of his t-shirt, dripping onto the tiled floor, slick and shiny.

His face did not register the injury, or realisation of what he had just done. Instead, it conveyed an expression of curiosity and – Amy thought through her disbelief at what she was witnessing – apathy.

The crisis forced her into action, and she grappled the nearby chair to help her to her feet, looking at the scene before her with horrified eyes.

"We need to get the hand on ice," she said. "We'll bandage your arm as best we can and I'll rush you to hospital."

John said nothing but continued to observe the bleeding stump, turning it in front of his face.

Grabbing a nearby ice bucket, she ran over to the refrigerator. As she opened it to get ice, John reached down and removed the knife from the chopping board with his left hand, and set it down beside his disembodied other. Amy grabbed a bag of ice, and ripped open the top, before pouring its contents into the bucket, the sound of solid water echoing in the kitchen.

"Amy," said John.

Amy stopped in her tracks and looked at him. It was the first time he'd said her name since he'd returned.

"Come and see," he said to her, his voice calm despite the horror of his arm.

Amy froze, transfixed, her mind reeling. She watched as John lowered his arm, blood now thickening in a deep red to the point of blackness, and he placed it on the edge of the counter. He picked up his amputated right hand in his left and placed it next to the stump. Amy had the perfect view of where the wound at the wrist met the edge of the hand.

John closed his eyes and stood very still. For a moment, it felt as though he was not in the room, a statue stood in the kitchen, but then he opened his eyes again.

Amy, looking at his face, looked back down to his arm, and gasped.

The white of the severed twin wrist-bones now jutted out of the wound, searching out the joining point in the hand, and connected – knitting together before her. Eyes wide with disbelief, Amy witnessed the bone fuse back together. The blood vessels, waving like tiny snakes emerging from the arm, found their corresponding connection in the hand and joined. The hand, which had been pale and lifeless, now regained colour as the blood flowed back into it. She stood rooted as the nerves, muscles and skin also connected. The tessellation of the healing was flawless - smooth and perfect – astonishing to behold.

Amy looked at John's face. He was smiling at her.

Instinct took over.

With a cry, she ran, pumping her legs to get out of the room. She smashed her shoulder through the nearest door, which led into the garage. The force of her entry sent her tumbling into the side of the Range Rover, causing the side mirror to collapse into the window. Racing to the garage door, she lifted it open and sunlight streamed in, the heat of the day washing over her.

Risking a glance over her shoulder, John had not followed her, but the panic still lingered – her head reeling and her stomach churning. The keys to the car were still on the hook in the hallway inside the house. She shook her head. She was not going back inside. Instead, she unhooked the mountain bike hung on the garage wall, and without any further hesitation, she cast her leg over the seat. She half pushed and half pedalled away out of the garage to the front of the house. Letting the incline on the driveway build up her speed, she sat on the seat and put her feet on the pedals. She wore sandals, which flopped as she pumped her legs.

The wheels bounced as she hit the dusty road. With no clear idea of where she was fleeing, she steered down the side of the hill, heading inland, the handlebars wobbling as she struggled for balance.

Risking a glance over her shoulder, she saw John. He stood at the bottom of the driveway, watching her – arms hanging by his side - as she made her escape.

VIII

Her thoughts as she pedalled further from home were disparate and confused. Her rational mind, always her support in difficult times, refused to accept what her eyes had seen. Maybe he hadn't chopped his hand off, and he managed to perform some visual trick to deceive her?

But the blood. All over the kitchen. The dark red blood spilt everywhere.

Could she, herself, be suffering from an acute psychological episode? If the last few days had proved anything, it was that she had suffered a great deal of stress – followed by the huge relief that John was alive – but then this...

Indeed, he seemed to be someone else entirely. Some *thing* else, if she could trust what she had just seen.

She had arrived on the outskirts of Soufriere, where the road leading up to her home met the main highway through the island. She could head into town and maybe find help.

Her thoughts were confused. She needed time to process this. Time by herself. Conscious that she would appear insane if she went to the nearest building and began to rant about how her husband had suddenly - and seemingly magically - reattached his disembodied hand. She needed to think.

Turning away from the town, she travelled along the main tarmacked road that led inland away from Soufriere northwards and into the central area of the island. She felt hot and confused, the exertion of pumping her legs as hard as she could meaning she became drenched in sweat. The sun's heat relentless. Passing vehicles gave her a wide berth as she wobbled by the side of the road, unsteady in her haste.

Around her, as she travelled through the mountainous interior, the hurricane had brought down many trees and flattened huge areas of undergrowth. Branches and logs ripped from their roots littered the carriageway, joined by palm fronds and leaves blowing around in the breeze. As she rounded a corner, following the road rising into the high ground, she spotted a crew clearing up the remnants of the storm.

She considered speaking to them for help. But the thought that they may see her as some crazy person returned to her. Maybe she was at that.

No. She needed some time alone to think.

She passed them, her breath coming in gasps, and drew their attention. They removed their helmets, scratching their heads and pointing, as they wondered why this woman rode alone, just after a hurricane, not dressed for cycling, and looking scared and exhausted.

Almost without realising, her body operating on automatic, she recognised where she was. A narrow road, up ahead, led to a track where no car could travel. A place she frequented when she felt the need to be alone: whether working through a thesis or just to be by herself. Just to get away from life for a while. She turned off the main road and took a more leisurely pace, her tiredness catching up.

Halfway around the track, where the volcanic forces that had shaped the island had created a geological divide, a small waterfall cascaded over rocks into a pool. The sound calmed her and seemed to bring everything back into focus.

As she rode into the shade of the overhanging trees, the thought occurred to her that she had just imagined the whole event. He had been so convinced that he could fix himself, that maybe she just imagined the severed hand reconnecting to his arm. Perhaps the reason he wasn't following is that he was seriously injured and needed help. Was he now lying on the floor of their home, bleeding to death, while she fled in terror? Should she go back?

She hit the brakes, and the bicycle whined to a halt. Placing a foot down for balance, she took a deep breath. Her lungs burned, and she could hear her heartbeat in her ears.

Collecting her thoughts for a moment, she closed her eyes and listened to her laboured breathing, picturing what had happened, clarifying her thoughts, and falling back on what she valued above all else about herself – her keen mind.

Closing her eyes, she recalled what she witnessed. The thud of the meat cleaver, John examining the stump, and blood pouring onto the floor and workspace. She had not imagined it. It happened.

Suddenly, she felt very weary. Dismounting, she gripped the handlebars and pushed deeper down the track towards the waterfall, her mind trying to make sense of events that seemed to be spiralling away from rationality.

IX

Glistening and sparking as it caught the late afternoon sunshine, the waterfall splashed over volcanic rocks and into the deep pool. The spray chimed as it struck stone, and the churned water gurgled, flowing to the far side of the pool, where it drained away to a brook that led through the valleys to the sea.

Mesmerised by the waterfall, Amy practised her technique of clearing her mind of any concerns - concentrating on the simple. Nature was beautiful. It was calming. And it was logical. The way the land had risen. The geology of the island forcing the rocks to divide in height, causing the stream to drop over a cliff into the pool below. Simple, explainable, and scientific. As a teenager, beset with confusing thoughts about her own life, her mother's death, and her complicated relationship with an absent father, she had developed this exercise of the mind. To analyse something to the point of abstraction. It calmed her and made her take control of her thoughts once more.

Closing her eyes, she felt her heartbeat relax. Breathing in through her nose, and out through her mouth, concentrating on the tinkling of falling water. Sat on a stone by the side of the pool, feeling its coolness rise through her, taking away the heat of the afternoon. Over the waterfall, she heard birdsong and the fluttering of flying insects around her.

After a short while, she opened her eyes. Her head felt clearer, and she had calmed her nerves somewhat, turning her thoughts to what happens next.

Her options, as far as she could tell, were either to seek help – most likely from Samuel and the island police - or to return to John. She would face whatever uncertain future lay in store for her with a man who claimed not to be her husband – and proved that he possessed a talent beyond her explanation – but who still appeared, on the face of it at least, to be the man she married.

If she sought help, what would they find? Would John demonstrate this same power in front of them, or would he just claim that his wife was having an episode? Would he even admit to them that he wasn't John? Even if she could convince them of the facts, what would happen to him then? Would they commit him to an institution while they assessed his mental state? If she made the same outlandish claims – would she be subject to the same scrutiny?

If John did demonstrate this power, then it would be of interest globally. He would be studied, operated on, and kept as a prisoner while being subjected to various experiments as authorities tried to figure him out. She would also attract a huge amount of attention, and that thought was against everything that mattered to her. She wanted to go through life left to her own devices. Being in the spotlight, whether it be through scientific attention, or through the media, horrified her.

Was she in danger though, if she did go back to him? He was unstable – the image of him holding the meat cleaver high above his head, with that white gleam in his eye emblazoned itself on Amy's mind – but the truth was that if he wanted to cause her harm, he could have done so on numerous occasions since his homecoming.

Just maybe she could figure out what was happening to him over the days and weeks ahead. Relying on her intelligence and intuition was how she had lived and it had served her well. This was no different, if more extreme.

Taking a deep breath, she glanced at her watch. It felt like hours since she had fled her home, and the light was beginning to fade. Her stomach growled.

Over the sound of falling water, she heard footsteps approaching. She wondered if tourists were taking a walk through the forest, but somewhere inside her, she knew it was John. The bend in the path ahead obscured her view, with the trees growing thick and dense, but those footsteps echoed a familiar gait.

From around the tree, striding purposefully but not hurriedly, the large frame of a man appeared. He looked like John, walked like him, sounded like him.

She tensed, glancing at her bicycle standing against a tree in case she needed to flee again. If he wanted to, he could grab her easily; and they were in the woods, remote and alone. She swallowed hard.

"Hello, John," she said.

"Hello, Amy."

"How did you know where I was?"

"This spot – it's familiar. I drove as far as I could and then walked. I knew you would come here."

"How could you know that?" asked Amy.

"I can read all the memories," he said. "The brain, the neural connections. Thoughts and emotions."

She recalled how he had repaired the damaged limb, and wondered if he had a connection to all his physiological functions. His right arm hung by his side, hand attached, and not even a scar to show.

As if sensing her anxiety, he lifted the arm and examined it himself.

"I'm sorry for this," he said. "Since you left, I knew you would need time to yourself. I used that time to examine more about your husband. I went through his memories to find out more about you and what it means to be human. I understand your reaction."

"Who are you?"

"I don't know. I have no memory beyond this," John spread his arms and looked down at himself.

"Then why are you here?"

"Because I have a sense that something important – *critical* – is about to happen. It involves Vix, and it involves you."

"But you have no idea what you are?" asked Amy. "How can you be sure about these things?"

"I honestly can't answer that," said John. "I am driven by this one aim, and everything that I do wants to advance this."

"I am a scientist. I don't believe in body-snatching pods from space or some kind of demonic possession. How can I trust you if you don't even know what you are? Can you tell me anything? Do you feel…*human?*"

"I don't have any frame of reference to answer your question. The best reply I can give is that I feel as though I am a vessel inhabiting this body. It has levels to it. The levels are made of energy that ebb and flow at each moment. Energy that I can use to manipulate my environment. Does that sound human?"

She considered his response for a moment.

"I wouldn't put it quite the way you do, but certainly we all have energy levels. We eat and we sleep to replenish them."

John stood still and silent, waiting for Amy to process her thoughts.

"You look and sound like John. So to me, you are still

human. And I'm still not convinced that you are not in the process of some psychological episode. But then there's that…"

She pointed at his arm.

"I can't explain that," she said.

Amy stood from her rock, smoothing down her clothes, and issuing a large sigh as she took an intake of breath.

John made no move.

"I suppose I could believe that you are an alien of some sort?" she said, keeping a careful eye on him. "I certainly know that statistically there should be life in the universe beyond our own."

"I have no inkling of coming from another world," said John. "Wouldn't there be a spaceship…"

"I'm speculating," said Amy. "I don't have any answers, just more questions. I still believe that you are the man I married, but something is happening which is beyond our explanation."

"If it helps you to believe that I am still your husband, then I can be," he said. "Everything John was is still here. His likes and dislikes, his memories, and the people who were important to him. You are the most prominent person in his life. And I find that me being here with you is of consequence and reason."

"What reason could that be?"

"Vix," said John. "I'm here because of Vix."

For a moment, as the tenseness between them began to evaporate, the only sound they heard was the splashing of water into the pool.

"Then I guess we start smashing protons together and see what happens," said Amy.

She approached the bicycle and placed her hands on the handlebars to wheel it out. Heading down the path, she neared John cautiously, her eyes never leaving him. As she arrived at arm's length, she stopped still.

"You're not intending to hurt me, are you?" she asked.

"Exactly the opposite," he said. "I intend to do *everything* I can to protect you. To me, you are the most important person who has ever existed."

"Keep thinking that," she said as they walked away from the pool. The gentle gurgle of the waterfall continued, as it had - unchanging – for centuries.

"Tell me, John," she asked, as they made their way back along the trail. "If you chopped your head off, could you put that back on again too?"

"Shall I try?"

"No. No, please don't," said Amy, hastily.

She looked at him and recognised the smile as it spread across his face.

Chapter Six – Mani

I

The white-hot sphere of iron and nickel rotated - generating a magnetic field that extended for thousands of kilometres beyond the atmosphere of Earth. Despite the immense pressures, causing the temperature to approximate the surface of the sun, the core remained solid – the peculiar nature that existed in such extreme densities prevented it from being molten.

Direction did not mean anything at this level – north or south, up or down – every direction was the same hellish construct. The engine of the Earth, heating it from within and creating the barrier that prevented radiation from the nearby star from eating away at the thin and precious gaseous layer.

Rising from the centre of the globe, the mantle filled the space between the solid core and the crust. A vast, planet-encompassing ocean of magma that seethed and broiled, travelling in convection currents. The chaotic maelstrom of viscous molten rock filled the planet as it had done for four billion years.

His consciousness observed this. Not a physical presence, nothing living could survive a hostile environment, but an extension of that which he had become.

As he rose from the core, through the mantle, he hit the discontinuity – where molten rock became solid, but still under huge pressures and scorching temperatures. Detecting fractures in the weak spots, where the slightest jolt would cause huge repercussions for the life above it, he considered the amount of energy it would require to cause that geological nudge.

Then, a fraction of a second later…

Mani opened his eyes.

A skeletal hand grasped the lip of the giant rock, and he pulled himself out, grime covering his face and hands. The accumulated dust and soil, not to mention his own sweat, covered his shorts and vest, the accumulation over the ten days of his seclusion.

Around his rock sanctuary, empty plastic water bottles and chocolate bar wrappers littered the area, blowing around by the keen breeze he could feel on his face. Turning to face the sky, juggernaut clouds heavy with the promise of rain, but reluctant to unload, drifted by.

The hurricane had flattened much of the vegetation; but out to sea, dots of boats going about their regular business were a sign that daily life was continuing. The storm was a blip in their lives, nothing more.

He knew what he wanted to do next – but he could not attempt that just yet. Energy flooded into him at every moment, building up inside the shell, but it would take every resource he had to make the next move.

Large amounts of his reserves were sustaining this fragile body. The lack of adequate nutrition, exercise and sunlight meant spending some of his precious energy on its functions. His priority was to find shelter and sustenance, ready for his next move.

He looked around from his viewpoint on the hillside. A mountain reared up behind him, now only sparsely covered by vegetation, but the slope ran in a curve to the sea. The waves rolled in constant motion, and Mani set off towards the coast, his feet sliding a little on the loose rocks as he did.

Heading downslope, with no clear destination occurring to him, he searched through the mind and memory contained within the neurons he inhabited. The slippage caused by his feet carried all around him, sliding down as he descended the steep incline. His internal focus honed in on hazy thoughts of his life on the island, the fractious nature of the memories caused by the frequent abuse of biologically unfriendly chemicals. It appeared as though this life had been mainly concerned with getting enough money for the next bottle or joint.

Perspiration had begun to form on his scalp, still a patchwork of hair and baldness, and his hand smeared the grease on his head as he wiped it. Ahead he could see the coastline approaching, and noticed that the slope ended at a cliff rather than a beach, but he continued his stride. As he neared the cliffs, he could see small settlements and villages; and the dots of boats he had seen from his vantage were now clearer, the white trails of their wakes vanishing into the blue. Some were fishing vessels, others pleasure craft for tourists. Normal, regular people for this place.

One of them may know the reason he was here, and at this moment in time.

He should go about the island and pick up as much information as he could, during this recovery period. Knowing his target would make the task so much simpler.

Not that collateral damage was an issue for him, far from it. He would sink this island below the waves if he could, but he would not need to if he knew where to strike.

He found a trail, nothing more than a walking track on the side of the slope, and headed down towards the nearby village. He needed to blend in, look like one of them, and draw no attention to himself.

II

The cyan sea engulfed him, and he allowed himself to sink deeper. Swimming out far enough so the deep blue obscured the sandy bed below the surface, he emptied his lungs and descended. Gravity dragged him ever deeper, but more slowly than he would above the waves. The water felt colder and he noticed the body temperature falling to a more comfortable level as the taste of salt assailed his lips and the back of his throat.

The water cleansed the body, wiping clean the grease and dirt. The mind lit up with a feeling of refreshment and a sense of clarity.

He stopped descending and paused for a moment – hovering underwater. The sun's rays dappled through the surface casting rippling spotlights around him, and a school of colourful fish swarmed just below his feet. Air bubbles rose from his lips and nostrils, and brown eyes paled in the blue depths.

What was his fate, what had brought him to this place?

He had no answers – the mind he inhabited was too occupied with thoughts and memories of self to be concerned with the overall state of the place he lived in – and he wondered if all humans shared this trait.

His legs kicked, catapulting him upwards; the lungs wouldn't take much longer without oxygen. He breached and spat out warm salt water. The clouds had disappeared, and he felt the hot radiation from the sun heating his face.

Ahead of him sat a beach. Tourists had stayed away

from the island in the days following the storm, but a few had begun to return – sat apart - each in their patch, towels spread below them, bags and cool boxes embedded in the soft yellow sand. A few swam in the shallows, playing with inflatable beach balls, or doing backstroke with their faces up to the brightness. Laughing – joyful in the sunlight.

Between them, a scruffy dog passed close by to each group, hoping for scraps, but shooed away by the impatient holidaymakers, annoyed that such a mangy creature was disturbing their slice of paradise. Mani watched it for a few moments, stirring a sense of familiarity within him before it disappeared into the undergrowth behind the beach.

In that undergrowth sat his shack – the one he had found himself in when self-awareness began. He needed shelter during his revival. Somewhere concealed, where he would not be disturbed.

Wondering whether the shack was still standing following the high winds, he swam towards the shore, biceps and legs pumping as he propelled through the waves, feeling the coolness slicing over the exposed skin on the scalp, he avoided the area where the people were. Arriving in the shallows, he placed his feet into the wet sand and felt the under-nourished muscles complain as he made his way out of the sea.

His clothing was sodden as he headed up the beach, the tide swarming around his ankles. With water dripping from him, he looked around to make sure nobody was looking in his direction; the tourists were busy soaking up the rays or playing in the sea several metres further away. Spotting a lone beach towel, he realised that the owners must be taking a dip, and so made for it. A red and white-striped cool box.

Behind which he spotted the thin trail through the palm trees that led back to his shack.

Without breaking stride, and looking around him to ensure no witnesses, he grabbed the cool box and strode into the undergrowth.

In the shade, he paused and looked behind, back out onto the beach.

Nobody had spotted him.

Without further hesitation, he pushed on further towards his shack.

Wandering through the flora, he mused over how the theft of the box had come so naturally. With the knowledge that Mani had spent his life performing petty acts of criminality, it seemed that such theft was second nature. Opportunistic events had supplemented his daily life before his death, and he would take anything from anyone if it advanced his survival. Tourists were rich, by their nature, and he had felt justified in ensuring some of their possessions became his own.

A fallen palm tree blocked the path, flattening the aloe vera and ferns around, creating a clearing where none had existed before the hurricane. The wind had stripped it of all branches and leaves, leaving just the woody, circular trunk. Clambering over it, he saw leaves had fallen over the trail, but he knew that the shack sat just through the next line of undergrowth.

Carrying the cool box in both arms, he entered the glade.

Half of the structure still stood, but the side closest to the trail had collapsed completely. Walls made from the sheets of corrugated metal had blown over, and the roof had fallen, propped up by the other half. Strewn over the area were bottles, bowls and cans that had littered the interior. The large Jamaican flag lay snagged on a bramble, torn in the high winds.

Placing the box down, Mani got to work repairing. First lifting the metal sheeting, he moved it out of the way so he could look at the roof. Going back out of the glade, he dragged the fallen tree trunk back towards his shack. It was very heavy, and he had to use every amount of strength from the weakened muscles. Hand-walking up the log, he propped it up vertically before manoeuvring it against the sloped roof. Using the trunk as an anchorage, he lifted the roof edge from the ground and balanced it on the shorn-off tip of the log. With the roof out of the way, he could place the walls where they belonged, creating the interior square space, before lowering the roof and sealing them in place.

It remained an unsafe structure. Any high winds or falling trees would cause another collapse, of that he was sure. Nevertheless, it was secluded and private.

The darkness of twilight descended, but by that time he had shored up the shack, bolstering the walls with the wood and twigs lying around, he had cleared out the litter that had remained inside, including the stained mattress, which reeked of death. He discarded it on the other side of the glade, away from the entrance.

With the knowledge that sleep was a crucial part of maintaining biological functions, he gathered leaves and fronds, scattering them across to stone floor. Comfort was not a priority.

As the moon began to peek through the palm canopy, he moved the stolen box inside the shack and opened it up.

Grabbing a plastic bottle of lemonade, he twisted off the cap and downed it in a single gulp. Tossing the bottle aside, he grabbed a second bottle – this was water – and consumed that too.

Fishing around further in the box, he located several sandwiches wrapped in foil. The white bread surrounded tuna and cucumber, along with ham and cheese. He ate them, chewing them voraciously, before pausing for a moment as he assessed the digestion process: the sparking of neurons and the release of dopamine in the brain.

Glancing in the box again, he saw sliced pineapple near the bottom, but his glance moved to a pocket, and a flap of paper poking out of it. Removing it, he unfolded it to reveal a tourist map.

The map displayed the best beaches around the teardrop-shaped island, along with the places worth visiting. At the southern edge, a beach had been circled – and Mani realised this must be where he was based. Further, around the western side, he saw the double peaks of the Pitons, and the town of Soufriere adjacent to them. This town may be worth a visit. This would be a place full of tourists. It would provide opportunities to steal more food and maybe obtain information on any island news that he may find interesting.

Grabbing a slice of pineapple, he munched into it.

Further northwards on the island, he saw the capital – Castries. Next to it was a picture of an aeroplane, indicating an airport, and below that a large ship – a cruise liner. This looked like a port, an embarkation point. Lots of tourists with their travel possessions.

Perfect.

This town would be worth a visit.

III

The largest town, the St Lucian capital, thronged with activity. Along the main street, with its shops and bars, the pavements bustled with the local population going about their business. Tourists mixed with them, the difficulties of the recent hurricane becoming a memory as normality resumed.

Along the thoroughfare, traffic made slow progress down the single-carriageway as the major roads on the island met in the centre of the town.

A fortnight had passed since Harriet and, despite the trauma and death it had wrought, the island had recovered. The general feeling of the locals was that a storm of that ferocity was a once-in-a-lifetime event, and they had escaped relatively lightly. They had experienced a rare catastrophe, meaning it would be many years, if not decades, before they would have to face anything so destructive again.

Mani sat in the park, listening to their chatter.

How secure they felt, how unprepared.

He sat listening, as he often had over the last few days, for any indication of what may be happening on St Lucia that was out of the ordinary. Anything that may suggest to him what he needed to prevent. All the time his energy grew, becoming stronger, and it was almost back to where it was before the hurricane.

His shack in the south was his sanctuary, a place of retreat and repose. But during the daytime, he needed to find food and water and exercise his body. The healthier this body became, the more self-sufficient it ran, and the less he had to expend from his reserves. It was sixty kilometres from his shack to Castries, and he had attempted to walk, following the eastern coast road as it ran next to the ocean, and through the central high grounds. After walking for six hours, his body temperature was high, and he was expending more energy to keep going than he was ingesting. Having barely reached halfway to the capital, he had turned back. On his return, he spotted a bicycle parked outside the gates to a hotel. A steel chain secured it to the gate, but a quick burst of energy from his fingertips snapped the links, and the vehicle was his. He then attempted the journey the following day; it had taken just over two hours.

The food and drink he needed to maintain his body he had stolen from shops – the odd piece of fruit or vegetables from a shelf outside grocery stores, a packaged sandwich down his shorts from a refrigerated display. Skills he had picked up from the mind and muscle memories of this man. He found that he could keep a low profile as nobody seemed to notice, or if anyone did, he was ignored. Just another vagrant going about his business.

He eavesdropped whenever he could during his travels. Patience was in infinite supply as he watched shops and people, taking advantage of any relaxation of vigilance, anything left unattended. During his wait, he took in everything he heard – from local gossip concerning friends or adversaries, to business owners ordering their staff to do jobs, and many discussions on the recovery from the hurricane and the tribulations they had faced.

He turned a careful ear as he reclined on a park bench. The sun hit the top of his bald head directly, causing the sweat to spring forth. One of his first acts since arriving back at his shack was to shave the remaining clumps of hair from his head. He hand found a ladies' disposable razor in a bag he had taken from the beach and smoothed off his scalp to the skin. He now felt truly anonymous sitting in the park, alongside many other locals, with nothing better to do than to watch the world go by.

He had chosen this spot specifically as he had learnt that today was the first time a cruise liner was coming into port since the storm, a little bit of news he had heard the day before on the same spot from passing tourist reps. More out of curiosity than for any potential opportunity for larceny, he had risen early in his shack – before sunrise – and cycled over the island to take a position on the park bench. He had watched the golden orb rise over the tips of the mountains as he cycled, and it turned the sky red as he arrived in Castries. The town had been quiet then. Soon after arriving, the gigantic liner – the *Vista of the Seas* - drifted in from the horizon and manoeuvred into the dock – mooring ropes flung by the crew to the dockside workers, and the gangways reaching up to the side of the ship to let the passengers depart.

Across the bay from the dock, the main airport of the island also hummed with activity. Propeller aircraft landed, turned around, picked up passengers, and took off again – island hopping. Security was tight in the airport though. On the previous day, a suspicious, conspicuously armed security guard eyed him as he walked through the automatic doors and eyed the rack of candy bars. Mani decided at that point that the airport was not worth the risk – he needed a low profile. He had turned around and left immediately.

Cruise liner passengers were different. Disembarking to

spend a day on the islands, they were far more susceptible to thieves as they walked around with their large bags, often trying to corral children, and not paying attention to their belongings. A perfect environment for sticky hands.

Sensing an opportunity, he stood up from his bench and made his way through the park. Further, around the bay towards the open sea, the dock also had a container ship unloading, the cranes removing the steel containers and stacking them in the holding area. He paid them little attention as he crossed the road, the fumes from the cars and motorcycles creating a brown haze, and joined the pavement leading to the moored liner.

Passengers thronged along the gangway emerging from the side of the hull – tourists dressed brightly and wearing sunglasses. Many had their mobile telephones out, pressing the buttons and filming their arrival – both handheld and on sticks to film their reactions as they disembarked. This was perfect, the more distractions the better.

Gathering on the quayside into small groups, tour guides were speaking to them, explaining their itinerary – it seemed most of them were travelling south in flatbed buses, the seats in the rear covered by a thin canopy, to the Pitons and the volcanic mud springs further inland. Excited chatter from the tourists drifted over the harbour area as tour guides directed them, like cattle, to their vehicles. Mani noticed some others were ignoring the tour guides and going off into the town, finding their way around. He figured these were more adventurous and therefore more aware of the pitfalls of travelling in a new country. He would avoid them.

Then, he spotted what he was looking for. A plastic suitcase, wheeled, with its handle raised above it. The mother it belonged to was busy rubbing sun cream into her son's face, whilst messing about with the brim of her oversized sun hat. The boy was no older than seven years and grimaced as she drenched him in oily liquid.

She paid no attention to her case.

Bodies moving around, intersecting and dividing in the chaos of the quayside, was the perfect scenario. To be caught up in the confusion and anonymity of a crowd. Everybody was busy making sure they were in the right place, searching for their markers, and keeping track of their excited offspring.

The light was dimmer in this area due to the shadow cast by the huge ocean-traversing vessel.

He began to move, eyes focused on the suitcase. Entering the crowd, he slipped through bodies as they chattered around him, eager for the day ahead, children screaming and tugging on the shorts and shirts of their parents. It smelt of lotion and deodorant.

The suitcase lay just ahead, the woman and her child still looking the other way, towards the parking area – searching for their ride. She held the hand of her son, who stood open-mouthed trying to make sense of the maelstrom around him.

Smoothly, Mani grabbed the handle and continued walking through the crowd. He risked a glance as he made his escape. She remained oblivious to the theft, still looking towards the transportation. Swerving past the last few people, he could see the clear ground beyond the quayside. Across the street and into an alleyway, and he would be clear.

Emerging from the crowd and the quayside, the sun

beat down on him once again and he made his way over to the road.

Behind him, he heard the woman start to panic as she discovered her missing suitcase. A general commotion ensued, with the people around her looking around them to see if they could spot her missing luggage.

Mani, suitcase in tow, crossed between the traffic hurriedly, glancing behind him. The woman, making the theft known to a tour guide, waved her arms angrily. The boy with her was looking like he would start crying.

Looking forward again, Mani stopped on the spot. Ahead of him, a St Lucian policeman – dressed in his uniform of a white shirt, gloves, and blue trousers – had appeared from the side street. He was staring right at him.

Mani, frozen in place, stared back at him.

Instantly they both knew.

Mani gripped the suitcase under his arm and sprang away from the officer. Avoiding the stationary traffic, he sprinted across the corner of the carriageway, the policeman giving chase, and slipped into an alleyway. His pursuer was lean and muscular, a man who looked after himself, in the prime of fitness.

The suitcase was not helping, and he dumped it over a high wooden fence. Even unburdened, he could not win a foot race against this man. Maybe he could lose him in the narrow streets and gardens. Rounding a corner in between the rear of the town buildings, he found himself in another passageway behind the main street.

He took the shortest moment to assess his surroundings, with his pursuer chasing just twenty metres behind and closing. The alley contained several trash containers, the large ones about as high as he was. He didn't aim for the nearest one, as he needed to build up his speed, but instead sprinted to one halfway along. Leaping onto it, he jumped and swung for the raised ladder of the fire escape from the building. His grip latched onto the lower rung and he began to climb up, hand over hand.

The policeman halted below him and jumped to try and grab Mani's ankles. Just out of reach, weighed down by his heavy belt and kit, he then searched for a ground-floor entrance.

"Stop where you are," he insisted.

Mani continued to climb and reached the window-level platform on the first floor. The window was open, and inside he could see people sitting at desks, wearing suits and shirts, typing into computers. A ceiling fan spun above their heads.

Down on the street, the policeman tried the nearest door handle, and the door opened, just as Mani climbed inside the upper-floor window.

The surprised workers shouted in alarm, but he ignored them as he searched for an exit. To his right, a stairway descended to the lower floor, and he could already hear the policeman's heavy panting as he was climbing it. Wooden partitions, with frosted glass, divided the office. In each area, staff worked on desktop computers, and Mani's attention snapped to his left as a water cooler machine bubbled suddenly.

Running through into the next room, looking for an exit, he found more desks and computers. The people in that room, shocked at the commotion, stopped typing and stood, shouting and pointing at him. One tried to obstruct him, but Mani pushed past – scattering him over the desk in a pile of flying papers and pens.

Chasing further down the building, the next room was an office, and it was the last room on the floor. A large desk occupied the centre of the room, and an overweight man – the office manager – sat behind it. A standing fan tried to keep him cool, but the sweat patches around his shirt displayed its ineffectiveness. Busy padding his face with a handkerchief, a look of surprise struck him as he registered the intruder.

Mani – spotting the large open window – ran toward it, and dived out.

Headfirst.

With no thought to what lay beyond it, he exited the window. Time seemed to slow as the hot sun struck him, along with the sounds of the traffic and pedestrians around. He fell, six metres, onto the main street.

His launch from the upper floor took him over the pedestrians below, towards the road, legs and arms waving for purchase. Landing hard, he struck the kerb. He felt the bone break, and then pierce the flesh on his forearm. The concrete kerb opened up a gash on his bicep as he scraped along it, adding to the blood of the compounded fracture, which stuck out of his forearm like the ends of broken twigs.

The crowd around him cried in alarm at his sudden leap from the window. He had managed to avoid falling on them by pure chance, and the traffic had stopped, with people getting out of their cars. Somebody mentioned an ambulance, and another started to dial on her mobile telephone.

From the window above, the policeman popped out his

head, searching the ground below. Spotting Mani laying on the ground, he shouted down to the crowd to prevent him getting away. He pointed at him before turning to exit the building.

Mani spotted the policeman as he lay on the ground. Despite the damaged body, he struggled to his feet, his left arm flopping by his side, and used his right hand to push the crowd away, blood seeping down his forearm. The crowd parted and he limped through them.

Crossing the street between the halted cars, he dodged into another alleyway – keeping a close eye to see if anyone was pursuing him. He didn't have time to repair the broken arm, despite his mind registering the pain. Neurons fired in alarm and consternation, but his expression did not display agony or fear. Grabbing his left wrist in his right, he snapped the bone upward and it went back inside the skin with a crack.

He had bought himself a little time, but back through the alley, he could hear the crowd informing the policeman of the alleyway.

Making a decision, cold and dispassionate, he needed to find somewhere secluded. If he was spending more energy to escape this situation, he may as well make sure that he was safe. With that in mind, he jogged down the alleyway, which led inland – away from the dockside area.

The policeman appeared behind him, some distance away. Mani made sure he saw him, holding up his damaged arm. His pursuer, believing that the hunt was now in his hands with his quarry disabled, jogged at a more leisurely pace.

"Hey, you there," shouted the policeman, his voice

echoing down the alley.

Mani looked directly at him and smiled with a grim rictus.

"Stop where you are. You are under arrest, but I will get you some medical attention."

"Come and get me, copper," said Mani. It was something said many years ago, back in Jamaica when being chased by the police, and it popped into his mind before he spoke it. Jogging down the adjoining passageway, not in as much of a rush as before, he noticed that it led to the outskirts of the town.

The policeman rounded the corner behind him, closer, but sensing a new threat from this thief. Why was he being so belligerent with a broken arm, surely he would be in agony.

Maybe he was on something...

Mani emerged from the end of the alleyway, where the buildings ended and the vegetation began. A hill rose, and to his right, the line of the sea curved around the other side of the bay. The fugitive pushed into the ferns and trees, leaving an obvious track.

Following him into the undergrowth, the policeman stopped running. Patches of sweat had formed on the underarm areas of his shirt, and he breathed heavily. The sound of the town lay behind him, but ahead he could hear the rustling of the leaves as Mani attempted to make his escape.

"Stop now, and we can deal with this like civilised men," said the policeman.

No response.

The policeman could not see him, but he sensed his

presence in the bushes. He withdrew his white baton from its holster – not taking his eyes from his surroundings. Pushing further in, and using the hard wooden truncheon to move branches aside, he searched. He was sure he could hear laboured breathing.

The sun burned through the trees overhead as noon approached, and the policeman removed his hat, wiping the sweat from his brow. The thief was close.

Should he call for backup? His radio sat on his chest; it would be a simple task. But then the thief may hear him and flee.

Just up ahead, a clearing came into view. Stepping out from the undergrowth, the policeman spotted Mani at the other side – lit by the shafts of the sun.

He was smiling at him.

"Don't move," said the policeman, and pointed his baton at him with word of a threat.

Mani stood motionless, his chest rising steeply, sucking in oxygen.

The policeman took a few steps towards him.

"Turn around, and put your hands behind your back," he said, reaching for the handcuffs on his belt.

Mani obeyed and turned his back on him. He crossed his arms behind his back.

Ready for the arrest, the policeman saw the gaping wound on the arm – and the white of the bone beneath the redness of the flesh and muscle.

"You are injured," he said. "I'll need to cuff you, but then I'll get you straight to the hospital."

The policeman put a hand on Mani's shoulder and proceeded to put the handcuffs on, snapping them together with a click.

"I'm arresting you on suspicion of theft," said the policeman, "You don't have to say anything, but you may…"

The handcuffs dissolved into nothingness – solid metal evaporating into the atmosphere around.

The policeman gasped, what was happening?

Mani turned around, hands now free and placed a hand on the startled policeman's arm.

Utterly astounded, the policeman watched as his arm disintegrated – no pain reached his startled, doomed brain due to how rapidly the limb vanished – but the flesh and bone, seemed to go with a crackle. As it reached his shoulder, the decomposition spread across his upper torso and neck.

The final expression on the policeman's face was one of shock and incomprehensible terror. Unable to scream as his flesh dissolved to dust, the white of his skull, and the grey jelly of his brain, popped through for a fraction of a second before that too dissipated.

The remaining frame collapsed as all life departed, and a few moments later, the uniform lay on the ground, filled with the dust of the former policeman.

Mani stared at this pile of clothing, and as the breeze caught it through the undergrowth, brown powder floated away from the sleeves and the trouser legs. Placing a bloody index finger on the shirt, it began to smoke. A few moments later a small - but intense - fire burned. The leather soles of the shoes melted in the hot flames. Mani picked up the baton from the ground, and added it to the fire.

The flames glowed on Mani's visage as he waited for the remaining traces of this human obliteration. The final moment when his atomic structure changed into its constituent parts. Recycled back to the cosmos.

He only let the fire burn long enough to destroy the evidence. Aware that the smoke may bring the curious, or police reinforcements, he held his hand out to the fire – the broken bone still dripping blood - and it extinguished.

IV

The handlebars of the bicycle rested on the warm metal of the shack wall, the steel frame glinting in the moonlight. Retaining the heat of the day, the walls radiated warmth through the fern-carpeted interior, attracting flies and other buzzing insects.

Mani sat inside and consumed a bottle of fizzy orange soda he had stored from a previous day's theft. His arm showed no sign of injury.

The stolen suitcase sat before him, unopened. He had managed to balance it on the bicycle for his return journey, jamming it between his legs and handlebars. Sneaking in the shadows, he had found the suitcase still lying behind the wall where he had discarded it during the pursuit. The town seemed to have resumed to normal, with the excitement over as far as the locals were concerned – nobody was yet aware that any murder had taken place.

He had kept to the back streets as he departed town and then found his ride. Keeping to the verges and tracks between the undergrowth to avoid suspicion, he made his way back south. As he left, Castries had become busier, and police cars started appearing around the streets as they searched for the missing officer.

As he arrived back, he decided he needed to stay here and lay low for a few days at least, maybe even a week. He had stockpiled his stolen food, drink - an untidy stack of plastic bottles, wrapped sandwiches, snack bars, cans of beans, soup, and rapidly spoiling plantains and pineapples - sat in the corner of the room. His view of conserving as much energy as he could for the times ahead had taken a blow. Today's endeavours had cost him more than he saved, and so would put him back on his timescale for a few days – but he had enough stocked now to last him. Time would tell if it would be enough.

Turning to the suitcase, he inspected the clips, and then unfastened them. Flipping it open, he unhooked the elastic that held the contents in place.

A towel. He flung it aside.

Below this, clothing for a child – shorts and a T-shirt. Useless to him,. Below these, a woman's swimsuit – also useless.

Various bottles containing sun tan lotion, after-sun cream, a tub of painkillers and self-adhesive plasters for cuts. He threw those over his shoulder.

Checking the pockets, a woman's magazine showing the latest fashions, and a comic book for the child. Some paperwork – documents relating to their trip on the island – and itinerary, and some money – around fifty US dollars.

He pocketed the money. No food or clothing he could use. Given the amount of energy he had expended, it had not been a profitable enterprise.

Kicking the suitcase aside, he reached for another can and then collapsed onto the leafy ground.

Chapter Seven – The Voice of Vix

I

Humming energy radiated from the machine and into the surrounding bedrock. Nitrogen mist descended from the super-cooling towers surrounding the accelerating magnets, and in the half-light of the clean room, Vix resembled a monstrous ice beast, rumbling and steaming through the shadows.

For the last two days, they had run vacuum systems to clear out any remaining dust from inside the clean room. Harriet had not compromised that area, but they still wanted to ensure complete sterility.

Now, they wanted to run a complete test – a dress rehearsal for the main event.

"Confirm power cells fully charged?" said Amy. She sat in the control room, in her white laboratory coat. She had a series of screens in front of her displaying the status of the collider.

"Confirmed," said John, also in his lab coat. He sat at a right angle to Amy, around the corner of the operations console. His station was to action each stage of the experiment.

"Klystron and electro-magnetic power up," said Amy, referring to the generators that created the microwaves on which the particles ride, along with the superconductors that kept the beam narrow.

John pressed a button on the console and confirmed.

Amy spent a moment inspecting the detection equipment situated at the base of Vix. In what she referred to as the "womb", they had built several chambers, separated by magnetic coils. The vertex detector tracked the position of the particles following collision events as they travelled through the drift chamber, these particles were then fed into further detecting chambers using directed electromagnets. These measured the radiation, energy, and type of sub-atomic particle created, such as fermions, quarks, hadrons and bosons.

Happy that they all appeared to be working as intended, she resumed her checklist.

"Coolant at maximum levels," she said.

John pushed four sliders upwards to increase the amount of liquid nitrogen flowing through the acceleration coils. Huge amounts were required due to the intense heat created during the acceleration process to prevent the copper tubes from expanding or melting.

"Coolant at maximum levels," repeated John.

Amy paused, giving the appearance of monitoring her screens; but in truth, she needed a moment. Everything seemed to be happening so fast. From John's seeming resurrection to his reason-defying display of self-healing, and now here they were about to witness their first real test of Vix. Glancing over at him as he sat poised over the control panels, she could not believe her husband had not returned. His behaviour over the last fortnight gave her strong reason to believe this – his mannerisms and the way he spoke appeared, on the surface, that of the man she married. Whether this was because he was *still* the John that she had met and fallen in love with, or whether this was some entity doing a very good job at impersonating him, she could not tell. His keen sense of humour still eluded him, despite everything else, and Amy wondered whether this aspect of his personality was a step too far. Nevertheless, here they were, running tests on Vix in readiness to smash particles together like a cue ball striking a pack.

It was what John had wanted.

She inhaled deeply – apprehensively – and reminded herself that this was her ambition too.

"Confirm injection of hydrogen," she said.

A hiss came from the clean room, like air escaping from a scuba tank.

"Confirmed," said John.

Amy typed into the keyboard in front of her to switch screens, watching as they reflected rainbow colours from the display of charts and graphs.

"Confirm power connection to electron field?"

He pressed the next section of buttons in front of him, fingers dancing. "Confirmed," said John, as Amy took a note from the volts per metre.

He disconnected the power from the electron field generator and switched it to the superconductors. Different LEDs illuminated the console ahead of her.

"Confirm power to the superconductors."

"Confirmed."

"Fire up the Klystrons," she said, and John switched several buttons on the console.

"Do we have magnetic field generation in the acceleration chambers?" asked Amy.

"Confirmed magnetic field generation in both left and right chambers," said John. "Field generation sufficient to cause predicted acceleration of the protons."

Amy looked up through the giant reinforced pane of

glass at the front of the control room. Vix stood in the chamber, illuminated by spotlights, wreathed in nitrogen fog. She could feel the hum of power through her seat.

"Confirm divergent magnetic field into collision chamber?" she asked.

"Confirmed," said John.

"Both left and right?" she asked, referring to the twin copper tubes on either side of the collision chamber.

"Confirmed. In both left and right tubes."

"Confirm operational detection in calorimeters?"

"Confirmed."

"And in sub-detectors?"

"Dual electrical insulators confirmed operational, along with time-stamp velocity measuring device between them."

A giant sentinel stood just metres away from them. She could not help but stare through the glass at it and wonder what mysteries it would reveal. Particles predicted by the supersymmetry model, along with the nature of the Higgs Boson, would be a dream discovery for her; but the actual excitement of seeing the practical and scientific models she had studied her entire life gave her a feeling of intense satisfaction. Einstein, Newton, and Feynman were her heroes - her inspiration in her academic life. She would never be as presumptuous to admit that her work may one day rank her among those luminaries; but John's return instilled a renewed sense of the importance of what they hoped to achieve. His belief that her discoveries would rank amongst the greatest – if not *the* greatest – in the history of scientific discovery had both encouraged her to continue but also instilled a certain discomfort. He was so convinced that she felt that whatever they found could never represent this hero scientist image he had of her.

"We have a slight issue," said John, looking at the output on the monitor.

Amy snapped out of her thoughts. "What is it?"

"The collision chamber. I'm getting some interference from the detectors."

"Any idea what may be causing it?"

"A bit of residual dust perhaps," said John.

"Could we proceed within this level of tolerance?"

"We can," said John. "But then how could we trust the data with the knowledge it could be contaminated? Do you think we should replace the equipment?"

"That will take ages," said Amy, "Set us back weeks potentially. And we don't even know if it will be an issue."

"You think we should go ahead then, despite this?"

Amy considered his question for a moment, before answering hesitantly.

"I do, but not today," said Amy, "Let's leave the vacuums on overnight, and see if we can get rid of the last bit of dust. It may still not work, but at least we'll have an initial run. If it's still an issue after that then we know we'll need to fix it. Also, there might be other issues that we're just not seeing that will only come to light once we've completed our first run. If we need to fix the machine - take it apart again - then let's try to capture everything. After our first run, it will be weeks before we'll have enough power to do another one anyway."

"I could correct the issue without dismantling it?" said John, turning around on his chair to face her.

Amy did not look him in the eye, not liking the reminder of his new nature.

"I don't think so John. If we have to, we do this the old-fashioned way."

John nodded and returned to his station, turning on the vacuum pumps.

Her beating heart began to wind down as she realised they would not be able to go further today. She needed a drink.

II

Sipping her wine, she let it mellow in her mouth before swallowing. A sigh came from her and she put up her feet on the wall on the edge of the terrace while she watched the sunset. The dusk seemed to linger longer than usual, almost as though the sun did not want the night to fall on this particular evening.

Placing her glass on the table beside her, she glanced over at John, who was sitting and silently contemplating the setting sun. His wine lay untouched.

Amy wondered what was going on in his mind. Was this person her husband, still inside somewhere? Or was he now something wholly alien?

In the days that had followed his self-immolation, she had not witnessed any further indication that his nature was anything but human. She found herself in denial at his assertion that her husband was now dead, replaced by whatever now resided within his body. Every day he seemed to become more like the man she married. From his silence when he first returned, to his halting words and alarming actions following, he now seemed to be resuming a normal human persona. Although it lacked any intimacy or indication of affection, he spoke to her as she would expect him to. He knew of their history together when she mentioned events before the hurricane, and he still knew all the technical details from Vix.

Indeed, John ate, drank and slept just as much as any normal human would, although they no longer shared a bedroom. It seemed a step too far at this time to let someone pertaining to be a stranger back into the marital bed, and he seemed to accept this as necessary. His memories were intact, and he was regaining a sense of personality. If she had not seen the event in the kitchen, she would almost believe that John was back to his old self again.

Yet, she could not help but feel that something was still off. He would not laugh or joke. John had always been amiable and sociable, far more so than her, and never took anything too seriously. Humour was his method of coping with stress, and it had worked for him, especially during the renovation and construction of their home and laboratory when every day seemed to throw up another obstacle. Many times when she had considered giving up the project, John's light-hearted comments calmed her down and made her realise that her life wasn't so bad after all.

Now, he had become very serious about their work. Once they resumed their experiments, he had relented his insistence and thrown himself into making sure that they were ready – including the clearing up of the house. Amy knew they needed a productive environment to work, making their lives as simple as possible during their experiments – such as cooking, sleeping and the general environment they lived in. He had done this domestic work with gusto, but generally unsmiling and efficient, rarely speaking and working every second he could. Directed by Amy, he also never seemed to take action from his initiative, relying on her to guide him in each tasks.

Even now, sat as they were, on the eve of their first run of Vix, he sat next to Amy. Not drinking, smiling, or making conversation. They had eaten, with a generally one-sided conversation – Amy making small talk – and then she decided they should watch the sunset together on the newly cleaned terrace. John joined her without comment.

An atmosphere lingered between them, but she felt this was outweighed by a feeling of excitement and – she had to admit – foreboding around the work they were about to undertake. This was what they had led up to for almost five years. Now it was here, despite the hiccup of today, and she felt a keen sense of her catching up with the future. What lay ahead of them was a mystery. In her bones, she felt it tied in with the man sitting opposite. Prior to the recent events, she would have expected the collisions to produce a collection of sub-atomic particles. Splitting bosons would produce quarks – and she had hoped that their work would initially lead to this outcome as it proved that Vix worked as intended, matching the work of other quantum physicists around the world. Once this had occurred, they could take the next step and continue their research into the various theories, including the elusive supersymmetry, which would unite the world of the huge with the world of the tiny. The Higgs boson fascinated her. Its properties, proposed to explain why certain particles had mass, meant the discovery of it in an unstable state proved the theorists correct. Nevertheless, the Higgs boson, which decayed almost immediately into other particles, was almost impossible to find, and she had not held out much hope that she would be lucky enough to detect it with Vix. Her machine was impressive and held a great deal of innovation, but the fact remained that they only had a fraction of the resources that were available in the Geneva Laboratories – most notably the amount of power required to run the collider.

Yet, John had convinced her that they were on the precipice of something game-changing.

Sighing again, she looked at him. His face was inscrutable.

"What are you, John?" she asked.

John turned and looked at her.

"I don't know," he replied.

"Let me rephrase the question. What do you *think* you are?"

"Are you asking my opinion on the nature of my existence?"

"Yes," said Amy. "It gives me something to work with."

She took a sip of wine and watched his face with interest.

"I get the impression that I have become a scientific curiosity for you," said John.

Amy nodded. "Answer my question. Are you human, alien, or…other?"

"What *other* could I be?"

"I don't know. No human can repair themselves as you did, and if you are some kind of alien, this implies that you have travelled here through space. That there is a planet, or someplace in the universe, full of your kind that can fix themselves. I get the impression that this doesn't seem likely to you either. You don't have any vehicle that we are aware of, and the astronomical distances you would need to travel make this idea seem unlikely."

"I agree," said John.

"So that just leaves...*other*."

"Do you have any theories of what this may be?"

Amy gazed out at the darkening sky, the clouds turning vermillion as night replaced day. The sea shushed in her ears, and a gentle breeze tousled her locks.

"Various thoughts have occurred to me," she replied, "Most outlandish, and all improbable. But honestly, without further study, I can't subscribe to any of them. Samuel examined you, and you seemed human enough – at least biologically. I guess a good starting point is for you to let me know what your experience of being here is like and whether that compares to the experience of a regular person."

"How can I compare myself to a regular person?"

"I'll ask you some questions."

"Go ahead."

"How do you *sense* the world?" she asked. "Do you see through your eyes? Do you taste the wine you are – not - drinking?"

"I should imagine I sense the world in the same way you do. Visual images are seen through my eyes and made sense by my brain, and this gives me a view of the world."

"And your sense of touch? You repaired your body just by willing it - does that mean you don't feel pain?"

"My experiences are signals in this brain. I feel like I am a reservoir of energy, this does enable me to function and interpret this body, but also disconnect from it if I have to."

"*Disconnect*? What does that mean?"

John picked up his wine and took a drink.

"This wine elicits a response in my brain. On some level, I can sense its taste from the chemical reaction taking place on my tongue and my nasal passages, but it is also igniting neurons in the pleasure centre of my brain. Since I am achieving a level of consciousness from John's body, I can react in a way that you would describe as human, or I can just be analytical."

John took another drink. "Mm – that's delicious," he said and smiled warmly at Amy.

Memories of happy times flooded her mind as he flashed that smile, the same one she saw as she walked down the aisle on her wedding day.

"The longer this energy spends in this body, the more I can adopt the consciousness of the host. But I can switch it off too."

In flash, her memory vanished.

"Does that apply to your emotional responses too?" asked Amy.

"Of course. Being dispassionate is an advantage in some situations, but I've discovered that being complimentary and enthusiastic about your work makes you more likely to be enthused about it yourself."

"That sounds like you are being deceptive and – well – manipulative," said Amy.

"You are applying your own emotional response," said John. "I'm driven by a singular purpose, and that is to get you to perform experiments with Vix. I will do whatever I can to get this accomplished."

She stared at him for a few moments, and he did not seem to mind her scrutiny.

Amy then reached for her glass and stared over the terrace out to sea. The inescapable feeling of the link between John and Vix pervaded through her, and yet how could he even know what they were likely to discover when they started their work?

The wine had gone to her head, and with the combination of the warm evening, she felt tipsy. Her light-headedness compounded the excitement that she felt for what was to come. Tomorrow was the first real trial of the machine they had spent years designing and building, and now her husband – imbued with a power she did not yet understand – was claiming that it was the most important scientific experiment ever undertaken. Humanity will change irrevocably as a result. Could she trust his assessment? Could she trust him?

III

Amy shifted, settling in her seat to make sure she was comfortable. LED lights illuminated the console, and a bank of monitors above these gave her access to every piece of information she could ever need. The read-outs and data access fed into this station – everything from the electrical and magnetic measurements to the ambient temperature of the clean room – and it in turn fed into a bank of solid-state drives that lined the wall behind her seat. Here she could call up any previously recorded data that she may use for repeated experiments or results comparisons.

Ahead of them, through the glass wall, lay the clean room where they could look at Vix. During the construction, John had argued that it was not necessary to be able to see Vix, as all the measurements occurred inside the machine. Making a glass wall, which had to maintain the ambient temperature in the room beyond, had been expensive when a regular wall would have served them just as well. Amy had countered that she based her methodology on both the visual and the abstract. To fire her imaginative ruminations, she needed context - she needed to *see* the subject. She argued that if she were merely looking at numbers on a screen, rather than viewing Vix in action, it would hamper her acuity. Knowing, through looking at Vix as the experiment progressed, that the events appearing on her screen were taking place just a few metres away, she could engage the part of her mind that worked its magic.

John had conceded her point, despite his reservations that she was romanticising the machine too much. They spent many stressful weeks making sure the glass was fit for their purposes – with the interior attempting to remain as sterile as possible, ensuring no hairline cracks formed between the frame and the airlock they had built on the right side of the wall.

Despite these precautions, they found it a constant struggle to keep the clean room truly sterile. Extensive purging of contaminants had taken up a significant amount of their time before today, including the halt of their run the day before. Their first action when they arrived at their stations was to check the collision chamber, and ensure that the vacuum pumps had eliminated the last remaining traces.

That morning they both had a leisurely, but hearty breakfast of eggs, bacon and toast. A cafetiere full of John's favourite Guatemalan coffee had washed it down and Amy felt fully awake and refreshed by the time they descended into their lab. Leaving the sunlight behind in the entrance corridor, she felt prepared for the day's events.

Fully focused, she had been jiggling her leg since she had woken, the excitement giving her nervous energy. Her gaze had taken on a glassy look as her mind drifted away from the day-to-day issues and into her head space. She wanted to lay all other concerns aside. His normal behaviour that morning had reinforced her view that he seemed to be like her husband of old, and she had no desire to give any thought to what may be going on with him.

She adjusted herself in her seat once more. It was high-backed and had padded armrests as they figured they would be spending many hours sitting in them. A flask of cold water lay in the drinks holder built into the seat, and the cooling flow of the air conditioning came through the vents.

"I think we are ready," she said.

John spun in his seat, waiting for her instruction.

"Let's power up," she said.

Without speaking, John pressed the button that sent power to Vix. It thrummed as the energy passed through the circuits, giving life to the machine. They could feel the power transferring into the rock around them, a slight vibration that only added to Amy's nervous excitement.

Amy watched the screen as it displayed the rising levels indicating the main power input.

"Maximum optimal power reached," she said.

"Understood," said John.

"Inject hydrogen into chamber A," said Amy, and switched her attention to the next display.

John pressed the button, and they could hear the hiss

coming through the glass as the hydrogen gas made its way into the first chamber.

"Injected," said John.

"And chamber B."

Another button press and a hiss.

"Done," said John.

"Confirmed hydrogen insertion in electron field chamber A," said Amy, her gaze fixed on the screen. "And now chamber B too."

"Understood."

Amy allowed herself a moment to breathe. She glanced at John, who didn't seem to spot her as he glared at the console in front of him.

They had successfully powered up Vix, and introduced hydrogen gas. The next step was to remove the electron particles from the hydrogen atoms, achieved by passing them through an electric field. The positive charge of the field attracted the electron, leaving the hydrogen atom with just a neutral proton, ready for acceleration.

Amy watched the screen carefully as the gas flowed through the manifolds and into the two chambers. She imagined the electron particle as a tiny spark, disconnecting from its host, and filling the chamber with flickering blue light.

A few moments later, the readout confirmed the step as successful.

"Protons ready in Chamber A, and Chamber B," said Amy.

"Confirmed," said John.

Amy prepared herself for the next stage. The power requirements for acceleration were enormous as the klystrons surrounding the coiled tubes had to fire at certain intervals to ensure the increased velocity of the protons. Superconductors had to focus the proton beam in a precise manner so collision events could occur, and the coolants had to flow to ensure the whole thing did not cause a meltdown. Any loss of power or any fault in any of the components would cause a failure. Vix would be running on its highest possible setting as the protons approached the speed of light. The sheer energy output in the next room was more than the whole island used for a day.

Amy bit her lip and then inhaled deeply.

"Okay, introduce protons into the acceleration coils. Coil A first please," she said.

John pressed the button, and the flashing red LED reflected on his face.

A new sound began to emanate from the clean room, a sound of a high-pitched whine. John had commented during their testing that it resembled the washing machine on a high spin cycle. It was an adequate comparison, thought Amy as she looked through the glass at Vix.

"Insert into Coil B please," said Amy, raising her voice above the noise. The thick glass did not eliminate the entire din.

John pressed the next button and had the pair of them flashing red.

The sound doubled up as the twin coils, surrounded by superconducting magnets, fired up. White nitrogen steam fell from the top of Vix to the floor, where it found its way out through vents. Inside the coils, the temperature was dropping close to absolute zero. Amy watched the screen for the deep cold to register. The whining sound reached a zenith and became a constant drone.

"Are we ready yet?" asked John, his hand hovering over a lever.

"Not quite," said Amy. "A few more moments. The temperature isn't quite there yet."

They waited a few more seconds. On-screen, the twin bar graphs showing the temperature continued to fall. Then, when just a sliver, the box turned green indicating the optimal temperature for acceleration had been achieved.

"Okay, I think we are ready to go," said Amy.

"You sure?"

"Yes, but keep your hand over the emergency stop, just in case."

John turned and looked at Amy. Now that they had reached the point of acceleration, she looked anxious. After he increased the speed of the acceleration, they would be at a no-return point. If they wished to halt the process, they would have to hit the emergency stop button, which severed the power ties to Vix. It would be weeks before they could make another attempt.

"Okay, let's go," said Amy. "Keep your fingers crossed."

John pushed up both acceleration levers. He had designed them to resemble the volume and mixing controls in a music studio, and they slid up smoothly.

"You've never been superstitious," said John.

"I am today," she replied.

From the clean room came a noise of revving, low at first, but growing in intensity. Their laboratory shook with the vibrations. Amy caught her reflection in the screen she was examining. She barely recognised the ashen-faced woman staring back at her, and she wiped her perspiring palms on her white coat.

The noise continued to increase, as though the throttle were being pressed down hard on a racing car, and she wondered whether they should have invested in ear protectors for the experiments.

Too late now.

The screen ahead of her flickered, giving her the figures on the proton velocity. Tiny particles whizzing around these tubes: first descending them, reaching the lowest coil, before transferring in a larger loop back to the top to continue their power surge. Relativity made the protons increase in size as they approached the speed of light; and she saw them as shiny, glowing baubles flying through their space to their final destination.

"Next step, please John," said Amy. She now had to raise her voice considerably.

John's next step was to ensure that he released the full reserves of power to the magnets focusing the protons. As the particles travelled, the energy requirements needed to keep increasing their speed rose exponentially. Power, drawing from the geothermal plant and stored in huge cells, fed into the microwave generators surrounding the coils. This boosted the speed of the particles to just below the speed of light. It was a feat only equalled by the Large Hadron Collider and was the most intensive process of their run.

As the power surge hit Vix, Amy felt her teeth rattle in her skull, the gigantic amount of energy leeching into the cave around them.

Keeping her focus on the screen, which shook and

blurred her vision, she could make out the velocity measurements of the particles. The speed of light was 186,000 miles per second, and these protons — approaching this - were now speeding around the coiled chambers millions of times for every breath Amy took. It was a concept hard to fathom, even for her and her academic life as a physicist. Numbers on a screen replacing physical reality.

They had reached the top speed.

It was time.

"Get ready to open the collision chamber manifold," she said.

He rested his palms on the manifold buttons, awaiting Amy's instruction. "I guess now we'll see whether the calibration is okay," he said.

Too intent on the screen, Amy ignored John. Checking for the optimal moment, she held her breath.

"Now," she said.

John slapped his palms down on the buttons simultaneously.

On-screen she could see the protons flood into the chamber. Data streamed onto her monitor.

"Collision events occurring," said Amy, the excitement in her voice increasing, she half-stood out of her chair. A look of pure joy spread across her face.

John looked at her, as a smile broadened and eyes widened.

"Collision events happening, right now!" she repeated. She jumped up out of her seat, her face euphoric, and grabbed John around the shoulders, hugging him.

John accepted the hug but didn't return it.

Realising that they were not finished yet, Amy took herself back to her seat and checked the monitors.

"We're getting a bank of readings here," she said. "It will take me a while to get through them."

The noise and the shaking still rocked their laboratory.

"Particle events still occurring in the chamber," said Amy. "All protons should now be jumping back and forth in the chamber like ping-pong balls. I think we are now safe closing the manifolds and powering down the superconductors."

John nodded and brought down the acceleration levers first, before hitting the buttons that turned off the magnets.

Amy sat looking through the glass at Vix, expecting the noise to die down.

Nothing happened.

The whine and the shaking continued to emanate from Vix.

"Have you powered down the superconductors?"

"Yes," said John.

Amy flipped her screen with a key press and could see that the superconductors were powering down, and yet the sound persisted.

If anything, it was becoming louder.

"What is that?" she asked.

John looked up, through the glass at Vix. The machine shook, as though full of fury, and he could see it straining against the steel girders that anchored it to the rock walls.

Amy checked the screens again, trying to remain calm as the vibrations around the room intensified.

"There are still events happening in the chamber," she said. "Or at least, *an* event."

"What does that mean?" asked John.

"I'm not detecting any further sub-atomic particles hitting the detectors," she said. "But some other event is taking place in the chamber."

"Do you know what it is?"

The water bottle rattled out of its holder and fell onto the floor, rolling towards the window. The overhead lighting flickered.

"I've no idea what it is, but the data coming through from the sensors is huge."

"Should we be concerned?"

Then another sound joined. The sound of screeching metal. Vix was starting to lose its structural integrity.

"We need to be concerned," said Amy, still wondering what the streaming data meant.

John, still looking through at Vix, noticed the bolts holding the collision chamber were rattling. Tiny gaps appeared between bolts, and from them, a white light emerged. Like a star was trying to escape from the base of Vix.

"What on earth…?" exclaimed Amy as she saw it.

"What do we do?" said John.

The sound around them began to hurt Amy's ears, and it became louder still. The strip lights swung on their hinges casting light around them. She tried to focus on the screen; to fathom what was happening, but the vibrations blurred her vision.

The floor buckled under her feet, causing her to lose her balance. Holding on to the front of the console, she approached the glass. The lights were everywhere, escaping in shafts from the manifolds, holding a rainbow of crystalline brilliance.

The centre was in the collision chamber - made from inch-thick steel, lead-lined.

It was warping inwards.

Panic replaced the curiosity.

She leapt back behind the console, to where John was still sitting – his face blank and incomprehensible.

She made a fist and slammed it on the emergency stop button.

With all power cut to Vix, the lights went out, the noise muted, and the vibrations subsided. The strip lights continued swinging but began to settle.

For a moment, as the chaos died down, she stood – her fist still pressing the button. She heard the sound of her rapid breathing.

She looked at John, who returned her stare with a white glint.

"What happened?" he asked.

"I have absolutely no idea," she said. "But I do know that Vix was ready to implode. Whatever it was, it was destroying it."

She lifted her fist off the button gingerly and stood for a moment while her racing heart settled.

Returning to her seat, she spun it to face the screens and rubbed her eyes before checking the read-out. John watched her as she took in the data, she was breathing heavily, but her eyes were wide and full of wonder.

"These readings are off the scale," she said.

"Do we have data on what just happened?" asked John.

"Just measurements – pressure, temperature, radiation, energy – that kind of thing. We also have the reading from the plates on the sub-atomic particles created. I don't know at this stage whether that is related to this event or not. Whatever it was, the energy going into the collision chamber was feeding it, and it was growing."

"What's our next step?"

"We need to know what we're dealing with," she said. "It will take me a while to crunch this data. I'll then try and work out the event, get my blackboard out."

Amy turned her back on John, looking back through the glass. Vestiges of vapour still obscured the mass of metal and circuitry beyond, but her gaze sat on the base of Vix, on the chamber where an event had just happened. She had expected the collisions to create a variety of sub-atomic particles, but what just happened had surprised and shocked her; she could not shake the feeling that they had been moments away from something disastrous.

Chapter Eight – Eggs and Clay

I

John, dressed in white coveralls and helmet, shone his torch around Vix. They dimmed the lights in the clean room to preserve the depleted power cells, and the torch helped him focus on specific parts.

Returning to the laboratory the day after the event, leaving the machine overnight to cool and settle, Amy sat watching John through the glass. She had found sleep difficult. Her adrenaline had lasted hours after they had cut the power, and she knew it would be pointless to begin a rational assessment of the event while her mind raced. Better to calm down, rest, and reflect. Then the work would begin.

The first order of the day, however, was to inspect Vix. See the damage caused. Perhaps this would provide some indication, some clue as to the cause.

John swept his torch beam across the gigantic structure, searching individual components.

The top of the machine extended above him – all the entry points and valves that controlled the injection of hydrogen gas seemed intact and undamaged; along with the ellipsoid electrical field chambers on either side. The supporting girders at the top, twin struts of steel that stabilised Vix and dampened the machine from the vibrations, had not performed well during the run. He would have to look at strengthening these.

Moving his beam downwards, the acceleration generators and coils also seemed intact and still connected with the superconducting magnets. Damage here was minimal, but he would need to check the coolant levels if they were attempting another run. Recalling the memory of the build, this section proved to be the most tricky and complex. They had spent over a year of testing and retrying different magnetic field configurations to get the superconductors aligned. Thankfully, they still appeared to be intact and functioning.

The bottom of the machine was the most concerning to John. Covering the entire base of Vix, the two-metre high, four-metre-long steel box housed the collision chamber, along with the detection plates and sensors that gave them the output data. The construction was steel, inlaid with lead. On all sides, the metal had warped inwards, and the manifold areas – secured with four-inch bolts – had loosened and sheared, exposing parts of the interior. They couldn't hope to perform another run while this section was in this condition.

"How's it looking?" she asked, through the intercom.

"Not good," said John, "We're looking at several weeks of work to replace and fix the collision chamber. We also need to look at the whole structural integrity of Vix, I'm not sure it's safe or secure unless we do."

"What is your best estimate time-wise?" she asked.

"Six weeks perhaps. We'll need to order the replacement parts internationally, so longer, depending on how quickly they can be delivered. It will be costly too."

Amy thought for a moment and looked at the output on her screen.

"There is another option," said John.

"What's that?"

"*I* could fix it…"

Amy understood exactly what he meant by that.

"I don't want you to touch it," she said.

"You don't want it repaired?"

"Not right now," said Amy. "I'm thinking that the event may not have happened if Vix wasn't in its current configuration. If we change it now, then maybe we'll lose whatever feature in the machine caused it."

"So what's your plan?" asked John.

"Figure this out. Then we can make a decision about the repair."

For a moment, as she looked at him through the glass, dwarfed by the behemoth he was inspecting, she felt the weight of a future momentous discovery. It both thrilled and terrified her. The thrill of further understanding the nature of the universe, but the terror of the potentially destructive nature of this collection of components sat inside a cave on a small island in the Caribbean.

"Okay," said John, and headed to the airlock. "It looks like you have a lot of work ahead."

II

Even Amy acknowledged she had underused her study in recent weeks. While they finished the construction of their laboratory and Vix, along with the hurricane and dealing with John's condition, she had neglected to spend any time working in the space she had created for herself to do so.

Her study was her haven. A room where she could retreat and not be distracted or have any other concerns than her work. They had converted one of the bedrooms in their home, and it had a pleasant outlook over the bay to the Pitons. Knowing how important daydreaming was when she formulated her theories, she had placed a reclining rattan chair in front of the floor-to-ceiling window that gave that aspect. When she needed to escape, she could sit and gaze over at the twin, green-covered mountains and let her mind wander.

A desk sat in the centre of the room, and her computer sat on that. The computer fed directly into the data banks from the laboratory below their home, and she could access any information from this hub. Bookshelves lined the walls, full of scientific works – mainly physics and chemistry tomes – but others that dealt with engineering and computing.

The only other item of furniture in the room was a small table next to her thinking chair, and against the outer wall, a blackboard.

Amy sat at her desk, the clicking of the keyboard and the swish of the sea through the open window the only sounds in the room as she transferred the data from the event into her spreadsheet. The pages of the sheet fed into each other, which gave her visibility on the relationships between the measurements where she could spot patterns. It was the first stage of understanding what had occurred with Vix the day before: once she had organised the information, she could begin to formulate the reasoning and the theory.

So intent was she on the screen that she did not see John come through the door. As he did so, the dress that Amy had hung on the back, swished outward, and he smoothed it back down.

"Must we go to this tonight?" said John, indicating the

dress.

Amy jumped, startled out of her fixation.

"Yes – we must," she said. "It's the least we can do for Samuel after his help when you returned."

"I thought you hated social gatherings," said John.

"They are a necessary evil sometimes, and he's been very kind to us over the last few weeks."

"You're not planning to stay here and continue your work then?"

Amy paused and leaned back in her chair, and rubbed her face. "Listen, John…" she started, looking for the right words, "…I still don't believe that you are not my husband. But John loved going on a night out. He always had to talk *me* around going out. And now you're here trying to persuade me otherwise."

"You still think your husband is alive?"

"Yes, I do. I mean, you said so yourself – you don't know *what* you are. Who's to say that you are not still the John that I married, and whatever energy is inside you has altered your brain chemistry? You claim to have a consciousness, but not have life – I refuse to believe that. I *can't* believe that."

John stood in the doorway, staring at her with a blank face – he seemed to be searching for an appropriate response.

"I won't mourn my husband's death while he is standing right in front of me, no matter how differently he behaves. And another thing – do you really think I can be in the correct headspace if I'm grieving over the man I love? The only thing pressing me onwards with Vix is the hope that by solving this mystery, I can find out what has happened to you."

She looked at the screen and the cells full of numbers and formulas. At that moment, from her distraction, that's all they were to her. Shaking her head, she clicked the save button with her mouse and closed down the sheet.

III

The taxi's headlights swept around the paved entrance road to the Paradise Hotel. The marble frontage, illuminated by soft spotlights, was a vision of palms, colourful flower beds and tinkling waterfalls. The nameplate for the hotel, built from hollowed-out sandstone, had gas-lit flames burning inside each letter.

The Paradise Hotel was an upmarket retreat for tourists, one of the many on the island that enjoyed a sea-front location, several swimming pools, and private access to a sandy stretch of beach; but also it had a restaurant open to the public, and an evening entertainment area with a stage and dancefloor.

The attendant opened the door and Amy exited first, adjusting her sleeveless black dress and teetering on her heels. Her make-up felt as though it was melting on her face with the warmth of the night. John followed, dressed casually in trousers and a white shirt – jacketless – and looked even more uncomfortable.

The attendant welcomed them and unhooked the rope, which led to the covered walkway. Along the walkway, leading to the beach, poles with lit torches guided them to the restaurant area. The flickering light illuminated Amy's face as she linked arms with John. He looked at her as she did so, but made no motion to remove them.

"I need you to be John tonight," she said.

"What does that mean?"

"It means that whatever inside you that is my husband needs to be present this evening."

"I'm not sure that is possible," he said.

"Just...try your best," she said. "Samuel still thinks you're suffering from shock, so we have a little leeway, but you need to at least show a glimpse of the man."

The walkway opened out into an area with tables and chairs arranged around a stage at the front of the room. Every table had a red glass cup with a glowing candle inside. The torches still provided their subtle lighting around the edge of the room, covered by an open, palm-thatched wooden roof. At this time of night, the room was empty as the patrons enjoyed their evening meal, but a small band of entertainers milled about the stage, setting up their sound equipment.

They skirted the room, and the salt smell of the sea reached Amy's nose from the darkness beyond the torches. The odd glimpse of light catching the waves in the darkness offered her the idea of the beach beyond.

Extending into the sea, a wide pier glowed in the night, brightly lit with yellow lamps swinging in the night breeze from the rafters. Tables lined the pier in neat rows, and smartly tailored waiters and waitresses wearing crisp white uniforms served the diners enjoying their meals.

Amy realised with a certain nostalgia that it had been a while – months - since she had heard the sound of cutlery on plates, clinking glasses, and the general hubbub of people enjoying themselves.

The head waiter, smiling, looked at his guest list and

greeted them at the pier entrance. Amy spotted Samuel at a nearby table and indicated to him, and the waiter led them over.

"Sorry if we're late," said Amy, checking her watch.

"No, no – I'm early," said Samuel, standing to greet them.

Amy returned Samuel's smile and gave him a polite kiss on the cheek. Going for a handshake with John, he had already sat down, unaware of the protocol. Samuel looked on, the smile remaining on his face, but his eyes scrutinising John's behaviour.

The waiter handed over menus, and they decided to order a bottle of white wine. The speciality of the restaurant was the local seafood; the flying fish in particular featured in several varieties, along with red snapper, swordfish and grouper. The waiter left with the wine order.

"Thank you for this evening," said Samuel, as they perused the menu.

"It's our way of saying thanks for what you did for us – especially for me – just after the hurricane," said Amy. "I'm not sure I would've coped without your kindness."

"It was nothing," said Samuel. "Just being neighbourly."

The waiter returned with the wine and poured three glasses, wiping the lip of the bottle with the napkin draped over his wrist after every pour.

"I'm not sure I would've been that neighbourly," said Amy.

"Ah, you're not as misanthropic as you would have us believe," said Samuel. "If kindness were needed, you'd be first to deliver it."

"Shall we have a toast?" said Amy, lifting her glass.

"What shall we toast to?" said Samuel, lifting his glass in return.

John, looking uncomfortable, looked at them both – and Amy stared at him meaningfully – and lifted his glass.

"To good neighbours," said Amy.

"Good neighbours," repeated Samuel.

"Cheers," said Amy, and clinked her glass.

John, watching the dinner ritual, looked confused as to who he should connect his glass with until both Amy and Samuel aimed theirs at his. They tapped his glass in unison.

"Cheers," said John, muttering.

The waiter hovered over their table, with his order pad in his hand and looked at his patrons expectantly. Amy chose the flying fish, and John chose the same, looking at Amy as he did so.

"Get what you like, John," said Amy. "You don't have to have the same as me?"

"No this is fine," he said.

Samuel chose the vegetarian option – curried cauliflower on basmati rice.

"Not very Caribbean," he said, "But I'm watching my meat intake at the moment." He patted his belly to illustrate.

The waiter went away, and an awkward silence descended before Samuel broke it.

"So, how have you all been?" by all, he meant John.

"We've been fine," said Amy. "Haven't we, John?"

"We have," said John, "We've been fine."

She couldn't be sure but thought she saw Samuel's eye twitch just a little when John spoke.

"Did you hear about that policeman who went missing

in Castries?" said Samuel, being conversational.

"I've not," said Amy, "I've not caught up on much news recently. Where was he last seen?"

"A number of witnesses saw him chasing a thief through the streets. The thief had apparently grabbed a case from a tourist, and the policeman had chased him. I've heard reports that the thief had jumped from a first-floor window to escape."

"And he went missing after that?" said Amy.

"According to the news reports the chase took them into some alleys that led out of the town," said Samuel. "He hasn't been seen since. The authorities have combed the area, and they've had divers in the sea nearby, but nothing found so far."

"Have they managed to track the thief?" John surprised them both by asking the question, showing a sudden interest in this news.

"No, not a thing," said Samuel. "They've managed to capture a blurry image of the man's face on CCTV, but the quality isn't great. The picture is in the newspaper, in case anyone recognises him."

John leaned back in his seat, seemingly deep in thought.

After a short wait, their meals arrived. They ate politely, stopping to comment on how delicious their food tasted, but otherwise, the sound of cutlery on porcelain drifted over the table. The bottle soon emptied, and they ordered another.

As they neared the end of the meal, their bellies filled, the alcohol freed their tongues. Even John relaxed as the evening progressed. Much of the chat was about Samuel's work at the hospital and how busy he had been dealing with the injured, along with problems of keeping up with the medical supplies. He asked about their work, and Amy mentioned that they had begun their experiments, although she did not elaborate on the event that had occurred in Vix. No sense in revealing too much information.

As they finished, she wiped her mouth with her napkin, and noticed a smear of lipstick on it. She excused herself to the bathroom where she went to the mirror to reapply the make-up. A quick tousle of her hair, and she returned to the pier.

As she approached the table, the guests were starting to gather for the entertainment – which appeared to be steel kettle drums and dancers. Stepping onto the pier to return to her table she noticed that Samuel was trying to talk to John. Hanging back for a moment, she examined her husband's face. He was unsmiling, but replying in very brief answers. No doubt, Samuel was asking how he was feeling in his doctor's capacity, and she wondered how John would respond when she was not around.

As she neared, a smile came over Samuel's face, and John turned to face her – looking a little abashed.

"What were you two talking about?" asked Amy.

"I was asking John if he could now recall anything from when he went missing," said Samuel.

Amy turned to John, hoping that he had not admitted anything about his new nature.

"I have no memory of it," said John. "I just remember arriving back home that night when you found me."

She breathed a sigh of relief. Samuel could become involved if he suspected John's mental health had become an issue – but John had appeared to understand this.

"That's right," said Amy, and she smiled at John, who

returned the smile. "He can't recall a thing from that time. I still think it was a miracle he survived."

"It certainly was," said Samuel, "And without a scratch. Miracle isn't a strong enough term, I think."

With their meal finished, they gathered themselves, ordered more drinks, and took their seat in front of the stage. Burning torches flickered in the night air, joined by the glowing red candles that sat on each table. The band began to play, starting with a gentle, warm tempo. Jangling drums echoed across the audience, and three young women dressed in the traditional outfits of the island, long colourful dresses and stacked head wrappings, began to sing in patois.

They sat and watched – Samuel looking misty-eyed as he tapped his finger on the table to the music, as though reliving his younger years and evenings spent with his late wife.

Amy allowed the music to fill her mind, and she felt transported to another time and place. One where everything in life was simple and happy, with palm trees swaying over golden sand beaches, and the gentle hush of the sea bringing calmness and serenity.

John's face was rigid and inscrutable, the sheen on his skin showing the warm, humid night. He caught her looking and returned her gaze, his irises white as they reflected the firelight.

The volume of the music increased as the band played to encourage the audience to become involved. Many guests rose from their seats to dance.

Samuel looked at Amy expectantly.

"Oh, I don't know…" began Amy.

"Please, indulge an old man," said Samuel. "John, do

you mind if I borrow your wife for a few minutes?"

John looked at Samuel, surprised and unsure of what he was asking. "Erm, not at all," he said.

Samuel stood and held his hand to Amy. She took it. Normally, she never danced – but she'd had many glasses of wine, and she felt some of her inhibitions relaxing.

The wooden dance floor felt bouncy under her heels. Taking Samuel's hand, and placing the other on his shoulder, he took her on her hip with a light touch.

"Mary and I used to dance to this a lot, back when we were younger," he said.

"You must miss your wife so much," said Amy.

"I do. Every day feels tough and – well, *empty* – without her."

"Loneliness is a terrible thing," she said, recalling her feelings when John disappeared.

"Of course. But as a doctor, you get to realise that death is the way of things. This world is for the young, and those of us that have had a happy and productive life must make way for them. Like you and John."

"She lives on in your memories," said Amy, suddenly uncomfortable.

"And in that way, we can all live for eternity – as long as you are remembered for the good you did during your life. But come, this talk is a little morbid. Tonight is about celebrating friendship."

They moved around slowly, not paying attention to the music too much as the band struck their metal drums lightly, producing a haunting, almost ethereal, sound.

"So how has John been since we last spoke?" asked Samuel. "He seems much better, but not back to his old self as yet."

"That pretty much sums it up," said Amy. "Every day he seems to come back to reality a little more. He can remember our life from before the storm, but he still seems to disassociate himself from it."

"That's interesting. Have you thought that counselling might help? I can put you in touch with an excellent therapist."

She shuddered a little when she considered how John would react to a therapist. He would be committed for sure, if he revealed his belief that he was no longer human, and then if they discover his talent…

"I think we're both reluctant to go down that path," said Amy. "Just being at home and getting back into a routine seems to be working for now. He's coming out of his shell a little more."

"Fair enough," said Samuel, "I'm not sure why you wouldn't want to take therapy, as it could help, but you know where I am if you need me."

Amy nodded her thanks and continued dancing in silence until the song stopped. They clapped and retook their seats.

Picking up the bottle, and pouring herself another glass of wine, Amy drank deeply as the band struck up their next number.

IV

Reclining on her sofa in the study, gazing outside through her rust-coloured sunglasses, she saw that the day's weather had arrived damp and misty. The lenses filtered the outdoor light that assailed her throbbing temples. Massaging the bridge of her nose, lifting the glasses as she did, she tried to ease her pounding headache. Hangovers had been rare in recent years, she enjoyed a glass of wine, but she rarely drank anything more than a shared bottle.

Through the open windows, she could just about discern the Pitons across the bay through the mist and her darkened lenses. Overnight, the cloud base had descended over the island, covering windows and vegetation with a sprinkling of dew. Nevertheless, it was humid and she felt overly warm. Whether caused by the weather or the alcohol, she could not be sure.

Despite her discomfort today, she had enjoyed the night. The food and the drink along with the music, and even the dancing, had given her back a taste of normality and good times. She had to admit, as averse to social situations as she was, being around people once again felt pleasant. Even John seemed more himself – whether due to him being more like her husband, or whether he was acting the role – she could not be sure. But it was the closest they'd had to a date since his return.

Samuel had been his usual lovely self too. She had sensed that he was assessing John's condition. Otherwise, he had seemed to enjoy the night. Amy was glad. He must have had a tough time since the loss of his wife – something she could begin to relate to – but he had shown them nothing but kindness since they became neighbours. It felt good to show their appreciation.

The end of the night for her was a blur. She had a vague memory of getting into a taxi – the three of them had shared one home – but she could not remember entering the house. She had woken in the early hours, minus her shoes but still wearing her dress, and felt awful. She was alone. She had stopped wondering what John did during the night, although she was positive that he did not share her same hangover, despite him matching her drink for drink. He did not even seem to be tipsy during the night at all.

When she woke, she took some paracetamol. They dampened the ache in her temples without curing it. She made herself a large jug of ice water and decided to relax in the peace of her study. Today, she could not face the drama of recent weeks. She wanted solitude. Even the weather, damp as it was, seemed to calm her with its gentle fog blanket and tinkling moisture.

The jug of ice water sat on a three-legged table next to her sofa, and next to it lay a glass. Her mouth had been dry ever since she had woken, and her skin felt tight and uncomfortable. It was a side-effect she suffered due to wearing make-up, especially so since she hadn't removed it when she returned home. The shower when she woke had done little to alleviate it, and she knew she had to keep on hydrating.

It seemed an effort to move, but she swung her legs to a sitting position and picked up the glass. She poured the water from the jug into it and heard the ice cubes clunk as they slid down and struck the base of the glass. The sound alone felt refreshing, but she watched as a pair of ice cubes, frozen together, drifted upwards from the base, spinning gently as they rose – a pair of dancing cubes waltzing around in the water.

<u>V</u>

Standing at the back door, looking out over the terrace,

John could not see the ocean due to the mist, but he could still hear the waves and the air had a tang to it. It disturbed something within him. Something was coming. Something that would threaten their work and the very reason he was here.

And it was getting closer.

If Amy had seen him staring into space, she would be upset. Following her comments, he knew that, for her to flourish, she needed him to be like the husband she remembered. He needed to turn inwards to discover what had made this man the person he had been. She still thought that John was alive. That this power to manipulate the world around him was just another scientific question for her to find a solution. Once it was, then her husband would be back.

Maybe she was right.

The sound of smashing glass interrupted his musings. He flicked his head around to the sound of the source, before bounding through the house, up the stairs, and bursting open the door to where she was working.

Amy sat upright on her sofa, her mouth agape and eyes wide – but staring into space. By her feet, broken glass and a water stain spread around the carpet.

"What happened?" asked John.

She looked at him and seemed to snap out of the daze. "The glass fell when I tried to put it on the table," she mumbled, her tone absent-minded.

"Are you okay?"

She didn't reply but continued to look around with unseeing eyes as her focus lay inwards.

"What if I told you that I may have figured out what

happened with Vix?" she said, snapping from her fixation.

John stared at her questioningly.

"I need to talk it through," she said, and John could hear the excitement growing in her voice.

"Okay, what do you need?"

"Eggs," she said.

"Eggs?"

Amy nodded. "We have some in the fridge."

She got up from her seat, without bothering to clear up the broken glass, stepped over it, and pushed her way past John. He followed her bare feet as she padded down the stairs, through the lounge, and into the kitchen. Opening the refrigerator door, she took out a carton of eggs and placed them on the counter.

"Okay," said Amy, composing herself. "I need you to listen and make sure what I'm saying makes sense."

"I'm listening," said John, standing on the opposite side of the counter.

"So I see three steps to progress our work," she began. "The first step is to figure out what happened with *Vix* to create that event. Then we work out what exactly the *event* was."

"And the third step?"

"The third step is to decide what we do next about it."

"Makes sense," said John. "So why the eggs?"

"Because I may have sussed the first step," she said.

Pausing for a moment, her head full of ideas, Amy had a sudden flashback to John chopping his hand off in the exact spot she now stood. She dismissed the thought, not wanting to be distracted.

"I'm listening," said John.

"So, we fire protons at each other," said Amy, and she removed two eggs from the carton and held them in front of her. It was not necessary to use the eggs as a proton illustration for John, but doing so aided her thought process.

"So we whizz them around the coiled tubes until they reach ninety-nine per cent the speed of light...," she spun her hands around in a circular motion, "...and then..."

She slapped her two hands together. Using as much force as she could muster in her hungover state. The eggs exploded, with bits of shell flying out and the contents oozing between her fingers, dripping on the work surface.

"So the detectors around the collision chamber then pick up what is thrown off when they collide," she continued. "So the shell would be a quark, the yolk a muon, and the egg white a gluon, for example."

John looked at her questioningly. "This we know already," he said. "What's your point?"

"What I've just demonstrated is what is *meant* to happen," she said. "But in our case, it didn't. Something happened that we did not expect."

"What was that?"

Amy padded over to the sink and rinsed her hands under the tap, washing off the bits of raw egg, before drying her hands on the kitchen towel. She then returned to the counter, flipped open the egg carton, and removed two further eggs.

"So we planned that the protons would travel in a straight path to the opposing particle, and smash into them."

She illustrated her point by placing the two eggs on the counter facing each other, the thin points of the shell on the inside. Propelling them along the counter in a straight line, she brought them together until the tips of the shell touched.

"This didn't happen, at least not in this way," she said.

John folded his arms and waited for Amy to continue her demonstration.

"There was a factor, built into Vix, that we did not anticipate," she said.

Pulling the eggs apart again, she took them back to their starting position.

"The protons are accelerated in the coils. Surrounded by the superconductors – their magnetic field *spun* the protons around the coils. So the protons were not just travelling in a straight line, they were also spinning."

In her demonstration, she twirled the eggs on their spots. As she continued to spin the eggs, she brought them closer together until they touched once again.

"So it was the coils in Vix that introduced this element of spin?" asked John.

"Exactly."

"So what does this mean?" asked John.

Amy looked around her, looking over the kitchen counter and the table behind her. "I need something sticky," she said.

"Modelling clay in the tool shed?" said John. "We have some left over from when we were mocking up the construction."

"Perfect," said Amy.

Leaving Amy behind with her thoughts, John left the room and exited the back door. Ignoring the dampness that clung to his clothes, he crossed the terrace to the wooden tool shed adjoining the house. No more than a lean-to, it opened inwards to a musty pile of well-worn tools and heavy packs of cement stacked against the far wall. John entered the shed and went straight to the shelving on his left. Picking up a plastic tub full of brown clay, he returned to the kitchen. Placing the tub on the counter, he peeled off the plastic lid. Amy's hand dived in and scooped out a dun lump.

"You grab some too," she said.

John obeyed and pulled out some more clay, just enough to fill his hand.

"Good, now make them into globes," instructed Amy, and she began to manoeuvre and work the clay around her palms, flattening and squeezing it into a smooth ball. John, watching her, did the same.

Grabbing the clay ball from him, Amy held up the two brown globes in front of her between her thumb and forefinger in each hand.

"So we have the two protons," she said. "Due to special relativity, they have increased their mass due to them travelling so fast, which means upon collision gluon interactions are more likely."

"You're losing me a little," said John.

"Basically, the protons seem larger to the observer the higher the velocity they are travelling at. And because of the sub-atomic properties of protons, which are made up of quarks, heavy ions and gluons, we are more likely to have gluon interactions at high speed."

"What is a gluon?"

"It's the sub-atomic particle responsible for the strong nuclear force inside the proton," she said. "The thing that binds the particle together."

"I see," said John.

"However, in Vix, we have *another* factor to consider. The proton beams are not fully calibrated. So even though we may have collisions in the centre of the beam – as intended – on the fringes we have a layer where protons are only *partially* colliding."

Amy took the two clay balls and brought them together so they were touching. But they touched at the poles rather than the equator.

"So on these partial collisions, the proton is not destroyed. Instead, we have the gluon interactions between the two protons, and they *fuse*."

"Fuse?"

"At least partially. The protons are super-heated due to their accelerated state, but not enough for complete nuclear fusion to take place. But also, they are not fully aligned for them to smash each other apart."

She squeezed the two balls together, until the top and bottom globes joined in a 3-dimensional figure of eight.

"Normally, this partial collision would only cause the protons to bounce off each other, but we also have the *rotation*. They don't bounce as their spin causes them to go into a mad orbit. Like the two particles are waltzing around, joined at the hip."

"Waltzing close to the speed of light," said John.

"That's right," said Amy, "And because of the energy of these partially fused particles, every other proton that comes into contact with them adds its mass and energy. So we have partially fused protons, spinning like water wheels in a raging torrent of the beam, gathering more protons and increasing their mass. The laws of quantum mechanics state that they will want to find an equilibrium, they want to *resolve* their state. But while the beam still has energy, it keeps spinning and spinning. They stretch as the mass increases – neither breaking apart nor fusing – unable to find their natural state."

Amy spun the fused clay balls around from the middle, using her free hand to stretch the balls outward as they move around.

"So what does this mean?" asked John.

"It means that we have broken the laws of physics," said Amy. "And to our current knowledge, there's only one place where this currently occurs in the universe."

"A black hole," said John, his basic knowledge of physics lending the answer.

"More specifically, the singularity at the centre of the black hole."

"So we have created a singularity in Vix?"

"It would be tiny and only flashing into existence for a moment, while it was still being fed with energy."

"Which is why it stopped when we cut the power," said John.

"And why it caused such damage to the collision chamber," said Amy.

"What would've happened if we hadn't cut the power?"

"It would keep growing as the mass increased," said Amy. "At some point, when the mass of the surrounding atoms came within its zone of influence – its event horizon – then it would feed itself from this and keep growing until no further matter could reach it."

"That sounds dangerous."

"It would be catastrophic," said Amy. "It would be incredibly catastrophic."

"Would it destroy Vix?"

"It would consume Vix, and then the laboratory, and then this house."

Amy paused and looked out of the window, through the mist and across the bay. It looked so calm and peaceful. So normal.

Her thoughts took her to a dark place, and when she spoke, she said the words quietly.

"Then swallow St Lucia, in all likelihood. And would continue to grow and expand as long as it had mass to consume. It would be a global catastrophe."

Chapter Nine – Dual Nature

I

The white screen reflected in John's eyes as he scanned the pages of the internet, sitting at the desk in the study. Ahead of him, Amy in front of her blackboard, chalk stick in hand, making calculations on the equations littering her vision.

"That policeman is still missing," said John, as he perused the local news pages. "It looks like the suspect is also wanted for several shop thefts too."

Amy hummed an acknowledgement, too engrossed in her formula to pay much attention. Her chalk squeaked across the board, but she shook her head as she assessed it, and then erased it with a cloth.

"A face matching the man wanted in connection with the missing policeman has been put up on the website. They've managed to capture the same person on CCTV."

Amy began to re-write the numbers, not paying him any attention.

"He looks familiar to me," said John. "Do you recognise him?"

Amy turned to him, the irritation at the interruption clear on her face. Swivelling the screen so she could see, she sighed and approached the desk. A grainy, black-and-white picture of a man wearing a beach vest and shorts looked back at her. The man had a bald head and appeared to be of Caribbean origin. He was also rather thin, with hollow-looking eyes, and Amy wondered if he was an addict.

"No, I've never seen him before," she said and returned

to her blackboard.

"Strange," said John. "Something about him…"

He did not finish his sentence, and Amy caught his tone.

"Could it be someone you remember from before the storm?" she asked.

"Possibly, I can't be sure," he said.

"This isn't someone I've ever met," said Amy. "I'm pretty sure of that, so I'm wondering why he's sparking your memory."

John shook his head, unable to answer.

II

Mani extended his arms, propelling himself through the water. The spray glistened in the moonlight, but otherwise, his night swimming could have looked like a shoal of fish from an observer on the shore. With every stroke, he dipped his head below the water for a few seconds, before returning to the surface with a splutter. He could detect the muscles in the body aching and complaining about the exertion, but he knew this was making the muscles, bone and sinew stronger and more resilient for what was to come. This was not necessary for his plans, but he could see the advantage of fitness, especially following the foot chase with the policeman.

He had considered changing the physiology, altering the bone structure and musculature, but that would use precious energy; and he was so close to being where he needed to be for the next step. The body could repair itself, and he could change his look cosmetically. Losing his hair had prevented recognition from anyone that may have known him on the island, and his body shape was altering through his diet and exercise. Anything more would be a waste.

Swimming towards the dry land, with the tide assisting his progress as he caught a wave, his feet sunk into the wet sand as he emerged from the water. The horizon was just beginning to glow red as the daylight arrived. He was naked, but the beach was deserted.

Avoiding the hours of sun, when it shone its warm rays over the browning tourists, he had opted for a fitness regime under cover of darkness. He spent his days resting, sleeping and eating in his shack - conscious of the attention he had brought upon himself. He had believed that getting rid of the police officer would eliminate tracking, but he had not banked on the cameras, and the willingness of the public to track down the suspect of a potential police murderer.

So he kept his routine to the hours the sun disappeared around the other side of the planet, but he still required vigilance. Couples taking a romantic midnight stroll, and even one adventurous pair, who had also decided to go skinny-dipping, had almost seen him. He avoided them by swimming away underwater to the edge of the bay and taking cover in some rocks. He could have made them disappear, but he had learned that missing people drew more attention. One missing policeman was something, doubt would still exist to his whereabouts; but if more were to vanish - that was something the authorities would come down upon hard.

The last few weeks, despite his isolation, had been productive. He had not expanded any further unnecessary energy, and his physique had improved. Mani had not been in as good shape at all in his lifetime, now that he had flushed out the poison. The muscle tissue had honed with the exercise. Any person that knew him would barely recognise him.

He worked his way back through the trees to his shack. The glow of the dawn had begun to creep over the silhouette of the mountainous interior, and that meant the first visitors of the day would arrive. The shadow of his shack emerged from the undergrowth and he slipped inside as the sun's first bloom shone overhead.

Inside, stacked in a corner of the room, discarded plastic water bottles, food containers and wrappers. Opposite these were his remaining supplies, dwindling rapidly. It would not be long before he would need to refresh his inventory and that meant being out under the watchful eye of the public and the authorities.

On the other hand, he felt he had almost reached his target. A few more days perhaps, and he would be strong enough for what was to come. If he were successful, then his need for food after this would not matter. In fact, he was unsure of what would *come* after. Once he had achieved his purpose, what would become of him? The human mind had a reward complex – every action undertaken should come with some benefit – whether for survival, sustenance, reproduction or personal gain. Inhabiting this body, which had for so long sought chemical stimulation in the reward centres, had no doubt instilled and reinforced this feeling. It was imperative, more than that – it was *crucial* – that he achieve the destruction of the future problem preventing the timeline. A reward for this was not necessary.

What comes afterwards: unimportant.

Soon he would find his shelter once again. The location

of the giant rock he had sought sanctuary under when the hurricane struck was fresh in his memory.

Getting to that place and releasing the power that had built up within was his sole intention.

III

"So this proves it then?" said John. He was examining the formula scribbled in white chalk on the blackboard. "This proves your proton spin theory."

Amy nodded in reply but was otherwise deep in thought, sat on her couch.

"So what next?" asked John.

Amy stood and came over to the blackboard. She flipped it to the blank side, the empty surface brimming with potential.

"Now we see what the event actually was," she said. "This is the real meat of it. This will take me a while."

"How long?"

"As long as it takes," she said, frowning at his impatience.

"Can I help?"

"You can get out of my hair," she said and motioned to the door.

John stopped and looked at the door for a moment, before heading towards it and exiting the room, the hurt puppy expression back on his face.

Shaking that thought from her head, she went over to her desk and turned on the computer. Readouts from the measurements taken by Vix throughout the event flooded the screen. She intended to take each reading – one by one – and work out the mathematics behind what would cause such reactions in temperature, mass, magnetic distortions and the electrical charge readings; along with seeing what type of fundamental particles were blasted out in the successful collisions. She would do a separate calculation for each one, and that should give her some thought to the theory of the event.

It was a great deal of work, and she knew it. But she also knew that this is what she had come into her field for. Excitement mingled with curiosity, and a sense of foreboding as to what she may find. She had already proved that the potential damage Vix could cause if left unchecked was devastating, but it could also provide science with answers to help in its understanding of the universe.

She would need to be thorough, and careful. Outlandish scientific claims littered history. The community sought more punitive reactions, seemingly not satisfied by simply disproving theories, they often ridiculed the discredited ones. Punishing those who had the temerity to try and prove their claims against the status quo. If she got one equation wrong or typed a decimal point a digit too far, it could give her false results, and send her on a path to humiliation.

Whatever her findings, she had no doubt it would shake the science to its very core, so it was important to make sure it was accurate, and also have watertight, replicable proof of her research.

Closing her eyes, she tried to blot out everything in her life. Thoughts of the hurricane, her father, John, and even Vix fell into a corner of her mind; a dusty filing cabinet in some unimportant room of her brain.

She opened her eyes to the spreadsheets full of data.

Numbers littered her vision, flying around her full of meaning and intent. Scanning the cells, she allowed herself to fill with resolve and comprehension.

__IV__

Samuel sat in his garden, looking back at his home, illuminated in the red flickering light of the fire pit. He rubbed his hands in front of the flames. Despite living his whole life on this tropical island, he had found warmth hard to come by in recent months. Sure, his bones felt chilled, but he had to expect that when approaching his seventh decade on Earth. A few extra layers of clothing, a few more sheets on the bed – that was the way of things. His body just couldn't retain the warmth it did when he was a young man.

But he had found that loneliness added to that too. In the months since his wife's death, it had crept over him like a slow fog, chilling him with despair and the thought of facing the future by himself. It seemed to strike at random moments. A glance at an empty chair. Eating a meal for one that they both used to enjoy. Waking up to silence rather than snoring in the middle of the night.

Work helped. He found travelling to the hospital most days alleviated the boredom; speaking with staff and patients, and making sure the hospital ran as efficiently as possible. And yet he had found himself returning home from the shift exhausted. His mind wandered during his office hours, and just earlier that day he had found himself nodding while sat at his desk. It was perhaps time to consider retirement, even though he found the thought of spending more time alone horrifying.

His son – Simon Frankland - contacted him from Miami only occasionally. Once a fortnight or so he would receive a phone call. Just checking in, he always said. He might as well say, just checking to see if you are still alive.

Simon had returned to St Lucia for his mother's funeral but departed soon after. Samuel could not begrudge him. His son had built himself a life, and he was doing well as a lawyer. He had a lot of friends in Florida even though he remained unmarried; and lived for his career, much like his father. Family life was not a high priority. Samuel was unsure whether he would see any grandchildren in his lifetime.

John and Amy had been a comfort, and he had enjoyed the night out. He had found he got on well with his current neighbours. When Amy arrived, and then married, along with renovating their home, he knew they intended to remain on the island long term – and he was glad of that. To have good relations with your neighbours at such a time in life was a boon.

From his position, firelight dancing across his features, he could see around the curve of the headland, towards the Hunter residence. His own home sat at the end of the road, with his and the Hunter's the only houses on this stretch – which was not even tarmac – clinging to the hillside as it rose from the sea and into the interior of the island. Over the top of his own home, he could see the tips of the Pitons during the daylight, but now hidden in darkness. The landscape also obscured the Hunter residence – but it was only a hundred metres or so to walk – and he could often see the glow of their terrace lights illuminate the headland.

Reflecting on his friendship with them, his concern

grew. John had not recovered from his hurricane episode, and Amy – charming as she could be – preferred to keep their problems away from inquisitive eyes. And who knows what they were doing below the ground under his own house?

He would need to keep a close eye on them. Any sign of serious mental illness on John's part and he would need to alert the authorities.

When she confided with him during John's absence, she had revealed that she had lost both her parents early in her life. He did not doubt that she felt the abandonment of being an orphan.

But more concerning to Samuel was the fact that she could not have children.

Not only denied the security of parentage into her adult life, she had been also robbed of her future.

Of being a mother herself.

The only relationship she had was that of being a wife and a partner to John, and Samuel doubted whether she would ever risk that. It would be to lose not only her past and her future – but her present too.

He would keep an eye on her, and John. If Amy buried her head in the sand, convincing herself that all was well, then getting him to seek treatment would require some tough love to convince her to release him. To lose her partner again would be hard for Amy.

Ultimately as he gave thought to the friends he had made up the road, he missed his wife. Her photograph sat on the table beside him. She stood where he now sat, in their garden, taken on the day they moved into this house. She had her hand on her belly, and she smiled as one beset with happiness.

He raised his glass of rum to the fire, holding it in the dark, smoky atmosphere for a moment, and then swallowed it with a gulp.

"I miss you," he said to the night.

V

Amy woke with a start, just as John bumped the door as he entered the study. The crockery on the tray he carried was laden with her breakfast, and the smell of grilled bacon and toast reached her grateful nostrils.

Having almost fallen off the couch with the rude awakening, she turned to a sitting position and rubbed her eyes.

"Have I been in here all night?"

"It seems so," said John, and laid the tray on the desk.

"I was dreaming," she said.

John walked over to the blackboard. It was full of chalk scribbles ranging over several lines, haphazardly written in Amy's frantic script.

"What were you dreaming?" he asked, looking over the mathematics.

"I dreamt of Mars," she said. "But it wasn't the planet we know about today. It had flowing water, seas, and a gigantic waterfall. It was beautiful. Olympus Mons was erupting in the distance. I don't know how I realised it was Mars, to be honest. Dreams. They don't need exposition."

"Mars is just a desert…"

"It never used to be," said Amy. "It used to have water flowing on it – seas, lakes…"

"What happened?"

"It lost its atmosphere."

"How does a planet lose its atmosphere?"

"Nobody really knows, but the current theory is that the iron core stopped spinning. That in turn meant it lost the magnetic field that protected it from the Sun's radiation, and most of the atmosphere was lost into space."

"Unfortunate," said John.

"I remember reading about it when I was young. I thought about Martians. What they may look like. I loved watching the movies and cartoons when I was a kid, with the little green men and the flying saucers. But when I found out what actually happened on the planet, I thought it incredibly sad. Complex life could never develop in such a place."

"*Complex* life?"

"Life evolves by adapting from its environment, which is why it flourished on Earth. Mars lacked oxygen from its thin atmosphere and lost all the water that it once had. But life may cling on in some pocket of dampness, possibly below the surface. It would be minuscule, microscopic – but it could exist."

Amy yawned, and the memory of the dream began to fade as reality took over. Blinking several times, she stretched and realised she needed a shower.

"How is this coming along?" asked John, motioning his head towards the blackboard.

"Slowly," said Amy, and she moved over to the desk, following the aroma of the food. "It's not making much sense to me at the moment; it's just the reading and measurements expressed. No kind of order to it."

"I'm sure it will all start to make sense as you work

through it."

Amy picked up a slice of toast and dipped it into the yolk, before taking a large bite from it.

"If you are trying to be encouraging, John, you are not doing a very good job," she said munching.

"Then how can I help?"

"I've said before," she said, "Stay out of my way and let me work. I don't like distractions. I work best on my own."

John nodded and headed toward the door.

"But thanks for breakfast," she said, and he turned around and a little half-smile spread on his face.

<u>VI</u>

The blackboard mocked her. Sitting on its pedestal, full of her numbers and formulas, it laughed at her. Deriding her for being so stupid. Taunting her for not being able to solve the puzzle it posed.

It was insulting.

She hated that blackboard and everything on it.

Picking up the board cloth, she felt tempted to wipe the whole thing out of her sight and out of existence. The scribblings represented a week's work trying to figure out what had occurred when Vix created a singularity, but none of it made sense. The mathematics did not work. She should erase it all and give herself some peace.

It took every ounce of her resolve.

Instead, to release her frustration, she kicked the base of the stand with her foot. Her toe throbbed, as the blackboard shuddered, but it didn't matter.

Her original scribbled workings were gone, and she had re-arranged them into neat lines, one representing each part of the equation, in logical order: her haphazard scribblings turned into organised functions. She had hoped that, once she had done this, it would all come together, that it would make sense – that when listed the numbers would stimulate her imagination and present the answer to the problem.

It did not.

They did not stack up. The equations just didn't work and gave outcomes way in excess of any reasonable, and even unreasonable, assumptions.

In the face of this, she went back to the drawing board. Wiped the formulas clean, and started again. Maybe she had made a mistake somewhere. Had she put a divide when it should be a multiply? A lambda instead of an omega? Was the Planck's constant in the correct place?

Repeating the process, she put the workings in order once again and produced the same result.

Checking in on her now and again, trying not to disturb her, John provided food and lots of coffee. On the fourth day of her work, she realised that she had not bathed for those days; on the fifth, she forced herself outside and onto the terrace, as she hadn't left the house. All the time, even with the sunshine warming her face, her mind knotted in the puzzle of the Event.

Now, as she finished going through her figures yet again, she felt at the point of giving up. Never in her career had she felt so stumped trying to work out the physics equations.

Vix was on her mind. How reliable was the data she had obtained from it? They had been rigorous when checking the integrity of the computer software during the build of Vix. All components built and designed by world-renowned suppliers and engineers, given the minute measurements needed.

If they could not trust the data from Vix, then she was in real trouble. Something happened on that day when they performed the experiment, something unprecedented and powerful. Faulty readings meant that she would never be able to decipher it.

As these thoughts passed through her mind, she went over to the desk and slumped into the chair. The screen in front of her listed sheets of figures and formulas, but she refused to look at it as she descended into depressive thoughts. Was this the end of it? Could she do nothing about it?

Her stomach growled, reminding her that she had not eaten all day. Looking through the window, she saw the sky darkening. She needed to eat.

Leaving the study, she went downstairs to the kitchen. In the dining area, John sat watching the small television they had sat on a shelf next to the wall. The sound of serious voices from it pointed to the twenty-four-hour news channel he had taken to watching. It made a change from staring out to sea, she thought. It was as though he was trying to garner as much information from the world around him as he could.

He spotted her as she entered the kitchen, and noticed the glum look on her face.

"Everything okay?" he asked.

"I'm hungry."

"You want me to make you something?"

"I'll make it myself," she said. "I need something quick and unhealthy. How about pizza?"

"Sure," said John.

"Do you want the usual?" she asked.

"The usual?"

"Half and half," said Amy. "We buy large pizza bases so we can share. You like to have pepperoni on your half, and I'm a Hawaiian girl myself."

"Sounds good," said John, and turned his attention back to the TV.

Amy went to the food cupboard and fetched her ingredients. A packaged pizza base, a pepperoni sausage, and tomato puree. And from the refrigerator, sliced ham and pineapple, and a packet of yellow, grated cheese.

Placing all the ingredients on the kitchen island, she switched on the oven, and then prepared the pizza. On the base, she spread the tomato puree and then sprinkled cheese over it. Slicing the sausage, she placed the circles of spiced pork on one half of the base; and on the other, she placed torn chunks of ham and small cubes of pineapple. She did all of this without any thought, working automatically, the aroma of the salted meat and cheese not registering. Making pizza was second nature to her – a simple dish, but one they had both enjoyed and indulged in over the years.

She placed the pizza in the oven on the shelf and closed the door.

As she let it cook, she joined John in the dining area. Placing a hand on his shoulder, she looked at the TV.

"What's going on in the world?" she asked.

"East and West are at odds, and conflicts in the Middle-East," said John. "Floods across various countries in Europe after record amounts of rainfall, and wildfires in parts of Australia and the US."

"The usual then," said Amy, and sat down on the seat next to him.

"Does it seem as though the planet is suffering more problems than it used to?"

"I don't like to think about it. I just want to concentrate on myself and make sure I'm living the life I want to live. The rest of the planet can sort itself out."

"Do you not feel as though your work here has a global significance?"

"Do you honestly believe that whatever we may uncover here will impact the globe in a positive way? The reality is that people are *selfish*. Their sole purpose in life is to get money in their pockets."

"That is very cynical," said John.

"Is it? Altruism is a fallacy. People can show kindness and generosity, but only when it doesn't cause themselves any harm or hardship, or where their status is increased by the act."

"So why are you doing this? What is your motivation?"

"Curiosity, a sense of accomplishment, to prove to myself that I'm capable of understanding the universe around me," said Amy. "I was born into privilege, with family wealth – otherwise I'm sure I'd be doing it for personal gain. But I'm not doing this for some kind of global recognition. I don't care about the rest of the world. I simply want to understand nature to satisfy my own curiosity. Answer those big questions about our reality."

A moment of silence passed between them. John scrutinised Amy's face to decipher her mind-set and her driving force, but Amy's gaze remained on the television, watching the horrors of the planet unfold on the screen. All the time, the salty aroma of pizza wafted from the kitchen.

Amy's stomach rumbled once again, and she checked her watch. It needed a few more minutes.

"I need some fresh air," she said.

Exiting out of the back door, she walked onto the terrace. It was a cool evening, breezy. The sky darkened rapidly.

Gazing out over the sea, she followed the line horizon southwards until the Pitons broke the line across the bay. Their green slopes turned into conical silhouettes. Two pyramids locked together for millennia.

Two pyramids….

Two…

The acrid smell of burning reached her nostrils. Snapping out of her thoughts, she raced back into the kitchen and opened the oven door. Wafting away the smoke with her oven gloves, she turned off the power and lifted the plate off the shelf.

"Hope you like it a little burnt," she said

The smell of cooked pizza made her mouth water. From her utensil drawer, she took the stainless steel pizza wheel to slice the dough in half.

Orientating the dish, so that the split down the middle ran from top to bottom, she placed the circular knife against the top section of the crust. She began to slice, pushing and pulling the slicer to split the pizza in half.

She stopped.

The pizza sat in front of her, in two halves, split in the middle.

Amy looked, frozen in place, at the two sections.

Two…

John still sat in the dining area and noticed Amy in the kitchen – standing and staring at the dish. "Everything okay?" he asked.

Without replying, Amy dropped the pizza wheel, and it fell to the countertop with a clang. Without acknowledging him, she rushed out of the kitchen.

Leaping out of his seat, John followed and he took the steps two at a time to keep up with her.

Amy burst through the study door and headed straight for the blackboard. Picking up a piece of chalk from the blackboard ledge, she stood in front of the equation – the lines scribbled white, dusty and smudged in some places.

Pausing in front of it, she appeared lost in thought.

John knew better than to disturb her at such a moment.

Without thinking, she drew a circle in one wide sweep of her arm around the whole equation. Drawing around it several times, the edges of the encircling chalk became ragged, and she wore down the stick until it was a nub in her fingers.

She dropped the chalk in the waste basket, and stood back, looking at her work. Her eyes narrowed.

"Chalk," she whispered and held out her hand.

John realised she was addressing him, and he sprang into action. On the desk, a cardboard box of new chalk sticks sat. Fetching one, he placed it into Amy's palm.

She took a step toward the blackboard, and again, without hesitating, she drew a single line from top to bottom, bisecting the equation as though it was pizza. Taking a step back, looking at the formula again, she moved her mouth without speaking, working through the calculations.

She shook her head.

That did not work.

Grabbing the board wiper, she moved down the single line she had drawn, erasing it, carefully avoiding the sums and the numbers. Holding out her forefinger, she started at the top, drawing her digit along the line. As she reached the end, with just a single formula remaining, she stopped. The chalk in her other hand drew a dividing line at that point.

She then moved to the second line. Again, her finger moved from left to right as the mathematics spoke to her. On this line, she almost reached the end again, although not quite as far as the first, and she drew another line of demarcation. Onto the third line, repeating the pattern, reading across and marking the split.

On each line, the split fell just before the one above. She made her way down the equation, line by line, making the calculation, before a quick downward swipe with her chalk to mark where one part stopped, and the other began.

Reaching the final line, she only read the first sum before she drew her line.

Then she stepped back for a moment and looked at her work. Returning to the top, she began to connect the vertical lines she had drawn with horizontal ones and then connected the top and bottom to where they met the circle.

John, standing silently and watching her work, looked at the blackboard. Her equation, now surrounded by a circle. Divided in the middle by a stepped pattern zig-zagging from bottom to top.

Amy, not liking the look of the pattern, instead took her chalk and smoothed the right angles, running the chalk over them so that they curved rather than stepped. The final look was one of two teardrops nestled against each other.

Amy took several steps back, and tears began to well in her eyes.

Her voice was barely a whisper.

"It's so beautiful…"

VII

Amy Hunter, Personal Log.

I've given myself a day to absorb the enormity of my discovery. Following my epiphany regarding the split equation, I confess to becoming rather emotional. I've always managed to pride myself on my ability to remain detached and objective when it comes to my work, but this is beyond any expectations I had for Vix or had in my career.

To put it bluntly, and without humility, I believe I have discovered the nature of the universe and – indeed – its purpose.

It has taken me a day to collect my thoughts and to try and put them in some kind of order. I have not slept since my discovery, as my mind is full of excitement, but also conflict. The implications for the future of the planet, and all life on it, I am only just coming to terms with. But I've realised that I need to write down my initial thoughts, along with a brief explanation of the theory, as they are bunching up in my mind. I feel overwhelmed by the knowledge. So here I am, on my laptop with my word processor open, to try and make sense of what I've found.

I've attached a photo of the blackboard I've worked on. This contains the full equation, which is based on the various results obtained from Vix during The Event that I relayed in a prior entry. The equation is now enclosed in a circle, with a dividing line following a curve through it, which makes it look something like a yin-yang symbol from Far-Eastern cultures. I felt that this is appropriate given what the equation is revealing.

I've decided to call it my Theory of Duality.

Where to begin…

Let's start at the very top, and work our way down. I'll go into detail further, but let's talk about the reason, I now believe, the Universe exists.

The purpose of the Universe is to create, develop and support life.

It seems so simple an explanation, and yet so obvious when you consider it. Life, or if you prefer, *matter given consciousness*, is such a unique condition that it would be foolish to believe that it is some kind of cosmic accident or by-product of physics. Given the sheer scale of the universe - with billions of galaxies, billions of stars within those galaxies, and billions of planets orbiting those stars – it strains credulity to believe that life on Earth is the only consciousness in the universe. Far more likely is that the universe is teeming with life – each going through its various stages of evolution as it endeavours to adapt to the environment it was created in.

Given the prohibitive distances between these oases of consciousness, it is also reasonable to assume that each pocket of life is developing in its bubble ready for the day it advances enough to leave the cradle of its creation and venture out into the universe. Could this be the measure of the success of life? If it evolves to the point where it understands the universe and can traverse around it?

So how does this equation explain this reasoning?

The answer to that is in the duality of energy that is combined to make up the fabric of space-time.

When the Event took place in Vix, it split space-time as a prism may split light into its constituent parts. Vix created a singularity when partially fused, infinitely spinning protons could not resolve their states in a stream of high-energy particles. What this achieved is the division of space-time.

Imagine if the very fabric of the Universe – space-time – were a sheet of two-ply tissue. Together this tissue represents all matter and energy, and the continuation of time. Vix took each ply and forced them apart.

The properties of these two halves are equal and opposite – just as Newton theorised – and they follow the pattern set out by the Universe that everything seems to happen in twos.

Two, it seems, is the answer to the question of the universe.

Matter and anti-matter. Life and Death. Egg and Seed.

Two.

The very beginnings of life on earth were caused by two amino acids merging, and creating the first protein. Everything occurs in pairs wherever you look.

Now I've uncovered that space-time is also built around two merged forms of energy. This energy cannot be detected or measured, at least not using any methods I'm aware of with our current technology, but the effects of this energy can be seen in a universe that is in constant flux.

What the equation tells us is that these forms of energy also exist in the universe in their *raw* state. They are *everywhere*. They are all around us, and gathering together in clumps. More of this energy exists in the cosmos than anything else – around seventy per cent of everything in the universe. This is the explanation that scientists have been searching for which explains the dark energy phenomenon. These energies can both create, and harness matter – keeping it together and preventing galaxies from flying apart by gravitational forces; and the opposing force can cause destruction, ripping apart matter and recycling it, such as in the hearts of stars and supernovas.

These twin energies can manipulate matter. It has the ability to create the nuclear forces that bind atoms together, or indeed break them apart into their constituent elements. The purpose of which is to ensure the best path for the flow of time.

We already know that space-time is in a constant state of creation and destruction. But what we can now also conclude is the *intent* behind it. Where the existence of life is going down a dead end, the universe will intervene. It is reasonable to conclude that if the existence of life is at odds with the environment around it, then *intervention* will also occur. As white blood cells seek infection, so does the universe.

The *nature* of this process is what we refer to as time. The process of time, which seems so linear to us, is anything but. Time is constantly assessing itself, making sure the optimal path is followed.

To what aim?

To create, develop and support life.

Duality is the DNA of the universe. Time runs along its twin helix of creation and destruction. In every moment, the future of the universe is being moulded and is adapting to the chaotic element of life, guiding it along a path to ensure the optimal outcome for existence.

Given this, what future lies in store for life on Earth? We are a lifeform on the verge of immense discoveries that would lead us to the stars, and a full understanding of the universe we live in. Yet we are at odds with each other, and with the planet. Would the universe embrace us with open arms, or would it not accept such a lifeform spreading itself out among the void?

The more I consider these implications, the more I can see the problems facing humanity. Is our version of life a benefit to the future of the universe, or a threat? It seems we are at a junction – and not for the first time on this planet. I'm convinced that at every evolutionary crossroad, every shift in the geology of Earth, the universe has decided how the course of time will play out, guiding life to reach the optimal path to flourish.

Are we still on this optimal path? Has civilisation and the expansion of human intelligence brought us to a utopia or the brink of global destruction?

This brings me to my husband.

John, since his confessed "death", has shown that he possesses energy, which can affect the atoms and molecules in his body and the environment around him. I can now surmise that each cell in his body is being animated. If we take this equation, we are all bombarded by this invisible force constantly – what if this is the energy that fuels the "creation" side of Duality?

Is John a representative on Earth as the universe tries to resolve the dilemma of humanity?

Also, worryingly, if John exists for the creation side, it stands to reason that the "destruction" side would also be among us.

John seems blissfully unaware of his new nature. This makes sense to me as this energy can only exist as a non-conscious entity, submitting to the whims of space-time and the direction it seeks to take. It has no mind of its own, just a compulsion to resolve the constant paradox of time and the vagaries of future events. It can only inhabit a human, not replace it; animate the shell to move among us and steer us into the future. The kinetic energy that motivates a water molecule to flow down a river does not do so with intent, but physics impels it to do so regardless.

So where does this leave the man I married? Is John still alive if this force has resurrected him?

I suppose it is a question of biology. The seat of consciousness is the brain. Remove the mind and you remove the person. You remove their identity and personality. John's mind is still active. He knows me, he knows our past. His mind is still present and the neurons still firing – even if they are doing so by artificial means.

He is still my husband.

But now I know that his presence here is for this very reason. He returned to me so I could carry on with our research with Vix in the knowledge that I would discover Duality. The universe is guiding me, guiding humanity, towards a hopeful future where science can overcome any challenges presented by our nature.

Is the future set?

I don't think so. Duality is equal on both sides. Are we to be saved or condemned? If John is here to guide us towards a bright future, is an opposite working *against* humanity – seeking its destruction?

Are our actions and our nature causing the universe to seek our removal from the celestial equation?

What form would this take?

Another unanswered question is a more personal dilemma. If I accept that John is still alive, he's the one person I have ever met that I have fallen in love with. He is my lifetime partner.

The last few weeks have been difficult for me to accept, and I have been treating him as though he is suffering from a mental illness, rather than being a vessel for universal energy, in the hope that I will wake one morning to find John – back to his old self – waiting for me with open arms.

He is getting to grips with parts of the theory – how Duality mixes and creates space-time – but I don't think he yet understands that the force inside of him is part of this energy. It won't take him long to figure it out. He believes he is no longer human, so it doesn't take a huge leap of intellect to see the association with the creation energy. Do I tell him? If I do so, I may remove that part of him that seems to become more like my husband every day. Perhaps I should allow him to come to terms with this more organically.

If one issue exists with physics, it is that it is such a cold science. It deals with facts and evidence, and very little with the emotional side of being. Without a doubt, this is a discovery that has the potential to change the face of science and the way we understand nature. This equation, for all its elegance and beauty, does nothing for this situation. It doesn't help me get my husband back or give me hope that one day his character will return. And I find it difficult to feel elated with my discovery while this thought pervades me.

This is joined by my growing fear that the planet is heading for catastrophe. Strange global weather patterns, increasing natural disasters, the destruction of nature and the atmosphere through our actions, and our warlike nature with any others who may hold differing ideologies to our own. If I ask myself the question of whether life on this planet is on the right track for a golden future, I only have one reply…

But maybe John is the result of the following equation: the equation that sums up Duality. Negative zeta plus positive alpha equals sigma:

$$(z) + \alpha = \Omega$$

VIII

Amy closed the lid of her laptop.

John stood, looking deep in thought, as he studied the calculations on the blackboard. He turned when he heard the laptop close.

"Are you done?" he asked.

Amy nodded. Suddenly, she felt very weary.

"Can we talk about this?" asked John. "I get parts, but I'm not sure I fully understand it."

She looked out of the study window as she considered his request. The sun was starting to sink below the horizon.

"These twin forces," he continued, "Their interaction creates space time, and they still exist in their raw state. What happens when these opposite energies interact?"

Amy tilted her head backwards and closed her eyes, massaging the back of her neck.

"The reaction would be….vigorous," she said. "Like

matter and anti-matter. Explosive."

"And yet the outcome of this reaction generates the fabric of the universe," said John. "How does this relate to me?"

A huge yawn stretched her cheeks.

"I'm tired, John," she said.

He turned around and looked at her. She returned his gaze, with heavy-lidded eyes.

"You need to get some rest," said John, and Amy detected a note of concern in his voice.

For once, she was too exhausted to argue. Her mental exertions had translated physically, and she felt her head nod even as she spoke.

"Thanks, John," said Amy, and headed for the door. "I'll see you in the morning."

John watched her leave the room, and then went over to the window. He looked out over the sea.

Crossing the landing in her bare feet, she went into her bedroom. She closed the curtains against the red sunset, sinking the room into the half-light. Her cotton pillow and sheets felt soft and comfortable as she lay on the bed.

On the side table lay her wedding photograph. Dressed in a white gown, she was smiling, John's arms around her, on that happy day on the beach. As sleep overtook her, she allowed her mind to wander through that memory.

Chapter Ten – Second Wave

I

What was that?

Amy roused suddenly. She had been in a deep sleep, but she snapped open her eyes. Woken by the sudden sensation of falling, she grabbed the edge of the mattress.

She looked around her bedroom. Through a crack in her curtains, the morning light filtered through, and she checked her watch. It was a little after seven.

Yawning, and stretching, she realised she had slept for twelve hours. She had needed it though, and it had refreshed her. Pulling the sheets aside, she stood up and pulled her arms above her head. Standing on her tiptoes, stretching out her back and neck, she proceeded to strip out of her pyjamas and changed into a fresh pair of shorts and a T-shirt from her bedside drawers. She would shower later – a good wash would complete her quiescence – but after such a long rest, she needed some breakfast.

Flinging aside the curtains, a morning of blue skies and sunshine greeted her. The sea glittered in the morning light, and the horizon was hazy.

Looking out, she had the odd feeling that something felt out of place.

The view didn't look quite right.

Dismissing the thought, she padded over to the end of the bed and slipped on her pumps, peeling them around her bare heels.

Breakfast and coffee on the terrace, she thought, *that's what I need.*

As she made to leave her bedroom, the wedding photo she had been looking at the night before had fallen to the floor. Frowning, she went over to it and picked it up. It lay face down, and as she turned it around, the glass had cracked, splitting the picture in half in a jagged line.

Making a mental note to reframe the photo, she placed it back on her bedside table but lingered for a moment to look at the picture.

On the landing, she headed for the spare room. The door was ajar, and the room beyond lay empty. Inside, edges of the white sheets tucked under the mattress, he had made his bed.

No sign of John.

Rubbing her eyes, she descended the stairs and into the kitchen. It was not unusual for John to go missing, especially when she was working. He spent much of his time watching the news or exploring the locality. The feeling Amy had was that he was re-learning everything about life and the environment. He had the memories, but not the experience.

The morning light diffused through the windows, dappling the kitchen and dining room. Flicking on the coffee machine, absently going through her morning routine, she placed a cup and headed to the cupboard to fetch the beans, she stopped as the coffee began to splutter into the cup. John must have been up before her and filled the hopper.

Grabbing a quick bowl of cereal, she poured over the milk and wandered through the open back door and onto the terrace. The warmth of the day swept over her as she passed through the doors. A gentle breeze tousled her hair as she walked over the patio to the terrace wall. She half-expected to see John staring out across the blue horizon, but he was not here.

Unable to shake some unease, she looked out at the sea. The haze was clearing, but the dividing line from the sea to the sky looked indistinct and difficult to discern. Shielding her eyes from the light, she looked out, considering where John had gone.

Had he had gone to the laboratory, or out on the boat?

Placing her coffee on the wall, she took a mouthful of cornflakes and peered over the edge. She could not see him on the stairs or the jetty. Of course, if he were in the lab, then she would not see him anyway.

Again, something did not feel right.

Finishing her bowl, it clattered as she placed it next to her cup. Picking her coffee up, she took a sip.

She looked again over the edge, leaning out to see more beneath her.

Below stood the jetty, with *Higgs* moored to the wooden post. From her vantage, it looked as though it was *hanging* from its mooring, its bow dipping into the sea, and the engine pointing into the air.

Something else — could she see more of the rocks around the cliff than usual?

"Are you okay?"

The sudden voice made her jump.

Turning around, Samuel stood at the other end of the garden, having come through the gate.

"Sorry, I didn't mean to startle you," he said. He held up his hands, but his eyes showed concern. "Just making sure you and John are safe after what happened?"

"What's happened?" asked Amy.

"The earthquake?" said Samuel. "Did you not feel it?"

"I was fast asleep," said Amy. "But something woke me up."

She recalled the wedding photograph that had fallen to the floor.

"It was a big one," he said, approaching her across the paved area of the terrace. "Bigger than I can remember. It smashed some plates in my kitchen, and my shed is a mess. I was just getting up to start my shift when it happened."

"Come and look at this…"

She motioned to the terrace wall, pointing down to the sea.

Samuel quickened his pace and came to stand next to her. Following her indication, he looked over the wall to the sea below.

"Sea level has lowered," he said, and she heard the sudden panic in his voice.

"Does that mean what I think it does?"

"We need to get down to town and warn them," he said. "Where's John?"

"I've no idea," said Amy.

"Could he have gone into town?"

They both began to head back, across the terrace towards the house, jogging through the flower beds.

"It's possible," she said, "Although he never mentioned that he was going. I'll grab my car keys."

The thought of John repairing his severed hand returned to her, and she knew he was well-equipped to get through it.

"John can take care of himself," said Amy, "We need to warn people."

Samuel looked at Amy, surprised at her lack of concern. "Are you sure he'll be okay? Do we not need to find him?"

"Trust me, Samuel," said Amy, "Just know that if John's absent, it's for a reason. More important right now is the town."

Reaching the house, they went inside hurriedly, and Amy grabbed her car keys, which hung on a hook next to the garage entrance. Going into the concrete-walled carport, she pressed the button that released the door. It rolled upwards with a hum.

Amy jumped into the driver's seat, with Samuel next to her, and fired up the engine. It burst into life with a growl.

"Do you think we have enough time?" he asked.

Amy reversed the car at speed from the garage, sunlight sweeping through the windscreen as she twisted the wheel to face the road.

"I've no idea," said Amy. "The magnitude of the earthquake will decide how much energy is transferred into the sea, and the size and speed of the waves."

"You know about tsunamis?"

"I know about wave theory," said Amy. "I did a thesis on it at Cambridge."

She popped a gear, put her foot on the accelerator, and heard the engine roar.

"Part of the thesis was how waves appeared when affected by gravity, and I used tsunamis to illustrate the theory."

The tyres kicked up the gravel and stones on the road, and the palm trees and ferns on either side flashed past.

"What did you learn?" asked Samuel, pulling on his seatbelt.

"Some of the largest can travel at five hundred miles an hour," she said.

Samuel looked at her, shocked and surprised. "That fast?"

Amy nodded.

"We don't have long then," said Samuel.

Amy wrestled with the steering wheel, struggling to keep the car on the road while travelling at speed. She winced as the edge of her tyres, hitting a corner, slipped off the track and onto the verge, her wing mirror struck by the branches and leaves of the undergrowth. She righted her position and resumed her haste.

"How did the earthquake feel?" asked Amy. "Was it a strong one?"

"Strong enough," said Samuel, "The nearest fault lines are off the coast in the sea, so we weren't at the epicentre."

"This has to be a tsunami then," she said.

The rear wheels scrabbled for purchase on the loose surface, causing the back end to fishtail. Amy struggled with the wheel, but managed to maintain some measure of control despite her speed.

Gaps in the vegetation gave them views of the bay below, and the Pitons beyond. During a normal drive to Soufriere, it would take Amy around fifteen minutes to reach the centre of the town. She believed she could halve that time.

As she drove, Amy thought of her discoveries. Of creation and destruction. And John. She wondered where he was and if he had a warning. Images of him standing on the terrace at their home, or out of their window, or on the prow of *Higgs* – looking out to sea…

Had he known all along?

The road, descending gently before, now became steeper as they reached the last corner. As Amy rounded it, a full view of the town appeared on their right side.

"Stop the car!" said Samuel, looking out over it.

Amy pushed both feet on the brake, and the car slid to a halt, swerving as it reached inertia.

"What is it?" asked Amy.

A look of horror was on Samuel's face. "Look," he said.

At the mouth of the bay, between the headland and the Pitons on the other side, Samuel pointed out to sea. The shallow convex tide travelled at speed, approaching the mouth.

Exiting the Range Rover, the pair stood on the edge of the road. From their vantage point, they could see all spread below them.

A smooth crest caught the morning sunshine, glittering as it flowed toward the inlet. At this distance, the wave did not appear high. The boats moored out beyond the mouth of the bay bobbled over the top, barely displaced by it.

Soufriere was just coming to life. Shutters opened. Cars milled about. Locals ambled towards their place of work. On the shoreline, the concrete pier held fishermen and pleasure boat crew organising their forthcoming day's activities. Some of them had noticed the low tide and stood scratching their heads – not making the connection between the quake. They had left their craft the previous evening as normal – now they had to descend the gangplank to board.

The Lady of the Pitons, moored on the pier had lost her gangplanks into the water, and from Amy's vantage point, she could see the captain, wearing his hat, arguing with the dock master as to what had happened.

Amy and Samuel looked down with an impending sense of horror as the disaster unfolded before them.

The wave hit the headlands on either side of the inlet, and white water burst over their rocky prominences, which disappeared under the deepening surface. Ever growing, as the sea bed became shallower, the wave sped towards the town. A few outlying ripples spread out in concentric arcs in the bay between the headland and the town, precursors of the following giant.

Samuel cupped his hands around his mouth and began to yell.

"Move, get out of the town!" he shouted, hoping someone was looking up at him. He had no chance of anyone hearing him, he was a quarter of a mile away, but he shouted in the hope some people may be looking up in his direction.

Amy, feeling equally helpless, joined in waving her arms and yelling.

On the harbour front, people began to look out on the bay, hearing and watching the waves crashing over the headland, and the horizon diminishing rapidly. Fascination turned to horror rapidly once they realised what was coming. The height of the wave doubled in size, filling their vision, and the outlying ripples splashed over the quayside rocks and onto the road at the front of the town.

Some, lucky enough to have a vehicle at hand and a presence of mind, jumped into them; the rules of the road, abandoned in their haste, caused two cars to clip each other as they turned from the front and into the town. Causing minor damage to their front wings, they did not stop. Separating, their wheels squealed as they fled, following several others racing toward the mountains.

Most people on the quayside seemed rooted, pointing in alarm to the wall of water bearing down on them, their minds unable to fathom the horrific vision before them.

The wave hit the pier. The concrete strip vanished in a moment. Swallowed up in less than a second. All too late some began to run but were overwhelmed.

The Lady's bow rose, her nose pointing almost vertically in the air, moorings snapping like twine. It rode the crest, hanging high above the harbour, and then plummeted back downwards. Caught in the wake, it capsized onto its side, and its red and white hull smashed into the rocks at the front. An explosion of debris, from the wood and fibreglass hull, rained down across the town, bouncing off the roofs and splashing into the advancing wave.

The water kept pace and struck the harbour. People and vehicles swallowed. Even from her position, Amy could see the stricken as they threw up their arms to protect themselves from the wall of water crashing into them, before they vanished a moment later. She could do nothing but watch, her hand covering her mouth and her eyes wide. Samuel stood next to her, his face grim.

Striking the frontages of the harbour buildings, the sound of smashing glass reverberated around the bay above the low roar of the rushing water. It flowed down every street, filling up every inch of space in the town, roads replaced by rivers.

By the side of one building, they saw a man jump on top of a parked car, and then leap up attempting to grab a first-floor window. The wave struck the car as he leapt, and he slipped, catapulting himself into the onrushing river.

The flooding in the streets spread to the central park, just ahead of the church - the green lawns vanishing and the trunks of the trees struggling against the surge.

People fleeing on foot could not outrun the wave. The town of Soufriere had become an extension of the sea, the white church steeple standing out of the water like a lighthouse, and a single bell peal reached their ears as the water flooded the base of the tower and struck the ropes.

The wave did stop on the outskirts of the town. After submerging every road, it continued over the acres of farmland, filling that space as a lake would fill after the burst of a dam. Choking all the ground. The water filled the valley, splashing up on the slopes, and forming a choppy, mud-coloured lake.

The rushing noise from the town fell quiet. The water rippled in the sunlight, forming channels between the buildings, lying where the streets had been. Amy heard the chirruping of bird songs. Nature continued as it had ever done.

From where Amy and Samuel stood, the water had passed them below. Once it had reached the limit of the slopes, it seemed to pause for a few seconds, and then the tide reversed its course and began to flow back out to the sea.

The water level over the fields started to drop as the energy of the wave gave way to gravity. As fast as it had flown inland, it retreated, the sound of a waterfall reaching them. In the harbour, the stricken pleasure boat sat on its side, awkwardly positioned on the rocks by the frontage. The retreating water took down the remaining trees, the logs floating on the surface, crashing into structures. Cars drifted past them, bobbling like apples.

"Look," said Samuel, pointing down the road.

Amy followed his direction and noticed that at the junction where the road up the hill met the town's streets, further down the hill, a collection of people had started to gather. Some had managed to escape the flow by seconds, but others were pulling themselves out of the floodwater. In turn, they linked hands with each other and helped anyone flowing past, yanking them out of the stream.

Another small group of people, at least twenty, had left the main group and begun to drift up the road towards them, a mixture of exhaustion and terror written on their faces. The shock forced their limbs forward, seeking the sanctuary of high ground, supporting each other with arms around their waists.

One elderly man - propped on either side by a teenage girl and a middle-aged man dripped in flood water - looked at the point of collapse as they made their way up the road. Many others were dripping wet and filthy, covered in all the kinds of waste that had mixed with the incoming tide.

Samuel expressed concern at some of the survivors displaying injuries. Most appeared to be cuts and bruises, but a few looked more serious and needed urgent treatment. As the disparate groups approached, making their way up the road, several nursed their arms, grimacing in pain; others hopped, broken legs and ankles rocking as they moved.

As the people grew in number and approached, Samuel

sprung, his decades of emergency training flowing, galvanising from his initial shock. From his pocket, his mobile phone, pressed a quick dial number and put it up to his ear.

Amy, still reeling, tried to collect her thoughts.

And they began to take her to a dark place

"I need to get a triage station set up," said Samuel, down the line. "We have a perfect spot where I am for emergency tents and ambulances. It's flat and wide, just above the flood line, and close to any walking wounded…"

Amy took several deep breaths.

The water had almost retreated from the town, but rivulets in the streets still flowed back towards the sea. In a flash of realisation, she recalled her knowledge of wave dynamics in tsunamis.

It was the second wave that was the most powerful.

The *second* wave…

Recalling her dissertation on the Boxing Day tsunami that had struck south Asia, most of the victims died when the second wave, now filled with the detritus from the first, crashing and grinding together in the water, struck a few minutes after the first wave had retreated.

Even now, she could hear the cries and screams of people in distress in the town. The unfortunate ones caught in the water or others sheltering in the upper floors. Seeing the tide reversing, they perhaps did not realise that other waves would follow and that they would be more destructive.

"I need to get down there," she said. Her eyes had taken the wide, fixed look of fear.

Samuel paused, taking the phone away from his ear.

"What do you mean?"

"There'll be another wave," she said.

Samuel knew from the look in her eyes that she understood the situation.

"Do you have enough time?" he asked.

She looked at the bay fearfully. The tide still appeared to be receding, driftwood and floating rubbish floating out to sea, but what lay further beyond remained hidden.

"I don't know, but I have to try," she said. "I can't just stand here and watch."

Without further procrastinating, she grabbed her car keys and returned to her vehicle. She opened the door and turned to Samuel.

"Please stay here, don't come after me," she said. "You need to sort things out, make sure help comes."

Samuel wanted to argue further, and keep her safe, but knew it would no effect other than to delay her. He nodded at her, and she jumped into the driver's seat.

As she revved the engine, the survivors approaching up the road split to the verges. The Range Rover clicked into gear and shot down towards the town in a cloud of dust and gravel.

II

The wide tyres of her car hit the flooded outskirts of Soufriere. The treads threw up an arc of water as the car twisted around the bend in the road on the edge of town, where a few single-storey homes gave way to the larger buildings in the centre. The first wave had all but retreated, vanishing almost as quickly as it had arrived, but it had coated the streets in a greasy film, as though the town had just suffered a heavy rain shower. But the wave had littered the streets with rubble, wooden planks, domestic waste from upturned dustbins, and smashed glass. Piles of these obstacles made driving through difficult, and Amy had to find a path to advance. Her speed, along with her twisting path, meant that she did not get more than a passing glance at what lay amongst the shattered buildings and piles of detritus. Keeping an eye out for the injured, the streets appeared deserted. Everyone had fled or were sheltering. In one of the homes, she saw the first sign of life: a solitary middle-aged St Lucian looked out of his upper-floor window at her as she drove past. Water dripped from the broken window sills at street level - the paint discoloured from the brine, but the upper half of the house looked clean and bright. The man appeared to be in his sixties, and somewhat in shock to open his window upon waking to find his town partially destroyed.

Opening her window, Amy looked up at him.

"Get to safety," she shouted up at him.

He looked down at her, quizzically.

"Find shelter," she shouted again. "You're not safe here – get to high ground!"

The man nodded to indicate he understood, but in a casual manner, as though the words registered, but his brain refused to take them in. He went back inside, closing the wooden window shutters behind him.

She had no idea whether he would listen to her, but she had no time to convince individuals. It would be his choice if he heeded her warning.

Over-revving the engine, causing wheel-spin, she resumed her path to the harbour, looking for survivors.

As she made her journey, more of the walking wounded appeared – the ones too far towards the front to have evaded the first wave. Some had escaped with soakings or just minor injuries, but all held shocked expressions, the fear fresh in their wide eyes. The church seemed to be attracting them, the lost souls attempting to find salvation in their pain and confusion.

"You need to get to high ground," she shouted to them through her window. "There will be another wave – get to safety!"

Their worried glances deepened, but they pointed to the roads leading out of town, making for them as fast as they could manage.

Turning around a kerb littered with dripping seaweed, she saw a small hatchback car, parked on the leeward side of a building, protected from the full force of the wave. Inside, she spotted four individuals – a family, it seemed – and she could hear their panicked argument. A mother and father, with two young girls sat in the rear seat. Their car was not a modern vehicle, it looked at least twenty years old and sea water dripped from the wing mirrors. The husband was trying to start the engine. It choked and spluttered as he desperately turned the key, his partner urging him to get it going, but it refused to start. The young girls were crying.

Amy spun her steering wheel to do a U-turn, slowing to crawl behind them, and rode up to the car's rear bumper. The man behind the wheel, seeing what she was doing, waved his hand out of his window encouraging her forward. She tapped the rear fender with her front, and the car started to propel forward. The driver turned the key again, the engine still choking and coughing. A few more metres forward and he tried again.

With a huge backfire and a plume of black smoke, the engine growled to life. The spinning wheels found traction, throwing up spray behind them. Waving his thanks to her, he turned the corner towards the town limits.

Amy hit reverse gear, sweeping back around the kerb, and then popped it into first. The park area sat in a square a street away from the harbour. It was a beautiful, shaded area of trees and park benches, usually filled with the town residents and tourists, relaxing and conversing. Enjoying their day in the sunshine. Now it was a pile of damp rubble and fallen trees, collected from the damaged buildings and vegetation around, and strewn across the park in a crazy, haphazard fashion. Piles of concrete rubble with broken wooden beams and planks mingled with palm fronds and dripping, slimy plant life. The whole area reeked of sour spoil and sewage.

A pile of rubble and wood blocked the short road that led to the quay from the park. Braking, she snapped opened her car door. Still wearing her pumps, they soaked through as she stepped out. Squelching between her toes, it felt greasy and unclean.

She left her car door open, and the engine running – prepared for a rapid exit.

The rubble ahead of her was three metres high, and she clambered over clumsily, he wet soles slipping on the loose material. It consisted of wooden planks, but she noticed broken sections of fibreglass that had smashed off damaged boats. Amy summited over this and beheld the harbour beyond.

From street level, it looked a lot different from her

vantage above the town. The water continued to retreat, falling through the harbour rocks like rapids, and flowing through the smashed concrete of the pier, jagged and cracked, damaged by the force of the wave and the pleasure craft caught upon it. Several upturned hulls bobbed around in the bay, their painted bottoms facing up to the sky. The *Lady* sat on its side. It had not fared well. Caught in the maelstrom of conflicting tides, the port side of the ship had submerged, but the pointed bow sat at an awkward angle on the harbour rocks, pointing at the town like a threat. Somehow it had held together, but a crack ran down the down the centre of the hull, and she heard the sound of straining metal above the backflow of the water.

The smashed windows and doorways on the buildings across the road from the quayside indicated the force of the wave as it struck land. Upturned cars lay amongst the rubble against their frontages. Green, oozing seaweed mingled with fish, some of whom still flopped around on the pavements and tarmac.

She viewed all of this in a second, her mind working on pure instinct. The sight was too alien for her to register fully, but her priority was to get as many people as she could to safety.

Playing at the back of her mind: the hurricane and the wave - once-in-a-lifetime disaster events - both occurred within weeks.

And the Vix revelations. Universal energies working towards creation and destruction for future resolution.

Coincidence?

She forced these thoughts to the back of her mind as she saw two women – one in her late teens and another in her forties – emerging from the ruined remains of the supermarket. Amy recognized them from her weekly grocery shop. The concrete frame of the building still stood, but the glazing had gone in the lower floor, and wood piled high against the structure.

The teenage girl, who usually carried Amy's groceries to the car, was named Kath; her mother, Amber, worked the counter. She called out to them.

"We've got to get out of here, there'll be another wave coming."

They both looked out to the harbour, their expressions of fear plain to see. Amy waved them over to her, pointing to her car beyond the rubble. Amber, more heavyset than her daughter, found it difficult to move quickly through the mess. She wore a colourful, wraparound skirt and sandals, further hampering her progress. She had dressed for a normal day. Kath, seeing her struggle, put her arm around to help – she wore shorts and a T-shirt, with sneakers – and was more dextrous over the obstacles. Their progress was painfully slow to Amy, and she knew the second wave could strike at any moment. Shielding her eyes against the glare of the morning sun, she glanced at the mouth of the bay. Conflicting channels of water appeared to be fighting against each other, causing a chaotic maelstrom of flow, but she couldn't see any large waves.

Maybe the first one would be the only one…

Reaching the barrier, the pair began to clamber over, water rushing through the cracks between the stone, soaking their clothing as they climbed. Amy offered her hand. Amber took it gratefully, her daughter pushing her up from behind.

Turning back to her car, the exhaust still smoking, Amy pointed to it and instructed them to get in. They obeyed without a word and made their way towards it.

Doing a quick survey before she followed them, she took a step down from the rubble. To her left, she heard a noise, and her head flicked in that direction.

A small boy, maybe ten years old, stood in a doorway. She did not recognise him. He wore a vest and shorts, and nothing on his feet. He shook uncontrollably. In his arms, he held a black and white dog, its fur soaked, and tail firmly between its back legs. It was almost the same size as him. It was obvious to her that they had been hit by the first wave, most likely soon after he had awoken and before he'd had a chance to get dressed properly. Perhaps he had managed to cling on to something, one hand clutching safety and the other holding onto his dog, as the waters flowed and rose around him.

Where his guardians were, Amy dared not ask.

She was about to call him over when, out of the corner of her eye, she spotted what she had been dreading.

From the opening to the bay, not too far out to sea, she discerned a rolling curve of water as it caught the sunshine. It grew and began to fill the horizon. Already it looked ten metres high, but as it hit the shallows, the height increased.

She didn't hesitate for a moment.

"Get in the car, now!" she shouted at the boy and pointed over to her vehicle. The two women from the supermarket were opening the back door.

Struck from his shock, his head flicked from where she was pointing, to the wave. Realising the danger, he ran toward her and over the rubble, the dog bouncing around in his arms.

She could not afford to go over to help and turned her back on the wave as it crashed over the rocky headlands that marked the entrance to the bay. The remaining water level around them drained away rapidly to feed the approaching tsunami.

The boy was lithe and agile, and made good ground over the obstacles, despite the weight of the dog. His bare feet seemed to grip the wood and stone, even though the sharp edges dug into his soles.

Amy reached the car, and the two women got into the back seat, adjusting their position.

"The wave is here," she said to them, her breath coming in gasps.

They both started shouting in panic.

"We've got to go."

"We must leave now."

Amy got into the driver's seat and shut her door. Reaching over, she opened the passenger side as the boy arrived.

She could hear the roar of the overwhelming volume of flow echoing across the town.

The boy got into the car, and his face was a mask of fear, but he remained silent. The dog remained gripped in his arms despite it shaking. It licked its nose anxiously.

Amy did not wait for him to close the door, she plunged her foot on the accelerator and put the wheel on full lock. The impetus closed the passenger door, and the car spun to face the opposite way.

She sped in the direction she had come from, the gears grinding as she changed up. Her eyes flicked up toward her rear-view mirror, and she could see the two women looking out of the back.

Dodging the strewn debris, she made her way past the park and towards the church at speed. At such velocity, she was not in full control and it bounced around as the wheels clipped flotsam. Hoping the objects she was driving over would not cause a puncture, the suspension on the car worked overtime.

Passing the buildings at the back end of the park, she once again looked in her mirror.

The ground shook beneath them. Hearing a huge crash, the row of buildings at the harbour side exploded in a cascade of rubble and water. *The Lady of the Pitons* crashed through the structures, smashing them to rubble, borne on the huge, terrifying wave.

The women in the back seat, as they glanced through the rear window, screamed in terror and disbelief. Their panicked cries to go faster did not fall on deaf ears. The boy remained silent, but shook visibly, his eyes wide open looking over the snout of the dog, fixed ahead, refusing to look behind him or even at the wing mirror.

Amy had to keep her head, but could not help risking several glances behind her as the wave pounded through the town, *The Lady* barrelling through homes and businesses. The water level around them was creeping up at an alarming rate. She put her foot down even further as she realised the speed of the water was far quicker than the travelling car and would catch them up in seconds.

The ship had split along the crack in the hull, but remained attached, held together by a deck of twisting steel girders.

Ahead of her, Amy saw a pile of wooden planks and boards that looked like collapsed fencing, with buildings at either side. She knew she had to go over them, no time to go around.

"Hold on," she shouted as she aimed right for them.

Mother and daughter gripped the back of the seats in front of them, and the boy held onto the dog tighter, burying his face into the damp fur.

She struck the wood, and the car lurched upwards, the tyres scrabbling on the loose planks. The front smashed into a fallen telegraph pole, denting the passenger-side wheel arch, and sending the wooden beam spinning away. Everyone in the car winced as the smash reverberated through them. The Range Rover burst over the summit of the wood and left the ground before landing on the road beyond. Bouncing in their seats, the four people and dog gripped the hand holds tightly. The force of the landing rippled through the frame of the car, and the front windscreen cracked – a thick, jagged line cutting horizontally across her vision.

The first outliers of the tide struck the rubber tread beneath the vehicle. Turning the wheel, she could feel the car losing traction.

Rounding a single-storey building, she saw the road that led out of the town, back up to where Samuel was setting up the emergency station. The road cut back on itself, before climbing up the side of the hill. To her dismay, she saw that the flood was already high enough to cover the exit, cutting off her escape.

The main bulk of the wave was not far behind, a wall of raging torrent obliterating the buildings and vehicles in its path; carrying everything it picked up and smashing them together in a deadly, grinding cascade.

The Lady smashed up against the church, and the building exploded in a mass of bricks and wood, leaving just the tower standing alone. The wreck split along the crack, jack-knifing around the tower as the tide crashed over it.

Crying in alarm, Amy went off-road, bursting her way through a picket fence towards the farmed area at the rear of the town. The previous wave flattened the rows of corn and plantains, and soaked the ground. Ahead of her, half a kilometre or so, the banks of the interior mountains rose high above the valley. Her tyres kicked up the mud, along with the spray from the encroaching sea, quickly seeping around the buildings ahead of the wall of water.

Pointing the tip of the hood to the tree-lined slope, she engaged low gear and slammed her foot on the accelerator. The wheels spun for a second, painting the mudguards and side panels brown before they found grip and lurched forward.

The wave was gaining, and the water around them rising and, from driving over muddy fields, she now forded through the rising tide. The dun flecks of mud made way for brown arcs of water splashing onto the windows. The wipers just smeared the dirt over the windscreen.

Her passengers had gone silent, willing the car to go faster and reach safety. They had stopped looking behind, and Kath had closed her eyes, anticipating the crash of tonnes of water. Amber uttered a silent prayer, her fingers working through the beads hung around her neck. The boy's eyes remained transfixed ahead, and his arms still embraced his dog.

The noise of the engine, growling from rough treatment and harsh conditions began to fade, replacing the roar of the angry sea. Around them, the level rose above the middle of the wheel hubs, and extended ahead of them at speed, reaching the lowest level of the slope. Amy felt the car slow as it tried to make its way through.

Then the wheels struck an unseen boulder below the water line, and it lurched sideways. The two women screamed in alarm, and the boy shut his eyes. Amy attempted to regain control, but she overcompensated and the car lurched the other way, spinning through 180 degrees and skidding to a halt.

Ahead of them, they saw the wave approach. It had engulfed the town.

"Hold on," said Amy, and gripped the steering wheel.

The wave struck.

For a few seconds, they were submerged. White water washed over the windscreen in a torrent, flashing by the side windows. The Range Rover, caught in the flow, jumped backwards, lifting off the ground. The wing mirrors melted off - lost to the tide. For a moment, Amy thought that they would be upended front to back as her seat rose higher than the back seats. The cries had stopped, the shock of the wave silencing them. The crack in the windscreen expanded, with jagged lines appearing across the glaze in web-like patterns.

Then it passed. Blue sky appeared, replacing the white water through the cracked pane. But they were drifting, floating on the flood. The engine smoked and sputtered out, and the water seeped through the slim gaps between the doors and the frame, filling the foot wells rapidly.

Looking around, Amy could see that they were floating

along the flow of the tide, and heading towards the safety of the mountain slope. The bulk of the wave had already struck the slope, and the car bobbled around in the wake created. Grateful for the sturdy frame of her car, she resisted the temptation to steer the wheel in an attempt to guide them, they were at the mercy of the flow.

From the back seat, cries of terror hurt Amy's ears as she felt the cold water creeping up her calves. The electrics on the dashboard flickered and died. She also heard the scrape of objects carried in the surrounding water as they struck, but the force of the wave had put her in a state of shock.

The energy borne through the tsunami calmed, the water now lapping the bottom of the windows. Leaks increased, filling the car up at an alarming rate. They needed to abandon the vehicle before it sank.

Amy snapped out of her hesitation.

Turning to the boy on the passenger seat, she saw he had lifted his bare legs out of the water and put his bare feet on the seat, just above the rising line. He was shaking, and the dog was becoming restless and nervous as it leant on his knees.

The car was drifting as the nose began to rotate. Amy tested the electric windows, preparing for escape, but they had stopped working.

"We have to open the doors," she said. "When we do, the water will flood in and the car will sink. We have to get out as quickly as we can, or we'll get sucked down with it. Can you all swim?"

The two backseat ladies said they could. The boy, still in shock, did not reply.

The water was high now, and the car was sinking. They needed to act. The car, spinning freely, turned sideways, bobbing around.

"Are we all ready?" she said.

They took a deep breath, preparing for a soaking. Amy hoped they wouldn't strike anything underwater.

With an effort, she forced open her driver-seat door. The weight of water made it heavy, and as soon as it opened a crack, the flood washed in. The front of the car dipped downwards alarmingly.

With just enough space to get out, Amy went swimming. She exited the car and kicked her legs. Unknown objects brushed past, and she forced her mind not to concentrate on them.

Amber struggled to open the rear car doors against the weight of water. She had not the strength against the pressure. The water submerged the front, covering the engine and creeping up the cracked windscreen. Fighting against the undertow, Amy went over to the rear passenger door, put a foot on the side panel and pulled the latch. It opened but then the water forced it back. Pulling again, Amber pushed on her side and managed to slip out just before the weight closed it again. She spread herself into the water, her head just floating above. On the other seat, Kath pulled on the latch to open the door. Younger and fitter, she still had to use all her strength against the pressure of the flow. After pushing the door with her feet, the strain showing on her face, she managed to open it and slipped out into the swell. Joining her mother, they trod water as the flow carried them inland.

The boy and his dog were still inside.

"Open the door," shouted Amy through the car, the unclean water slipping between her lips and into her mouth. It tasted salty and metallic.

The boy seemed frozen, but the dog was scrabbling at the closed passenger side door. The cab was filling up quickly – now most of the way up the windows – and the front end pointed downwards as its lateral flow turned vertical.

The half-submerged car drifted towards the eastern bank as it rose to greet the precipitous slopes of the Petit Piton. Twisted trunks of trees overhung the floodwater, their leaves dipping and dripping as the branches swayed. Mother and daughter, seeing a potential escape ahead where woody stems were within reach, kicked their legs toward it.

Amy, leaving them behind, manoeuvred her way around her sinking car, grasping onto it to keep with the flow. The rear pointed to the sky. She made her way to the passenger side, the back tyres out of the water.

With the front half fully submerged, Amy dipped her head below the surface, grabbing onto the door handle, and yanked on it. Opening a fraction, she could see the dog was trying to put its snout in the gap and escape. Air escaped its nostrils, causing the invading flood to bubble around it. With an effort, she managed to pull it open enough for it to squeeze through, scrabbling with its front paws. It rose to the surface and began to paddle. The force of the water closed the door once again, leaving the boy trapped.

The two ladies stood on the slope grasping onto the vegetation, securing their footing. They were drenched, their hair lank against their scalps, clothes clinging to their frames. They called the dog over, and it swam towards them. Jumping up into the mud, it did not stop and sprinted into the undergrowth, disappearing from view.

Amy surfaced, out of breath.

The Range Rover had sunk below the waves, with just the rear fender now poking out. Gulping in a lungful of air, Amy dived below. She kept her eyes open but could not see much in the murky grime. She banged on the passenger window, but it remained firm. She caught a glimpse of the boy, still stuck in the passenger seat – his eyes were open now, and he was gulping in a lungful of water. His eyes showed panic as he realised he was about to drown.

Moving to the cracked windscreen, keeping hold of the frame, Amy kicked with the heel of her pumps. Pointing to the glass, she instructed the boy to try and help. Inside the car, the drowning boy – floating around over the dashboard – hit the windscreen with the heel of his hand.

Amy was running out of oxygen, and the car was sinking. She kicked upwards and emerged into the sunshine once again. Taking another gulp, she slipped back beneath the water and forced herself downwards with a stroke of her arms and a kick of her legs.

The boy was still hitting the glass, a dull thud reaching her ears as she swam back to him. She grappled on the roof of the car, pointing down at a forty-five-degree angle, and managed to get a good handhold. Swinging her body in the weightless depth, she managed to get some force behind her kicks. The weakened glaze cracked further as they both hammered it, but with the boy's efforts waning. Then, the side of the glass cracked and gave way, and half the windscreen – now racked down the centre – split and wafted in the underwater current. Amy, grabbing the boy's arm in a fist, dragged him out of the gap and kicked her legs upwards.

They both breached the water with a splutter.

Checking on him, Amy found that he was conscious but could barely keep his head above water. Amy cupped her hand below his chin, keeping his head high. Gasping for air, the boy did not struggle against her.

On the bank, Amber and Kath had followed their progress, scrambling over the rocks and the bushes, and they had managed to get a little ahead of them. Kath grabbed hold of a twisting trunk that overhung the flood, seeing the stricken pair floating towards her. Her mother stood by the bank, waiting to assist.

Just behind them, the rear lights sank beneath the waves with bubbles, and then a swirl on the surface as it sought the ground below.

In the flood, Amy spotted the girl and, even as she felt her strength fading, kicked her legs towards the bank, still holding onto the boy, her palm firm under his chin.

Dipping the tips of her fingers into the water, Kath waited for the tide to bring them to her. With Amy swimming the best she could, Amber called out to them to make sure they were on track. Then, as Amy lifted her spare arm out of the water, she managed to grasp her wrist.

Without the strength to pull herself out of the water, Amy twisted the boy around so they could help him first. Amber, stood on the bank, reached out and grabbed the hem of his shorts. With an effort, she managed to drag him onto the bank, grateful that he was of small stature.

With the boy safe, Amy could use her other arm to hold on, and Kath yanked her out, her shoulders complaining and her whole body dripping, from the flood. Scrambling into the mud, her feet and calves sunk into the sodden earth, and she forced herself up the slope and to safety. Lying on her back, her soaked clothing clinging to her, her breath came in deep moans as she gasped to get air into her lungs. Beside her, the boy vomited out water and started to cough, tears striking down his dirty cheeks.

After a couple of minutes, her heart rate began to level out, and Amy looked up at the concerned faces of Amber and Kath.

"Thank you," she said.

"No, thank *you*," said Amber, "If you hadn't come along, we'd be at the bottom of that flood right now."

Kath nodded, shivering from both dampness and shock.

At that moment, from deep in the undergrowth around them, the leaves rustled and the dog emerged. It was panting and still sodden, but otherwise uninjured. It ran straight over to the young boy, sniffed his face once, and started licking it.

The boy stirred and sat up, shaking from the damp and the shock. Tears came from his wide eyes, but he reached out and hugged his canine companion.

The dog whined and licked the boy's face in grateful reunion

III

Samuel had not been idle. Using his phone, he contacted the government's emergency committee, and their recovery plan came into effect. He'd heard the wave had struck the government offices in Castries, but the infrastructure was still in place to start the initial rescue effort and the treatment of victims. From the storage depots located in the central region, within minutes trucks began to arrive at his location delivering medicine and tents to set up a local triage and patient treatment area. Two helicopters appeared, buzzing around, assessing the situation, and the coastguard mobilised to search for survivors.

The flat space jutting from the hillside, that Samuel had designated as a sanctuary, was now a gathering area for hundreds of people, both civilians who escaped the town, and rescue workers, doctors and nurses deployed to help. They had arrived along the higher internal roads that were above the floodwater.

As he had begun to organise, the second wave had hit. Witnessing the destruction of the town as *The Lady* acted as a wrecking ball on the tide, he had also kept a keen eye on Amy's Range Rover. Seeing that she had picked up some of the town's residents, he watched anxiously as she fled the town just as the wave struck. She had disappeared around the slope of the Petit Piton just as the wave bore down, and he had not seen her since.

A thumping sound from the helicopter's rotors overhead distracted him from his thoughts. It hovered, directing the rescue workers in boats trying to locate anyone trapped, with the other sweeping over the local area, assessing the extent of the damage. He knew they were likely to find many bodies, and wondered how many people had perished. Very likely people that he knew. He thought the hurricane would be the worst disaster he would face in his lifetime, but now this compounded the horror inflicted upon the island in such a short period. Once again, it was a grim task ahead, but one he had trained for his entire life.

Within minutes of their arrival, the emergency rescue workers had put up three blue canvas tents, sat across the road, taking up the entire carriageway and run-off area. The first, no more than a canopy, housed the walking wounded. A single nurse administering bandages and painkillers attended them. Those caught in the flood sat wrapped in silver blankets. Many of the victims were in shock and sat on the wooden benches whilst they mentally processed their narrow escapes.

The more seriously wounded lay in the second tent. Two nurses were plastering broken limbs and stitching gashes. Several people lay in camp beds, unconscious from head injuries, some of whom needed urgent hospital treatment. Samuel heard that ambulances were struggling to cope with the volume of call outs, and so it was likely to be hours before any would arrive. They would have to treat them in this makeshift hospital as best they could for now.

The final tent had a second canvas sheet around it, and it lay a distance away from the other two. Samuel opened the flap and glanced inside. Rows of bodies lined the floor, covered in white sheets, identifying tags tied to their toes. A cadaverous odour lingered despite the face mask he wore, and the heat of the day was raising the temperature. Flies were gathering.

Outside the tent, he located two orderlies wearing white face masks and scrubs; they were piling crates of bottled water. He instructed them to make further space available inside. He had to anticipate the worst. Moving the deceased to a morgue was a priority.

He paused for a moment, looking out across the

devastation. Wiping his brow with his forearm, he saw *The Lady of the Pitons* in her final spot abutting the church steeple. Around it, despite the receding tide, the dinghies buzzed around like pond skaters, looking for survivors, the injured, or the dead. Samuel let out the deepest sigh he had ever uttered and shook his head.

How could anyone hope to compete with nature's fury?

At that moment, from the undergrowth at the side of the road, Amy emerged. Two women and a boy with a dog joined her.

Samuel spotted her, covered in mud and looking exhausted.

"Amy, my lord!" he said, unable to contain his delight, "What a sight you are."

He went over and hugged her, but she didn't have the strength to squeeze him back, or even speak. She almost collapsed into his arms.

"Come, let's get you seen to. Let's get you all seen to," he said, turning to the others.

Taking them to the walking wounded tent, he gave them bottles of fresh water and silver blankets. Amy took her seat wearily, and - after unscrewing the cap – drank deeply from the bottle, ending by pouring the last dregs of the liquid over her face.

Samuel watched with concern.

"That was just about the bravest thing I've ever seen anyone do," he said.

Amy didn't reply, she still had a mouthful of water, but she gave him a baleful stare. She had acted on instinct. She was no hero, and she did not want anyone to regard her as such. Swallowing the water, she took a deep breath and closed her eyes, rocking back on her chair, her visage pained.

The disaster, and its possible cause, playing on her mind.

Coming back to the present, she looked up the road. Ahead the bend turned the corner of the hill that led back to her home.

"What happened to you?" he asked. "I saw you escape the town, but then lost sight?"

"We were hit by the wave," she said, her voice quiet. Around, she heard cries of distress from the survivors facing ruin from that morning.

"I lost the car," said Amy, "But managed to escape the flood on the far side of the town. We worked our way back round here, through the trees. I knew you'd organised the recovery."

"You saved the lives of those people," said Samuel. "So many others haven't been as fortunate."

"I need to get home," she said.

"You're concerned about John?" asked Samuel. "Have you not seen him at all today?"

Amy shook her head.

"You mentioned that you thought he'd be okay though?" said Samuel. "How do you know this – was he at home when I called?"

Amy could not find the words to explain, and fatigue was starting to overwhelm her.

"I promise you that he will be fine, wherever he is," said Amy.

She tried to think of an excuse, some reason to explain her confidence in her husband's wellbeing without causing suspicion – but she had nothing.

"You're just going to have to trust me, Samuel," she said. "Things are going on that I can't explain to you right now."

"What do you mean?" he said. "When people tell me that there are things that can't be explained, that's usually a cause for *more* concern?"

Amy's exhaustion made her sway in her chair. She had no energy to speak further and placate him. She needed to think. If she told him what she knew, could she trust him to keep it private rather than go to the authorities?

Would he keep it secret?

Samuel saw her sway and placed a kind hand on her shoulder, and then noticed a new batch of injured people making their way towards them. Another helicopter arrived, chopping the air overhead.

"You rest up now," he said. "I'll come back shortly and we can talk further. I'm worried about you both."

With that, he left her alone and went to help the casualties.

She watched him leave and looked up the road again to her own house. After Samuel disappeared into the tent, she stood up.

IV

Amy approached her home, her feet kicking up the dust from the road as she used her last reserves. A helicopter still hovered above, but she was immune to the rapid thumping as it swept above the ruined town. Smoke had begun to rise in a haze in the valley, fires catching as the waters receded.

None of these registered as she reached her driveway. Her eyes were as heavy as her mood. Dark thoughts followed the harrowing escape, and they threatened to overwhelm her. One thought, in particular, had rooted in her mind.

Samuel had just called her actions heroic, but she felt another emotion growing within.

A hurricane and a tsunami had struck them in the space of a few weeks. An unfortunate coincidence? Possibly – both of these disasters could occur in St Lucia. It was prone to occasional hurricanes and was located near a fault line. Had these occurred throughout her lifetime, they would both be terrible events, but not surprising.

Just mere weeks apart, however…

As a scientist, she could still explain these away as just unfortunate timings but ultimately down to natural forces. But with her discoveries on the fabric of the cosmos and Duality, thoughts about this universal nature began to cloud her logic. These two disasters, although affecting hundreds of thousands of people across the Caribbean, seemed directed right at her. Right at her home.

Right at Vix.

What if her research had been the cause of nature targeting this attack on her, and the people affected were the collateral damage? Her luxury home, with its elevated position above the town, like a castle above a village, may have been the catalyst for the disaster. She had no way of proving if this was the case, but she found it hard to shake the feeling.

She did not feel heroic.

She felt guilt.

She reached her front door and found it unlocked. Entering, she moved through the lounge and spotted her reflection in the large mirror: her hair unkempt and wild and her skin and clothes covered in dried mud. The red circles around her eyes gave her a haunted look. It felt as though someone else was looking back at her.

Moving into the kitchen, she grabbed a bottle of water from the refrigerator. It was warm. The flood had caused a power outage. Downing in a single gulp, she wiped her mouth with the back of her hand and placed the empty bottle on the counter.

"John, are you here?"

She did not get a reply.

Fighting the urge to go upstairs and curl up in her bed, she left the house back into the hot sunshine on the terrace. She put a hand on the door frame to steady herself as she felt her head spin in the humidity.

Crossing the terrace, she smelt a mixture of wood smoke and diesel drifting over the coastline from the town. Looking out over the wall, a haze lingered, but she could see several lifeboats floating just outside the mouth of the bay area. She leaned out further and discovered her jetty had gone. Washed away by the wave. No sign of *Higgs* either.

No doubt, their lab had been flooded. Vix, with all its knowledge and power, destroyed.

Fearing the worst, she took the steps down the side of the cliff to the laboratory door. As she descended, she saw the broken planks of wood littering the rocky shoreline, the remnants of their little pier. She saw no sign of the dinghy.

Reaching the foot of the stairs, she had to drop a metre to the rocks. Parts of the walkway remained but were damaged and hung from their anchors. The seawater lapped her feet, and she shrunk away from it as she felt the coldness, the memory still close.

Moving the short distance to where the doorway lay, she found her eyes dazzled by the sun's reflection. The sea itself was calm and placid. It seemed hard to fathom the energy and fury it had unleashed just a couple of hours ago.

Amy halted and looked back up at the cliff. The doorway would be at the line of the now destroyed walkway, but now it wasn't.

It was all just solid stone.

She looked around. Had she missed it? Walked past it? Maybe being at a different level, with the sun in her eyes, she had not spotted it. She walked back a few steps.

No, it just wasn't where it should be.

Being so familiar with the lab, she knew where it lay. The curves of the cliff, the steps required from the staircase were all second nature to her. But now, the cliff just came down right to the damp rocks beneath her feet. The face smoothed like the rocks had been spread over the slope like butter over bread…

"John – are you here?"

Nothing happened for a moment.

She repeated his name. Louder this time.

The sound of cracking began to reverberate around her. In the space where the door should have been, a line appeared in the rock, descending in a vertical, jagged line down the face. Small stones started to fall around her, and she took a step back to avoid them as they splashed in the sea.

The cracking became louder, and the stones larger. An area around the door began to open up, and she saw the rusted blue doors of the entrance appear behind the clearing rocks. A mini-landslide now fell, tumbling over the rock shelf where Amy stood, bouncing and sinking into the sea below. The salty water splashed her face, and she let out a yelp as she retreated for cover.

Her arms went over her face defensively as the rockslide continued for several moments. Then, it quietened. For a moment she stood, blocking out her vision with her arms.

As it subsided, she uncovered her eyes. In front of her, the doorway to the lab stood as it always had – just a metre or so above her position. With a clang, the doors swung outwards.

John stood at the entrance, looking down at her. He looked exhausted.

Amy's vision swam, but it was more intense this time. The last thing she saw before passing out, was John leaping down from the cave.

Chapter Eleven – Aftermath

I

Darkness greeted Amy as she awoke. A thread of moonlight entered her room through the gap in the curtains, and her bedside clock displayed the time – it had just turned 3 am. Next to her clock lay a plate, with another upturned plate on top of it, and a glass of water.

She wore her pyjamas, and her skin and hair felt washed and clean.

Lying silently for a moment, she tried to recall what had happened. The rock face crumbling to reveal the entrance to the lab, the sound of falling rocks into the sea, and the door opening. John, standing in the doorway, looking exhausted.

Then it went black.

The stress and shock of the tsunami had overwhelmed her, along with the growing belief that her experiment may be involved. Hazy memories lingered of the hours following, as she fell into a mental stupor. Being in John's arms as he carried her back to the house. Stripped from her filthy clothing, he then bathed her clean. The water was cold, but it felt cooling after the heat and exertions. John washed her with a soapy flannel and shampooed her hair, his touch gentle and caressing. She must have been in and out of consciousness as parts of her recollection were missing, but she had not protested when John towel-dried her and dressed her in clean, cotton pyjamas. Indeed, rather than feel awkward and ashamed from her loss of control, she found her recall pleasant.

The actions taken were something her husband would do.

She must've been out as he put her to bed.

"I'm sorry."

Amy jumped in surprise at the voice, and she sat up in bed.

In the corner, on the wicker chair next to her dressing table, sat John. His eyes glinted white as the moonlight struck them, but otherwise, he was a dark silhouette.

"I'm sorry," he repeated.

"Sorry for what?" she asked, rubbing the soft skin on her cheeks.

"For not being there for you," he said. "It won't happen again."

Amy's stomach growled, the noise echoing around the stillness of her bedroom. She hadn't eaten for hours.

"I've made you a sandwich," said John.

She clicked her bedside lamp, and it took her a few seconds to recover from the sudden glare. Lifting the upturned plate, she saw two slices of bread. Separating them, grated cheese appeared.

"The power's back on then," she said, before eyeing the sandwich.

"It's not - I switched the house from the island grid to the power plant while I was down there yesterday."

"So the lab is completely undamaged?"

"Yes."

She shook her head, the solid rock face fresh in her mind. But first things first: she grabbed the sandwich and took a large bite.

"I think I'm still processing what happened," said Amy, her mouth full. "I nearly died yesterday."

"I know," said John. "And I'm sorry. I shouldn't have left you alone. You were safe in the house when I went to the lab. I didn't think you would leave before the wave came."

"You went to protect Vix?"

John nodded.

"I knew it would flood and destroy Vix," he said.

"We would've lost our only proof of my theory," she said, swallowing a mouthful.

John stood and went to the window. Parting the curtains, a sliver of water-dappled moon rays played on his face as he looked outside.

"We have to protect Vix at all costs," said Amy. "Otherwise, how do we prove to the world that Duality exists?"

John didn't reply.

"You don't need to apologise," said Amy, and she shifted herself to get back under the sheets. "You did the right thing. But I'm too tired to think of this right now. I need some sleep, and figure things out in the morning."

She reached over and turned out the light. John remained at the window.

"Vix is not as important as you are," said John, as she felt sleep returning.

Her last thought, before they were lost to her dreams, was wondering how he knew the wave would come; and if he possessed that foresight, why he didn't know that she would leave the house.

II

The night continued.

Mani lay under his rock, undetected. The sound of motors from helicopters, boats and road vehicles - as they continued the flood relief effort through the night – echoed around his location. The sound reached the tympanic membrane, but the brain did not register it. Not enough energy lay within the body to animate all the functions.

He had all but resumed the death state.

A flicker of energy still existed, creeping around the body, preventing decomposition; maintaining enough of the molecular integrity contained within this person to resume animation once recovered. Every moment it grew stronger, as the energy that flowed amongst all the matter, and the absence of matter, drifted through the body.

Space-time, the very fabric of the universe that existed by the duality of the two combined energies of creation and destruction, fed into him.

Was it done?

Have we reached a resolution?

No. It wasn't.

Uncertainty still existed. Space-time demanded settlement, one way or another.

Lying beneath his rock, growing stronger with every moment, he still had work to do. His massive expenditure of energy had achieved nothing.

Time to start again.

As the energy grew a fraction, the neurons in the brain began to fire. Senses restored. He could hear the sound of vehicles nearby.

Something else began to return. Something that only existed within life.

Emotion.

Replacing the cold logic of the universe was a very human reaction to failure. As the brain fired, and Mani began to return, the emotional state followed. And a single feeling overwhelmed him.

Fury.

III

Amy emerged from the rear of the house, and out onto the terrace. The heat struck her, and she squinted up at the clear blue sky. The days had been increasingly warm despite heading toward the end of the year.

"It's a hot one," she said.

John grunted acknowledgement back in the kitchen. He was checking the larder for their stock of food – supplies would be hard to come by in the following days.

Amy still felt tired, her limbs weak and she ached. Despite her physical exhaustion, her mind was working overtime, working on a link between the island devastation, the condition of John, and her discoveries with Vix.

Looking over the wall, the water below was the busiest she could ever recall. Countless boats dotted the seascape. The coastguard vessels, providing the relief effort, were easy to spot. The Royal St Lucian Constabulary ran the coast guard, and they had the word "Police" stencilled to their grey hulls. Many other smaller boats, belonging to private individuals, mingled between them. Fishing boats and pleasure craft – lucky enough to escape undamaged – drifted around; they were looking for anything to salvage from the wreckage of the town.

Feelings of overwhelming responsibility were growing within her; but she was beginning to plan how she would spread her findings. No doubt, the key was Vix. John's miraculous resurrection, and his ability to manipulate the matter around him – be it his own body, or the rock face – all fell on one side of the Duality equation. The events taking place on the island – Hurricane Harriet and the tsunami – felt as though they were on the opposite side.

As she stared down at the commotion on the sea below, and the smoke-filled air from the now smouldering remains of the town, a sense of despair came over her. They had designed and built Vix to enhance, or dispute, the current understanding of the quantum universe. Instead, it revealed the very nature of a violent and uncaring one. A universe that displayed no distinction between creating life and destroying it, depending on what lay in the future.

The future…

The progression of time. Past. Present. Future.

Was that the key?

Physics as a science was concerned with the properties of nature, and everything in it. Physics was predictable, given enough data.

John emerged from the house, curious about her musings.

"Hey, question for you," said Amy, calling him over.

He approached, and she turned to look out at the sea once again.

"Last night you apologised to me for leaving me just before the wave struck," she said.

John nodded. "I meant it," he said, "I shouldn't have

left you."

"Answer me this," she said. "You *knew* the wave was coming before it was here. All that business staring out to sea, and taking that boat trip to the middle of nowhere. And yet you *didn't* know that I would leave to help the people in town?"

"I had no idea you would go," said John. "And my responsibility is to protect you and Vix – to make sure nothing happens to either."

"My Duality theory states that the universe is in constant flux between the forces of creation and destruction. Time *itself* is a construct of the two forces interacting. Each force must constantly monitor the passage of time, and crucially – the *destination*. Where each action taken will lead in the future."

"I did these things on instinct," said John. "Using humanity as a frame of reference, I would guess you would call it a feeling."

"What's that feeling telling you right now?"

"That everything is right. As it should be."

Amy looked across the bay and the grey haze over emanating from the remains of Soufriere.

"Your actions yesterday prevented Vix from being destroyed. You knew the wave would hit because it was affected by the universe."

"I have no knowledge of the future."

"That's because - if you are just made of pure energy - any intelligence or information you possess comes from John."

"What's your point?"

"That the energy inside you – the one that heals your

body and changes the rock to protect the lab – *does* have knowledge of the future. And it guides you to make sure that this future comes to pass. The problem is, judging from recent events, it appears we have something out there with an *alternate* future in mind. It's trying to stop us by destroying Vix. Trying to stop you."

"How can I, or this other force, know the future?"

"Physics," replies Amy. "I can go into my study right now and, using my knowledge of physics and maths, tell you what location planet earth will be in, a million years from now. But what I cannot do is tell you where *I* will be this time tomorrow. Life is not predictable - but as the universe obeys the laws of physics, we can project time, backwards and forwards, and know exactly where it will be and what will occur. It's no stretch to think that this energy that defines the very fabric of the universe also knows its outcome."

"So you think that life on Earth has caused some kind of universal dilemma?"

"Exactly!" said Amy. "We are the chaos element when it comes to space-time. It is so obvious to me now. We have caused a *problem* for the future. Does the universe *want* humanity, the dominant species on this planet, and maybe the first ever to extend itself off its home world, putting itself about in the cosmos? If we continue as we are, we'll ruin this planet. We go to war with each other, and we destroy the very world that gave us life. And yet we are intelligent. We possess emotion and artistry. We've all but figured out the story of the cosmos. The universe doesn't know whether to destroy us or embrace us."

She paced over the paving on the terrace, speaking

faster as her thoughts and ideas overtook her. John watched in patient admiration, allowing her realisation.

"The two forces of Duality work together to define the future of life," she continued. "The whole story of the development of life, from a single cell to complex organisms, has been defined by the actions of these forces. Ensuring the correct chemistry existed on Earth to form long-chain molecules and amino acids before they formed into the first thing that could be considered alive. Even throwing a lump of space rock in our direction when it realised that giant lizards would never evolve to understand physics and leave the planet. Maybe even *after* civilisations formed, every genius scientist, and messiah – along with the other side with evil dictators, pandemics, and every other ill that has ever befallen us – are the ones that have shaped our history. Guiding us to try and resolve this uncertain future."

Amy, in her excitement, wobbled on her feet. She put a hand out to the wall to steady herself, and John rushed over to help. She put a hand to her forehead.

"I'm sorry," she said with an apologetic laugh, "It's a lot to take in. I guess I'm not quite over yesterday."

John held her arm as he moved her out of the sunlight and into the shade of the kitchen. It felt cooler inside. Sitting her down, he grabbed a bottle of water from the counter and handed it to her.

"I'm okay," she said. "We should go and see Samuel at the relief station. He could probably use our help."

"You're not going anywhere," said John. "You need to stay here and rest."

"I can't rest. My mind is racing. It's too much to take in."

"Then all the more reason to take it easy," he said. "Work things out, process your thoughts. Once you have, we can discuss them, and then start getting them down in writing."

Amy nodded in agreement. She was still tired, her aches and pains firing over her body and her head swimming.

IV

Arching his back against the rock, Mani felt the heat return within him. The stone, heated by the midday sun, transferred its warmth into the skin and muscles as he stretched his spine across it. Spreading his arms out wide, face up to the sky, he allowed the rays to beat down on him - feeling the body returning to a lifelike state.

He remained a pale shadow of how he had entered the rock two days before the wave. Well-fed and exercised, he had been lean and strong physically. Inwardly, the force that had grown inside him had reached huge levels; and he needed every part of it to nudge the fault line. Transferring so much of that part of him that kept the body functioning had caused a near-death state once again; with the brain shutting down almost all its regulatory processes, and just keeping the heart pumping and lungs inflating. His nervous system, digestion, senses of taste, touch, sight, smell and hearing had all ceased.

The gradual build-up of energy that flowed across the universe had revived him as time progressed, but it would take several days before he could function fully.

His vest lay on the ground next to him, and he put it back on despite it being filthy. Around the rock that he sought shelter in during his attack lay snacks and bottles of water. Grabbing a chocolate bar, he unwrapped it and consumed the melted contents, stripping the brown ooze from the wrapper with his tongue. He discarded the wrapper into the air and picked up a plastic bottle. Drinking its contents, he also dropped it, adding to the litter around him.

Rotating his head around the orbit of his shoulders, his neck muscles cracked.

Above him, a helicopter thumped over at speed. It was heading west, towards the Pitons. From his viewpoint, the twin cones dominated the landscape, their green tips poking out from the surrounding hills. Out of his view line, their western slopes descended into the sea.

He shielded his eyes against the sun to get a better view of the area. He knew that the wave would have affected the whole island, and no doubt most of the Caribbean, the coasts of Central America, the northern shores of South America, and even the edges of the desert in North-west Africa. The thought brought satisfaction, but he had not completed the task.

Something on this tiny island was preventing the future from happening. He needed to destroy it.

So far, he had hoped that natural disasters would bring about the outcome. That widespread destruction would stop the obstacle preventing his future, but that had not worked. Time was short. He needed something more targeted, more direct. The problem he faced was that he did not know his target. This body, this mind, did not know about the event taking place on St Lucia. Tramping around the island had not revealed anything either.

It was time to come out from the shadows and find out

what he needed to know.

Keeping his gaze on the Pitons, he followed the direction of the helicopter.

<u>V</u>

Dr Frankland removed the tetanus needle from the arm of the boy and swabbed the site with a ball of cotton wool.

"You're done," he said, trying to sound as cheerful as possible. The boy had lost his home and all his possessions. He was one of the lucky ones though. His parents had survived and were looking on as he had his injection; their faces were a mixture of concern and gratitude. They had suffered cuts and bruises when the wave struck them, before the coastguard, drifting by on an inflatable, rescued the family. Having nowhere else to go, they slept along with hundreds of others, under the stars, on camp beds.

During the night, more casualties arrived from across the local area.

The tide had fully receded by late afternoon. Replaced by small fires igniting in the heat of the day, fuelled by piles of wood from the destruction. As the hours progressed, the rescue effort changed from finding survivors to finding the deceased. Samuel made it his priority to make sure he moved the cadavers in the covered tent to a morgue as soon as the ambulances could reach them. The potential for disease preyed on his mind, and keeping the dead stored in an unrefrigerated tent was something he wanted to avoid. Nevertheless, the rancid, rotting stench of death lingered over the station despite the rapid movement of the bodies. It was a grim task, and despite trying to remain as upbeat as possible for his patients, he was starting to feel the toll of the pressure and the dark thoughts that came with it.

He needed a break, but he was on duty for another four hours before his relief would arrive. After only two hours of sleep overnight, on a spare camp bed from the station supplies, his energy was flagging. It seemed a thick atmosphere covered the whole camp. Not just from the smouldering town, but also from the dead and injured. It was a constant battle trying to prevent the insects from swarming, even though they had set up blue-light traps; and the heat was unrelenting. Samuel's sweat-drenched handkerchief had made a damp patch on his shirt pocket.

He needed to go on his rounds again and assess the patients still in recovery. They had a range of injuries from severe lacerations to broken legs and arms. Several concussions, along with the unconscious required constant monitoring. The island hospitals were overwhelmed with casualties, and so this was the best treatment they could receive until beds became available.

He had heard through his communications that the international community were rallying to provide a relief effort: sending aid workers to the island. The tsunami had not just been a disaster limited to St Lucia, it struck most of the Windward Islands, and the flat island of Barbados had suffered especially badly.

As he rose from behind his makeshift desk, shaded under a temporary gazebo, he spotted a figure walking down the road from the direction of his home. John Hunter was making his way towards him and the camp.

Here was that enigma that had been on his mind since Hurricane Harriet struck. That man just had not been the same, and where had he been yesterday when Amy saved those town residents so heroically? What was going on with their laboratory experiments? Some kind of particle physics, they had said. It was not Samuel's field, but they were playing around with nature. Just at the point they start their experiments, two of the worst disasters in the island's history had struck just weeks apart, and John had been acting strangely after a miraculous survival.

As John neared the camp, Samuel wondered at his thoughts. Being suspicious was not in his character, and these thoughts may just be down to stress. He needed to remember that John and Amy were his friends and neighbours, recalling the night in the restaurant. He did not think they had some wicked plan, but many questions remained.

John spotted Samuel as he reached the edge of the camp, and the doctor went to meet him. They shook hands, with John looking at the handshake with a certain curiosity.

"I'm here to help," he said. "What can I do?"

"It's great to see you, John," said Samuel, "I'm sure we can find you some tasks, thanks for coming here to volunteer. How's Amy?"

Samuel led John into the camp, with his hand on his shoulder.

VI

His feet sank into the mud that, despite the heat, persisted around the fields to the rear of Soufriere. Feet that blackened as the dirt clung to them and the sandals that offered little protection. He cut an ethereal shape as he passed through the white-grey smoke drifting over from the town, but his stride was measured and purposeful as he approached the ruins.

Around him, emerging from the haze, piles of jagged timber and broken concrete. The sun shone pale, but no breeze stirred the mist. Small fires had ignited in places, fuelled by some unseen spark; they came to life for a moment before they disappeared, only to reappear again a short distance away. He looked on at the church steeple as it formed before him; and from the mist the impossible wedge of a ship's bow emerged, defiant but crippled, *The Lady* hugged the tower. It was an abstract tableau amongst the destruction. It featured alongside countless cars, some upturned or on their sides, buried in what remained of the structures. Flashes and sparks strobed in the thick air around him as welders fired their cutting tools to free the stricken vessel.

Puddles remained in the spaces between the rubble piles, and the odd stench combination of burning, dampness and death lingered over everything.

People wandered through the remains of the town. Hazy outlines of ghosts, shades in the mist, drifted around. Aid workers and residents, many of whom seemed to be scavenging what they could find in the detritus.

He felt a tap on his shoulder, and he turned. An aid worker smiled at him, his face also etched with concern. He was an islander, and had a heavy accent, but wore a high visibility vest and carried a first aid kit.

"Are you okay, brother?" he asked. "You don't look too well?"

"I'm fine," said Mani, turning to leave.

"There is an aid station just up the hill there," said the aid worker, pointing to the road leading up to it on the far side of town. "If you need any help or assistance, that's the place to go."

Mani grunted, and left the aid worker behind, looking bemused.

He made his way to what remained of the harbour, and the slopes of the Pitons emerged, along with the sound of motor boats in the bay. Uprooted palm trees lay in a line next to the collapsed ruins of the harbour-side buildings, and many people clambered on top of the rubble, sifting through it for possessions or anything worth salvaging from their shattered lives.

About halfway along the line, he found a steel shopping trolley on its side, and lying around – in between what remained of shelving and wooden planks – were tin cans full of food. Tins of pineapples in syrup, condensed milk, and various soups. A wooden sign laying on the floor near the road had the word Supermarket painted on it in white, its wood now stained and the planks cracked.

Righting the supermarket trolley, Mani began to pile the cans inside it. Not to pass up an opportunity to find sustenance, this would save him much time hunting for food.

At that moment, he noticed two women a few metres away on top of the rubble pile. They seemed to be trying to clear away the remains of the building, hunting down any mementoes or personal possessions. One of them was approaching middle age, the other in her late teens – but their similar features suggested to Mani that they were mother and daughter. They seemed not to have noticed him and were deep in conversation as they moved away the wood and concrete chunks that once were their home and business.

Wanting to hear their conversation, Mani stopped collecting the tins and moved closer to them, using the mist to conceal himself. Going down onto all fours, he clambered over the rubble as quietly as he could.

"What've you found there, Kath?" asked the older lady.

"Just piles of clothes, mam," she replied. "I think it's what's left of the T-shirt rack."

"Just put them over there, with the rest of the stock we've found."

Kath picked up the loose and dirty pile of fabric and moved them over to another part of the rubble pile.

"What are we even doing here?" she asked. The weariness evident in her voice. She slumped down the T-shirts onto the rubble.

"We can't give up. As long as we are still breathing, we keep going,"

"But we've lost everything. Our home, our business…"

"But we still have each other. We salvage what we can, and we rebuild."

"I think it's about time I got off this island," said Kath.

"That's your choice, child, I won't stop you. But there are good people here. Friendly people. We live in paradise, but now and again, god sends us a test. We have to make sure we are up to the task."

"How could a kind god do this to us?" asked Kath, looking around at the tangled mess around her.

"Don't you blaspheme here," her mother crossed herself. "Yes, he sent this wave. Remember your bible, child. Remember Noah? Remember what he did?"

"It wasn't Noah this time - it was that English lady that

lives up on the hill. She's the one that took us in, two by two."

"Indeed, and that's the spirit we need to get through these times. God sent us that woman, and because of her, we are still here today. Praise be to god."

Mani clambered a bit nearer as they moved around the patch of rubble, listening intently. The mist was starting to lift, and he needed to be stealthy to remain concealed.

"I've heard other things about her," said Kath.

"What have you heard, child?"

"I've heard that she's some kind of scientist. That she's running some kind of experiment up in that house of hers. Some unnatural experiment."

Her words struck Mani to his core. Surely, this was it, what he had been looking for. He crept closer so he could hear every word.

"Don't be silly, girl," said her mother. "Don't talk ill against the person who came here and saved our lives. She was sent by The Lord, I have no doubt."

"Maybe," said Kath. "But what if all these disasters have something to do with what she is doing up there?"

"You have no idea of what you say. What possible experiment could she be doing that would cause our town to be flooded by the sea? Or cause a hurricane to hit us?"

"Don't you think it strange that they happened so close together?"

"No. It's unfortunate, but living in paradise means we have to pay the price occasionally. Hurricanes have hit St Lucia before, and so have waves. It has nothing to do with experiments, whatever you and your gossiping friends have heard."

Mani heard nothing for a few moments except the sound of them moving rubble.

"What do you think they are doing up there then?" said Kath. "How did she know that another wave would come after the first?"

"I have no idea," her mother replied. "But what I do know is that she came, and she saved us. We owe her our lives. Not only that, but she and her husband have always been good customers, and been very nice and polite to us both when they've shopped here. Now, I'll hear no more talk of what may or may not be happening up in their house on the hill."

She waved her hand over in the direction of their home, and Mani looked over towards the hill at the mouth of the bay, that overlooked the town. He could not see anything, his view obscured. He crept back from the rubble pile stealthily, until the two women were out of his earshot, and stood up.

The mist had begun to break up. It streaked across the bay, its tendrils drifting between the remains of the streets and the rubble mounds. Blue sky crept through in the gaps, and Mani wandered down the ruined harbour side, the people still searching amongst the wreckage ignored him.

The far side of the bay opened up through the clouds, and he followed the line of the cliff face as it swept around the headland. Seeing the camp refuge, he followed the line as it rose adjacent to the sea. Just as it disappeared around the hill, he could see the tip of a villa nestled against it, and his eyes narrowed.

VII

The sudden hum of the air conditioning roused Amy from her nap with a start. Wiping her eyes, and feeling groggy, she stirred from her slumber on the sofa and looked around her. She clicked on a lamp.

Standing from her seat, she went into the kitchen and turned the tap on, the water sputtered from the tap, splashing her t-shirt, but then the regular, steady flow.

John had switched the laboratory power plant back to Vix a few hours earlier. Marvelling how quickly power and water had been restored on the island, she stretched her arms and shoulders. Feeling refreshed, the nap had done her the world of good.

John had not returned, but he had asked her to check on the lab. It had been a few days since she had been down to it, so she resolved to check that everything was what it should be and power was flowing into it once again. John had assured her that everything was fine, that Vix had been unaffected by the wave due to his intervention, but she wanted to reassure herself.

Leaving the house, crossing the terrace, she paused to look out over the mist that streaked over Soufriere. The Pitons seemed to have a white moat surrounding them, but the haze obscured her view of the destruction.

Descending the staircase, she navigated the rocks outside the lab doorway, avoiding the planks from the destroyed walkway, and wondered where their dinghy may have ended up – out to sea, or more likely at the bottom of it.

Clambering up to the doorway, on a small lip of rock in front of the iron doors, she took the key out of her pocket that opened the padlock. She swung one of the doors open and entered the passageway, noticing that the whine of the door hinges had disappeared.

Maybe John had fixed that too.

She clicked on the lights, and they spotted down the corridor down to the lab in pools. It was dry inside, with not a trace of moisture.

Reaching the inner door, she opened it and pressed the light switches for the control room. They flickered on.

Pausing, Amy looked at the glass dominating the far wall. The room beyond, housing Vix, was still in the dark, and, as she stared at the blackness, a shiver passed through her.

Just metres away stood a doomsday machine.

She found it hard to calculate was damage Vix could cause if left unchecked. Repeating the experiment without making sure safeguards were in place was not an option. Those safeguards had begun to work through her mind, but she first needed to make sure Vix was otherwise operational.

On the left side of the control room lay a smaller antechamber filled with spare parts for the electrical equipment and hardware, along with circuit control boxes and air conditioning access panels. Analogue displays showing the electrical current passing up from the generator – housed through another door that led to the further depths of their lab – sat embedded in the concrete walls. She checked the pointers as they waved a little left and right, monitoring the flow from the power plant to the storage cells. Satisfied, she left the room, closing the door behind her.

As she made her way to exit the lab, she paused – looking at the glass once again.

A panel next to where she stood turned on the

monitors. Pressing the button, it fired up and the familiar operating display illuminated her visage. She took the mouse and clicked the program on the screen, which displayed the charge sitting within the batteries. The incremental measurement read that it was full. The batteries were charged and Vix was ready to use.

Being adjacent to such a machine, she felt a temptation to press the required buttons to activate it. In some corner of her mind, whisperings.

Just turn it on, they said.

Here – in front of her – it lay.

Horrific technology.

They had assembled metal and circuitry in such a way to manipulate energy that broke down matter and split the very fabric of the universe.

Turn it on…

Her life had begun to spiral out of control at the very moment they had completed Vix. They had meant to improve their understanding of the universe through the collider, but instead, it had shown her the true nature of it.

A universe that was ambivalent about life on Earth.

It had the bigger picture in mind. If life on this planet meant that existence in other parts of the cosmos may suffer, then the universe would intercede – recycling this speck of consciousness back to its constituent parts – put back into the atomic mix.

On the console in front of her, Amy pressed a different button and the lights illuminated the clean room.

Vix seemed to stare back at her - almost mockingly. It was a trick of her mind, she knew, but despite the amount of time, money and effort they had spent making Vix, she felt resentment toward the machine in the next room.

They had created a monster.

"I hate you," she said out loud.

Turn me on, it whispered back.

She looked to her right. Against the wall was a recessed cupboard. Inside lay a fire extinguisher and a fire axe. It would be very easy for her to take the axe and end it now. Go to town on the machine. Smash it to pieces. The thought so overwhelmed her that she swayed where she stood, feeling dizzy with the sudden rush of adrenaline. She saw herself swinging it around like a maniac - bits of electronics, nuts and bolts, chunks of manifolds and pipework flying around her while she screamed in despair.

Amy caught herself. Relaxed her imagination. And in a moment of clarity, she realised that it was not Vix that was the problem.

It was humanity.

Attempting to convince the world would be impossible without Vix. Picturing herself trying to persuade a panel of scientists that they were on a path to destruction: that the twin energies of creation and destruction were at work constantly, their forces passing through the earth and the life that called it home, measuring out the path of time and the potential future. The panel, their arms folded and heads shaking, listening with increasing incredulity at her Armageddon theory. Reading her thesis full of mathematical equations showing her evidence, but not able to demonstrate where the data originated. Her refusal to collaborate with the rest of the scientific community would also count against her. She was a lone wolf, a science maverick determined to put herself ahead rather than work with others, seeking fame and glory no matter the price or the integrity of the data. She would end up going to the press with her theory to get it heard, to get it out into the public domain, trying to convince the planet to change its ways. Conspiracy theories would arise, people ridiculed for following them, and she would become the object of contempt by the very people she was trying to get through to.

No, Vix must stay. The cost was too high.

But she needed to make it safe to use first.

Switching the lights off in the clean room, Vix was plunged into darkness once again. Musing over her thoughts, she departed the laboratory but turned around as she did so.

She looked at the black glass and saw her reflection in it.

VIII

John pushed away his empty plate.

"That was delicious," he said.

The evening had fallen, and the sun had sunk to the west. His face flickered in the light of a single long candle in the centre of the table. He had changed into black trousers and a white linen shirt following his day at the camp.

"You're welcome," said Amy, "Glad you enjoyed it."

The sound of rumbling drifted through the open terrace door. Heavy plant machinery brought into town to clear the debris. It was distant enough not to be a disturbance to them both.

Amy wiped her mouth with her napkin, leaving a red stain lipstick mark. She had also changed into a floral shift, loose enough to allow the breeze to cool her on this humid evening. She reached for her wine glass.

"You not drinking?" she asked.

John did not reply but took a sip from his glass.

Amy felt the silence that followed and continued to drink her wine. The sea breeze made the hem of her dress dance, and the candle flame flicker.

"So how was Samuel? What did you get up to in the camp?"

"He was fine," replied John. "Very tired, you could see it in his face. The strain of the last forty-eight hours was catching up with him."

"I'm not surprised," she said. "At least I managed to get some sleep last night - I bet he's had to work right through."

"He's being relieved tonight," said John, "But he's back on duty at lunchtime tomorrow."

"What sort of things did he have you doing in the camp?"

"Menial stuff, mainly," he said. "Fetching fresh bandages, linen, that kind of thing. Moving beds around to where they needed to be. Filling up buckets of water from the tanker to cleanse the medical stations."

"Were there many injured?"

"Quite a few, yes. I'd say more than fifty. The more seriously injured were assessed and taken to hospital, and some others could be treated in the camp. Medical supplies were delivered and emergency care workers from the USA and Europe had just arrived."

"And how was Samuel?"

"Tired, as I said?"

"No, I mean - how was he about you and me?"

"Oh, I see. Well, as I was leaving he asked if he could

have a private word."

"A word?"

"Yes – he said he was too exhausted to think about things at that point, but he's asked me to go around to his house in the morning at breakfast for a discussion."

"He suspects something going on with us?" said Amy.

"He's shrewd," said John. "With two disasters striking the island at just the point we started with Vix, along with him perceiving that I am not quite the John he remembers, he's putting the pieces together."

Amy thought for a moment, listening to the faint sounds of the machinery rumbling in the town.

"I think we should tell him everything," she said.

"Everything?"

She nodded.

"Aren't we worried he would report us to the authorities?" asked John. "That he may bring scrutiny to what we are doing here?"

"At this stage, I think we need to start having scrutiny on what we are doing," said Amy. "I trust Samuel to do the right thing once he finds out, and it would be good to have another brain working on this with us while we work out our next step."

"It's a risk," said John. "If we tell him just how dangerous Vix could be, he may decide to take it out of our hands rather than risk the safety of the island."

"Vix could be even more dangerous than that. I just don't know how destructive it could be without safeguards."

"So what do we do?"

"Make Vix as safe as possible before we use it again. Automatic power cut-offs after the event reaches a certain stage, reinforce the collision chamber and introduce sensors that are dedicated to providing data on the space-time split."

"That could take months, years even. Not to mention the expense," said John.

"Then that's how long it takes," said Amy. "We'll need to budget for it. And in any case, during the refit, I can concentrate on my thesis. Make it detailed and watertight. There can't be any ambiguity with it if we need to convince the world. The credulity of the theory needs to be perfect; any uncertainty will just pour scorn on it."

"But if we have other forces working against us, do we have the time to do all this?" said John. "It's only been a few weeks and already we've had a hurricane and a tsunami, who knows what will come at us next?"

"What choice do we have?" said Amy. "Admittedly it's a strong argument to say that one half of nature seems to be working against us, and we should be ready for whatever it throws our way, but something I've realised that we also have the other half in our court."

John looked at her quizzically.

"You covered the entrance with a rock face," said Amy, waving her arms to exaggerate the incredible nature of his actions. "*You* are our defence against this. The creation side – the side that wants humanity to succeed. We have to rely on you to make sure we're protected from whatever comes our way."

"That's quite the gamble," said John. "Can we not think of any other way? Months of expecting and anticipating disasters while trying to refit Vix could draw this out even longer. Even if we succeed, there is no guarantee the world will go for this."

"We are in a battle for the future of the planet. The universe is facing a dilemma with us and is seeing on which side we fall. Either we go down with our violent and destructive ways, or we plough forward with our ingenuity and creativity."

John drained his glass of wine and looked out through the doorway into the nightscape beyond.

"And that is why we need people on our side," Amy continued. "Convincing Samuel with this is just the start. If we can recruit him to our cause – maybe even give him a demonstration of what you can do – then it stands us in good stead for the future when we'll need to prove it to everyone. Having a respectable doctor on our side can only help us."

John did not look at her. Instead, he continued to stare into the night. He seemed to be thinking – distant and contemplative.

A moment of quiet passed between them, a pregnant pause.

"Penny for your thoughts?" said Amy, noticing his preoccupation.

"We'll do what you think is best," said John, not meeting her eye.

"Do you not agree with me?"

John looked down at his hands.

"If you have an alternative I'm all ears," said Amy.

"I don't right now," he said. "So I'll get up early tomorrow and go and see him. I'll tell him everything."

"We'll both go," said Amy.

"No – he asked me to go alone," said John. "I think he's worried that I'm somehow coercing you into claiming that everything is normal."

"I don't think he has any idea of what is about to be revealed to him, but okay. Go around, tell him what we know, and then he'll no doubt want to speak with us both. Just try not to act like some crazy person predicting the end of the world."

"I'll do my best John impression," he said, smiling at her.

She smiled back and reached for her wine. The sound of distant heavy machinery had abated for a moment, and all they could hear was the gentle waves of the sea lapping the shoreline.

"I meant to ask," said John. "This was a lovely meal you prepared tonight. I enjoyed it very much, but it seems a little out of place, given the circumstances?"

Amy looked back at him, a smile on her face.

"What?" asked John.

"You really don't know?"

"Should I?"

"Come on, John - look back into that mind of yours."

She moved a little closer to him, shifting her seat so that they were together. She did not remove her gaze from his.

John thought for a moment, searching for an answer to her inference internally.

"It's our Anniversary," he said, after a moment.

"It sure is," said Amy. "Seven years ago today, we tied the knot on our beach. It was a beautiful day, and we partied way into the night. Do you not remember?"

It was a loaded question, and she knew it. John hesitated before he replied, searching within himself.

"I can *feel* the happiness of the day," said John, "The

love felt for you when you took your vows."

"For better or for worse," said Amy.

"Until death us do part," said John.

"Maybe even beyond that."

"I can never replace your husband. I can only hope to imitate him."

"What makes a man, John?" asked Amy. "Are we just a bunch of neurons firing? Is everything we are held within the synapses of the brain? I always believed so."

"What's your point?"

"Are those neurons firing right now? They have to be. You *are* my husband, John. I do not doubt that. Maybe the energy firing them has changed, but everything you were – everything you are – is still there."

"Do you believe that?"

"I do. You're my miracle."

"What if I am not? I could leave this body and it would just drop dead."

"Don't speak like that. You are my husband that is my firm belief."

Moving her chair next to his, she put her arm around his waist and rested her head on his shoulder.

"Do you not feel like my husband?" she asked.

"I…I don't know," he replied, unsure of his next move.

"Then I do. I know for sure. You are John. And we are married. And I miss you. Every part."

She moved her face from his shoulder and placed her other hand on his chin. Gently, she moved his head toward her own and met his lips with hers. He was hesitant at first, but then a change – a spark. He responded, and at that moment, they forgot their fears.

He put his arm around her body, and the other behind her knees. With ease, he lifted her, still locked in the kiss. Only as he carried her toward the staircase did she release and bury her head into the curve of his neck.

Chapter Twelve – Division

I

When Amy awoke, it was a natural and gradual progression from contented oblivion to alertness.

Her head felt fuzzy from the wine the previous evening; but as the morning light filtered through the curtains, she roused, sweeping her hand below the sheets, fingertips caressing the imprint of where John had lain – it was still a little warmer than the mattress around. Grabbing the partnering pillow, she hugged it with her arms and legs, and buried her face in the downy softness, taking in his smell.

She wondered where he was. But then recalled how he had said he would visit Samuel early before the doctor was due back at the camp. He must have slipped out, and left her to continue her early morning slumber.

Sitting on the edge of her bed, noticing the outline of John's frame, she afforded herself a smile. Whatever may be ahead of them, whatever challenges were in store, she felt a better about it all now her husband had returned.

No doubt, he would come back soon, and maybe Samuel would be with him after the news they had decided to impart. She should prepare them breakfast.

They had quite the story to tell.

Standing, she unhooked her silk robe from the door, and covered her nakedness, heading to the bathroom.

She showered quickly. As soon as John started with his tale, Samuel would be either concerned at his state of mind or concerned that Amy herself did not have stable thought processes. Trying to second guess what the doctor may think was a trap she did want to allow herself to fall into; hoping he would keep an open mind, she also must be sensitive to his reaction.

Returning to her bedroom, she pulled on a pair of denim jeans and a T-shirt, towelled her hair and pulled it into a rough ponytail. She thought about putting on a little make-up but decided against it. She wanted to appear normal and level-headed – scientific and academic.

At that moment, just as she turned away from her bedroom mirror, she stopped.

Was that a noise downstairs?

"John, are you back?"

She must have slept in longer than she thought, or maybe Samuel did not want to hang around.

Keeping still and silent for a moment, she listened.

The palm trees flapped around on the terrace - it was a breezy day. That must be it; maybe some fronds struck a window downstairs.

She checked herself in her dressing table mirror one last time and mused over breakfast. Maybe something continental. Croissants, perhaps? She'd bought a selection from Soufriere the day before the flood, and they needed eating. Along with butter and strawberry jam or marmalade.

She'd do a pot of hot coffee too – keep them all alert.

In the mirror, she saw a reflection. Beyond her open bedroom door, in the shade of the landing, two points of red. They formed into a face, and then the silhouette of a man.

Her ponytail flicked as she spun around.

Mani stood in front of her, in the frame of the bedroom

door.

For a moment, they stared at each other, as though not quite sure what was to come. Fear rose from the base of Amy's spine.

"Who are you – what do you want?" she said, her voice a quiver.

Mani did not reply but instead looked at her, maintaining eye contact.

Her pulse quickened. Who was this man, and why was he here? Was he a looter, trying his luck with the houses that survived the wave?

His face looked vaguely familiar…

"I have a TV and a little cash downstairs," she said, "Take what you want."

She pointed back down the staircase, hoping that he would help himself to whatever he came here for. But he remained cold and still.

He did not look in good physical condition. He wore shorts and a vest common with beach vagrants and trinket traders that frequented the tourist hot spots, but his dark skin was pale and clammy. Beads of sweat fell from him so profusely that his clothing was sodden, and it dripped from his shaven head to the carpet of her bedroom. Nevertheless, his lithe and sinewy muscles popped out of his arms and legs.

But his stare gave her shivers. It was empty, devoid of emotion or empathy. It did not even show hate or the nervousness one would expect from a home invader. It was heavy-lidded apathy, and it terrified her.

She backed off toward the window doors that led onto her bedroom veranda. Taking small steps, she reversed, keeping her eyes on the stranger. Mani made no move towards her, but continued staring, as though trying to work out her intentions.

At that moment, recognition dawned on Amy. She knew where she had seen him. His face had been over the island news reports in connection with the missing police officer, and he was a wanted man. But why was he here? Was a maniac on the loose?

The thought just increased her terror, and she continued backing away, her mind racing at her next move.

"Where is it?" asked Mani, his voice flat.

Amy registered the words but was unable to answer. She just wanted to escape, flee to safety.

Where is it, thought Amy, desperately? *Where's what? What is he talking about?*

His cold expression and even tone reinforced her view that he was dangerous, and she needed to get out.

Rational thought eluded her. Escape was all that mattered. She doubted she could talk her way out of this, or offer him money or her possessions. To flee was her only option.

In a fraction of a second, she had turned and burst through the doors and onto her bedroom veranda. It was only a small space, about a metre wide – just enough to open the doors outward. The hot sun beat down over the garden terrace below, and a keen breeze struck the sweat on her brow.

Flicking a glance over her shoulder, the man had not moved but was looking with detached interest at what she was doing. Without hesitating, she grasped hold of the wrought iron railing and climbed over it. Her fingers grasped the iron bars as she swung her legs over the ledge to hang down. Her palms slid down the rails as gravity pulled her to the terrace, and she felt the heat in the metal, with the wind swirling around her armpits. Reaching the base of the veranda, her feet were still a couple of metres from the patio below, but she let go and collapsed onto the concrete. Yelping as she fell, her knees absorbed the impact and forced her onto her backside. Sitting for a moment to recover her senses, she looked up and saw him looking down at her.

Without a second thought, he hopped over the railing himself, as though he were jumping a fence, and fell the full height of the first floor.

Amy ran through the kitchen door as he fell, and she heard him crash into the flower bed next to where she had landed.

Her mind now raced, and she headed straight for the knife block on the counter. Grabbing the largest handle, she yanked out a steak knife. The sunlight from the open door glinted on its jagged steel surface.

Mani, seemingly uninjured from his jump, but covered in dust and leaves from the planter, stood in the doorway. His demeanour remained calm, but Amy thought she caught a glint of resolution in his otherwise dead eyes.

"Don't come near me," she said, holding the blade out in front of her.

"Where is it," said Mani, taking a step indoors.

"I don't know what you mean," said Amy. "Just take whatever you want and leave!"

Mani, looking around the kitchen, as though searching for something, took another step toward her. He ended by turning his neck around and fixing his eyes on Amy once again.

"Where is it?"

Her breath came in gasps, her chest heaving.

"Don't step any closer," she said, "I mean it!"

She thrust the knife ahead of her once again, stabbing it towards him threateningly. He did not seem deterred.

She took a step back and bumped into the kitchen counter.

"Where is it?"

"Where's what! What are you talking about?"

He had her boxed into the corner, and she glanced around to see if she had any escape route. She would have to go through him.

Another step forward.

Amy gulped, but it felt like she was swallowing a rock. Her hand shook, and her legs felt weak. She felt like crying – she did not want to do this.

"Where is it?"

The next step was the line crossed. Amy let out a cry and sprung forward, swiping the knife ahead of her. She connected with him and continued slashing. She hated the violence and closed her eyes against what she was doing.

In her panic, she felt his arms grab hold of her – they seemed unnaturally strong. He embraced her around her upper arms, restricting her movement and stopping the slashing. Trying to twist from his grasp, crying incoherently, she continued to wave the knife around, but he was too powerful for her. With his arms grasping around her biceps, she waved around the knife in futility with her forearm, before collapsing, dropping the blade in the process. It clattered on the floor, and the bounce seemed to play out in her mind in slow motion.

Those arms around her were powerful, but she could see she had connected with them. A ten-centimetre gash had opened up on his shoulder and blood seeped from it, a scarlet stain oozing onto Amy's T-shirt. He refused to let go despite the injury, and she struggled in his hold.

Noticing the injury, and without relinquishing his grip on her, he turned his concentration on the cut.

Amy could not help but release a small scream as the wound began to knit together. She was so close that she could see the skin itself healing and connecting, stitching.

The realisation hit her.

John's opposite.

It now made sense. The future of the planet, the solving of the dilemma humanity presented to the universe, was playing out in front of her; and Vix was central to it. Such clarity swept through her, despite the fear for her own life. Her terror focused her thoughts.

"Where is it?"

His voice was now almost a whisper, and his breath – foul smelling – reached her nostrils. Indeed, he stank. Being enveloped by him came with a stench akin to rotting meat, and she gagged, her senses overwhelmed by fear and revulsion.

"Let her go."

She had not even seen him walk in, and neither had her assailant. He jumped around, keeping hold of her.

John stood at the entrance to the kitchen but walked into the room with caution. Behind Samuel accompanied him, standing at the doorway, looking shocked and surprised.

Mani tensed up, Amy felt his grip tighten, his muscles clenched.

"Stay where you are," said Mani, and wrapped his hands around Amy's throat. He was not gentle, and her face went red as he restricted her oxygen.

John stopped, and held his palms outward to placate him.

"What do you want?" asked John.

"Everyone, let's just calm down here," said Samuel, and he circled away from John, towards the back door. "I'm sure we can find the best resolution for all of us."

Mani's eyes flicked to both of them, but on John mostly. Amy could feel the muscles in his body contracting when he looked at John, and she wondered whether he knew how dangerous this proximity was. Creation and destruction. Opposing forces: akin to a matter and anti-matter reaction should they meet.

For them to touch would be catastrophic.

John, still with his arms outstretched, took another step closer.

"John, don't come any closer," said Amy, her eyes bulging at him, but managing to speak despite the grip on her windpipe. "You…you know what will happen."

John halted his advance, the sweat now visible on his brow.

Samuel looked at them both, back and forth, with confusion.

Mani, still looking at John, looked confused. "What will happen?"

Amy did not speak again but stared at John. It was

clear from the dawning on his face that he recalled their conversation about the meeting of opposing forces.

Mani, now sensing John as a threat, moved towards the rear of the kitchen, keeping Amy close. A careful dance played out as Samuel moved away, trying not to spook him. He wanted to tell John that they should rush the intruder - two grown men against one should be enough to subdue him, even after a struggle. John was a large man. It should be easy. He carried no weapon. But he could assess the room and could see that something he was not aware of was taking place.

Mani now bared his teeth at John. The animistic gesture sent shivers through Amy as she felt the spittle on the side of her face. She wanted to wipe the filth from her, but could not move her arms.

"What do you want?" asked Samuel.

Mani looked at the doctor, and then back at John. "Where is it?"

"Where's what?" said Samuel.

"I know what he refers to," said John. "And I will tell you. But first, you must let her go."

Mani hesitated, sensing duplicity on John's part.

"You know what it is I'm looking for?" said Mani.

"I do," said John. "But I'm not telling you anything until you've released her."

Mani let go of her throat, but moved his arms, and grasped her around her waist instead.

"You know what I could do to her," said Mani, his eyes glaring at his counterpart.

"I do," said John.

Amy swallowed hard, thinking about his flesh knitting

back together moments before. No doubt, he could do the reverse to her, along with far worse. Her skin crawled with the thought of his touch.

For a few moments, a stand-off ensued. The four figures stood around the kitchen, John at the doorway to the lounge, Samuel next to the kitchen's island, and Mani still holding onto Amy near the open back door to the terrace. They all looked at each other, attempting to second guess the next move, anticipate the heading of the flashpoint.

"Let her go," repeated John. "And I will tell you where to find what you are looking for."

Mani considered his demand.

"If I let her go," he said, "You will tell me. If you trick me, I will make sure none of us leaves this place."

"Understood," said John.

Samuel, still not understanding the full danger of the encounter, looked at them all in turn, confused but unsure of his next move.

"I will make sure you and I…come together," said Mani.

John nodded.

Mani released Amy, and she scrambled forward, her bare feet slipping on the tiled floor. She reached John, and he gently moved her behind him.

"Now tell me," said Mani.

"Don't tell him," said Amy. "If he turns it on, I can't imagine the consequences. Vix is the only way to prove Duality."

"We have no option," said John. "If I don't tell him, he'll destroy all of us – along with Vix."

"Vix," repeated Mani, his eyes narrowing. That name

reverberated through him.

Vix.

This was why he was here. This is what he had been attempting to destroy since his arrival.

The future, playing out around them, was now uncertain.

John looked at him eye-to-eye. As the morning sunlight filtered through the windows, it reflected red from his irises. Returned as white from John's gaze.

"It is below the house, down the staircase in the rear of the garden," said John.

Mani paused in front of him for a moment and licked his lips – just a quick flick to moisten them. Then he sprinted out of the back door of the house, as a rabbit would flee a fox.

"What have you done?" cried Amy, collapsing to the ground, "Do you know what he could do if he gets to Vix?"

"We need to get you out of here," said John.

"Agreed," said Samuel. "We can make it to the camp and contact the authorities from there."

"It may be too late," said Amy, but allowed them to pick her up, and lead her out of the kitchen. As they departed, she looked to the vacant back door.

<u>II</u>

Mani raced across the terrace, his greasy skin on his brow bursting forth as the hot sun struck him, but whipped off by the wind. Spotting the staircase leading down the cliff face, he made for it, his flip-flops smacking the steps as he descended, the soles spanking his heels as he ran.

Seeing the destroyed walkway at the base of the

staircase, he leapt over to the small ridge at the base of the cliff and edged his way along it, keeping his eye on the choppy waterline. Boats from the emergency services, powered at speed to the bay.

The metal handles on the iron doors held the heat of the morning, and they rattled as he pulled them due to the padlock. Taking it in his hands, he looked at the lock. Between his thumb and forefinger, he began to rub at the bolt, transferring some of his energy into the steel. The inch-thick metal disintegrated as though melting; it warped and flattened, and eventually, it snapped and fell, bouncing off the rocky ledge, and splashing into the sea.

Swinging the doors open, he stepped into the cool corridor that led to the laboratory. The dark tunnel illuminated as he flicked on the light switch at the entrance. Guessing that his time was short, that the authorities would be on their way soon, he hurried down the corridor. He had no idea what he would find but knew this was his path. The people he had just accosted would be informing the police as soon as they could, so he needed to act fast. He felt no anxiety about the police, or anyone else – he could defend himself against any human, survive any attack – but they could make his work difficult.

That aside, another obstacle had been placed before him.

Another player, like him, was on the table.

They had both beheld each other and understood.

Maybe the energy that coursed through this human flesh recognised like. Or indeed recognised opposites. This man's path was different to his own, and he was the reason his current efforts had been unsuccessful. He should not fail this time.

The doors to the laboratory swung inwards, and Mani breezed into the dark room. Locating the light switch, the strip lights blinked on, illuminating the control room. Taking a moment, he assessed the space. Two seats sat at right angles against the console bench that occupied the centre of the room. At the front of the room, he saw his reflection mirror in the glass, the room beyond in darkness.

He had no idea what he was looking at.

Going over to the desks, he saw that buttons lined them had name plates below them. He paid little attention to the idle monitors but began to read the words below the buttons. None of them made any sense to him in the context of what to do next, but as he glanced at them, he noticed one that said "Interior Lights".

He pressed it.

The clean room beyond the window illuminated, and Mani beheld Vix for the first time. A human would describe the moment as a chill of excitement running through their spine, and Mani registered the reaction in the brain, but his overriding feeling was one of destiny.

This colossal machine, just a few metres away, would decide the fate of the planet.

He approached the glass, laid both palms flat against it, and pressed his cheek on it, feeling the coolness of the glaze. As he pulled away, he left a sweaty impression of his palms and face.

It was time to decide his next move.

III

"We cannot give him access to Vix," protested Amy. John, his arm around her waist, forcefully propelling her up the driveway towards the road, was leading her away from the house. Samuel followed behind concern on his face. He did not understand what was taking place but knew it was serious enough to leave quickly.

Amy squirmed, trying to free herself from his grasp, wanting to return. John held onto her, as gently as he could, but firm enough to keep them moving.

"We have to get away from here," said John. "You must be protected."

"John's right," said Samuel. "If we can get to the camp, there are police – stationed to try and deter the looting. We can let them know, and keep us safe."

"We need to evacuate the camp too," said John.

"Why?" asked Samuel.

"Because if that man manages to turn on Vix," said Amy, "It could devastate everything."

"What is she talking about?" said Samuel.

"Don't worry about Vix," said John. "I'll make sure that doesn't happen. But we need to get you to safety first."

"What kind of a machine have you two created?" said Samuel, anger mingled with incredulity in his tone.

"The doomsday kind," said Amy, grimly. "We must go back, stop him from using it."

"Is she right?" said Samuel, turning to John.

They reached the corner of the road, where it led around the headland, heading towards the town, and the makeshift camp set up for the relief effort.

"It's more likely that he will try to destroy it," said John. "But she is right. That's why you and Amy need to get out of the area."

"What about you?" asked Amy.

John ignored her question and they continued at a jogging pace. The wind lashed up the dust from the surface, biting into their faces, and reducing their visibility to a few metres.

"It's not much further," said Samuel. He was out of breath and sweating.

"John, what do you intend to do," asked Amy.

"I'm going to see you safe, and then I'm going back to stop him," said John.

"How will you do that?"

"I don't know. But it ends here. I must stop him if we are to have a chance."

She wasn't sure if he was referring to her, or the entire planet. She stopped in her tracks, resisting John's pull.

"I can't lose you again, John," she said. Her fear from the encounter replaced by sudden concern for what her husband intended to do.

John halted, facing her. Samuel went ahead.

Amy and John faced each other in an embrace. Her expression held unadulterated fear, horror for what may occur on this day. John's, by contrast, a mask of resolution.

"I can't promise what will happen," he said, "But what I do know is that the future is not certain. Right at this point, none of us can tell what's to come. Not me, you, or even those forces in the universe that decide the course of time."

The orange-brown dust from the roadside swirled around them, obscuring everything from view. For just this single moment, only the two of them existed.

"How can the lives of two people, living on such a small

island, hold the fate of the planet?" said Amy.

His eyes glowed passionately as he spoke.

"During his life, the man in this body always believed that every decision, made by each and every one of us, every day, had a momentous impact on the future."

John took a step closer to Amy, making sure she heard every word he said.

"Even small choices in our actions and the way we choose to live our lives have a profound impact," he said. "Our task in life is to face responsibility for the decisions we make. Good and bad."

Amy embraced him.

"That was the most like John I've heard you speak," she said.

"Right now, at this time, the most important move to make is to make sure *you* are safe," said John, holding her embrace. "Everything depends on *you*."

"But if Vix is destroyed, we have nowhere to go. And if he switches it on…"

"I will not allow that to happen. But you must go now. Get to safety, continue the work. Machines can be rebuilt, but you cannot."

"Vix cannot be rebuilt," said Amy. "At least not in the way it functions now. I can't think of any other way to show the world."

John pulled back from her, but his arms still held her tight around her waist. His eyes never left hers, focused and insistent.

"There is always another way," he said, not hiding the passion in his tone. "It may seem that Vix is our only option right now, but there *will be another way.*"

Amy returned his gaze, her look one of love and adoration for the man, but also of confusion. John backed away from her releasing his hold.

"Another way?"

"I *know* you will find it," he said, moving away from her back towards the house, his eyes never leaving hers.

Amy remained, watching him move away, helpless and confused. He became a silhouette in the swirling air.

"Get to safety," said John, and was gone in the sweeping air, obscured by the dust from the road.

Her knees felt weak and a sob sprang from her.

IV

The buttons seemed to follow a logical fashion, from left to right, on the console. The first one was a large red button that Mani surmised switched on the power to the machine.

Why was he even looking at this? Surely, all he needed to go into the next room and smash it to pieces? That had been his intention all along – to destroy the item that was preventing the future. It would be easy to use his energy to disassemble the machine in the same way he had dealt with the padlock. Easier still would be to take the fire axe against the wall and start chopping. He aimed to achieve the end of life on Earth, and the device in the very next room interfered with that outcome.

But something had changed.

The woman had called it Vix. And what else had she said?

Vix was the only way to prove Duality...

Mani had no idea what that meant, but she must have

figured out the importance of the machine for the passage of time.

"*...if he turns it on, I can't imagine the consequences.*"

She had stopped using Vix because she was afraid of what it could do.

He had to destroy this machine, but in a manner which caused the most devastation. The more of a calamity he could cause, the easier the future flowed to resolution.

He should turn it on.

What was the worst that could happen? That he overloaded it and caused it to explode? That in itself sounded like the ideal scenario.

He slapped his hand on the red power button – given its prominent position on the console, it was clear this turned the thing on.

With a hum, power surged into Vix. As a great and terrible beast would rouse into life from its den, the power vibrated through the rock and the walls. Mani felt it through his feet, before travelling up his legs and through his body.

Looking through the glass, Vix sat – patiently waiting for him to proceed.

Mani wondered what he should expect next. None of the console monitors had switched on, not that he would need them - the information they would display would mean nothing to him. He was not interested in the science, the measurements or the information displays. He just wanted to blow it apart, along with anything else that he could envelop in its destruction.

Adjacent to the power switch lay a series of buttons – four in total - grouped under the printed title of "Electrical Field." They flashed red. Without hesitating, he pressed all four.

Nothing seemed to change with Vix outwardly, but Mani saw that the next two buttons began to flash – "Hydrogen Injection." Tube A and Tube B – both were blinking red.

He pressed them.

The vibrations intensified just enough to notice that something was occurring in the machine chambers. It was of a higher pitch and seemed to be coming from the upper part. He took a moment to look through the glass, and his thoughts went to what may be taking place inside it.

At this point, on the console, a whole series of buttons flashed. He'd got the pattern now, as he was proceeding from left to right, but the next group seemed to be listed under the heading of "Proton Coil Insertion" – again showing an "A" and "B" section. Also, an entire row below this just said "Superconductors."

Looking at the machine, he could see the two bulkheads at the top of the machine that sat on a pair of wide circular manifolds surrounded by white-cased devices, which Mani guessed were these superconductors.

With no regard for protocol or safety, he swiped his hands across the console, depressing every single button that now flashed. Next to these, a pair of sliders, which he pushed all the way up.

The change in noise level was dramatic. Vix now began to whine and the clean room beyond filled up with vapour as the hydrogen coolant attempted to keep the temperature of the superconductors down. The sound intensified every few seconds, so he left it running. When it reached a crescendo, he would press the final button. This would be the last – the one that opened the collision chamber. Whatever was due to happen would then occur.

At that moment, the door to the laboratory burst open. John stood at the doorway, stern-faced.

Mani halted, his hand hovering over the final button in the sequence. He looked at John and gave him a large, toothy grin.

John stepped onto the laminated floor, into the room, towards him.

Seeing the larger man nearing, Mani hesitated for a moment. What was his intention? Nothing he could say or do would prevent him from pressing that button, even if it led to the destruction of his own body. He did not fear for his corporeal self.

John knew this too. This was not a battle of strength between two men, nor was it an effort of persuasion between two diplomats.

This was the moment the universe set the fate of life on Earth. The next step in the resolution of time and the evolution of that most important of natural energies – consciousness.

John stepped closer, glancing at Vix. He knew that the protons were whizzing around the coils, driven to increasing speeds, ready to initiate the Event.

A single button press was all that was required.

He looked at the red power button. If this man pressed the final one, he would need to make a dive for the power button to switch it off. Or, if he could delay the button press, the power would run down eventually. The batteries would not have enough energy stored in them for another run, so the machine would be safe.

But the console was just out of reach, and Mani's palm was mere centimetres away.

Another step towards him.

Still grinning, Mani pressed the final button.

From the clean room, the pitch changed. Vix had been whining, but now it began to rumble, and they could feel it all around them. As John found in the first experiment, the whole laboratory began to shake, with the strip lights swinging and throwing around shadows.

John made for the console, but Mani – second-guessing him – leapt back to his left, covering that part of the console with his body. Stopping in front of him, John left a clear gap to avoid contact between them.

The shaking increased, the vibrations reaching the point where they both found it difficult to remain on their feet. The noise deafening, but they both knew they could afford to suffer injuries.

Joining the rumbling came the screeching sound of metal bolts losing their integrity. Vix shook violently. A white light began to beam out of the collision chamber, moving and sweeping around the clean room.

The chain holding the overhead lights snapped – and with a spark, the lights went out. Vix now providing the only light in the cavern, and the white rays blinked off and on around them as the singularity grew and began to consume the material around it.

With a smash, the window to the clean room exploded, shaken to destruction by the quaking. Shattered glass, bursting outward, sliced into their skin - tiny cuts as the shards showered over them.

John moved around the room, his feet crunching on

glass crystals. The vapour from Vix spilt into the control room, and the noise now obliterated all other sounds. He never let his stare leave the man who was determined to bring everything down. The flashing lights strobed around them, throwing them from blinding white light to utter blackness in fractions of a second.

The already damaged collision chamber imploded - sucked into the singularity. It vanished in an instant as it lost structural integrity against the immense forces.

The Event continued to grow.

The two figures began to feel drawn to the space-time split. It felt like the room itself was flipping on its side. Gravity moving sideways. The laboratory a stricken ship, sinking beneath the waves.

They both stumbled and slipped, and Mani had a look of panic in his eyes. It was not his destruction he feared. Rather, he feared this other man, his opposite, would stop the process before it could overwhelm and destroy everything. He grabbed the edge of the console as he felt himself dragged towards Vix.

The light was more constant now, streaming from the tear created by Vix, and vapour rushed past them, towards its core.

John now needed to grab the console to prevent himself from falling inwards, but managed to move closer to Mani by going hand to hand over the bolted-down metal units. His fingers slipped as he moved, threatening his downfall. He must reach the power button.

But at every moment, the Event strengthened.

It was consuming Vix.

Warping metal and twisted wiring fell into the tear.

Consumed by the monster it had birthed.

From John's perspective, the singularity was now below him, ready to accept him as he fell. Ready to free his energy from this body and take him back to the cosmos. He clung onto the console, his legs dangling towards the empty window frame. Four metres away, Mani also held on – but he had reached the end of the unit and could proceed no further.

Inching along, John came within reach of the power button. The force working against him made it risky to release his hold, but he had no alternative. Letting go with his right hand, suspended for a few moments, his arm flapped by his side. Regaining his strength, he lifted his arm back so his hand was at the level of his chest, where the button lay below, and he struck out.

The button depressed.

Nothing.

The chaos around continued, and he struck the button again.

It was too late. The space-time tear was now self-sufficient. It no longer needed the power from Vix.

It was its own entity.

John looked to his right, to Mani. The other man glowered back at him, but despite everything going on around, he also managed a malevolent grin.

He'd won.

The tear would continue to grow, devouring everything it came to contact with, sucking it into a place where space and time broke down. Where matter became irrelevant and the only state to survive would be energy.

John knew this.

Knew this was the End.

But he had one last card to play.

Maintaining his grip on the console, he resumed edging toward Mani – hand over hand. The strain began to tell on his body, tearing at his armpits. Blinding light glowed from the clean room, Vix lost utterly to the power of the raw exposed energy; the machinery destroyed, never to create this Event again.

John felt the horizon of its power cross his feet, stretching the flesh.

Mani felt it too, but he was determined to last as long as possible, until the very last moment that it consumed his body. He could leave this state with the knowledge of his success.

John had to stop this the only way he knew how. He was two metres away from his enemy, and he stretched out his right arm to reach him. To touch him.

To bring them together.

Mani, seeing what he was doing tried to move away. John's intention became clear to him, but he had nowhere to go. Once the horizon overtook them, he could not be stop the expansion. Their twin energies would feed back into the universe. Going home. Consciousness lost. Mani just needed a few more moments.

Trying to move away from John, his left hand slipped from the edge of the unit. Helplessly flapping as the tear drew on it. The faltering energy remaining in this body could not resist the pull.

Seeing the loose arm, John used the last reserves, moving the biceps, to stretch towards Mani. His index finger extended.

Just a little more.

Mani held a wide-eyed, manic expression. Caught between two minds – should he let go, or let John touch him?

Just a fraction away, Mani made up his mind.

The event horizon surrounded their lower legs, and as Mani released his grip, time seemed to slow. His lower half stretched, legs distorting, but the inflexible flesh below his hips ripped apart in gory striation. As his body slipped downwards, consumed, breaking apart in stretched-out meat, his arms flipped above his head

At the last moment, the tip of John's forefinger brushed the tip of Mani's.

Time stopped.

All matter and all life hesitated. Time meant nothing. The future not set.

A tableau of two energies, in a vague approximation of human beings, fingertips touching, lingered. Neon shadows in a place beyond space-time.

The meeting of Creation and Destruction occurred in a small cave below the island of St Lucia, just as it had - in the time before time, and the non-place at the start of it all - on a more immeasurable scale fourteen-point-nine billion years ago.

A flash, and all flesh, bone and sinew vaporized. As the combination of the energy released from the interaction of opposites, along with the tear in the universe created by Vix, merged, the flow of the continuum paused.

The raw energies left over from their interaction with life travelled into the tear. They prevented the resolution. Creation and Destruction announced a draw.

The outcome undecided.

The future not set.

The seconds began to tick once more.

<u>V</u>

It had been just a minute since the quaking started, but to Amy, it felt like hours. The ground shaking under their feet, emanating from the home she had just evacuated, only meant one thing.

Vix had been turned on, and the Event was out of control.

She felt terror she had never experienced. Mixed with her fear, was a sense of guilt that she had created something so destructive. Was she the person responsible for bringing life on Earth to an end? From her humble beginnings, did her hubris for wanting to understand the universe lead to the downfall of this special – this *unique* - planet?

Around her, in the camp, Samuel was attempting to round up people and get them out of the vicinity. Paramedics loaded ambulances with injured, still being treated in the camp due to the overwhelmed hospitals and clinics on the island. Nurses and orderlies jogged around, helping people into wheelchairs and assisting others on crutches.

The wind whipped the flaps of the tents and the bandages on the legs of the injured. Sudden panic, heightened by Samuel's frantic attempts to motivate them, meant a lot of worried and scared faces around the camp. Expressing their confusion, they knew something bad was on the way when they felt the trembling of the ground beneath them. Would they have to go through an earthquake now too?

Amy knew it would be fruitless if Vix passed the point of no return. She felt helpless – caught between her desire to make sure these people were safe, and knowing that time was not on their side. How far did they need to run to escape this?

Her answer came quickly.

The quaking became more intense. She struggled to keep her balance standing on the edge of the camp, looking back towards her home.

But then it stopped. As though taking a deep intake of breath. Everyone in the camp halted and looked around, eyes wide with anticipation.

The shockwave knocked everyone off their feet. As though the ground were imitating the tsunami. The epicentre was from the coast, from where they had just fled.

Just for a moment, where the hill met the sea, the very ground seemed suspended in mid-air. The force of the subterranean explosion and gravity seemed balanced and the entire half of the seaward side of the hill separated. Shearing from the land, the tonnes of rock, soil and surface vegetation hung in mid-air.

Sitting on her backside, staring in wonder, Amy thought she saw a white light, only briefly, at the centre of the destruction.

Earth's gravity kicked in, and the collapse began. Just ahead of the camp by metres, the hillside slipped into the sea. Rolling and crashing, boulders flew into the air leaving dust trails like failed booster rockets, and the hillside fell into the water – the spray visible from their camp.

Amy knew her home, her laboratory, and everything she

had worked for were collapsing into the waters. Samuel's home too.

But her thought was for John. She knew he was no more.

An explosion this large could only mean that he had sacrificed himself. His energy had come into contact with the opposite and obliterated Vix and the singularity with it.

This time, her husband would not return.

Part Two: Duality

I have put duality away. I have seen the two worlds are one.

Rumi (1207-1273)

Chapter Thirteen – Zeta

I

Overcast clouds greeted Robert Birch as he stepped off the tram, which hooted as it departed the platform and snaked away through narrow streets. It threatened to rain, but remained dry and gave the dark red Victorian architecture of central Manchester a gloomy quality in the morning air.

He tugged on the tie that seemed to constrict his windpipe, and the starchy collar of his shirt irritated the back of his neck. Unused to the suit, the professor had asked him to wear one today due to the visit of a potential investor. For a mid-November morning in Manchester, it was unseasonably warm even just in his jacket. It would reach twenty-two degrees, according to the weather reports, which were breaking centuries-old records year after year for this part of the world.

Rob felt dissatisfied with his job, a growing sense that his administrative duties were wasting his education and keen mind. He had been grateful that the University had given him an institutional role following his graduation, but after almost a year, his job lacked any kind of responsibility. He reported to his old lecturer, Professor Bell, who had said he would need to work up to taking on tasks that he was eager to develop. Rob figured that the ageing professor distrusted the youth element of his department, and was after the quiet life in the few years before his retirement.

Crossing gridlocked roads, he entered Sackville Park – no more than a city garden - towards the University buildings and disturbed a flock of pigeons feeding from the discarded plastic fast-food containers. Last night's revellers must have left a decent amount of kebab. They fluttered up to the leafless branches, and eyed him as he made his way along the path.

It was quicker for him to avoid the small park to get to his work, but he liked to say a silent good morning to the seated statue of his hero. Cast in bronze, Alan Turing sat on a sculpted park bench – apple in hand – gazing away at the feasting pigeons. Mathematician, computer scientist, and key code breaker in the Second World War – he had been persecuted and prosecuted for his homosexuality; and committed suicide by eating an apple laced with cyanide. His posthumous pardon, given royal assent, came sixty years too late.

Arriving through rotating doors, he took the marble stairs to the upper floor. Acknowledging the "good mornings" from the other staff with a polite nod, he arrived at his archaic office, with its wood-panelled walls and sash windows.

He was fixing himself a cup of tea when Professor Bell arrived.

"It's ridiculously warm for this time of year," he said, carrying his raincoat in his arms.

"The jet stream has an unusually deep trough, according to weather reports," said Rob. "Which is bringing warm air up from the Azores."

The professor grumbled under his breath, muttering about opening some windows, and went through the door to his office.

Ditching the dripping tea bag from his mug, Rob

looked across to his desk at the pile of letters in his in-tray. This was his least favourite part of the job: opening and assessing the letters sent to the Science and Tech department by unsolicited scientists and the general public. Invariably this meant spending several hours a week reading a variety of Armageddon theories, concocted by some rather disturbed individuals, who had come to some pseudo-scientific conclusion of how the end was nigh.

Taking his seat, he blew on his steaming mug before placing it down next to his desktop paper shredder. He reached over and flicked the power switch, before grabbing a pair of latex disposable gloves from the carton box next to it. He had learnt, to his cost, that it was advisable to wear hand protection as some letters arrived anointed in bodily fluids, presumably by those tainted minds that believed their own DNA held some mysterious power, or by others who just saw it as some sick joke. The first time he had opened a letter containing paper with a distinctive brown stain on it, he knew – after washing his hands thoroughly – that gloves were advisable.

He had appropriated his letter opener – a stainless steel knife - from the staff canteen. Inserting it into the corner of the first envelope, he ripped it open and removed a folded page of A4.

He scanned it for a few moments. It was handwritten, and the scrawled writing was difficult to read. But – hang-on – the writer had written the important part in capital letters – that was always a good sign…

"ANYONE WHOSE NAME WAS NOT FOUND WRITTEN IN THE BOOK OF LIFE WAS THROWN

INTO THE LAKE OF FIRE."

Ah, good old Revelations, he thought. Quoted as fact by the mentally unstable for centuries.

He placed the letter, along with the envelope, into the shredder and watched the paper sliced into long, narrow ribbons.

A pile of letters still faced him – they had been growing in number since the increase in disastrous events that the news associated with climate change. The reports seemed vague to Rob – with the phrase repeated so often as to lose any kind of meaning. So frequent had these come in, many of the public were convinced that this was the beginning of the end times, that we were nearing the day of reckoning. Robert Birch had taken a degree in Earth Sciences to explore humanity's impact on the planet, but his lack of faith made him cynical towards the doom-mongers.

The fan on his laptop hissed to life as he reached for the next letter. He also had the email inbox to look forward to.

He grabbed the next from the pile and opened it. It was an A4-sized envelope, and the page inside was not folded. Removing it, he noticed the entire sheet was covered in mathematical equations. From top to bottom, symbols and numbers had been written in ink by a neat hand.

The words of one of his former tutors came back to him.

You can show the probability of the moon being made from parmesan cheese by using mathematics.

Words that had remained with him whenever he saw someone trying to prove their theory by blinding the reader with equations.

Who was this even from? No covering letter, and no name or address on the page itself?

Looking back inside the envelope, he noticed something at the bottom. Taking it out, he flipped it over and it was a photograph of a young woman. Indeed, she looked to be in her teens – perhaps fourteen or fifteen years old – unsmiling, and on a black background.

"My word they are starting young these days," said Rob out loud to himself, and shook his head, wondering what sort of conspiracy websites this girl subjected herself.

Flipping the photograph, he noticed an email address written on it, but nothing else. No name, no home address.

The photograph went in the shredder, along with the page full of equations. It screeched as it sliced through the paper, and Rob reached for the next.

Opening the door to his office, Professor Bell stuck out his head, speaking to Rob.

"She's here," he said, "In reception. Would you be kind enough to bring her up?"

Rob nodded and headed for the door, grabbing his jacket and smoothing his suit trousers as he did. Their guest today was a representative from Design Venture Projects - DVP - who had shown an interest in forming a commercial partnership with the University. They had become the leading firm in the UK for large-scale engineering projects - the go-to for the Government for any construction work of national significance. From buildings with unique architecture to advanced transport networks, DVP had built a reputation for taking on a variety of tasks and had the resources to plan, build and complete all of them. Their CEO was well-known in the UK and around the world, named Vic Macken. Scottish, and a famous eccentric, he was one of the wealthiest people in Europe and globally. Building his fortune on solar technology, he expanded into construction. A man who had both an entrepreneurial spirit and a taste for adventurous pursuits, it was rumoured that he was planning to begin commercial and tourist activities in space.

The woman who greeted Rob in reception looked formidable. Dressed in a grey trouser suit, she had the demeanour and confidence of someone approaching middle-age, but from meticulous detail in her appearance, Rob found it hard to guess her years. Her stylish blonde hair was immaculate, and she had applied her make-up conservatively.

He shook her hand and she introduced herself as Kathryn Powell.

"Pleased to meet you, Robert," she said, as he led her through the corridors towards the stairwell. "Have you worked here long?"

"Almost a year," he said, "Just after I graduated."

"I see, and what is your degree?"

"Earth Sciences," said Rob. "With a minor in Physics."

"Interesting, are you happy here?" she asked, their steps from the marble floor echoing as they ascended a staircase.

He paused before he replied. "It pays the bills," he said, wondering at her line of questioning.

Reaching the office, Rob introduced her to Professor Bell, who invited her to sit in the hard wooden seat opposite his desk. The professor took his seat behind his enormous wooden desk, and Kathryn Powell sat opposite – an underling in the professor's eyes. As he departed to leave them to their meeting, he spotted her regarding him with interest, albeit with an expression that Rob decided was conveying a certain bemusement.

Rob resumed his letter-opening duties; his mind occupied with the discussions taking place in the next room – or as more likely the monologue the professor was giving. Recalling an occasion, when he had received a letter from a geologist who had claimed that recent exploratory digging for gas had caused seismic activity in Lancashire, he was reminded how fruitless it was trying to get through to the professor. The geologist had readings on the corresponding digging activity and could prove the correlation between them and the quakes. Requesting the University's assistance in proving his findings to give his research credence for a possible legal challenge, he had written to the Earth Sciences department. Rob had taken this to Professor Bell, who had quickly distanced himself from it, and asked Rob to discard the letter. When he attempted to convince the professor otherwise, he treated Rob to a long glance down a bespectacled nose. "We don't get involved with *environmentalists…*," said the professor – not disguising the disdain in his voice – "…and we certainly don't get involved in legal cases". The professor had a policy of turning a blind eye to anything controversial, which may risk bad publicity for his department and subsequent impacts on student intake.

Their meeting ended at lunchtime, and Kathryn emerged looking as though she had spent the morning in one of the professor's lectures. They shook hands, and he asked Rob to escort her out.

"How did it go?" asked Rob, leading her out of the

room. He was genuinely interested.

"It went fine," she said, but in such a breezy tone that he could tell that it was far from fine. "But what about you? Can you see your future here?"

"It's useful experience," said Rob, diplomatically. He did not want to bad mouth the university despite his misgivings about his job, but also confirm that he could not see his long-term career in this place.

She seemed to sense this, and as they arrived in the reception area, she reached inside her jacket pocket and handed him a card. It contained her contact details.

"If you are ever interested in a more promising career, give me a call," she said, and before Rob could reply, exited the rotating doors.

Rob turned the card over in his hands.

<u>II</u>

Loch Ryan's grey and choppy waters filled Rob's vision as he gazed out of the window. It merged with the ashen skies above. He wasn't sure if he was nervous or excited.

It wasn't every day you met a world-famous industrialist.

The DVP Research facility that Vic Macken had built a decade earlier stood on the shores of the loch. It was not a production facility, but rather a series of laboratories dedicated to giving a home to the scientists employed to provide the research required for whichever project DVP was working on. It sat as a satellite facility to the head offices located in Glasgow and employed many from the nearby town of Stranraer. Rob had purchased a small flat in the town when he switched jobs.

Vic Macken swept into the office like a strong gust of wind. He was of short stature, but broad and doughty. His greying hair, cut short and balding in places, made him look older than his years. He wore jeans, training shoes and a white woollen jumper in sharp contrast to Rob's suit and open-collar shirt. He was carrying an electronic tablet.

Rob, a little taken aback by his sudden entrance, regained his composure and held out his hand.

Vic shook it gruffly.

"It's a pleasure to meet you, Mr Macken," said Rob.

The industrialist waved him away. "From now on you call me Vic," he said, his Scottish accent strong. "No more of this Mr Macken shit."

Rob nodded his understanding.

Vic ignored the desk in the centre of the room and headed for the sofa against the wall. Lounging on it, he put a knee up onto the cushions.

Rob took a seat in the armchair next to the sofa; the scenic loch appeared misty through the large window.

"Do you like the view, Rob?" asked Vic.

"It's beautiful," he said.

"Aye, indeed it is," said Vic, "But we're about to ruin it by building a godawful bridge here to connect Scotland and Northern Ireland."

"It's been confirmed then?" said Rob. He watched the news reports about the Government wanting to press ahead with the bridge.

Vic nodded and opened his file. Pulling out a few papers, he scanned them.

"You've been working under Kathryn for the last three years," he asked rhetorically. "She has nothing but praise for you. You've been working on the repurposing of the offshore platforms that we acquired. She says that you saved us millions by recycling the scrappage. Good job."

"Thanks," said Rob.

Vic got to his feet and headed for the door. "Come with me," he said and walked out of the door without waiting.

Rob scrambled out behind him, and followed down the corridor, his feet scrabbling to catch up.

"Do you have a family, Rob?" asked Vic.

"My parents live back in Manchester," he said.

"What about a wife? Girlfriend? Boyfriend?"

"No, nothing like that," said Rob, feeling uncomfortable. "I'm not one for relationships."

"Me – I've had two wives and two messy divorces," said Vic, who looked back over his shoulder at his understudy, and winked. "I think you're the wise one."

Rob wasn't sure of an appropriate response, mumbling something incoherent.

They descended a set of stairs and began to walk past several rooms on either side – the glass panels in the doors displayed tables and laboratory equipment in them. Within each lab, many white-coated scientists worked.

"Reason I ask is that you may be finding yourself short on time in the coming months," said Vic. "Not the best situation if you have a family to look after."

"I understand," said Rob.

They entered another laboratory, but this one was empty. It was a large room, well-equipped with computer equipment and scientific apparatus. Posters lined the walls displaying all manner of graphical representations of spacefaring ideas. Space stations, orbiting satellites, and rocket boosters for ships designed to break out of the atmosphere hung from the walls. Rob took them in rapidly, but they fired his imagination.

"This used to be my own private development lab," said Vic. "I was exploring the possibility of space tourism. Had a mind to set a launch site right here on the coast of Scotland."

"Looks like you had gone quite a way down that road," said Rob.

"Aye – it was a dream of mine," said Vic. "But it was way too expensive, not sure I'd ever make the money back. The problem is getting up in the first place. The amount of fuel for a single launch just to make orbit is so pricey, it's just not practical."

"Makes sense," said Rob, "But I share your passion for space. I grew up staring through telescopes and staring down microscopes. My parents bought me my first telescope when I was five, and I spent hours looking at the planets. I was fascinated by Mars in particular."

Vic smiled at him. "I'd travel there tomorrow if I could," he said. "To stand at the peak of Olympus Mons and look out across the red planet. What a view that would be."

"It would be incredible," agreed Rob.

"Well we have more worldly tasks to be getting on with now," said Vic. "I'm repurposing this facility to provide the research science for the bridge. I want you to head up the research division. We'll need bedrock samples, sea depth gauges, and extreme weather reports – that kind of thing. You'll work closely with the engineering departments to get the bridge built. You up to the job, Rob?"

"I can't wait to get started," he said.

"That's the spirit," said Vic. "Give me a shout if you need anything."

III

The needle on the compass spun right and left, refusing to settle on the north position. Rob frowned and shifted his location. Looking around, he could not see anything locally that would disrupt the magnetic field. The grass stood up to his waist and obscured his view of the coastline, but the unmistakable smell of salt in the air and the cry of a lone gull indicated the presence of the sea.

A light drizzle hung around Rob and his team of four. The wind from the Irish Sea swirled, but Rob and his team, well protected from the damp in their dew-covered waterproofs, had their measuring equipment covered in clear plastic to prevent the dampness from damaging their circuitry.

"Janet, can you get any compass readings?" he shouted over to the research assistant. She was busy setting up a survey tripod, ready to obtain accurate ground-level readings of the area where the bridge foundations began. Just over thirty kilometres away, across the narrowest section of the Irish Sea, stood the opposite coastline. Another team were taking similar readings near Carrickfergus, Northern Ireland, in preparation for the precise bridging plans.

Janet, hearing Rob's query on the wind, reached inside her coat pocket and pulled out her compass. After a few moments of rotating her position, and looking around her, she shook her head at Rob.

"No, it just keeps rotating," she said.

The weather worsened, the wind and rain increasing; and Rob looked up to the sky in consternation.

"Okay, let's wrap it up for today," he said. "We won't be able to get measurements while it's like this."

Ending their field trip early and with no success, Rob jumped into his hatchback, and retreated to his office a few miles away. As he arrived back, he shook his waterproof jacket free of droplets before hanging it on the hook on the back of the door and took his seat.

Pausing in thought for a moment, a chill caused more by his ominous musings than his sodden clothing ran through him. Janet appeared through his office door, her hair still damp. She had been checking the more powerful equipment they held in the laboratory.

She shook her head, her eyes wide with alarm, before exiting to continue gathering measurements.

Picking up his landline, he dialled a number committed to memory. A few moments later, he was holding a conversation.

"That's what I'm saying," said Rob down the telephone, "We can't get any readings whatsoever on our magnetometer. We've checked and it's in full working order."

In the next room, his team were busy collating the data they had managed to measure, but with the lack of any accurate directional research, they were struggling to pinpoint the precise location for the start of the bridge construction. Their colleagues over the strait had also experienced it.

It may just be a local anomaly: certain places on Earth

experienced a weaker magnetic field, but he needed to be sure. Certainly, the west coast of Scotland was not one such area, but perhaps it was just a temporary weakening. He had decided to contact his old colleagues at Manchester University to see if they were experiencing the same issue.

"You neither?" he said, into the mouthpiece. "What's going on?"

IV

Vic Macken's Glasgow Head Office was not how Rob had imagined it. In keeping with the stereo-typical image of wealthy entrepreneurs, he had expected paper-sliding doors, exposed air conditioning pipes, and bean bags everywhere. Instead, an old Victorian Mill housed the base of his whole operation. Exposed brickwork and hardwood flooring replete with old, wrought-iron radiators, kept the cold weather at bay, and leaded windows let in the air during the warmer months.

His office was not spectacular with a desk constructed from flat-packed, and an old tube-television mounted on the wall. The one indulgence he seemed to have was a huge leather-bound desk chair, and a bar area which had every malt Rob could think of. Dwarfed as he sat in his impressive chair, Vic had been joined by Kathryn – who sat on a stool at the bar, eyeing the liquor.

He felt like he needed one right now.

"So what are you saying," said Vic, impatiently tapping his finger on his desk. The news station was on mute, but Vic could read the captions detailing various strange happenings across the world, such as planes making emergency landings due to technical errors, an unexpected grouping of dolphins beaching along the south coast, and people panic-buying toilet paper because they thought the apocalypse had arrived. Vic asked Rob to come around and explain what was happening with the magnetic field; while Vic's expertise lay in business rather than science; he had been contacted by several government agencies in a state of panic, asking if DVP could help out with the situation.

"So the Earth has an outer core made of liquid iron and nickel, along with some other minor elements," said Rob. "It acts like a dynamo. Convection currents from the mantle in the intense heat around the core cause the liquid metal in the outer core to rotate, and these generate a large-scale magnetic field that surrounds the Earth. If you look at the Earth in these terms, it looks just like a huge bar magnet."

"And this is what gives us protection from the harmful radiation from the sun?" said Vic.

"Exactly. Along with making our compasses point north."

"So what is happening to our magnetic field?"

"That's the question," said Rob. "We don't know for sure. But it seems that the Earth is losing it rapidly. We believe that something has affected the rotation of this outer core. Some external influence has stopped this liquid metal from rotating and generating the field."

"What could do this?"

"Various theories are being bandied about, but I don't subscribe to any of them," said Rob. "What we do know, is that over the last two thousand years, pretty much since the start of advanced civilisation, the Earth seems to have lost about thirty per cent of its magnetic field. But in the last couple of years, that's increased to eighty per cent, and we estimate in another year or so it will be gone completely."

"Could human activity have caused this?" asked Kathryn. She had been silent so far but listened intently.

"I'm not sure what activity could have caused the core to stop spinning," he said. "But I do think that the damage we have done to the planet will have implications for how this affects us."

"In what way?" asked Kathryn.

"We've pumped a lot of carbon and other pollutants into our atmosphere," said Rob. "So once the magnetic field has gone, we will have nothing to protect us from the Sun's radiation. Opinions are differing on this, but I believe that the planet will heat up. This will cause some crazy weather patterns to begin with, and cause mass extinctions of animal and plant life around the globe. Eventually, the water in the oceans will evaporate into the atmosphere. Some of it will be lost into space, but with the amount of water and carbon in our atmosphere – joined by the decomposition of life – thick clouds will blot out the sun. This in turn will cause the sun's radiation to become trapped between the surface and the upper atmosphere, causing the air pressure to rise and creating a runaway greenhouse effect, heating the planet well beyond tolerable levels for life to exist. Take a look at Venus, if you wish to see how that ends up."

"Are you saying that this is the end of the world?" asked Vic, a look of horror on his face.

"The scientific community are divided, as usual," said Rob. "I've been taking on opinions from all sources – from the most optimistic, to the direst. The optimists are saying that this is just a natural fluctuation in the Earth's core, following convection tidal patterns in the mantle. They are in a minority though. Most are saying that this is unprecedented, and spells our potential extinction."

"What's your opinion?" asked Kathryn.

Rob moved out of his seat and looked out of the sash window. The river Clyde drifted towards the Sea, and on the quayside, people went about their daily lives.

"I like to think of myself as an optimist," said Rob. "I've always believed that as a species we overcome any challenges set in front of us. However – on this – I'm struggling to see what the answer would be."

"How long do you think this would take?" asked Vic.

"I reckon the process will be complete in about four centuries. A speck of time in astronomical terms."

"Well that doesn't sound too bad," said Vic. "If we have four hundred years to solve this, I'm sure we can come up with something. Not only that but I'll be long gone anyway."

"That's for the *process* to complete," said Rob. "I think we have maybe thirty to forty years at most before the planet is uninhabitable. And for that time, we'll lose animal and plant species we rely on for food. Water will become scarce as the planet heats up. The implications for civilisation don't bear thinking about..."

The three of them remained silent. Just the ticking of Vic's desktop clock was the only sound.

Kathryn broke the silence.

"I was brought up Catholic," she said. "And this to me is punishment for our sins. It's Noah. It's our flood."

A moment of contemplation passed between them before Rob spoke.

"I'm not remotely religious," he said. "But in the absence

of any other data, that's as good an explanation as any."

"Noah," said Vic, almost inaudibly. "He had his Ark. With the animals going in two by two. Where will our olive branch come from?"

"We need a miracle," said Rob.

V

He spent the journey to Euston gazing at the countryside blurring as it sped past the window. He could not extricate himself from the grief, which had transformed into this black mood, which was so unlike his natural self. The journey seemed more dreamlike to him, with the bleary greenery of the meadows and hills merging with the grey concrete of the urban areas.

That morning Rob had buried his mother. The funeral had been a small, quiet affair with close family in attendance. Immediately after the ceremony, Rob abandoned the wake and rushed to Manchester's Piccadilly station for the train to London. The funeral coincided with the day he was due to meet ministers alongside Vic, so the timing was awful. Not only that, but the train was running over an hour late, so he knew he was not going to make the meeting, but he travelled down anyway. He needed to escape the mourning.

All this going on had conspired to defeat him, it seemed. But even the late train seemed to indicate that the world was losing grip, tearing apart at the seams. It was high summer, and the population were generally enjoying the soaring temperatures – every year they broke new records – but to Rob, it was just another indicator of what lay ahead. The deterioration of the planet, being paid lip service by the media, was put down to a temporary weakening of the earth's magnetic field, coupled with (untrue) reports of high sunspot activity, but not reporting on the ultimate outcome. It made sense to Rob. He wished that he lived in ignorance of the future.

Inflation was high and growing – eroding the value of savings and salaries. A collective sense of ignorance seemed to grip a population determined to bury their heads in the sand, and unwillingness to believe what was to come. Healthcare and transport infrastructure was collapsing, but imperceptibly. Death of society by a thousand cuts. He thought that it was perhaps the nature of humanity to believe that something would happen to solve all ills. Something would come along and fix it all.

As the train clacked along the tracks southward, he thought about his parents. His father had died a couple of years earlier, and now he was an orphan just as he hit his forties. Perhaps his parents were the last generation to live believing that the world was eternal – it would always be – that it was not breathing its last breath.

End times lay ahead on his watch.

Arriving at Euston, he made his way to the Tube Station. He had contacted Vic on his mobile phone to say he would miss the meeting and arranged to meet him at Southbank instead.

London stank in the heat. He wasn't sure if it was petrol fumes or effluence – or a combination of both – but it assailed his nostrils as he made his way through the packed station. The heat on the underground train was no better, and the air felt like treacle as he packed himself into the overfilled carriage. He hated the Tube, always had. It brought feelings of claustrophobia and panic, heightened by the multitudes of hot, sweaty bodies around him. He would jump into a cab instead, but city traffic would make him even later.

He emerged into bright sunshine and heat just outside the Houses of Parliament. The Thames oozed through Westminster Bridge, with more of the riverside banking appearing every year as water levels dropped. Checking his watch, Vic would be having the meeting at that moment and it was almost due to end.

Crossing the bridge to their meeting point, he heard an approaching clamour; a great noise of people on the move, and chanting that he could not make out. The traffic had stopped, and the procession arrived ahead of him, crossing back over the bridge towards the Palace of Westminster. He held to the pavement as they walked towards him on the road, their banners bright in the hot sunshine. Spotting a variety of displayed slogans on the banners regarding the extinction of wildlife, climate change, and the banning of fossil fuels – it seemed they were protesting at the state of the planet, along with the mishandling of human activity upon it. They banged drums and blew whistles to get attention, and many photographers surrounded them as they made their way. Rob found some banners curious. They seemed to display nothing but a far-Eastern symbol – the Yin-Yang.

At the head of the march, a young woman led the way. She was perhaps in her late twenties and wore a long, green dress. Her dark hair seemed to explode from her head in curls that bounced as she strode across the bridge, head held high.

Rob could not be sure, but she looked familiar.

Arriving at Southbank, he found a bench and took a deep breath. He still wore the black suit from the funeral, his shirt damp with perspiration, and black sunglasses against the late-afternoon glare. He had removed his black tie. The protest march continued over the bridge and he surmised that over ten thousand people must be part of it – men, women and children showing their profound concern over the future of life on Earth.

They were not wrong to be worried.

He spotted Vic as he crossed the bridge, ruddy-faced and puffing, and casting an irritated eye at the march getting in his way. Seeing Rob on the bench, he made over for him, a heavy sweat covering his face. Vic proceeded to wipe with his pocket-handkerchief as he took his seat.

"Bloody protesters," grumbled Vic.

"They are making some shrewd observations about the planet," said Rob.

"Oh, aye – they are quick to tell you about all the problems," he said, "But never offer any bloody solutions."

"If I was in the dark as much as them, I'd probably be marching with them," said Rob. "How was your meeting with the ministers? Sorry I missed it."

"Condolences, by the way," said Vic, regaining his composure.

Rob nodded in appreciation.

"What are you doing here, Rob?" asked Vic, looking around at the chaos going on in the capital. "Nobody would've held it against you for not being here."

"I couldn't face the wake," said Rob. "Too many people crying and getting drunk…"

"That sounds like a funeral to me," said Vic. "Getting

shitfaced and having a good bawl is the best healing, in my experience."

"You know I avoid alcohol," said Rob. "And I grieve in my own way. A lack of tears doesn't mean I don't care. I didn't cry when my dad died, and it's the same with mum. They raised me, I loved them both dearly, and I miss them. But crying is just not my nature."

"We all show our grief in different ways," said Vic.

"What happened with the meeting?" asked Rob, changing the subject.

Vic heaved a sigh, audible above the whistles and drums.

"I have both good and bad news."

"Let's have the bad news," said Rob, "Get it out of the way."

"They've abandoned the bridge contract," said Vic. "Under the circumstances, a bridge between Scotland and Ireland is suddenly not high on their agenda. Can't say I blame them."

Rob nodded in agreement.

"That's nearly five years of research, planning and expense down the pan. And the good news?"

"They've replaced that contract with a new one," said Vic. "Something right up your alley. They want to build an underground bunker. A big one. Large enough for all the country's bigwigs to shelter in once the shit hits the fan."

"Really?"

"Aye – they've identified a site. Its location is classified, but its somewhere in the north of England – a decommissioned coal mine by all accounts. They'll let me know where it is shortly. After we've all signed the Official

Secrets Act."

"So they've finally admitted the worse," said Rob.

"Not officially. They intend to keep going for the next few years, but they have realised – quietly, mind – that our economy and infrastructure are going to decline along with the rest of this bloody planet. They are throwing everything they have at this, but even they know that money won't be worth much as the years go on, they want to make sure the continuation of our species, and our way of life."

They both went quiet and watched the unending number of protesters cross the Thames. The sun beat down on them ferociously.

VI

The automatic lights switched on in his office, but it still looked gloomy. Rob's bespectacled face, illuminated more by his monitor screen than the low-energy light bulbs installed in the facility, was a mask of concentration. He hadn't shaved for a few days, and the grey was starting to show through the stubble.

Building a self-contained bunker, it seemed, was more complex than even he had anticipated. Recycling oxygen, maintaining a consistent power supply, ensuring that the living quarters were inhabitable, and that water remained potable had all occupied his team over the last few months. What was proving most problematic to him though was the food maintenance. Hydroponics was simple enough, the technology suitably advanced to grow enough sustainable plant-based food for the bunker population, but one of the necessities was for meat and dairy. Building animal pens underground, dealing with the waste they produced, along with their feeding requirements was problematic. In many respects, housing animals was trickier than humans. A large part of their agriculture would have to be dedicated to their feed, and with limited space to work with, and no possibility of access to open pastures, their welfare was not high on the agenda. Sacrifices had to be made elsewhere.

In front of him were several ideas proposed by his team. Some of them were better than others, but also more expensive. The decisions he needed to make were, based on the fixed budget they had, what he considered more of a luxury rather than a necessity. He found himself making choices based on the bare-bones necessity of living. They had to abandon any concepts of wealth and privilege at this stage to make sure they didn't leave out anything fundamental to the continuation of life. As the economy of the world began to falter, money became tighter; the budget did not go as far.

Vic had confirmed another addition to the bunker earlier in the week. They needed storage to hold the DNA of every living thing on the planet – or at least as much as they could save. Seeds of every plant and blood samples of every animal needed to be stored somewhere. Rob was running out of space. Not only did he need to house four thousand people, but also livestock, food and water for them all, and now these DNA samples.

Extra tunnelling would be needed. Which meant extra pipework for air, ventilation, sewerage, power conduits – the list was endless. Six months into their planning and they were nowhere near starting construction.

The Government had given an eight-year timespan to complete the bunker, but even at this early stage, Rob doubted they could achieve the deadline. They would need another couple of years of planning at the minimum, and then working underground to build all that was required would be difficult in the extreme. And all the time, the planet around them would be deteriorating.

Rob's appointed team of scientists and engineers from a variety of fields – all two-hundred and twenty-four of them – had gone home for the evening. He felt guilty asking any of them to work late under the circumstances. Many had families and loved ones. They needed to be with them in whatever time remained. He was also conscious that they were working on something to save the lives of others rather than themselves. It was not difficult to motivate them at this stage, where the effects of a dying planet were still minimal, but it would become more problematic as time progressed.

On the other hand, Rob lived for the job. He found that throwing himself into his work gave him purpose. To build the best bunker possible meant he could face the future with pride. Motivated with the knowledge that he had worked to preserve life.

Who the Government would invite to live in the bunker had been occupying his thoughts. It was a private contemplation: at this stage, everybody seemed reluctant to discuss such matters – as though everyone on the project was in denial of what would come after the bunker was sealed, regardless of whether they were inside it or not. But no doubt, the leaders of the country – politicians and royalty – would be first on the list. He also surmised they would need medical personnel, engineers, scientists, and botanists – along with their families. He wondered if the government were already working on a list. Whether he – as one of the chief design architects – would be on it. Would Vic?

More than once, he had spent the entire night working in his office, picking up a few hours' sleep on the couch in the corner. Tonight looked like it could be a repeat, and he worked towards midnight, assessing the various designs, and typing out emails to the departments instructing them to make improvements or to abandon them completely.

Just after midnight, he paused, squeezing the bridge of his nose under his glasses before removing them. His throbbing temples meant he had worked enough. Time to rest. It wasn't worth going home, so the couch would do.

Powering down his computer, he went over to the light switch and flicked it off. The room became dark and he lazed on the couch, massaging the dimples on either side of his forehead, eyes closed.

As he lifted his eyelids, his sight adjusting to the darkness, he saw that the room had a greenish hue – stripes of a verdant emerald created by the vertical blinds. Looking around, he attempted to perceive where the glow came from. He had not closed his blinds fully, and it seemed to be filtering through the gaps. He swept his legs out below him, and retrieved the glasses from the table, wiping them with his handkerchief before putting them back on.

His mind wasn't playing tricks; the room was glowing green, as though some kind of alien spacecraft were landing outside. Going over to the window, he separated the blinds with his fingers and looked out.

Astonishment gripped him.

Grabbing his loafers, discarded next to his desk, he ran out of his office. His shirt had escaped from the back of his trouser waistband, and it fluttered as he rushed through the laboratory and into the corridor beyond. That in turn led to the staircase to the ground floor – the hard soles echoing as he sped to the exit.

Down in the reception area, the security guard sat reading a book in the pool of a spot lamp, and he looked up in confusion as he saw Rob emerge, his expression one of incredulity.

Without a word, Rob went to the exit, and – curious - the guard followed behind.

Emerging through the rotating doors, Rob looked to the sky and removed his glasses, holding them loosely by his side.

The plant itself consisted of two wings, joined in a horseshoe shape, which lay on either side of the now deserted car park. Ahead of the plant, Loch Ryan sat as a mirror to the heavens.

The ethereal green illuminated everything.

Looking at the guard, whose face had taken on the tint, Rob gave him a look as if to say, *can you believe this?*

Above them, the sky was clear and cloudless. But a serpentine band, stretching across the upper atmosphere, obscured the stars. Writhing and waving above them, the aurora dominated the broad scape above their heads. The water reflected the ribbons, adding crystalline elements as the light glinted on the tops of the waves. It felt magical to Rob and utterly beautiful. He had always wanted to see the Aurora Borealis in the northern parts of the planet, common events above the arctic-circle; but now he did not need to travel. Parts of Scotland could see the aurora at certain times of the year, but never this close, never overhead – they were usually just a jade hue on the horizon. He felt inspired, energised, as he craned his neck to witness the charged solar particles as they interacted with the high atmosphere, gazing at them for several minutes, hypnotised by every aspect. The longer he stared, the more his sense of wonder grew – the power of nature in its endless and eternal variety. But he also became more perturbed. This display, so far south, was a sign that the magnetic field no longer deflected the solar wind at the poles, but was affecting lower latitudes.

Beside him, the guard stared open-mouthed at its majesty, fascinated by its beauty, not fully aware of its significance. Just living in the moment.

Rob envied him.

VII

The gateway to the bunker yawned open, its steel doors fifteen metres high, and two metres thick. Across the entryway area, busy with supply vehicles driving into the tunnel, Rob sat in the prefab office on the edge of the compound area. He stared through the dusty window but did not take notice of the activity. The overcast skies showed his reflection in the glass. His brown hair, thinning on the crown, made him look like his father, who had himself died just a few years older than he was now. More often, he had found himself thinking of his late parents as age began to make its presence known, and he found inevitable comparisons.

He had become sentimental, just as they had been. Nostalgic for the old days, for the music and movies of his youth that recalled a happy childhood. Friends made and lost throughout a life dedicated to his work.

He snapped himself out of his thoughts, his reflection replaced by the view of Vic Macken storming out of the bunker gateway, stomping towards the office. His complexion was ruddier than usual; even the crown of his bald head looked red. Rob was hoping it was down to the heat of the day but suspected it was his raging blood pressure. The amount of stress he had been under during construction had been immense, but now he was being held to reckoning by the financiers of the bunker, and the government committees could be brutal. With the continuation of the human race on the line, Rob figured that their view of what the bunker should be differed greatly from what time and budget had dictated.

The office door slammed open, and he exploded into the site office.

"That's it, I've had enough," he said. He threw himself into a chair and buried his head in his hands. They shook visibly.

"I take it our bunker residents are not happy," said Rob.

"I don't know what they expected with the money we were given," said Vic. "They wanted a Hilton or something."

"Considering it extends five-hundred feet below ground, I'd be surprised if any hotel chain could do better."

"One particularly irate politician complained that their room didn't have a TV. A television for god's sake! Who the hell is going to make television shows when the world has gone to shit?"

"I don't think the reality of the situation has hit home," said Rob. He tried to make his voice soothing. Despite the hardships they faced over the years of planning and construction, and the many heated arguments between them, the shared pressures of the project meant they had developed a keen friendship.

Early on, just before construction started, Kathryn Powell left the company to be with her family. She had moved to New Zealand in an attempt to get as far away from the rest of civilisation as possible. Originally, she had planned to go to a south pacific island, but most either had now sunk below the rising oceans or were likely to in the coming years.

Knowing that the world was declining rapidly, most people were reassessing their life situation; and some who were in a more privileged and wealthy position decided that family came first, and retired. One of the main issues they faced with the bunker was obtaining suitable labour and engineering skills from a population pool of increasingly disenchanted workers. When they found someone suitable, it usually meant having to pay them over the odds to employ their services. When Kathryn decided to leave, Vic did not hesitate to make Rob his second in command. Rob's lack of family, and dedication to his work, made him the perfect person for the task. He found himself suitably distracted by the job to spend too much time worrying about the future.

"So have you decided when you'll move in?" asked Rob.

Vic looked at him out of the corner of his eye but did not reply.

"You must be on the list," said Rob. "You made the thing!"

"Aye, aye, I'm on it," said Vic, sighing heavily.

He stood up and put his arm around Rob's shoulder. "Let me show you something," he said and led him back to the window.

Looking at the compound beyond, they saw a steady line of dignitaries, together with family members, walking into the gateway that led to the underground bunker. Invitations to see their sanctuary had gone to the people chosen to keep a semblance of their society maintained underground - once surface living became impossible. The visitors wore suits and uniforms and seemed excited about seeing their new accommodation.

"It's like they are going on holiday," said Vic.

Rob watched as an overweight military man – presumably a General – walked over the dirty concrete towards the entrance. Behind him tottered a young woman in a short leopard print skirt and heels, which sank an inch into the dusty ground. In his large fist, the General carried a heavy-looking briefcase.

"Believe it or not, that isn't the General's daughter – that's his wife," said Vic. "When he found out that he was on the list, he left his wife of twenty years and quickly married his mistress. Who of course was only too eager to dedicate herself to the man who was guaranteed a place in the bunker, away from the horrors to come."

"What's in the briefcase?" asked Rob, deciding not to mention Vic's now three divorces.

"What do you think?" said Vic. "It's full of money. Cash. Wads of twenties. These people still believe that their money will save them from Armageddon. That they can buy their way out of it. To be placed in the safe of his quarters."

"Money won't be worth much underground," said Rob. "But don't let that put you off taking your place. They'll need you in there."

Vic moved away and slumped back in the chair, looking defeated.

"The truth is, I've had a diagnosis," he said.

Rob turned, and lowered himself into the chair opposite, eyebrows raised in query.

"I've got a brain tumour," said Vic, simply. "Just a small one, but particularly buried in the centre of my head. It's inoperable. Even before the collapse of the Health Service, it would've been difficult, but now it's just not possible – my private doctor confirmed it a couple of weeks ago. No amount of money will save me."

"Oh, Vic – I'm so sorry!"

"Don't be laddie," said Vic. "I'm not after your sympathy. I'm fast approaching seventy, and I've had a better life than almost anyone I know. Truth be told, I might have years ahead before it affects me."

"Is that why you're not on the list?"

"No – no, I haven't told the powers that be. This is my own decision. When you see the end of the road, you reflect on the journey you've taken. I've spent my life in the pursuit of wealth, and I'm still going to end up in the same place as everyone else. Do I want to spend the end of my life locked underground with these people? No chance. I'll go down with the ship.

"Not that I believe that I'm any different from them. I have been part of the problem rather than the solution. I've worked hard to provide the ruling classes with an escape from the reality of the situation. What Kathryn said is ringing true to me. I don't know how, but it feels that we are being punished, and the very people that got us to this place are now seeking to abandon it. That won't be my fate."

"So what will you do?"

"Dissolve the company," said Vic. "And give the remaining staff any of the proceeds. Money is becoming irrelevant though, it's all about survival now. But you've made the largest contribution of anyone I employed – that's why I'm offering you my place in the bunker."

Rob didn't even have to consider it.

"No – I don't want it either," he said. "I can barely stand going in there. Claustrophobia."

"You'll get over that," said Vic.

It was Rob's turn to become reflective and looked at his mirror in the window once again. Vic looked at him quizzically.

"When I was young, I read The Time Machine," said Rob. "H.G. Wells – you know it?"

"Never read it," said Vic. "But remember seeing the movie years ago."

"Morlocks," said Rob. "I don't want to become one. I'd rather remain an Eloi – and take whatever that brings."

"Do you think they will last that long - underground?" asked Vic, getting the reference.

"Probably not," said Rob. "Authority and prestige will mean nothing. And it only takes one of the systems to fail before it all comes crashing down. It feels like all we've done here is delay the inevitable."

Vic nodded and remained silent for a moment, busy with his thoughts.

"Once we're done here, I'm going to retire to my home," he said. "A nice place, on the shores of Loch Lomond."

"Sounds lovely," said Rob.

"Aye – it is. But it's a large place, and I've no family to speak of – at least nobody that can stand my presence. You haven't either. Come join me."

Rob looked at him with eyes wide. "You want me to come live with you?"

"Don't look so surprised," said Vic. "I'm not asking you to share my bed!"

Rob laughed back at him.

"But it would be good to have some company in whatever time is left to us. The house is well stocked with food and fresh water, and it all now operates on my solar power."

For the first time in what seemed years to Rob, he felt a sense of optimism. This felt right to him. The completion of the bunker meant an uncertain future, but this invitation meant they both could share and support each other in whatever came next.

Rob accepted Vic's offer with gratitude.

<u>VIII</u>

Vic's lakeside house was a Georgian affair. Re-named after himself, altering it from the original and long-forgotten laird who constructed it, Macken House was made from white granite, and replete with long, floor-to-ceiling windows and ornate pillars. It sat within several acres of browning grass and the leafless trunks of trees that flanked the wide driveway. On the side of the house facing the water, across a wide lawn sat the banks of Loch Lomond, the sediments cracked and dry from the level dropping.

He had not lied when he said the house was well-provisioned. The cellar was stacked high with preserved and dried meats, canned fruits and vegetables, and a huge wooden vat of fresh water.

"I've been busy building this up for months," said Vic, as he showed Rob around. It felt nice and cool in the windowless cellar, unlike the oppressive heat in the rest of the house.

"Every time we sent supplies to the bunker, I had them send some here too," he continued, idly picking up a can of Scotch broth.

Above ground, Vic had decorated every traditionally. Tartan wallpaper and landscape paintings of the Highlands littered the walls. Above the fireplace sat a mounted set of bagpipes.

On the roof, Vic had installed solar panels. He had retained that side of the business, despite the massive entity that DVP became, and kept pace with improvements in solar cell technology. Nevertheless, they still had to ration their electricity usage due to a lack of sunlight: overcast skies were now the norm, trapping heat and retaining any vapour. Power stations across the country had closed as the infrastructure collapsed, and so the population were finding alternate sources. Diesel generators became popular for a while until the fuel ran out, and people looked at renewables. All too late, wind, water and sun provided the energy, but only on small scale to individual homes. Candles became popular once again, and as Rob toured his new home, he carried a copper candelabra as the dim light from outside faltered. He could not escape the feeling he was in some Dickensian novel.

Vic gave Rob the largest of the guest bedrooms, which

had an en-suite bathroom and window overlooking the retreating Loch. He moved some of his possessions from his flat and into his room, including a photograph of himself as a ten-year-old child, smiling with his parents in front of the Eiffel Tower. The picture evoked nostalgic memories of a happy childhood from a world unconcerned with its fate.

The journey from his previous home to move his possession had been a risk. Travel had become dangerous. As the planet descended into chaos, parts of the world had become uninhabitable: the temperatures between the tropics, covering the equator, had become too high for human habitation leading to mass migrations to more northern or southern climates. The impact on fossil fuel production meant that flights had all but ceased, and even journeys by sea had to rely on old-fashioned sail power.

Britain, as an island, meant it largely escaped the influx of people fleeing the extreme environments, but the hardships endured by those fleeing the broiling temperatures were only delaying the inevitable. Soon, the whole planet would face the same fate.

Rob owned an electric SUV that he kept as fully charged as he could and that he used to move from his flat in the south. It was a risky journey, since the deterioration of law and order, but he managed to bring the few possessions to Macken House without incident. Being not overly sentimental, he only brought a few necessities – mainly his extensive book collection and flash drives containing family photos.

The set up in this new home meant that they could be self-sufficient for a long time, years potentially, so he parked the car in the garage and covered it with a sheet. When he arrived, he felt grateful that he had not encountered any problems. With fuel running out, the roads were deserted, but that in itself was a reason not to draw attention by driving around.

Vic had prepared himself for any such incursion onto his property.

"If anyone does come knocking," he said, completing the tour of his house, "I have this to hand."

From a cupboard below the staircase, he produced a rifle, complete with a sniper scope and ammunition.

"It's my father's old hunting rifle," said Vic, "He used to shoot stag on the Highland estates, but here we can see anyone coming for miles around."

The first few weeks of staying at Macken House almost made them forget about the environment's slow deterioration. Rob and Vic spent the evenings chatting about their lives, reliving the good times – and quite a lot of the bad – that they had encountered on their journeys. Vic focused on his family. Of his now three ex-wives, one had died of breast cancer (he talked about her as the true love of his life); the second had remarried a surgeon who adopted their child (he had not heard anything about them), and his third wife had moved to America with his other two children.

"Lord knows what's happening over the pond," said Vic, over a glass of whisky. "If you think we've got it bad here, America must be suffering with everyone owning guns."

It had become impossible to obtain any news, or hear from any loved ones, as communication networks failed, and the internet ceased operating.

They managed to have a standard three meals per day, usually prepared by Rob, who adopted a rationing system. It was likely that this food needed to last years, so he tended to stick to the more perishable meats and vegetables first. Even though Vic had taken steps to preserve the food, it still had a shelf life. Freezers took too much energy to operate, so the food was mainly canned or chemically preserved. They were free with the wine though, with a well-stocked cellar, and with Rob abandoning his abstention (what was the point, he thought) they usually went to bed feeling somewhat tipsy.

Vic himself took more and more to alcohol. He began to suffer headaches, and experience tiredness. He would often fall asleep during the middle of the day, with a glass still in his hand. Rob did not see his place as someone who should be berating him for his drinking; indeed, with the end getting closer, why not indulge? Temperance abandoned, he found that alcohol just made him feel unwell if he drank too much. He tended to skip the drunken stage and head straight for the hangover. He learned moderation quickly.

As the weeks passed, he found a new problem with their situation. Boredom. They had a large TV and disc player, which Rob tended to watch old black and white movies as his host had a large collection. He also read from the library, along with his own collection of books, but the silence that settled over the house as he flipped the pages became oppressive. He longed for a newspaper, to hear something from the outside.

Vic used the computer, with video technology, to speak with the people entering the bunker. The UK no longer maintained mobile technology, and so the reliance on landlines became more important; the bunker itself only had landline connections extending to the outside world.

Through this, he learned that the transition of people - from government offices, military bases, science institutions and other key areas - to leave the surface world behind had increased. Westminster no longer operated, but the government attempted to maintain some administrative control by issuing edicts from their remote location. Retaining control over the military, their task was diminishing due to the lack of a functioning economy, causing the erosion of their power base. They could no longer keep the population in check, and living anywhere urban had become dangerous. Anyone of authority and importance, who were fortunate enough to have a place in the bunker, now evacuated to it. Rob often wondered what their thoughts were as they left behind the open air and the dark skies to enter self-imposed incarceration, and whether they fully comprehended their futures below ground.

Depression descended upon him as he realised that no end to this would come.

This was not a passing phase.

No hope rested on the horizon.

Days passed to weeks, and weeks passed to months. The passage of time became problematic to measure. Seasons, which were always the illustrators of the Earth's annual orbit, became indistinguishable. Every day seemed to have a repeat pattern of weather caused by a solid block of cloud layered over the landscape, but no rainfall at all. As though the clouds taunted the drying ground. Uncomfortably warm and dry, with very little wind to stir the browning grass on the lawn, and the surrounding moorland. It made everything gloomy around the house, with the silence almost as oppressive as the stale air. Vic – when not speaking with the bunker - spent most of the time in the lounge, either drinking or sleeping, his headaches getting worse. Strained conversations occurred between these two ageing men, but mutual respect still existed between them; they let each other handle each day, ensuring that they did not try to impose their mental state on the other. More than once Rob had passed by the lounge and heard the sounds of quiet sobbing coming from within.

The bunker, it seemed from Vic's contact with them, had closed its doors to the outside world for good. Fears of the desperate trying to force entry were forefront in their minds, and the government had long ceased failed to have any remaining influence in the affairs of state. They locked the great ironclad gates, stopping everyone from entering or leaving. If you were not already in, it was too late. The population were now on their own.

That had a certain finality to Rob, and rather than envy, he felt a certain sympathy for those now trapped inside the bunker they had constructed. Their rejection of the outside world spelt the end of their liberty in favour of protection.

In his own darkest moments, the desperation to hear another voice, and see another face made him question whether he should leave Macken House. How would Vic react if he did? But then it did not take much of a leap of imagination to realise how life and humanity were suffering beyond the boundaries of the property. They still had supplies and shelter, and relative safety, which put them above almost everyone in the country.

On one morning, perhaps a year into living on the

receding shores of the loch, Rob awoke later than usual. He had developed a cough. Nothing too serious, just annoying, probably caused by the drying heat and lack of fresh air. It made him more tired, needing more sleep, and when he was awake, he lacked his usual energy and vigour. On this morning, feeling more exhausted than usual, he dressed and descended the grand staircase of Macken House.

The glow in the study indicated that Vic was online with the bunker. As Rob neared the room, he could hear Vic speaking with an urgency to his tone. He bobbed his head around the door.

"Everything okay?" he asked, spotting Vic sitting at the desk in front of the computer.

Vic stared at the monitor, his face red and his brow furrowed. The long curtains were still drawn, and the electronic glow cast a pool of light across the mahogany furniture.

"Hello? Can you hear me?" he said to the image in front of him.

The face of an official, wearing a military uniform and hat, frozen on the screen mid-speech. His mouth was agape, and a look of anxiety was on his face. He wore a grey beard – shaving had become a luxury – but it was stained red with blood from a trickle down the right side of his skull.

"What's happening, what's going on?" demanded Vic, tapping the keyboard to see if the computer had frozen.

But the connection was gone, leaving the stuck image flickering in front of him.

Rob entered the room fully, and Vic turned to face him.

"Something's happened at the bunker," he said. "I logged on for my usual morning chat. It took me a while to get through, but eventually, the Captain here answered. Some commotion was going on in the background."

"Did he say what happened?"

"Not much," said Vic, "As I said, the connection has been getting worse recently, and I only caught a few words. One of them was *mutiny*."

Rob considered this for a moment, placing his fingers on his chin.

"It sounds like the population in the bunker may have rebelled after all," he said. "I can't say I'm that surprised. Humans were not meant to live underground."

"This was for the preservation of the human race, though," said Vic.

"Was it?" asked Rob. "Or was it so that a few important people could have somewhere to escape all of this? To make sure they were looked after while the rest of the world suffered."

Vic did not reply but stared at the image on the screen with a glum expression.

"Faced with the reality of the situation, having to abandon the lavish lifestyle they were used to, living hand to mouth in what was a glorified army base – it sounds like they've decided to reject it."

"The military tried to make them stay," said Vic. "For the sake of survival. When you've spent your life being free to go wherever you please, and then suddenly living in a windowless prison under an authoritarian regime…"

"A lot of powerful people went into that bunker," said Rob. "The psychology of so many living so close together would've created factions. Disputes. Arguments."

"Looks like these have spilt over to violence," said Vic.

Rob nodded and walked over to the curtains. With a swipe, he opened them. The dun landscape presented itself below the ceiling of grey, rainless clouds. He could no longer see the edge of the waterline from the window.

Vic, realising he was wasting electricity, turned off the computer.

"Did we create a white elephant?" he asked. "Are all those years spent building this wasted?"

Rob shook his head, still staring at the view.

"I don't believe so," he said. "It gave us purpose when all around us was turning to despair. Part of me always thought this would happen."

<u>IX</u>

After spending a morning exploring the dusty attic space, Rob found the answer to his growing sense of isolation. Sat on a wooden table, covered in dust, was an old two-way radio – a dirty cream colour, and complete with a microphone attached by a coiled wire. Rescuing this, he took it down into his bedroom and examined it. The plug needed a new fuse, which he replaced, before taking the panel off to give it a thorough clean. A couple of hours later, he replaced the screws and plugged the radio into a wall socket. The crackle of static coming through gave him a sense of elation he had not expected.

It took him a few days of turning the frequency knob and speaking into the microphone to get a reply. Through the crackling, a woman's voice came through. She sounded distant, but through questioning, Rob learned that she was about twenty-five miles south of them, just outside of Glasgow. Her name was Ruth, and she was fifty-two. She lived alone following the death of her husband from a heart attack two years previously. They had a long conversation about their situations, and Rob learned that, as a keen gardener, she was attempting to grow her food in the allotment she had at the rear of her home. The lack of rain and the warming temperatures though made it impossible, and she had lost much of her crop. She had resisted going into the city, as she was afraid of the near-feral mobs now trying to get food and water by any means possible, but if she could not get hold of any soon, necessity may force her.

Reports of starvation, and the increasing problem of getting drinking water, had reached her. Death was on every street in the land, it seemed, and only small pockets of the population remained.

The desperate situation outside the four walls reinforced Rob's view that he should stay with Vic, and hope that they could both survive longer than trying to move elsewhere.

"You learned much about what's going on in the world from your radio friend?" asked Vic. They were sharing a can of baked beans, heated in the microwave. Night had arrived and they sat in the grand dining room, illuminated by the flickering of candles.

"Not much," said Rob. "Like us, she doesn't dare venture from her home. Mostly, we reminisce about the old days, when we were young."

Vic smiled, lost in his pleasant thoughts.

"What do you miss most, about the old world?" asked Rob.

"Travelling," replied Vic. He was having a rare lucid moment, as he had not yet touched the alcohol. Half a bottle of single malt sat next to his bowl on the table.

"I miss that moment when you go somewhere for the first time," Vic continued. "The first time you see the Pyramids, or the Great Wall of China. Once, I stood on the edge of the Grand Canyon, after a rather mad weekend in Vegas, and marvelled at the splendour and beauty of it. I climbed to the summit of Uluru when I was in my teens, and I went just as the sun went down and turned it the colour of velvet. But just to experience the world, in all its glory and colour. The diversity of its cultures and beliefs. It's history. To lose that is the greatest tragedy of all to me."

Rob nodded in agreement; the smell and the smoke from the candles making him feel sleepy.

"For me, it's my childhood memories," said Rob. "I always seemed so happy when I was young. I recall my mother singing Silent Night to me just as I snuggled in my bed on Christmas Eve, and my father singing with the radio as we drove to Cornwall for a holiday. It was such a small, brief part of my life, but those memories burn so brightly in my mind – I dream about them often."

"Aye, family is important," said Vic, eyeing the bottle on the table. "How long have we been here now?"

"It's difficult to say," said Rob. "I wish I'd started logging the days when we first moved here. I honestly don't know what month it is, or even what time of year it is. Every day is just hot and stuffy. If I had to guess, it feels like a couple of years."

"We've missed birthdays and Christmases then," said Vic.

"I'm sure we have," said Rob. "Sadly, I haven't had the chance to nip out and get you a present."

Vic chuckled.

"How are our supplies doing?" he asked.

"I had a look earlier," said Rob, "We've had about three-quarters of the stores. So I'd say we have six to eight months left, maybe longer if we start rationing more."

"What I wouldn't give for a fresh, medium rare, steak," said Vic. "Covered in pepper, with a side order of chips."

"Right now I'd settle for a crunchy, green apple," said Rob.

"Aye, but at least we still have this," said Vic, and reached for the bottle.

Rob decided to make his excuses for the night, leaving Vic to his bottle. He would see if he could contact Ruth again on the radio. As he left the room, he looked back on Vic silhouetted in the candlelight on the table in front, halo-framed as he poured a glass.

X

"For the first time since I shut myself away, *all* my crops have failed, not just the least hardy ones," said Ruth, her voice had a gentle Scottish crackle over the static. "I just can't find enough water to put on them."

"Is your still not producing enough at the moment?" asked Rob, pressing the button on the microphone.

"No," she replied. "I've got a load of stills all over my garden, but there doesn't seem to be enough moisture in the atmosphere for them to gather the droplets any longer."

"Water is becoming scarcer," said Rob. "The loch here used to come right up to the house, but now it's a good mile away."

"Can you drink it?"

"No, it's just a soup of rotting vegetation and dead fish. Would make us very ill if we tried drinking that."

"It seems crazy that we have so much cloud cover, but no rain falls," said Ruth.

"Not really," said Rob. "The sad situation is that water is evaporating from the surface which is turning to clouds as it reaches the lower atmosphere, but then instead of falling back to Earth as rain, the clouds themselves are trapping heat, preventing the water from coming back down again. The water is gradually being eroded into space."

"A sad situation indeed," said Ruth. "Enough of my woes. How are you and Vic getting along?"

"Not too good," said Rob. "I found him yesterday collapsed in his room. He'd had a fit. His tumour is progressing, it seems."

"Sorry to hear that. Is he in much pain?"

"He managed to get a ton of painkillers from the pharmaceutical company we employed for the bunker supplies, so he's either high from those, or drunk on the scotch he's downing."

"Not a great situation," said Ruth.

"No – and it's not helped by this constant heat. There's no relief from it."

"I know. And I'm finding it increasingly hard to get a breath."

"The oxygen is thinning too," said Rob, coughing on cue. "I always seem to have a mild headache."

A moment of silence passed, with just the crackle of static in the darkness of Rob's bedroom.

"Well, it's getting late," said Ruth. "I'm going to sign off now. Good night Rob, it was lovely speaking with you."

"You too," said Rob. "Good night."

XI

Rob woke at what he assumed to be his usual time. Daylight was just a little brighter than night, the brown and grey clouds illuminated a little more, and the heat more intense. He just had a thin cotton sheet on his bed, it was all he could stand, and he usually woke up with it drenched in sweat. By his bed, a small bottle stood on his nightstand full of water. It tasted brackish and warm, but he felt refreshed as he swigged it.

He rose and dressed. Clothing was now functional, and he generally only washed once a week, using as little water as possible, and his denim jeans and cotton T-shirt were now threadbare in patches.

His radio sat on the side table near the window. He established a routine call to Ruth each night over the weeks, but last night he had not been able to reach her. Maybe it wasn't anything more serious than power supply issues, but the concern remained.

His hands gripped the balustrade as he crossed the landing. He knocked on Vic's bedroom door and put his head inside. Nothing. The curtains were open. Vic had either risen early or never gone to bed at all. Rob figured the latter more likely.

Going downstairs, through the hallway full of stag heads and bagpipes, he entered the lounge.

Vic was sat in the same seat as the previous evening, positioned to look out over the Loch, as the morning came through the long window.

Moving quietly, in case he was still asleep, Rob entered

the room and faced him.

The white skin, and lolled head, was enough to indicate that he had died.

Rob bowed his head, before placing a finger on Vic's neck to check for a pulse.

It felt cold.

Nothing.

"Oh, Vic," said Rob. He took a deep breath, and his exhale was a sigh.

"Farewell, my friend."

He sat down on a chair opposite while he processed the situation. Vic sat, with eyes closed, in front of him. His right arm still rested on the table, and his hand still clasped an empty tumbler. An empty bottle of scotch next to it.

Then Rob noticed a small, transparent, plastic box. The lid was open, and it was empty.

A pill box.

Picking it up, Rob examined it. For painkillers, perhaps? He had been on a lot of them as his headaches progressed.

Putting it back down, he then noticed another similar box, hiding behind the bottle. It had a tartan bow wrapped around it, and as he picked it up, it was sat on one of Vic's old company wallet cards. On the back of a card was a message for him:

To Rob

It's my time to go. Thanks for the company. I've left you something for when it is your time.

Vic

Rob swallowed hard as he read Vic's final words. He had always seen himself as mentally strong. Times of strife and grief were moments to endure, not to lose your head. You needed to be logical and to temper emotion.

He had not cried when his parents had died, and he would not cry now. That did not solve anything.

Swallowing the upset away, his throat feeling hard and lumpy, he took off the bow and opened the pill box. Inside, a single white tablet lay. It was lozenge-shaped, and when he picked it up, it felt soft and squishy.

He felt an overwhelming urge to pop it in his mouth right at that moment. To just swallow this little thing and go to sleep forever.

It would be so easy.

He looked around as he fought the urge, looking for something to cling onto. His eyes settled back on Vic's body. It looked empty, devoid of anything that made this man a human. He wasn't ready for that. Not just yet.

It wasn't his time.

XII

He spent the day in a fugue, lacking any energy. He just wanted to sleep. His mind unable to concentrate, to think, to get him through the day.

Delaying the issue of dealing with Vic's body, despite knowing the longer left, the worse it would be, he decided to spend the day sitting on what used to be the lawn of Macken House. Reclining on an old garden lounger, legs up and pointing to where the lake used to be, he closed his eyes and allowed his thoughts to drift. His body had to work harder to get any oxygen in his lungs, with every other breath being a cough, but over a few minutes, he relaxed enough to fall back asleep.

When he woke, he figured that it was mid-afternoon, although with the thick cloud it was hard to tell where the sun lay, and the temperature had to be over forty degrees. Husks of dead trees covered the surrounding mountains, black teeth to the sky, the former green moorlands now hard earth. Nothing would grow on them, and nothing could live amongst them.

The white house sat behind him, its crenulations framing the darker sky, but he got a sense that he was not sitting at sea level, but was perching on the side of a mountain. The water of the loch had receded so far that the once-hidden depths were now a cliff face in front of him. Farther away, a little water remained – but it was foul and rotten – and sat many metres below.

He had covered Vic with a white sheet, in a classic pose that looked like a ghost from children's stories. Body disposal was necessary, he did consider throwing it down into the depths of the drained loch, but that seemed callous, and the likelihood was that he would still be able to see it from the house as it decomposed in the heat. Burial was not an option – the ground was so hard through lack of moisture it would be like trying to dig into concrete.

So that left a final option.

Cremation.

It seemed the sensible choice. The house contained many items of wooden furniture and décor that he could use as a pyre. He would collect some, build it around the body, and ignite it.

But not today. He was too exhausted, and it felt both

physical and emotional. He just needed a few hours.

A sudden and intense loneliness struck him. He had not prepared for it, having considered himself emotionally stable and strong throughout his entire life. But looking at the bleakness around him, feeling his lungs burning, and knowing the corpse of his lifelong friend sat in the house - it struck hard.

As the day darkened, returning to the house felt hollow. Rob had never felt so alone, so cut off from anyone. Following the glow of a candle, he ascended the staircase and went through the door to his room.

On the table lay the radio, and he went over and sat down next to it, placing the candle by the side. Switching it on, it crackled to life and he was grateful the house still received enough light to power the solar panels on the roof.

Picking up the mouthpiece, he spoke into it. He prayed he could reach her, despite the problems he'd had the previous evening.

"Ruth, are you there?"

Nothing. Just crackling.

"Ruth, are you reading me?"

Still nothing.

Rob sat back in his chair and closed his eyes.

"Who's that," said a man's voice through the radio. The accent was Scottish, but he did not recognise it. Someone new, perhaps.

"This is Rob, who's this?"

A pause at the other end. "This is Andy," said the voice.

"Good to speak to you, Andy. Is Ruth with you there, or have you picked up this frequency?"

"Ruth?"

"Yes, I've been speaking with her for a few weeks on this frequency," said Rob.

"She's not here at the moment. You say you've been speaking with her?"

"Yes, is everything okay with her?"

Another pause. "Yes, she's fine. Where are you calling from?"

"Loch Lomond," said Rob, "Just on the northern edge, are you at Ruth's home? Who are you?"

Nothing, no reply. Rob repeated his question.

Nothing. Dead air.

He could have sworn that, as the man who identified himself as Andy was speaking, he could hear a commotion in the background.

He breathed deeply and spoke once more.

"Hello, anyone there?"

Rob waited for a few minutes to see if the voice would return but all that remained was static.

A creeping dread passed over him as he realised he had given away his location. If this man had invaded Ruth's home, it would not take him long to get here – especially if he had a vehicle. Worse, if he was part of some roaming gang, striving to survive by any means possible, they may be on the way. It was likely that people desperate to survive would be searching for any pockets of the population – anyone who potentially had supplies.

He could be being paranoid. It could just be a friend of Ruth's, although she had never mentioned one. And why the silence?

Just to be safe, he needed an escape plan.

XIII

Rob was not a fighting man. He was intelligent and considered himself a liberal. The thought of hurting anyone was against his nature. Yet here he was - Vic's loaded rifle over his shoulder, on the roof of the house looking out over the canyon that once held the loch. Vic's binoculars in his hand, he scanned the summits of the hills and the empty roads that skirted the former edges of the waterline. The dried-up bed of the lake had revealed peaks and troughs smoothed by water erosion over millennia.

It was the evening after his conversation with an unknown person, who had named himself Andy, and he had not been idle during the day.

Rob had checked his car and plugged it into the grid. The four-wheel drive had enough charge to get him around sixty miles, he figured, but perhaps less now he had packed it up. In the garage next to the property, he had loaded it with as much as it could hold. He had stacked boxes containing the remaining cans and dried food in the storage trunk. He had also filled every plastic bottle, flask and container he could find with the water from the dwindling vat in the basement. Scrounging together a survival kit, he had equipped a multipurpose penknife, a canvas tent and rolled-up sleeping bag, matches and candles. He had avoided the pressing issue of Vic's body during his preparation, keeping himself busy; he left the door closed to the room where he sat.

During the day, lingering in the back of his mind, he thought that he might be overreacting. Perhaps it had been an innocent conversation, but he knew that he could not afford to ignore the risk. The need for vigilance, even if this threat was unfounded, was now required. The planet, and humanity, had entered the final phase. Life would soon be extinct, and people were desperate.

Resting his elbows on the stone, he scanned the surrounding landscape. He was now using the ornamental crenulations for actual defensive purposes, and feeling an aching in his arms and legs. He had to face the fact that he was an ageing man (he must be in his sixties now, he thought, but he had lost track of his precise age), and his chronic cough plagued him as much as his daily aches and pains. He also knew he wasn't getting close to adequate nutrition living off old water and whisky, along with canned and dried food. The lack of vitamin D from the obscured sunlight, and the dwindling oxygen in the air, contributed to his malaise. It had become an issue of pride with him that he would hang on to his life for as long as possible. Only leave this world at the very last moment.

Tiredness crept over him as he looked. How long did he intend to be a sentinel here? He couldn't keep watch by himself every minute of the day. The darkening, overcast sky meant it was difficult to see anything. Maybe he had been concerned for nothing, and hunger was starting to set in – he had not eaten all day.

Heading back to the ladder down from the roof access hatch, he stopped.

Did he hear something?

Going back to the battlement, he grabbed Vic's rifle and placed his eye on the telescopic sight. Scanning the road, winding its way around the headland of a mountain, above the loch canyon, he aimed the crosshairs at the direction of the rumble. Spotting headlights as they swept around the heel of the canyon, he clicked the magnification to get a closer view. Five vehicles travelled on the road, heading in his direction, a couple of kilometres away.

Anxiety crept over him as he continued to follow them.

They reached the apex of the road, and pulled to the side of the bend, throwing up a cloud of dust. Rob rested his elbows on the stone to steady his view. As the dust settled, he could see that the cars were a mix of common hatchbacks and saloons, dirtied by the landscape - identifiable by the clean swipes on the windscreens. Emerging from them, he discerned several people, males for the most part, although he could not make out all of them.

Adjusting his position a little to get a better view, Rob zoomed the scope in even further.

In the light of their headlights, he could see them pointing up the road, in his direction. The men looked skinny and unkempt, with a gaunt, hungered look in their eyes. Moving his crosshairs across them, he spotted that they were carrying weapons. One had a shotgun, and others carried what appeared to be machetes hung on their belts.

They were not friendly.

Considering his options, Rob knew that he wouldn't stand a chance against all of them. He was not inclined to be violent, even in self-defence, and these people were probably used to taking what they want by force.

He needed to flee.

Decision made, not wasting another moment, he headed for the hatch, shouldering the rifle as he went. Climbing down the ladder, he made for the stairs.

Knowing he only had a few minutes, he said a silent

farewell to the house he had known for so long, and that had kept him safe and fed for so many years. Survival was now everything, he could not afford to be sentimental.

As he reached the ground floor, a feeling of hatred overcame him with such ferocity; it took him a moment to come to terms with it. Examining his reaction, he realised he did not hate these people specifically, but rather the capacity in each individual to commit atrocities to extend their existence a little longer. In a flash of perception, it all made sense to him.

Life on Earth was ending due to this.

He could boil down everything that had gone wrong to human greed.

To want more, to put oneself above others – *that* was our downfall.

And, what's more, *he* was not above this.

These attackers would want what he had. They would hunt him until they did, and he felt nothing but contempt for them and their lives.

It is our nature, he thought. Violence, vengeance and greed. Whatever the cause of Earth's destruction, the universe would not miss us. It would not shed a tear.

We were getting what we deserved.

Vic still sat where he had died, and the basement was still stacked with supplies that he could not fit in his car. If he could convince the attackers that he had never left, they had no reason to pursue him.

Pushing open the door to Vic's Study, a waft of death reached him. Trying to ignore this, he grabbed a candle on the desk and lit it with a match from his pocket. Taking the wax shaft, he went over to the window, parted the curtains slightly, and across the land could see the approaching headlights.

He put the candle flame on the fabric of the long curtain.

And repeated this on the other side.

Fire washed over the fabric, and rose to the ceiling in seconds. Black smoke began to fill the room and billowed across the high ceiling.

Bidding a rapid farewell to his friend, he also lit the sheet he had covered him with – and paused for a moment of silent reflection as it took hold. Vic would be his decoy. If they inspected the remains of the house, they would find the cremated body and assume the flames had caught him.

Becoming aware of the heat growing, alarmed by the rapid spread of the fire, Rob dropped the candle on the carpet and left the room. Running through to the rear of the property, the thick black smoke followed him through the doorway, clinging and spreading across the hallway. Sweat ran down his face.

Rushing out of the wood-panelled rear door, he crossed the paved area to the garage, the sounds of nearing engines echoing around him. The car, parked just outside the garage, pointed towards the driveway. Rob fished the keys from his pocket and jumped in. He had packed all available space around the driver's seat with supplies, and he had to adjust some slippage of containers so he did not obscure his view through the windscreen.

Starting the car with the ignition button, he pressed the accelerator and prayed that it was still mechanically sound. He had not driven it for months. It drifted away with a subdued whine, the car's battery silently propelling him.

Keeping an eye on the rear-view mirror, his face a red glow from the reflection, he was grateful for the quiet engine of the car so he could steal away. As he pulled past the outbuildings, and onto the tarmac drive, a fleet of vehicles rounded the far corner of the house and roared into the paved area.

He pressed his foot down further, leaving the headlights off, and he left the buildings behind. In his wing mirrors, he saw the silhouettes of several people getting out of the cars, but they were not looking in his direction. Instead, they faced the flames that now smashed the panes of glass in the windows, and licked around the stone façade.

Rob continued towards the exit, the incline rising above the glow of the inferno. Nervously, he still checked behind him. None of them looked in his direction as they watched the conflagration grow.

He reached the edge of the property, where the wrought iron gates hung open on the stone pillars. One of them had rusted away from its hinges, and it struck the side of the car as he sped through them. The bang made him jump, and the car lurched sideways. Correcting the wheel, he did not stop, but as the tyres struck the road, he headed northwards.

Travelling for fifteen minutes, he followed the road up the mountain to the rear of Macken House, and near its summit sat a lay-by area that gave a panoramic view. Pulling into it, he got out and looked back towards the red glow that now dominated the vista.

Black smoke rose from hellish red flames. The fire was out of control, forked red tongues licking from the shattered windows; and the smoke rose in a twisting pillar, rising straight upwards in the windless night, joining the black ceiling of cloud above his head. Through the crimson glow of the fire, the silhouettes of the invaders stood, arms held by their side – some holding machetes – watching the house burn. They had not seen him leave.

This had been their last chance. Their final gamble.

Rob stood mesmerised, eyes wide, pupils dancing with the flickering light, and watched the conflagration.

XIV

He knew he was dying.

Weakness and pain had become the everyday. He tended to move around in the late evening and early morning, searching for any available food and water. Finding none. Not even a blade of grass. Not even a fly, or any other insect. Not even on the bodies he had encountered.

Not such a long time ago, sea birds would have been everywhere here, on the north coast of Scotland; but now the sky was just dark grey, holding in the sun's radiation, creating his predicted greenhouse effect. Breathable air leeched way, and the sea had retreated so far that he could not see it. Instead, the cliffs he now sat on gave him a view of the former sea bed, covered in smoothed rocks. It stank from rotting fish and vegetation.

As he sat, pondering his situation, he reflected on the days that had passed since he fled Macken House. He headed north, through the Highlands. Figuring that it may be a degree or two cooler the further north he travelled, he also wanted to avoid any potentially populated areas. The towns and villages he travelled through were deserted. Between the grey stone buildings lay the emaciated bodies of men, women and children who had starved or died of dehydration, alongside pets and cattle decomposing in the heat.

Still, he travelled, through all the death, following the road, rifle close at hand.

During the day, when the temperature was highest, he would find a place to stop amongst the canyons and dark mountains. He would have a little food and water from his supply in the car. The vehicle was too hot to sleep in – with the insulating windows – so he tended to sleep out in the open. Outdoors, his tent could draw unwanted attention from any survivors, not that he had seen any, but he figured anyone alive would be desperate. So he tried to find shelter in barns and outbuildings where he could. The villages he encountered had homes he could use, but he resisted entering them with the knowledge that many would contain the dead. He doubted any houses would have any remaining food or water; the occupants having consumed every scrap before death found them. Many barns had remains of livestock, but they were too far gone to be edible, and many he found had been stripped of all their meat and were skeletal.

He would sleep as the temperatures rose, trying to block out the horrific, cadaverous smell that seemed to linger everywhere, and then as darkness fell and the heat subsided a little, he would move on – always northward.

As he arrived at the coast, the car battery expired. The supplies had kept him alive, but as he cracked open a can of soup, he noticed that it had begun to spoil. The cans were already years old, laid down when he first moved in with Vic, and now sitting in a boiling hot car, they were cooking. He was having to drink more water too, as his daily exertions left him dehydrated, and each day seemed warmer and more uncomfortable.

And his cough had worsened, and more than once, he had noticed blood-stains on his lips.

He had reached the end of the world.

He could go no further

The days passed him by and he did not notice them. He spent much of the time camped on the bare earth, pitching his tent close to the edge of the cliff, and using rocks to anchor it. Going through his remaining supplies, he discarded much of the food that would make him sick and began to ration the water he had stored in plastic containers, but that also began to wane.

Exploring the former coast, he wandered along the cliffs and beaches – now just cracked boulders and sand bordering on the smoothed rocks of the sea bed. It kept him moving, and he spent most of the day lost in thoughts and memories, with intense loneliness.

Sleep gave him some blessed relief. His dreams seemed to want to give him at least some hours of pleasant distraction from the nightmare of wakefulness. He dreamt of his childhood, of laughing with friends, swimming in clear, cool pools of water, and faces from his past appeared around him, whispering unremembered words of comfort.

That morning he woke and drained the last scrap of water from the plastic bottle that he had kept next to his sleeping bag. He had eaten a dry packet of crushed crisps the evening before, and that had been the last of the food. Examining his mental state, he was experiencing desperation, and fear of what lay ahead. His body starved of all the fuel it needed – water, food and oxygen – was waning. Looking at the desert around him, he could now count his lifespan in hours.

Maybe it was human nature, the design of the mind, he thought – but I just cannot give up. Not yet.

Soon, maybe…

Not yet.

He became weaker as the hours passed, and he gave thought to where he would like his body to lay as life escaped him. Perched on the cliff, legs dangling over the edge looking out to the sea bed, appealed to him, though he could not explain why. He positioned himself and let his thoughts drift.

In those dark hours, he thought about the world. He wondered if any survivors still roamed. It could be that other places had more successful bunkers and those pockets of civilisation existed underground – never to see the sun again – never to breathe natural air. But it did not stretch his imagination, after this time of seeing nothing but death, to believe that he was the last person alive.

He was weak. Hunger and thirst, along with the thin air, seemed to eat away his innards, and cloud his mind. A sleep, from which he would not awaken, began to overtake him.

A wail broke the utter silence. Like a banshee in the half-light, the sound roused him from his semi-conscious state, and he sat upright.

Another wail, low and pained. Gasping and urgent. Mournful…

Rob raised himself to his feet, feeling his thighs complaining. He tightened the belt around his trousers to stop them from falling and shouldered the rifle that sat on the ground. What was it? Could it be the death throes of an animal? A deer or a bird, perhaps?

He followed the sound, travelling on the cliff edge with a drop of around twenty metres to the dry bed below, trying to make out any sign of the disturbance.

The wail continued every few seconds, imploring. Desperate.

Finding a small trail, he followed it as it began to lead him down the edge of the escarpment, the sound nearing. He descended towards the former shoreline, and about halfway down, he found the entrance to a cave. The cries came from within.

It was dark inside, but from his jacket pocket, he produced a candle and matches. The candle flickered its jaundiced light, and he saw that it was a shallow cave, just a scoop in the rock of the cliff.

What he witnessed inside was horrifying.

On the ground, to the rear of the cave, lay the body of a young woman. She was gaunt and pale, but her death had been very recent. She looked no more than sixteen years old, but her black hair stuck to her skull-like visage, her sunken eyes fixed open. She had worn a large, loose-fitting dress. This had ridden up to her chest, exposing her stick legs and a swollen belly. Blood had pooled around the hard floor of the cave, staining the fabric of her dress and the rocks. Wrappers of snacks, crisps and chocolate, also littered the ground, some floating in the dark red pools.

He saw her lying down, with her head resting on a rock, her legs spread wide. Her bony thighs were red and became an indistinct mass of gore towards her crotch.

Between her legs, on the ground, lay a new-born.

A tiny girl.

Still attached to the umbilicus, the child waved undernourished arms and legs through blood and the afterbirth. She seemed to be trying to crawl towards her mother, her arms striking the sides of the thighs; but she just swam around helplessly, covering herself in the congealing carnage.

Rob took a sharp intake of breath as he saw the little girl. With everything he had seen, this disturbed him the most. A child born into this dying world.

He took his penknife from his pocket and squatted next to her. Pulling out a blade, he severed the cord attached to the belly of the girl, pocketed the knife, and picked her up with both hands.

The little girl cried incessantly, blood dripping from her toes.

Removing her from the cave, Rob took her outside, away from the horror. He thought about the dead mother, and the terror and pain she must have felt as the labour pains began. Surely, she had sought refuge in the cave in the final days of her pregnancy, wanting so desperately to see her child come into the world, and yet leaving it in intense pain and fear for her baby as the blood flowed out of her. He could not imagine anything more nightmarish.

As he reached the top of the cliff, he still held the child at arm's length in front of him. Covered in afterbirth, she screamed with every ounce of energy she could muster – sucking in the thin air. She was a miracle birth.

He wondered briefly about the father. The girl was alone, had she lost her partner? Or maybe she did not know the father? The few survivors of the past months had taken to feral ways, so who could tell what may have befallen this poor woman?

Arriving back at his camp, he took his towel and wiped the little girl down, cleaning her the best he could. Pink flesh appeared and he dropped the towel. In his pack, he had a white T-shirt. With one hand, the other cradling the new-born, he fished it out, and wrapped her in it, folding the sleeves so he covered her with just her face showing.

Her eyes remained closed, but her mouth moved around her cries, and she squirmed her arms and legs inside her wrapping.

He rocked her gently, trying to soothe her.

Rob had never had his own family, his dedication to his work taking him away from ever considering one. But here she was. A little girl, helpless, confused, wondering about the world around her. So much potential for life, and no opportunity for it to grow.

He wondered what her future might have held. Sleeping peacefully in the arms of her mother, laughing as she was tickled, going to school and making friends, finding her way in the world and falling in love for the first time.

Having a child of her own.

All denied to her.

She needed a name. Perhaps her mother had given her one, but Rob needed to name her. Give her at least some identity.

One came to him immediately.

Lucy.

So she was the first, so should she be the last.

"Lucy…" he said to her, in almost a whisper.

For a moment, Lucy stopped crying, and she opened her eyes, looking up at him directly.

They were blue.

He had never let emotion overtake him.

He did so now.

Whatever reservoirs he had in remaining him burst forth from his eyes. Tears streamed down his face, uncontrollably. He wept.

Wept at the hardship. Wept at how unfair it was that he could give no chance to this innocent. He wanted to be angry. Wanted to direct fury at someone, something that had caused this. He wanted to scream at them to fix it – to end this hell.

Two slivers traced a path through the dirt on his cheeks and dripped on the T-shirt blanket.

Lucy stopped crying, but continued to squirm, cradled in the elbow of his right arm.

With his left hand, he reached into his pocket and pulled out his penknife once again, and coaxed out the blade with his fingers. Placing it onto the ground in front of him, he reached back into the same pocket and retrieved a small, transparent plastic box.

Lifting the lid of the box, the lozenge-shaped pill sat inside. He took it out and looked at it for a moment. Then, he took the blade and sliced through one side of it. The pill was soft and pliable, and he shaved off about a quarter from the tip.

That should be enough.

He picked up the sliver and looked down at Lucy.

Her eyes were open now, looking up at him.

Rob looked back down at her, his eyes full of love, as he

gently inserted the sliver of the pill between her lips. She took it eagerly and willingly. Her trust was absolute.

Her mouth worked a little.

It only took a few seconds before her blue eyes closed forever, and Rob waited a few moments as the movement ceased and the small body went limp.

Rob rested his back on a rock and picked up the rest of the pill. With his free hand, he twirled it between thumb and forefinger, examining it closely.

It tasted bitter on his tongue.

It was time.

Chapter Fourteen – Alpha

I

"Anyone whose name was not found written in the book of life was thrown into the lake of fire."

Robert Birch watched as the words on the letter dragged downwards and sliced into thin ribbons. The paper shredder buzzed as it sliced. A shiver ran through him, though he could not explain why. He'd seen those words from Revelations many times in the correspondence received in the University office, but for some reason – this morning – he felt disturbed by them.

Casting his thoughts aside, he grabbed the next letter. It was A4 sized, and as he opened it, the sheet inside had not been folded. The page was covered in mathematical equations, written in ink, and had been circled with a diagonal line dividing the formulas through the middle.

Who was this even from? No covering letter, and no name or address on the page itself?

Looking back inside the envelope, he noticed something at the bottom. Taking it out, he flipped it over and it was a photograph of a young woman. Indeed, she looked to be in her teens – perhaps fourteen or fifteen years old – unsmiling, and on a black background.

"My word they are starting young these days," said Rob out loud to himself, and shook his head, wondering what sort of conspiracy websites this girl had subjected herself to.

Flipping the photograph, he noticed an email address

on it, but nothing else. No name, no home address.

He turned the photo and looked at the girl once again. She had a darker skin tone, piercing blue eyes and long black hair in wavy curls. She had allowed her hair to grow, and the explosion of curls took up half the image.

She had an eye for mathematics, which he could not doubt as he looked at the carefully formatted page, but he wondered about her mental state. Many outlets – television and internet news, social media, and the press – were reporting on the state of the planet, between both nations and beliefs, and humanity and the natural world. Destroying it, and each other. All the media surrounding her must have influenced this girl, and at such an impressionable age.

Maybe he owed it to her to look at the sheet of figures supplied. If nothing else, he could explain where she had gone wrong and put her back on the path of rationality. It was clear that she had talent, for one so young, but that needed to be directed in the right areas.

At that moment, Professor Bell's head emerged from his office doorway.

"She's here," he said, "Would you be kind enough to bring her up."

Kathryn Powell from Design Venture Projects had arrived, interrupting Rob's thoughts. Without thinking, he folded the letter and put it with the photograph in his jacket pocket, and raised himself from his seat to bring her up from reception.

II

Arriving back at his apartment, leaving the noise of the inner city traffic of a rain-soaked Manchester behind, Rob mused about his meeting with the business woman from DVP earlier that day. She had introduced herself as Kathryn Powell, and from her demeanour, as he walked her out of the building, it was clear that she was not impressed with the professor. That might cost the department the commercial partnership that DVP was proposing, but more important to Rob was that she had shown a professional interest in *him*, and had given over her card as a contact.

Stepping into the lift to his floor, he pressed his floor button, and ascended – still lost in contemplation.

When she had asked, he had not hidden his dissatisfaction with his job. Her offer was tempting. At the very least, he could go for an interview and see what they had to offer.

Arriving at his floor, he fished out his keys and reached his apartment door. Closing it behind him, he ditched the jangling keyring in the tray, switched on the lights, and ambled through to the main living area. The November evening had arrived with his single window streaked with greasy precipitation, but it felt humid. His apartment had central heating, usually a necessity at this time of year, but not required at the moment. The black silhouettes of the Mancunian skyline filtered away as he closed the window blinds. Flicking the switch on the kettle, he took out his laptop from his work satchel and flipped it open.

Unloading the contents of his jacket pocket, he intended to contact Kathryn; drop her an email confirming his availability for an interview. Strike while the iron is hot.

Dropping them on the table next to his computer, he found the card wrapped in a sheet of A4 paper containing a series of equations, along with a photograph of a teenage girl. Occupying his thoughts during the day was the offer from DVP. The letter he had opened first thing had slipped his mind.

The kettle steamed and clicked off.

The laptop fired up, and Rob returned with a steaming mug of tea, the teabag string still hanging over the side. Placing it down, he opened up his emails and typed out a message to Kathryn, adding her email address. He had kept his CV up to date, and on file, which he attached, and clicked send. A few moments later, he received a read receipt back in his inbox, and he indulged himself with a smile of satisfaction.

Placing the business card aside, he noticed the sheet of paper full of figures. Taking a sip of tea, he picked up the page, holding it up so he could see more clearly in the light of the laptop. Scanning the page, he did some mental calculations, his mouth moving as he worked out the equations.

At the bottom, a simple summing-up equation:

$$(z) + \alpha = \Omega$$

Placing the page flat on the table, he switched on the standing lamp. Taking another sip, he carried on with his workings, his finger tracing a path across the paper, his face a mask of concentration.

Whatever this sheet represented, the maths worked. If this girl had formulated the numbers on the page, then she had a genius level of mental acuity.

But what did it represent? All he had was a page full of numbers and mathematical symbols, with a summation equation at the bottom. No cover letter, just a photograph and email address.

Intrigued, Rob's initial cynicism evaporated, lost in the elegant logic of figures and symbols. He wanted to know more. The temptation borne from unanswered questions.

Looking at the photograph of the girl, he felt struck by her eyes, which seemed to pierce his own from the very image.

This was important. Why or how it was important, he could not fathom – but it *felt* as though the correct course of action would be to find out more.

Turning back to his laptop, he entered the email address and began to type a new message.

III

The sitting statue of Alan Turing, holding his deadly fruit, glinted back at him in the sunshine as he opened his sandwich box. Next to the bread lay a green apple. Rob had not planned that deliberately, but it still felt like a pleasant coincidence.

A bright, blue sky peered through the branches of the trees in the park. A few browning leaves clung to them, but most now collected around the trunk and the benches as nature, it appeared, still followed the path of seasons, even if the weather did not. It had turned chilly, but not freezing. He felt warm enough in his shirt and wool tank top worn below his suit jacket.

Today's lunch was a little different though. He received an email reply from DVP, inviting him to Glasgow for an interview. He had already accepted. That alone would make this an interesting day, but he also had arranged to meet someone, and he wondered if she would show.

As if on cue, a young woman stood before him – framed by the rays of the midday sun. Rob found it difficult to guess her age – perhaps fifteen or sixteen now he saw her for real – and she wore dark jeans, heavy-soled shoes, and a long black overcoat. Her long black, frizzy hair - tied back from her forehead in a rough ponytail - bobbed around as she approached. But her eyes glinted in the sunlight and conveyed to Rob an intelligence matched by a fierce determination.

"You must be Robert," she said, extending out a hand.

Rob stood to greet her. "I am, call me Rob," he said and shook her hand. She grasped it with both her own hands and kept eye contact with him.

Rob invited her to sit next to him on the bench.

"Would you like a sandwich?" he offered, not sure how to proceed.

"No, thank you," she said.

"Erm, do you have a name?" said Rob. "What shall I call you?"

"I like your choice of meeting place," she said, seemingly ignoring his question. She motioned towards the statue sitting on the bench opposite.

"Ah, yes – that's Alan Turing," said Rob.

"Instrumental during the Second World War in breaking the Nazi code," she said. "Saved countless lives by shortening the war, and then committed suicide after the nation prosecuted him for being homosexual."

"That's right," said Rob. "You know your history. The man was a genius, in my eyes. What happened to him was tragic."

"It certainly was," she said, nodding in agreement.

Rob could not place her accent. It was English, but he could not detect an element of regionalism in it. It was not a local Mancunian accent.

"You travelled far to be here?" he asked.

"What did you make of my letter?" she asked, changing the subject again.

"I found it...," he struggled for a word, "...*intriguing.*"

"Did you figure out what it was? Why it is so important?"

"I was hoping you could clarify that for me," said Rob. "I thought that was why we're here today?"

"I'm so happy you arranged it," she said. "You're the only one that replied."

"You sent other letters?"

"I sent hundreds," she said. "To every scientific institution I could think of. Universities and tech laboratories, state societies and amateur physics groups alike."

"And you've only had this response from me?"

"Just you, so far," she said. "I was delighted to get your email."

Rob began to wonder what he had let himself in for – if indeed, he had made an error of judgement in contacting her. If so many other places had not seen fit to entertain her, maybe he had missed something that they did not.

"I can see what you are thinking," she said, paying him a shrewd glance. "I fully expected to be rebuffed. After all, I offered no explanation as to what the content of the letter was."

"Why did you do that?"

"Because I hoped the maths would speak for itself," she said. "Seeing a teenage girl come along with new ideas about the nature of the universe would cause consternation. The maths however does not lie. I hoped somebody would see that."

"Is that what this is then?" asked Rob, producing her sheet of equations from his pocket. "Negative zeta plus alpha equals sigma? Something to do with the nature of the Universe?"

She shifted her position on the bench to look at him, eye to eye. The depths they contained once again struck him.

"This *is* the universe," she said, keeping her voice low and even. "That page defines the very ingredients of space-time. It describes the two energies that merged at the moment of the Big Bang to create all matter and set the course of time as we know it rolling."

Rob took a breath, taking in what she was saying.

"Those energies still exist in their raw form throughout the Universe today," she continued. "We can't measure them, but we can see their effects. The Physics community have labelled them dark energy. But what they don't yet understand is that they define the passage of time. One energy creates and shapes everything around us – lights the spark of consciousness - allows the evolution of life and the time it needs to develop. The twin energy destroys – it recycles those parts of the universe that serve no purpose, or is a danger to the positive flow of time, throws them back into the cosmic mix – so that they may be of use in the future."

Rob considered her words, recalling the divide showing

the delineation of the two energies. He felt he needed to look at the page again, given this revelation.

"What's the significance of this?" he asked.

"That it the real question," she said. "The universe *wants* life to flourish, *wants* to encourage its development and progress. But it is also cold if it feels as though that development is going down a dead end. We are at the point in our civilisation where we can destroy ourselves. If we travel further down the path we are on, then the destructive side will end all life on Earth so that it may start up again at some other point in space and time. Simply put, if we want to survive, we have to change our ways."

"It's no secret that we are destroying the planet, and each other," said Rob. "Science has known and warned for decades about the damage we are doing. But what you are describing is that time *itself* will bring its own Armageddon?"

She nodded.

"What proof do you have of this?" asked Rob. "I see you've managed to show your theory with equations, but science *needs* proof of this. Where did you find the data to formulate your hypothesis?"

She remained quiet for a moment, staring ahead at the statue.

"No proof exists," she said. "The data was collected by breaking space-time. And it seems the universe does not like this. I'm sorry for the vague answer, but you must believe that this is the case."

"You are asking me to take your theory on faith?" said Rob.

"I understand the scientific method," she said. "I also subscribe to that. We do need evidence to support a hypothesis. In this case, I cannot provide that – but I *know* it exists."

"Then you must realise that you cannot go forward with this unless you can show evidence," said Rob.

"That evidence will come in time," she said. "But it will not be through any human intervention. Something will happen – I can't say what that would be – but something will happen. And it will signify the ending of us."

"With that attitude," said Rob, "You may as well walk down the street wearing a board stating that the End of the World is nigh."

"I'm aware of that," she said. "But you are here. The thought of this has seeded itself in your mind. Even if you don't believe it right now, it is a start."

"Maybe if you reveal a little about yourself, you may be able to get more people to listen to this?" Rob suggested.

She looked around, taking in the surroundings of the park. Nearby, a pigeon feasted on some discarded, leftover fast food.

"I view myself as a messenger," she said. "I don't want any of this to be about me. It is not about me, it is about what humanity needs to change to survive. If I start introducing my ego and my personality, then the message will be lost as people may look at *me* rather than at *themselves*. I do not want to end up leading some kind of end-of-the-world cult."

"You are very intelligent and driven for someone so young," said Rob. "Do you not think you can use this?"

"No, it is not about who I am," she said. "And of all people, I believe you should understand my point of view. After all, you brought me here."

She pointed to the statue opposite, to the image of the man persecuted despite his genius. Rob understood her position immediately.

<u>IV</u>

Rob never regretted the day he left Manchester to move to Scotland. Standing in his lounge, looking out of his front window, he was lost in thought. From the view from his first-floor flat, he could see the shores of Loch Ryan, its wide waters never still, as they drifted northward towards the horizon.

He lived alone but spent most of his time at the DVP plant nearby. In the five years since he joined the company, he had worked up the ladder to become the lead in Research and Development. His current task was with repurposing thirty-five former rigs, once used for oil and gas drilling in the North Sea and other British waters. They had become defunct as the reserves dried up, and so the company snapped them well below market rate. Vic had parked them around the Scottish coastline, with the majority just a few miles away, at the mouth of the loch where it met the Irish Sea – outside of any shipping lanes. Vic Macken, who Rob had only met a couple of times, hoped that they could be repurposed to either provide a base for his solar energy business or branched out to give wind or wave power offshore. At the very worst, Rob could dismantle them for scrap, but he wanted to avoid that.

He had several ideas, none of which Vic considered profitable enough. The expense of refitting the rigs outweighed the profits from energy generation using current technology.

Frustrated, but determined, Rob was desperate to find a solution. Time was on his side though, Vic did not seem to view the project as urgent, and so Rob continued to probe his development ideas, certain that he could find a suitable answer to all this metal and machinery.

A fake telephone ringing noise emanated from his computer, and rushed over to his desk at the back of the lounge. It was time for his weekly catch-up.

He still didn't know her name; and whenever they chatted online, she sat in front of a blank white wall without any kind of identifying features. They always met this time of the week. For a single hour. Set in stone.

They discussed events going on in the world, from politics to military conflicts. Scientific and technological advancements were also a topic they enjoyed, but also ideological and philosophical concerns and assessments. Forefront as always was the state of the planet, the decline of the environment and the damage caused to nature and civilisation; the growing frequency of natural disasters, along with the ever-increasing temperatures.

Whenever he spoke to her, he marvelled at her intellect for one so young – she seemed to know everything – and never tired of talking. Just into her twenties, she was nevertheless gathering support in the scientific community for their shared passion for the future of the planet. Amongst the student population, in particular, many campuses had societies dedicated to her and the Duality Theory that she promoted. Rob had attended many himself and acceptance for it was growing. She travelled the country to deliver keynote speeches wherever she could.

Always being anonymous, nobody knew anything about

her. Not even her name.

More often than not, their weekly hour spent passed so quickly that they overran, talking passionately about the affairs of the world. Seeing her as a face on the screen was a highlight of his week – but his affection for her was an intellectual one. From an early age, he had known that intimate relationships did not interest him, preferring to interact with the people around him with a meeting of minds, rather than bodies.

Reaching for his mouse, he clicked on the connect button, and her smiling face appeared.

"Good evening Rob," she said.

V

"So you're telling me that we have no idea what is causing these magnetic anomalies?" said Vic. He was pacing behind his desk in his Glasgow office and casting glances out of his window towards the river Clyde.

Kathryn Powell was also in the meeting, and sat on Vic's couch, looking at Rob nervously. The world had started reporting issues with GPS and navigation systems. Along with an upsurge in global-warming-related events, nobody could now deny that the planet was in dire trouble. Governments, who had only paid lip service to the issues to this point, were now on board. Something needed to happen, the public demanded it as they were losing votes and their power base was diminishing.

"The scientists I've spoken to have no idea of what process is happening at the core to cause this," said Rob. "But what we do know is that both Mars and Venus had magnetic fields in their past. They both could've been earth-like planets – habitable and life-sustaining – but for some reason, millions of years ago, their cores stopped spinning."

"Is there any way we can stop this?" asked Kathryn.

Rob hesitated before answering.

"Well, come on man, speak up," said Vic, frowning at him.

"I know someone who has a theory about the nature of the universe that seems consistent with what is going on."

"Who is he?" asked Vic.

"*She*," said Rob, "I've known her for years, and she correctly predicted that some kind of catastrophe would affect the planet."

"Does she have a name?" asked Kathryn.

"Not that I'm aware of," said Rob.

"What do you mean – she doesn't have a name?" said Vic.

"She wants anonymity," said Rob. "But what I can say is that she is a genius. Everything she predicted is coming true. The fact the she is remaining secretive about herself is only adding to the convincing nature of her theory as its clear she is not doing this for her ego, or money, power – any of those."

"She sounds like a doom-monger to me," said Vic, "Some kind of charlatan."

Kathryn nodded her agreement.

"I think it would be wise to at least listen to what she has to say," said Rob. "She's already mentioned to me that she would like to meet you, Vic."

"Would she now," said Vic, raising his eyebrows. "And why should I meet this woman?"

"Because she seems to have all the answers," said Rob.

"And I have to say, I believe in her theory. She does have it backed up with mathematical proof. You seem to value my judgement, so I would ask you to trust me on this. What do you have to lose?"

Vic narrowed his eyes at Rob and paced around the room running his hand over his bald head. Pausing, he looked at Kathryn, who shrugged and nodded.

"Set up the meeting," he said. "But if this is some kind of joke, I'll be directing my anger at you."

VI

Vic Macken emerged from Rob's office, his mouth agape. His face was pale. Looking like he had seen the doorway to paradise and then had it slammed in his face.

"We have to do something," he said, his regular booming voice replaced by a quiet, determined tone.

Rob stood, gathered with his team of scientists in the laboratory outside his office. His team were already supporters of the Duality Theory, and Rob felt grateful for their backup when it came to introducing Vic to the source of their conviction. Vic had recently tasked them with gathering the necessary data to build a bridge across to Northern Ireland, but this had taken a back seat, as the theory was gathering momentum. Since the discovery of the weakening magnetic field, having Vic as a proponent would add a huge amount of weight to the cause.

"That is one persuasive woman," said Vic.

"She's something else," agreed Rob.

Through the window of his office door, he could see her sitting with her arms folded on her lap. Rob had arranged the meeting, but she had asked Rob to leave when

Vic entered the room, as she wanted to speak to the Industrialist one to one.

"Come inside, Rob, we have to talk about this," said Vic.

Following his boss back into his office, Rob took his seat behind the desk, and Vic went over to sit on the couch. She regarded them both, her face expressionless.

"Okay, let's say I'm on board," said Vic, and heaved a huge sigh. A weight had descended onto his shoulders, but a part of him relished what was to come and the challenges involved.

"It all makes sense," said Rob. "She predicted a global catastrophe, and it is happening."

She sat, looking impassive, in the seat opposite the desk. Her eyes held an inscrutable depth.

Rob turned his computer monitor around to face her, and she looked at her equation copied precisely into a spreadsheet.

"I'm working on a blurb to go with this, to explain what it all means to the scientific community. If we can put this together with the data showing the slowing down of the core's rotation, we'll have all the evidence they need."

"It won't be enough," she said. "Even if we do get a group of intellectuals together, it will not solve the problem. That's why I wanted to meet Mr Macken here."

"Call me Vic."

She nodded and smiled at him.

"We have to go further than just educating a few physicists," she said. "If we are going to save humanity, then we need to show the *universe* that life here can move forward, can adapt, can learn from our mistakes and evolve our nature."

"How do we do that?" asked Vic.

"By convincing the world to stop killing each other and to stop destroying the habitats of all life on Earth."

Vic huffed and crossed his arms. "Well, why didn't you say so, lassie, I'll get right on it."

Rob smiled. She may have convinced Vic, but he had not lost his talent for sarcasm. Raising an eyebrow, their guest also raised a grin, her mirth reflected in her eyes.

"Not asking for much, am I," she said.

"Do you have any ideas?" asked Rob.

"It's something I've given a lot of thought to over the years," she said. "But lacked the means to accomplish it. Having you and Vic with me on this, I think we could make a start. But we are going to need more people. *Influential* people. *Intelligent* people. And most of all, *wealthy* people."

"I thought wealth was the root of all evil to you environmentalists," said Vic.

"I wouldn't consider myself an environmentalist," she said. "My vision is on a larger scale. I see myself more as a survivalist."

"The two are becoming the same," said Rob, to which she nodded an agreement.

"I don't see wealth as evil either," she said. "Money isn't inherently evil, but the pursuit of it can be if a greedy person is willing to destroy the earth and the lives of other people. What we need to do is make it work for the benefit of all."

"What's your plan then, lassie?" said Vic.

She looked around and spotted a map of the world hung on Rob's noticeboard with coloured pins. Standing from her desk chair, she stepped over to it.

"The very first thing is to find us a base of operations," she said.

"Look at where we are standing," said Vic. "I can turn this whole facility over to you if it will help?"

"Thank you," she said, her voice earnest in her appreciation, "But we need somewhere with no affiliations concerning countries and cultures. Somewhere truly international."

"I'm not aware of anywhere that isn't owned by some country or other," said Rob. "Even the smallest speck of land in the middle of the sea is usually claimed by some nation. Antarctica, maybe…"

She shook her head. "Too remote, too difficult logistically. We need somewhere with a certain *prestige*…"

Rob and Vic exchanged glances as she studied the map, wondering where this conversation was heading.

"You're looking for a place that has prestige, is accessible, and is not owned by any particular country?" said Rob.

She ignored them as she continued looking at the map.

"Am I correct in thinking that DVP has some old deep sea rigs?" she asked.

"Too many," said Vic, "I bought them years ago in the hope I could use them for offshore power. No such luck."

"We couldn't find any use for them," said Rob. "We're in the process of taking them apart for scrap."

"Are they serviceable?"

"Aye," said Vic, "Some of them were only in used for a couple of years before we towed them to storage, others would need a refit, but none of them are beyond salvage."

"What are you thinking?" asked Rob. He walked over to the map and stood next to her.

She put her finger on the map, over their precise location. Sliding it eastwards just a little, she hit the prime meridian, zero degrees longitude. With her left hand, she placed a finger on the equator, zero degrees latitude.

Then she began to move her fingers together, following these invisible lines. Her right hand passed down through London, and then Paris before heading south to the Sahara; her left passed through Ecuador and Colombia, and over the Amazon before it struck the Atlantic.

Then her fingertips met, in the blue waters, just south of Ghana.

"Null Island," said Rob, in a whisper.

"What was that?" asked Vic, joining them both.

"Null Island," said Rob. "It's the name given to the fictional place where the equator meets the prime meridian. Zero degrees latitude and longitude. It's a little misleading as there isn't any island at that point at all, just lots of water."

"The centre of Earth," she said to them both.

Vic laughed out loud. "You want my rigs to be towed there – and set up shop? Like some kind of Atlantis rising out of the waves?"

"Is it possible?" she asked.

"Anything is possible," said Vic. "It will cost a small fortune though."

"Then we will need more money," she said.

VII

Vic Macken had a lot of influence over many of the wealthiest people across the planet. He was a member of the entrepreneurial elite, and his contemporaries were friends and industrialists in several varied business sectors, along with others in direct competition in energy and construction. When Vic arranged a meeting in London, for a group of contemporaries to discuss the future of the planet, he knew he could count on those who held him in respect. But once the word was out that such a gathering was taking place, an avalanche of interest came from other globally significant and wealthy business owners from every nation.

Rob looked out on the Conference Room with a sense of awe that such a conglomerate of the elite could come together. It was a grand space that Vic had hired to host the conference. Victorian architecture in red brick, dripping in clean marble, with long windows inlaid with stained glass. It was a suitable location, designed to impress; but more important was the message. They had accommodated just over a thousand people, but only a fifth of them were business owners. The rest were the entourages – financial advisers and accountants, lawyers and their aides. Some had even brought bodyguards.

Rob sat at the top table, along with Vic and Kathryn, looking out at people who held a quarter of the wealth of the entire planet. He stood to introduce the keynote speaker, and some uncertain applause went around the room as she stood up to the dais.

Wearing a grey trouser suit, and her hair tied back, the room went from a murmur to a hush. She smiled at the gathering. Everyone gathered to listen to her in that room would swear that she was addressing them personally, her smile so disarming that their attention was total.

"I'd like to welcome you all here, in this grand hall, during a time of such dire circumstances," she began. "Before I get to the purpose of the meeting, I would like to ask a favour from you all. In the next room, we prepared refreshments and a drinks bar. I would ask that any of you who are not the owners of your businesses go and enjoy this hospitality that Mr Macken has so kindly put on."

Both Rob and Kathryn raised to their feet as a noise of consternation rumbled around the room. The entourages were shaking their heads, advising that they remain in the room.

"I would ask that the only other people to remain are the translators," she added, in response to several confused glances from non-English speaking delegates.

Rob and Kathryn, smiling and being as courteous as possible, began ushering people out as the owners placated their retinues. The room echoed with the chairs scraping across the marble floor as they began to move, and seeing that some were going along with the request, the other Industrialists instructed their people to go along too – as though retaining their advisors and assistants was a show of weakness. Competition between them, it seemed, was still very real, and in this context, useful.

Rob and Kathryn heard much grumbling, in several languages, as the supplementary people departed.

As they entered the other room, Rob pulled the doors closed but exchanged a glance with her on the podium through the glaze. She smiled her thanks back to him and turned back to her stripped-down audience, ready to deliver her speech to them.

Over the next hour, Rob and Kathryn attempted to

entertain the supplementary staff who felt side-lined by the turn of events. Ensuring they had plenty of food and drink, their mission was to placate them while the speaker delivered her message in the hall next door.

At various intervals, Rob looked at her through the doors and, although he could not hear what she was saying, her strong body language conveyed how effectively she communicated her announcements. The expressions of the delegates - at first suspicious and cynical - turned over the course of the hour to become concerned and ended with stony-faced determination.

At the end of her speech, they stood in unison, fist pumping. Applause and cheers echoed throughout the gathering.

VIII

Rob never knew he suffered from seasickness, but as he hung from the deck rail, the ship lurched in the choppy waves of the Atlantic, and he felt his stomach heave. Flying would be easier, he thought, but for now, this was the only way to get to the new location of Null Island.

Construction had begun just over a year before the day of his arrival. They had towed several of the former deep-sea platforms from Scotland to the spot in the ocean where the equator met the prime meridian. Anchored onto the sea floor, they added more rigs as their project gathered investment and momentum – connected with bridges and walkways.

Standing on the deck of an electrically powered ship, it drifted almost silently (but sadly not smoothly) through the ocean. One of the first instructions they had set down was that they must preserve the planet from the moment their project started. With the movement growing beyond scientists and industrialists, the planet had already seen the benefits of living a life conscious of humanity's impact. Climate change had slowed, but not stopped. Habitat destruction had continued, but not increased. It was a start, although the Earth's shield was still weakening.

Even the supports below the rigs had been adapted to create natural underwater reefs for aquatic life. Carefully designed so that none of the utility pipes and cables created any pollution or destruction of habitat.

Just the very week Rob had travelled to Atlantis – a nickname that was starting to stick – he had learned that several governments were trying to ascertain who this influential woman was that was seemingly at the forefront of a global revolution. Many of the leading and respected physicists, economists, environmentalists, geologists and chemists had joined - adding to the industrialists from a wide range of areas, including communication tech, social media, space exploration, energy development and construction. Everyone was welcome it seemed, and the more powerful regimes had begun to see it as a threat. This new way of thinking was a direct challenge to the established order in their countries, and they were worried.

As he looked up from the deck rail, grey on the horizon, he could see the rigs rising from the water. Construction cranes towered over them. As the boat neared the dock, he could see several rigs attached in the central area, creating a platform over a kilometre wide. This area sat over zero degrees.

Null Island.

On its surface, a circular building had begun construction, split down the middle into two chambers. From above, the design resembled the Yin and the Yang.

This symbol had come to represent the Movement, showing as it did the Duality of the universe in a constant state of creation and destruction, but it also signified the Duality of life and death. It was apt that world was adopting the symbol associated with ancient Chinese spiritualism. By a world where faith and science were merging.

In consultation with architects, and funded by Vic, Rob had developed the designs for Atlantis. Other Tech companies funded designs for platforms in the development – with the intention of showing how they could shape the planet to come, given the appropriate investment.

Rob was now convinced that his friend was the most extraordinary person he had ever met. She had the vision, scope and ambition to see it through. She had approved everything that had come her way so long as it fit the narrative of healing the planet and improving life. She was tireless in her endeavours, and yet never lost her temper or seemed stressed no matter the issues they faced.

And they were many.

Rob had seen so many plans that were now gathering pace. Plans undertaken not for profit, but for the survival of the planet and of convincing people that the movement was a force for positive change.

As his sea sickness subsided, a sense of excitement remained in his stomach not caused by the roll of the waves. For the first time in his life, the future held a sense of optimism. The woman he had first seen in a photograph fifteen years earlier in his University office had inspired this.

And if he could believe reports, nobody had found anything on her. Given the resources at the disposal of the countries investigating her, none of them could find a birth record, a name, or anyone from her past.

She was a blank page; they could not figure her out. What were her intentions? Who was she and where had she come from?

Nobody knew, and Rob could not be any happier about this.

IX

In a cavernous hall, stood a lone woman.

She looked left at the director, sitting in the shadows by the side of the stage. He gave her the thumbs up as everything was working as intended. The camera was ready, links to outside broadcasts established, and television networking and internet streaming online.

The smell of freshly applied paint entered her nostrils, but the decorating work on the hall had ceased temporarily while she gave her broadcast. The lighting in the hall turned down in favour of a single spotlight centred on her, standing on the podium, facing the camera. The dark space felt cavernous to her, but full of potential.

In the last moments, before she spoke, she smoothed down her long dress and made sure her tied-back hair was secure. In an unusual step for her, she had allowed a make-up artist to apply her skills. She had bowed to the pressure the director had put on her about her appearance after he had insisted that she could appeal to more people if she looked flawless. She had taken the advice of Kathryn, who had spent her career perfecting the art of public speaking at conferences and sales events. This was on a different scale altogether, but the concept was the same. She did not feel nervous or lacking in self-confidence, she had told Kathryn, but she accepted that she needed to conform to a certain aesthetic for the focus to be on the subject rather than the way she looked.

A silence descended on the hall in the few seconds before she started to speak. A moment later, a red light appeared on the camera, and the director pointed at her to indicate transmission had started.

"It is an honour and a privilege to be standing here today. Speaking to the World. Delivering a message I have spent my life preparing."

She paused and sipped a glass of water placed on the podium, before continuing.

"Who am I? That is a question that I've no doubt many of you will be asking. Who am I? I am nobody. Nobody, because who I am matters not one bit in the grand scheme of the world and the Universe. I am Everybody. Everybody, because my life is of same value as every single person living today.

"Who am I? It is an important question. One that I would suggest we all have to ask ourselves. Duality exists in all of us. We are at once a force for creation. For productivity, for ingenuity, and for love. And yet we are tools of our own destruction. Each of us takes from the world more than we give back. I am no different. Duality exists in me too.

"I have been surrounded by people who believe likewise. Who want to give back to this world. Their genius and foresight have led to this building I now stand in to deliver this speech, here in what we can consider to be the very centre of the surface of the globe. They have also been hard at work delivering important projects that will help humanity move into the future. I would like to demonstrate one such project to you now."

She nodded to the director, who cut to an outdoor camera pointed at a neighbouring platform five kilometres away.

On the platform stood a large circular construction, ten metres wide and sixty metres high, anchored to the platform. At its northern end, pointing directly upwards to the blue sky, sat a barrelled tube. The whole construction resembled a giant snail lying on its back, with its head pointing up. On its circular side were inscribed the words "Space Launch Catapult."

As the viewers watched, the catapult began to vibrate. A tremendous sound as within it the mechanism accelerated. A whirring noise roared from it that increased in tone as the internal workings built to stupefying levels of power. A shot from the barrel: a projectile, flying faster than ten times the speed of sound, the cannon-ball-shape shot upwards. Behind it, two-thousand kilometres of thick cable, wrapped and coiled, starting next to the catapult but laid in the waters around the platform, whipped skywards. Dragged upwards. Moments later, the ground-based camera lost sight of the tip of the projectile as it passed through high-level clouds and haze, but the cable it towed continued travelling skywards, always unravelling.

The camera cut back to the hall. She stood behind the podium, watching the monitor with great interest, as the cable rocketed into space.

"This is just one of the inventions that we are now using to further our aims," she said into the microphone. "The catapult uses kinetic energy, rather than fossil fuels, to launch objects into space. Due to the g-forces involved, we cannot yet launch humans this way, but we can send drones and other objects into orbit – and we have been doing so for years. During this time, we have not been idle. We have not just been building on a man-made island in the Atlantic. We have looked into our future, examining ways this planet can survive and thrive. Scientists and engineers – supported financially by the wealthy who harbour genuine anthropological views – have worked tirelessly. This is all in preparation for what comes next if we have the foresight and desire to do so. More on that later.

"So how have we reached this point? Most of the world is now aware that the Earth is in grave peril. If the Earth's magnetic field disappears then that is the end for us. This is a fact. So what is the point of all this? Why bother?

"Let's face it, if the magnetic field had not been fading away, we would have brought down global destructions on ourselves eventually. Its decline needs to act as a warning to humanity. The damage we've caused both to each other, through wars and terrorism, along with the damage we've caused to the planet - in pursuit of our greed - means that destruction would have been a certainty. So what is happening here, and what solution do we provide?

"This planet has an internal engine that has provided a shield to life. From the very first single-celled organism, through the history of evolution, to the advanced bipedal mammals that now inhabit every corner, this shield has turned the deadly radiation of our parent star into life-giving energy. *Creation*. Many civilisations have worshipped the sun through the centuries, and so they should as it provided the necessary means for life to grow and develop. And yet it contains so much power that if the Earth's shield is turned off, it will cause life to fail. *Destruction*.

"Duality. Creation and destruction. Life and death. It is all around us. Everywhere. Every day. It is the way of the universe. What is happening on this planet, right now, is Duality in action. The universe sees our life as a threat to its continued existence. It needs to remove this infection, get rid of it, and recycle it so that it may – in time – be transformed into something more beneficial to the creation of life across the cosmos. Universal energy flows through us at every moment, and this same energy has slowed down the dynamo of the planet – the very object that creates the protection we need to survive.

"We have to show the universe that we are *worth* protecting. That we can adapt our nature so that we show that this planet is *worth* saving."

She paused to gather herself, before taking a large inhale and continuing her speech.

"I understand that many of you may not agree with my scientific appraisal of our situation. Some may refer to the universe as God. You may have belief and faith that life is divine, given to us by a higher power. I do not wish to dispute this with you, as our goals align. Not one major religion seeks destruction, but through the words of your scriptures, you can interpret the will of nature to be that of creation and rebirth. Faith is not the enemy of scientific endeavour – indeed, the best science springs from articles of faith. To take a leap of belief, to know in your *very being* that something is true is the starting point in our knowledge of the world around us. And as our scientific understanding of the universe expands, and religions absorb the increasing of our knowledge, we find that any barriers between them become blurred. But prayers alone will not save us. Knowledge alone will not save us. It is in deeds that we must show that we can change.

"These deeds must demonstrate our best qualities. They must show that we are a lifeform that can stretch itself out into the stars and be a benefit to the cosmos, rather than a threat. But before we can do that, we must show that we can embrace the planet we call home. We must learn to come together as a single species, rather than fight or live in fear of ideas and cultures contrary to our own. To achieve these aims, I have a proposal to offer. It is a proposal to every single country containing every single human on the planet."

She paused for a moment. Her speech flowed from her effortlessly, but she knew she tended to speak so quickly and passionately, that the message was lost or glossed over. Kathryn had taught her to slow it down and let the words sink in before continuing.

She took a breath.

"I am proposing a global alliance of countries to achieve the common goal. The aim of the alliance is to save the planet first. Bring an end to warfare and violence. Bring an end to the destruction of the natural world. Through this, we save ourselves. Once this is accomplished – and it *will* be accomplished - then we flourish and reach for the stars. Our ultimate destiny lies off this world, exploring the cosmos.

"This alliance will not be based on military protection,

nor is it to give an economic advantage to its members – although, through this alliance, those may become evident over time. This is an alliance of *humanity*. To ensure fairness and equanimity to every living person, and to eliminate prejudice and the fear of others. It is an alliance to *protect* the place we call home. To prevent further damage and to undertake a commitment to healing the planet we have treated so grievously over the centuries. We have named this the *Earth Alliance*.

"How can each nation qualify, and what will this mean for each member state? Sacrifices, accessions and submissions will be required from all. But this will be an alliance based on trust. Trust that those other nations will be making these same sacrifices in the name of a better world for all. Trust that the leaders we place in the positions of power have our best interests at heart. Joining this alliance will validate this trust.

"What must each country do to join the Earth Alliance? First and foremost, it must have free and democratic elections, free from bias and interference – something that the Alliance will verify – and that represents the people and the culture of that nation.

"Secondly, it must embrace the freedom of its citizens by providing laws that protect against any form of prejudice. It must allow for freedom of identity, gender, sexuality, race, faith or no faith, age, differing physical, mental or emotional abilities and allow its people to live the life they want to lead, in so far as it does not harm or oppose anyone else's right to live free. It must be enshrined in law that every single human be treated with equal rights and respect.

"With those fundamental principles in place, it must

also take steps to protect our environment. It must ban the use of fossil fuels to generate power, or for use in vehicles, including aeroplanes, ships, trains and cars. Our atmosphere is so fragile, that an immediate ban on these is necessary, especially in light of innovations that move us away from combustible fuel sources. It must also protect its rivers and waterways, and coastal areas – ensuring that no pollution contaminates the wildlife and ecosystems that rely on them. It must also ban non-biodegradable plastics and microplastics that are suffocating the oceans. New developments, homes and factories, and all new buildings must go through rigorous planning applications which will take into account their environmental impact rather than their economic benefit - in this new world we are building, the planet is more important than wealth. And for countries that hold areas of important and special significance to Earth – such as rainforests and reefs – these areas must be protected from all damage. We must build a metaphorical barrier around these unique and vital systems to protect the future of our home.

"What else must each country do? Once a member of the Alliance, you must disband your military. You won't require them. The council will resolve any disputes diplomatically, and steps taken towards violent and deadly action by a nation will lead to complete expulsion and exclusion from the Alliance, and utter isolation so that very quickly your country will become an anathema to the world. It will sink without a trace. You won't have the resources, the support, the money or the infrastructure to pursue any kind of military campaign against anyone.

"Countries must also destroy all stockpiles they may

have of nuclear and biological weapons and any other weapons of mass destruction. In this new world, planet-killing weapons will be outlawed, and the production of *any* kind of weapon will be strictly controlled.

"Once each nation has removed its threat of arms against another, the borders will no longer be required. Many nations have natural borders, such as islands or rivers, but those lines on a map that delineate one set of sovereign ideas from another will exist on maps only. Your sovereignty will be enshrined as part of the Alliance, but we live in such a world of cultures, that we should be free to move wherever we like. I understand that certain nations will fear the influx and migration of many people to the more affluent areas of the planet, but if our projections are correct, the development across the world will become equal. Anyone rarely wishes to leave a place they consider their home, but are sometimes forced to do so due to warfare or discrimination, or for economic prosperity or the promise of a greater opportunity in another part of the world. Removing the reasons for migration and the movement of populations will come down to the simple question of where I *want* to live, rather than where I *need* to live.

"But I understand that one of the greatest concerns of each country, which rightly values its own cultures and ideals, may still be worried about its own future *identity* if the physical borders between it and another country are removed. We form part of our individual identity from where we are born. Its values, its history and traditions, and its geography. How can we, in this Alliance, promise you that your patriotism will be protected?"

She paused again, moistening her lips with a sip of water, before then looking down at the camera lens directly. As she looked, a sound echoed through the hall. A clanging sound, deep and booming, echoed around the dark spaces around her for several seconds. The single chime of a large bell.

"We have named that the Alliance Bell," she continued, once the resonations had ceased. "That bell sits in the hall next to the one I am standing in right now. I stand in what will become the Council Chamber where delegates will gather. Next to this sits the Chamber of Culture, where we will keep a record of each nation and each culture, recording its history and its decisions as we move forward through time. We will protect your culture. Your cultural leaders – whether through a monarchy, tribal chief, spiritual or presidential – will find a place within the story of your nation. Your way of life will have a dedicated place within the chamber, where all cultures mix and all our wonderful variety will be on display for all to see.

"On entry to the Alliance, we ask for a simple gift from each sovereign nation. A *bell*. It can be of any size. But we will hang it high in the chamber, above the databanks that will contain all there is to know about your culture and way of life. As our ancestors painted their lives on the rock walls of their dwellings, so will we paint our stories in this hall. And as each country joins the Alliance, the bell will ring just once, to indicate its acceptance and its glorious commitment to its people, its future and the entire planet."

She remained silent for a moment, her words permeating the airwaves with the billions listening. Knowing her recorded words would be replayed over again, studied and picked apart.

"I know many of you would consider these goals noble, but ultimately idealist and impracticable. That the world I am describing could never happen, that too many obstacles and difficulties prevent the nations from coming together for the benefit of the planet and each other. I would respond by saying that, *by every measure*, we should try. What do we have to lose? And if you believe the scope of this is too ambitious, then allow me demonstrate to you how ambitious we can be."

Nodding to the director, the camera cut away from her. A black screen was all the viewers could see for several seconds before the drone camera rotated enough so that the blue-white marble of the Earth, as seen from space, came into view. Below it, the green edge of the western coast of Africa spread along the blue of the Atlantic. As the camera spun further, the viewers caught a glimpse of a line extending upwards from the surface and into low orbit. The cable, fired from the catapult, was travelling to its destination. As the end of the cable had reached the limit of the atmosphere, a small flotilla of drones grabbed it. No larger than a metre in size, the drones were powered by jets of air, and operated from Atlantis Base Control. They were directing it toward a massive metal structure, two hundred metres high and fifty in diameter. The structure was convex at its base, tapering off to a series of folded struts at its tip.

"This is Rose One," she said, providing a voice-over for the live feed. "The cable you saw shot from the catapult is being attached to it as we speak."

The drones arrived at the base of Rose One, and sparks flew as specialist welders worked to fix and connect it. The black robots, each spitting forth small, course-correcting jets, swarmed around the cable. Some were workers, and others were observers carrying cameras. After a while, the drones drifted away from the connection, and the viewers could see the whole of the structure. It looked like an unopened rose bud, with its stem extending back down through the atmosphere and the platform from where it had originated.

"Now that the cable is attached, we can go to the next phase," she said.

Silently, operated by a remote ground crew, the bud began to open. The struts at the top began to unfurl and spread outwards. The struts themselves also had folded portions within them, and they too began to spread out. As rose flowers when the sun shines, so did this platform. The bud split and widened, and as it did so, the reflective silver panels caught the sunlight, blinding the cameras for a moment before moving further and further outward. After several minutes, the panels were still extending and unfolding, offering up their silver innards to the power of the nearby star.

"Rose One is now active," she said, unable to hide the pride in her tone.

The reflection of Rose One overwhelmed the lenses in the drones, rendering them blind; but before they lost the feed, the world could see that the structure had extended out for several kilometres on each side, and was still expanding.

The camera cut back to the podium.

"This is our gift to the world," she said, her voice quivering with fulfilment. "Rose One will provide an unlimited amount of clean and permanent energy. Being above our atmosphere, it will receive the maximum possible amount of sunlight, and the platform will convert this to electricity, sending it back down the cable, and powering the planet. Our reliance on planet-killing fossil fuels is over. A new age of clean energy is upon us.

"We at the Earth Alliance have agreed to take a percentage of the GDP of each nation that joins the Alliance. This is not for profit, and will not be going into my pocket. Nor is it going into the coffers of the specialised teams and companies working with the alliance on these ambitions. The money received will go towards global, world-changing projects like this, and their maintenance. Such undertakings will be decided by the Council of Nations with the aim to further humanity, but not at the expense of the planet or individual freedoms. And to show our commitment, we will give the energy provided by Rose One – *for free* – to any nation that joins. Free permanent and renewable energy for all. That is our gift.

"No single leader, no one all-powerful figurehead, will lead the Alliance. Instead, the world's best scientists will ratify every decision made across a range of disciplines, together with economists, environmentalists and philanthropists who will examine the impact in terms of ensuring the continuation of life on Earth. Decisions made will come from the council members that represent each member nation.

"I myself have no desire to lead or to have power or wealth. I am a messenger. I am here to set the path for the planet to walk down, nothing more. However, I promise you that – if we achieve our objectives – I will open up to all of you. Tell you anything about myself that you wish to know. You will know my name.

As she approached the end of her speech, she stopped to take a breath and ready herself for her final statement. The camera focused in on her hands as she clenched them together, clasping them and holding them in front of her.

"The choice between oblivion and survival lies before us. Each of us, every individual, has to make this choice. It is easy for us to continue as we always have done. It is easy for us to go on with our lives, making no changes, and accepting the world the way it is until we can go no further. It is an option. Maybe we don't deserve life. Maybe we don't deserve this beautiful planet. Maybe the universe is *right* to bring about our extinction.

"On the other hand, we can make the hard choice. The choice that requires effort on our part – not just in actions concerning the planet and each other – but also in our *minds*. It is in our nature to hate. It is very easy for us to get angry. It is very tempting for us to accumulate wealth at the expense of others and the natural world. We must overcome these if we are to survive. Our minds can evolve too.

"Look into the eyes of the people you love – your families and your partners and your friends. All across the world, our basic humanity – our very essence - wants to love and be loved in return. But it takes effort to maintain. If we can choose to love, it will beat down every bad decision we have ever made – every small-minded choice made from anger, greed or fear.

"I believe that we *want* to fight. I believe that humanity does not want to leave this Earth and become a footnote in the universe. We must show that we are *not* some kind of cosmic mistake. We must show the universe that we are a species worthy of our place in the great scheme of Time. Be a child of Earth. Be a child of the universe."

She reached the end of her speech, and the feed faded to black.

<u>X</u>

Despite The Atlantis Hotel on Null Island becoming his home away from home, Rob nevertheless marvelled at its construction whenever he was in residency. The organic architecture, built around nature, sustained an ecosystem that recycled all the waste products produced by human activity. Trees, bushes and flowers growing in and around the structure and the gentle tinkling of fountains and pools gave a tropical aesthetic, and provided a home to humming birds, small colourful fish and dragon-flies.

The hotel served as living accommodation for the island's workers, along with the global delegations and diplomats that arrived by air and sea.

Rob picked the hotel to host his fiftieth birthday party, and he stood, champagne in hand, at an open window, watching a small slice of paradise play out in one of the many water holes as the humming birds hovered over pink and purple orchids, their bell-shaped flowers providing their sweet succour. Beyond this scene, in the distant haze, the thick cable of Rose One extended vertically. Scaffolding sat around the base as the next phase of construction had begun – a space elevator – to enable the quick and clean transition off the planet in search of resources.

Rob was not fond of parties, he would have preferred a more conservative celebration, but Vic had insisted. The Scotsman was putting himself about around the plush room, talking to the hundreds invited from across the world. Over the years, the Earth Alliance – with Vic and Rob at the helm – had made many strides and made many friends. In reaching his half-century, he felt it a time for reflection rather than a celebration; but Vic had insisted they make a big deal out of it.

Even Kathryn Powell had come out of retirement to attend, and she was looking her usual immaculate self, laughing along with Vic's booming voice. It had been a couple of years since she had visited the Island, as she had retired to New Zealand, and all the operations staff were delighted to see her, along with the corporate affiliations she had managed to attract.

As Rob sipped his champagne, watching his party from a distance with both Vic and Kathryn being convivial, he felt one notable absentee.

The figurehead of the Earth Alliance was in residence on the Island, he knew, but from her instruction, nobody tracked her movements. She made appearances whenever she needed to, but otherwise came and went to her own schedule. Given her tireless international visits delivering the message and ethos of the Alliance, they respected her privacy whenever she was present.

Realising that he was neglecting the guests that had made the party, Rob went over to join Vic. The Scotsman was busy talking about Rose One - how it had transformed the development of the countries that had joined. Free power generation provided the bedrock of economic and social development for the poorer and militarily weaker nations that had flocked to sign up. Respecting the caveats to join, they saw an immediate rise in their living standards, with growth coming through better quality education for their populations, along with freedom of movement for those that had signed the Treaty. Around one hundred nations' bells had rung within the decade since the Alliance was formed, but the wealthier countries – the ones that had traditionally held the balance of power – had resisted. The nations with freer, democratic systems had acknowledged the noble aims of the Alliance; but due to the stringent conditions for joining, had resisted signing up. Nations with less liberty, the ones with nationalist governments or dictatorships, had portrayed the Alliance as evil and in opposition to their way of life and culture. This had come as no surprise to anyone.

"The tighter they hold on to power," said Vic, addressing the issue to his audience, "The more they will lose it."

Rob nodded his agreement with his assertion. Rose One had been Vic's pet project as they commenced the work on Null Island, and he had made corporate connections through DVP – especially with the US Company that had designed the Space Catapult - to make sure his dream was realised. Since it came online, it had hooked up over three billion people to its limitless energy. Plans were in place to build Rose Two in the Atacama Desert of Chile, and Rose Three in either the Gobi Desert in Mongolia or the Western Desert of Australia depending on whether they joined the Alliance, as was looking likely.

Eighteen months before Rob's fiftieth, the Alliance had celebrated when the final African nation – Egypt – had become a member. Investment in these nations where power was free, borders were open, and conflicts eliminated, grew exponentially. The rest of the world watched on with interest, and mounting envy.

Smaller nations on other continents also joined, which posed challenging logistics on how to extend the power cables to these geographically isolated places. Many joined by necessity, their survival threatened by climate change and rising sea levels.

At this time, Rob took it upon himself to provide a solution to these issues. Together with his team, he hatched a plan.

The Saharan Canal.

Vast swathes of northern Africa were uninhabitable. Rising temperatures meant that even the nomadic peoples of the desert could no longer survive in these areas. Rob's ambitious plan posed that he created a human-made waterway extending from the Atlantic coast of western Africa, where the sands met the sea, to the now dried-up crater that was once Lake Chad. Following the natural contours of the desert landscape, this waterway would be around half a kilometre wide and almost three thousand kilometres long. At regular intervals along the canal, where the geology allowed, lakes filled with carbon-munching plankton formed part of the excavation, combating the pollution in the atmosphere. Such a huge canal would require trillions of litres of water, which would lower global sea levels.

As a secondary impact of this, the earth removed during the canal's construction provided material for coastal defences in places threatened by flooding.

Irrigation of the Sahara would turn the desert green once again, the crops produced would feed a burgeoning population, and natural havens created for wildlife. Rob had predicted that such large-scale vegetation would turn the arid landscape into a sub-tropical paradise, again causing the reduction of global temperatures due to the presence of water-vapour cloud cover; and it would provide opportunities for new settlements and townships to grow, reducing the burdens on over-populated cities.

As Rob sipped his champagne, construction on the canal was due to begin in a fortnight, with the electrically powered cranes and earth-movers gathering to commence work. It would take decades, but its schedule completed piecemeal as locks at each stage accepted water fed by the ocean. His sense of pride in this future accomplishment outweighed everything he had ever done. When the Alliance Council signed off on the project, he could not have wished for a greater birthday gift.

As he discussed the workings of the project with a Mauritanian diplomat, a hush descended on the room. The general chatter of voices was suddenly subdued as the doors to the room opened and a figure entered.

She always carries herself so gracefully, thought Rob, as she made her way through the crowd toward him. Smiling and courteous to those that greeted her, she made her way through them. This legendary figure, her hair flowing behind her, instilled awe and an air of mystique from the gathering. As promised, she held no power, no sway over the council – but her thoughts always lingered on the presence of Duality above all else. The universe around her, and humanity's place within it.

And yet, as she approached Rob thought she looked unusually careworn. The manner of her gait, a few extra lines on her expression, he could not place it, but he got the sense that she was putting on a brave face.

Reaching Rob, she embraced him. It was warm and full of love, and he accepted it gratefully.

"Happy Birthday," she whispered in his ear. He realised that they had never celebrated her birthday, as nobody knew when it was. Knowing that this was her choice, his brief and very British guilt dissipated.

"Thank you," he replied, picking up a glass of champagne from a table and handing it to her. "Is everything okay?"

She took him to one side, away from the guests. Smiling at him, the lines around her eyes displayed another emotion – that of sadness.

"Rob, I'm going to have to take a little time to myself," she said.

He was not sure how to reply. She had never taken any time off since the inception of the Alliance, diligently going about delivering the message and the cause; and yet if anyone deserved a holiday, it was she.

"Is everything okay?" he asked.

"I need a little time. Just to collect my thoughts. Reinvigorate myself."

It was the first time that he had known her to admit any kind of fragility. Concern arose in him.

"Can I help in any way," he asked. "Has something happened?"

She touched his arm affectionately. "This is just something I have to do," she said. "I'll be away for a month or so, but I'll be back and ready for what comes next."

"I see," said Rob. "Where will you go?"

"Home," she said. "I'll be going home."

XI

Across the Serengeti Plain, the distant mountains were framed in lilac skies. Their edges curved the horizon. A distant thunderstorm rumbled a few kilometres away.

The night was warm, but she did not mind. The thunderstorm was far enough away for it to lull her close to the edge of sleep as she reclined on the lounger she had positioned on the upper floor of the lodge. Downstairs, the walls closed off the structure to the elements, but the upper floor was open on all sides, just roofed with narrow, wooden pillars, and gave an excellent vantage point for the plain. A haven for anyone wishing to spot wildlife.

It was indeed remote. Small villages dotted the plains, but the nearest large town lay fifty kilometres away. The lodge itself, built two years ago, followed the environmentally-friendly guidance issued by the Alliance for all new constructions - built from sustainable wood – two trees being planted for every one used – and powered by the new infrastructure that threaded across Africa.

The Alliance hierarchy had been surprised when she announced that she wished for isolation. They had never suspected that she desired solitude as she had given no previous indication, but she now felt it important to sequester herself away, at least for a short time. One month, she said. Although her announcement had come as a surprise, the respect she had from everyone was one of complete acceptance. Over the last decade, she had travelled the world, speaking to delegations and diplomats, answering questions from governments, doing television interviews and school visits. Indeed, once the Alliance members heard her request, they expressed surprise that she had not taken any time off before.

Not wanting to reveal her reasons for being alone, now it was important for her to do so. She had dedicated her life to the cause, but so many obstacles presented themselves every single day that she had begun to lose sight of the overall objective – to have the entire world join the Alliance. She needed to reconnect. Quiet the multitude of thoughts and issues going through her mind.

But another, more personal, reason had occurred. As usual, she had kept this to herself for fear of being a global distraction.

On the table next to where she sat lay an urn. A vessel made of white marble but decorated around the sides with images of stars and planets. The lid itself was fashioned as a yellow sun, with rays streaming out of it. As she drifted through a half-sleep, she looked at it affectionately.

She couldn't fall asleep – not tonight. She wanted to stay awake and see the dawn. Rubbing her face with her palms, she stood up, went over to the edge of the floor, and looked out over the plain. The scent of rain was in the air, accompanied by the low rumbling of the storm that was travelling further away, but she could not see anything in the darkness. Around the corners of the roof overhang, low-powered electric lanterns swung in the night breeze, surrounded by nocturnal flying insects.

By the side of her chair, next to the urn, lay her favourite possession. She typically shunned any form of ownership or material wealth, but she did keep sentimental ones. The album held photographs from her life. Regarded as old-fashioned, when electronic devices were used to store still images, to have printed photographs stored in a book; she took great comfort in looking at her past and reliving the moments that counted.

Picking up the album, she stood in the pool of light created by the lantern. In the dimness, she flicked past the first few pages. She had spent many of her years looking at these early pages from her life, and could recount the images without concentrating; instead, she moved to the start of when the Alliance was founded, around halfway through the book.

The first photo was of her, along with Robert Birch, Vic Macken and Kathryn Powell, standing at the entrance to the Halls back in Atlantis – the huge double doors that opened into the Council Chamber. It had been empty then, but now member states filled around half of the chamber. Just out of shot was the great globe they had commissioned in the plaza just outside of the Hall. The plaza was a great circular space. In the centre stood a giant globe, four metres high and sculpted from bronze. Held up on the back of Atlas.

Below this photo was one of her delivering her follow-up speech to the United Nations. That treaty organisation had felt as though its mission were similar to that of the Earth Alliance, but its member states had less stringent caveats for membership. She had argued in her speech that, although their goals were noble, the UN had outlived its purpose, and that it was relatively toothless against the ravages of war and environmental catastrophe. A single powerful nation could veto any action taken, or simply give its subjective version of events to serve its interests, rather than the planet as a whole. Certain countries had too much sway and influence over the council, and it was becoming increasingly irrelevant with the Alliance forefront in the minds of world populations. It was a blistering speech, which left the delegates reeling as they heard many truths called out. From the time of her speech, the UN still existed, but in a diminished capacity. Nevertheless, its members had voted to support the Earth Alliance due to its aligned intentions.

In the next photograph, a picture of happier circumstances as she met the heads of all the major religions on the planet. They met at Null Island, in the Chamber of Culture, as she showed them around each of their dedicated sections, which contained databanks listing the history of their religions and all the verses and tenets from their holy texts. The Chamber was open to all visitors, and now that a full airstrip ran the length of a linked island, visitor numbers had increased. She had worn a head scarf in deference to her guests who all met together for the first time in memory, and had agreed that the Alliance was holy and righteous. The photograph itself was her standing at the arched doors of the Chamber entrance flanked by the leaders of the Catholic, Islamic, Judaic, Hindu, Sikh, Buddhist and Shinto faiths.

Turning the page, she came to a picture showing Rob and Vic standing at the very base of the cable that led up to Rose One, taken on the first day construction started on the Elevator. The platform where the cable arrived at sea level now expanded to accommodate the huge number of transformers and batteries required to store the energy. It had become so massive that it had grown to double the size of Null Island itself. A kilometre long bridge connected them with a monorail that moved people back and forth along it.

Soon after construction had finished on the power network, stage two of their plans kicked in. Space was the ultimate destination for humanity. In the expanse, the people of Earth could find an unlimited amount of every raw material they required. At that very moment, the Alliance had sent exploration drones to all the planets, moons, and asteroids within the solar system to search for possible locations for mining. But they needed to get people into orbit quickly, efficiently and cleanly. The cable attached to Rose One provided a wonderful opportunity to build an attached Space Elevator. The photograph showed Rob and Vic laying the first piece of the carbon framework that would extend up to orbit. It was another long-term project but was now attracting investment from every company eager to seek the wealth of the stars.

Flipping her page, she came to her final photograph. It was a simple shot of her standing amongst the dunes on the coast of West Africa, pointing out at the blue Atlantic. In the distance, stood the white domes of a village. The population of that village had been dwindling in recent decades as temperatures soared and families departed to areas that were more temperate. This location would be where the Saharan Canal would begin.

The countries of the Alliance had seen huge growth and development. With education and environmental standards came innovation and development. More countries wanted in. All the countries of Africa were now member states, along with all the islands in the Pacific and Indian Oceans. South American nations were in the process of reaching the requirements to join, which pleased the Alliance due to the increasing threat posed to the Amazon – the chance to protect and preserve that region was at the forefront of the their aims. But now, also, more liberal countries in Europe, Asia and North America who valued happiness and the environment above all else were seeing the growth of political movements subscribing to Duality and the goals of the planet.

Just before she came to the Serengeti, she had heard some encouraging news from the Alliance scientists spread across the world. They monitored the magnetic field constantly. Although still in a weakened state, it was not worsening. It was at a critical balance point where further erosion could undo all they had achieved concerning the elimination of pollutants and the taming of the human race. Most planetary scientists now agreed that human activity was responsible, and urged greater acceptance of the Alliance's terms.

And yet still just over half the planet had to accept the Alliance and were showing no interest in joining. Wealthy nations of Europe, the US and Russian Federation, the subcontinent, and the Far East had not been willing to surrender their arms and had all their industry and transportation geared around oil. Afraid of losing the historic power and influence they had globally, they held the Alliance at arms-length – acknowledging its aims but refusing to commit to them. In countries where freedom was valued, strong Alliance movements were forming and gathering pace amongst the populace that had begun to find a voice. In countries less free, protests had been put down – violently in some instances – by a population seeking regime change.

She felt frustrated in particular in these countries where powerful individuals kept control with iron fists, but knew that change came with time. Ageing leaders would not live forever, and these places were fast becoming so isolated with the rest of the world that even the most calculated dictator could not hold back the opportunities presented. Time mended all, and they were becoming increasingly aware that history would judge the forward-thinking leaders positively.

The hurricane of thoughts drifting through her mind, the tasks she needed to achieve, the people she needed to speak to, and the pressure of being the figurehead of the Alliance contrasted sharply with the peace and calm around her. The far-off storm had drifted away, and calmness had descended in the dusk around her.

Dawn was near.

Casting a glance at the urn once again, she fought against her drowsiness. It was her favourite time of day. An almost dreamlike transition from the death of night into the morning and the return of life. A gentle breeze stirred the grasses and leaves in the trees around the lodge, tousling her hair.

The horizon silhouette became clearer as it began to glow with orange phosphorescence, revealing the distant mountaintops in clear relief. Nearby, a single birdcall pierced the air, followed by a chorus of melodious birdsong in response, swelling and ebbing in chirruping intensity. She closed her eyes and listened to them, curious as to what they were saying – and whether they were praising the coming of the sun.

Throaty bellows from wildebeests met the symphony of

birdsong as they rose from wary slumber, herding together and feeding in the dusty meadows. Puncturing these deep murmurings, the unmistakable roar of the lions echoed over the plains as if to say - be aware, we are watching.

Opening her eyes once again, she walked over to the urn and picked it up. Moving it to the veranda railing overlooking the plain, she watched as stars twinkled out one by one above her.

At first, it was just a golden edge, hazy and dissipated by the atmosphere, but it moved quickly, forming from the horizon, and melting in reverse. The curve of the first rays cast light across the plain, blooming in her eye-line. As the glare passed, golden light illuminated all. The brown-green grasses, the tall trees, with high crowned leaves reachable only by the giraffe, and the parched riverbanks offering the promise of water from the overnight storm.

She released the lid of the urn, exposing the ashes to the air flowing on her platform. Taken up in the breeze, the ashes drifted out of the lodge and over the plain. They seemed to pick up the morning rays, glinting as the dawn broke, forming eddies and dancing before her eyes.

Nobody had ever seen her cry. But here, in the beautiful morning of the world, pure as the joy and hope of tomorrow's dream, the tears flowed unabated.

XII

He had returned to Macken House to die.

Surrounded by tubes and lines, feeding him morphine for the pain, and an oxygen facemask, Vic's life was nearing its end. A private nurse had offered him as much comfort as she could, under instruction from his doctor, who could do no more for him other than make his last moments more comfortable.

Rob sat beside the bed of his friend. Even though he had never lived at Macken House, he felt a sense of homeliness when he visited the place, as though the walls, the decorations, and the furniture spoke to him somehow. He could not explain it. Even the lake seemed to be an old friend.

At the window, gazing out through the rain-spattered glaze at the mountainous reflections in Loch Lomond, stood the woman they had grown to know and love over the decades. She had become the most famous person on Earth, her every move scrutinised by the media and her every word studied by scholars. And yet she had never forgotten her humanity. She had never regarded herself as greater or different from anyone else around her. When she heard that Vic had hours, rather than days, remaining she had jumped on the first hydrogen jet flight from Washington – despite having diplomatic talks remaining with the still-abstaining US president. Americans, it seemed, were still reluctant to part with their guns and their gasoline – this despite most of the planet now moving to cleaner and free energy, and consigning weapons to history books. The holdout nations were part of the old guard, still distrustful of other countries' intentions should they let their defences down. They had found that their new enemy was inflation as the Alliance now tended only to trade within due to the huge tariffs imposed.

Vic stirred into consciousness, his face scrunched in pain. Nevertheless, he lifted the oxygen mask from his mouth so he could speak to them, before pressing a button by his bedside that increased the painkiller flooding into him intravenously.

Recognising the glare from the window wasn't helping, she closed the blinds, sinking the room into a half-light.

"How are you?" asked Rob.

Despite the pain, Vic managed to give him a withering look showing how much of a silly question that was.

Joining them at his bedside, she took Vic's hand in hers and laid her other hand on his brow. A calmness seemed to descend on the room, and his tenseness abated. Taking a seat, her expression was full of love and concern.

"What do you think of the house?" asked Vic, his speech slurring as he slipped around a conscious state.

"It's beautiful," she said. "The view is extraordinary."

"Aye, it is," he said. "This is the only place I would want to be."

Despite their long years of association, she had never visited Macken House. Even in his final moments, Vic could not help wanting to impress her. Even the four-poster bed he lay in displayed opulence and style.

"To have a place to call home is very important," she said.

"I never thought I would die," said Vic, "And I don't want to. Money seems to make you think you're going to live forever."

"Nobody lives forever," she said.

For a few moments, he struggled. Discomfort and pain squirming within him as the flesh began to lose the battle. After a while, he managed to take a few breaths and quietly uttered a question.

"What happens when we lose life?"

Vic had his eyes closed, not addressing either of them in particular. He may have been asking the universe at large. Rob answered first.

"I like to think that, at the moment of death, we see everyone we have ever cared about that has gone before us – smiling, welcoming. I don't believe in an afterlife, but I do believe that as your reality alters, your mind will show you the way. Once mortality is no longer part of your experience, the energy of your body will still form that part of you that is human. We are so much more than flesh and blood and interconnected neurons. The choices we make, the things we believe in, will give you this transition into otherness – and whatever it may bring. For most of us, we will see the people we have loved at the moment of death. That is what I like to believe."

Vic remained silent, his breathing growing more difficult with each passing second. She simply gazed at him with a look of profound love. Then she began to speak, forming her words carefully and speaking in a deep, clear tone.

"Your consciousness belongs to the universe. You are part of it and are made from it. Dying is a transformative state where you become one with the cosmos. When we look up into the night sky, we see stars whose light has travelled for many thousands of generations. Like starlight, your life leaves an impression on the world you leave behind, in the memories of those who have known you, and in the ways you have changed the planet during your time. In your final moments, think about what you have achieved. Think of the world that now exists because you took a chance on a young woman who you found in your office.

"Don't be afraid. You came from the cosmos, and you are returning. You are going home, and the world you leave behind is grateful – life will flourish because one slightly grumpy Scotsman decided to use his gifts to benefit us all. The memory of you will live long throughout history, and your name will be celebrated. The very stuff you are made from, that came from the fiery furnace at the heart of a star, will be given back into the universe – death is the necessary recycling of life into something a little more perfect. It is the beginning of creation. Death and life. Duality."

She whispered the words to him, and a tranquillity passed across his face. His chest rose more slowly, and he closed his eyes forever. Placing her hand back on his forehead, she waited for the few moments of his passing, a single tear rolling down her cheek, and falling on her shirt.

Rob gazed at her in awe, before he turned to his friend lying still on the bed. He placed Vic's hands on his chest, and bid him a silent farewell.

"We will honour you," he said.

XIII

In the darkness of the Council Chamber, the space throbbed with anticipation. A thousand people in their seats in the darkened room: delegates from across the world. Councillors from the member states, some of whom had been attending for decades, remembered when the chamber was mostly empty. Others who had arrived recently found themselves at the centre of extraordinary times.

Despite the palpable excitement, the chamber was silent. The delegates did not utter a word or even shift in their seats. A complete hush hung over all.

On the podium at the head of the Hall, a single spotlight illuminated. Reminiscent of the historic speech that began it all. It cast a pool of light, a white dot, on the dais.

She stepped into the light, in front of the podium. Her once dark hair now flecked with grey and her skin creased with the years of life.

She was beaming.

Her eyes shone in the glint of the spotlight, and her cheeks wrinkled with the size of her smile that showed her white teeth. An expression of pure joy.

To her right, a holographic image of the Earth appeared. It began as a three-dimensional globe, transparent, and with the outlines of the nations of the Earth showing as it rotated. One by one, the countries began to glow green on the globe in order of joining the Alliance. As the globe spun, more of the land masses completed the jigsaw. At the same time, surrounding the image, a faint haze appeared around it that represented the magnetic field. It did not obscure the planet below, but it became more concentrated and complete.

Soon Africa was completely green, joined with various countries in Europe, the Middle East and the island nations of the Pacific. It seemed to stall for a moment, the haze surrounding the planet hovered, and it took a few rotations before Canada and Japan joined along with South and Central America. Most of the smaller Asian nations then followed, along with mainland Europe, Oceania, and then Scandinavia. After a few more rotations, the only countries left were India, China, Russia, the UK and the USA. The world continued to rotate.

With every new territory, the shield covering the planet became more distinct – from a shimmering blue glow to a surface resembling liquid – like looking at the globe under crystal waters.

The planet rotated further, and the five countries remained black.

From the adjacent Hall, echoing through the council chamber came the sound of a bell. It was low in tone, but deep and booming, and resonated throughout the room. Then came another – at a higher pitch, but still having a depth of sound. The third was higher still, and the fourth. The final fifth was the highest. The vibrations of the sound flowed through the floor, ceiling and walls - the delegates feeling it through their seats.

An expectant pause came over the audience. Tense anticipation.

The five remaining countries turned green.

Silence.

A wave hit the delegates, a sonic zephyr with a blast of a pillow strike. Originating from the Chamber of Culture, over two hundred bells rang in unison. Striking in a cacophony of golden, joyous noise.

The delegates rose to their feet in a unified wave of jubilation, joy, and amazement. Cheers erupted along with tears streaming down their faces. She stood on the podium, her arms outstretched as if she wanted to embrace every single person in the crowd.

The bells rang out across the island they had created, but they tolled for all.

They rang as, in the depths of the ocean, humpback whales sang their ethereal song surrounded by dappled sunlight. In the reefs, multi-coloured clown fish drifted amongst the swaying corals and anemones and bottlenose dolphins skimmed the surface as they raced each other.

They rang in a Chinese hospital, heard alongside the first cries of the new-born arrived to tired and emotional parents, holding the little boy in their arms; born into a world moving together for the first time since the dawn of civilisation.

They rang in the Amazon Rainforest, where an iguana padded along a fallen tree, each step placed, its head and eyes flicking around, but still not spotting camouflaged jaguar until it was too late. The predator leapt from the undergrowth, claws and fangs bared.

They rang in in the school room in Mali, where the new village had grown around a farming community, irrigated by the Saharan Canal, tall green crops hissing in the breeze. In the classroom, a teacher pointed at the blackboard with his chalk and asked a question. Twenty tiny hands shot up in the air.

They rang in Northern regions of Canada, where a polar bear mother curled up with her cubs in her icy den, her maternal instinct strong to keep her offspring warm while an arctic storm raged outside.

They rang in the Swiss Alps, where two young women just reaching adulthood, climbed the summit overlooking Lake Lucerne, where the snow-capped mountains overlooked the glassy water. One helped the other up a final rock face, pulling her up with her arms; and as she came to eye level, they knew it was love.

They rang as the condor glided over the Peruvian Andes, soaring on the thermals created by the mountains and the valleys. In the warm and cloudless skies, it uttered a single cry.

They rang as the astronauts floating around their station listened to them in low-Earth orbit; watching the footage on their monitors at the top of the Space Elevator. The hum of Rose One feeding power to the world.

They rang as the drones scoured the asteroids between Mars and Jupiter, surrounded by billions of points of light across the vastness of space, searching for the valuable minerals Earth needed, as automated mining machines stood by to fill their cargo holds ready to ship back to their home world.

They rang.

And the universe listened.

It listened as, for the first time in the long history of the planet, a single species came together to ask that most fundamental question.

Who are we?

It listened as energy flooded into the nucleus at the very centre of this cosmic atom of consciousness, the core of the Earth generating a magnetic field once again, and growing stronger by the moment.

It listened as time flowed forwards, confident that in this place, a lifeform would look outwards at the Grand Scheme: the preservation of the energy of awareness, rather than within at itself.

This species was worthy of its place.

It could stand tall in the pantheon of the cosmos.

These bells echoed at a far greater distance than anyone in the Chamber could fathom.

As she stepped down from the stage, the hem of her

long robes floated around her ankles. She walked up the central aisle, the euphoria in the hall reaching a crescendo. Some of the delegates close by reached out to touch her sleeves as she drifted past them. Turning her head left and right, the smile on her face clear for all to see, she bowed respectfully. This was *their* time. Time to move forward as a single planet, a united but diverse civilisation, celebrating the wonderful variety that brought colour to humanity. It would be up to these people to make sure they continued progressing to a future full of optimism and hope. To prevent any backward steps and any slide back into mistrust and the destruction of nature.

As she walked up the carpeted aisle, she approached the entrance to the Chamber's closed double doors. Stood next to them was Robert Birch – his face reflecting the joy of his constant companion during his adult life. As she neared, they embraced. Such emotion, such elation, such excitement for the future – Rob felt it overwhelm him.

The planet saved.

Nature saved.

Humanity would go on.

He recalled their first meeting, all those years ago, in a chilly park in the centre of his home city, his feelings of cynicism soon overcome by the truth of which she spoke. He thought of the close call everybody on the planet had managed to avoid because they chose to *listen*, and chose to *believe*, the evidence before their eyes.

As she returned his gaze, her own journey welled up within her. A journey that began long before Rob met her. A journey that began before she had been born to the world, but which gathered pace as her first cries fell on the ears around her.

Her mother had told her that she was her miracle.

Many years later, when she had been in her late teens, Rob had said to her, "I don't believe in miracles, I believe in cold, hard science."

To which she replied, "We are *all* miracles, every one of us. Science is the very study of miracles."

That simple conversation remained with them for their entire lives.

Rob turned and threw open the doors. Equatorial sunlight streamed in, warm and comforting. It basked them both in white light. The sound of the ringing bells echoed across the island and the waves.

Striding outside the Hall, and into the sunshine, she looked down the stone steps that led to the Plaza. In the circular space, the bronze statue of Atlas holding up the globe dominated the paved area. Around the Plaza, along the edges, media had gathered – their television and streaming cameras recording her every move, drone cameras buzzing around – it was the final part of the planned ceremony.

On her own, she made her way down the steps, the planet following her every move, and she stood in front of the circular sculpture. The ringing bells seemed clearer in the open air, and they seemed to ring up to the skies.

Still smiling, she nodded and gates opened on all sides of the Plaza. From each gate sprang children. From all nations, from all cultures and beliefs, they had come to Atlantis to celebrate. They ran, excited and giggling. As this day became a global holiday, each child was eight years old on that day and it would be a birthday they would never forget. She encouraged them to gather, and they did so, over two hundred children surrounded the sculpture of the planet.

Soon they were in a ring, and as the cameras panned around them, they saw the excitement and happiness written on their faces. Faces of every hue, wearing clothing representative of their cultures and their beliefs. Hijabs and Kippahs mixed with tribal headgear from Africa and South America, western clothing mixed with traditional outfits from the Far East – and they all formed a great circle.

She stood, her back to the Council Hall she had emerged from, holding the hands of the children on either side of her. Each child reached out and grasped the hand of their neighbour. The innocence of childhood showing the world that race and culture were not a boundary to friendship.

Once they had gathered, holding hands around the world, she encouraged them to start swinging their arms together. Laughing and looking at each other, this the proudest day of their young lives, they joined in.

Arms swinging, they reached their zenith – as the bells all rang in one huge final peal – and reached up to the sky.

The memory of that day remained in the collective consciousness of humankind, and the footage immortalised the joyous occasion. Statues were erected in celebration - each depicting a child frozen in time in matching bronze, hand-in-hand, their solidarity forming a ring around the world.

At the head of the circle, sculpted by the loving hands of a grateful planet, a bronze representation of the woman who showed the planet the way to its bright future. A woman who led the world in celebration of life within the cosmos. A woman who would be remembered in history as a messiah for *everyone*, regardless of belief, culture and way of life.

Below the statue lay a bronze plaque, it's writing in bas-relief:

TRUST IN
THE WISDOM
OF GAIA

Epilogue – The Return

The wheels of the Range Rover came to a halt on the dusty road, just a couple of metres away from the temporary barriers. They stated road closed, but in reality, the dusty carriageway had disappeared completely, along with half the hillside.

The driver's car door opened, and Amy Hunter stepped out into the warmth and sunshine. She cast a glance over the bay at the Pitons, their verdant twin peaks pointing at the blue sky. Their beauty stirring memories within her.

A light breeze ruffled her hair as she closed the car door, and she stepped towards the barriers. Beneath her feet, the reddish gravel on the road crunched as she approached.

She moved past the blockade and watched her footing as she moved to the edge. The road had collapsed into a rocky, tumbledown cliff. Sheared from the island, it had fallen, leaving tonnes of rocks and boulders littering the sea below. Glittering, the Caribbean had claimed the land and everything built on it. No sign of her home or of Vix – buried and submerged under rock and water. Amy leaned over as far as she dared, trying to spot a roof tile, or section of manifold, or a duct pipe.

But nothing remained.

Everything from her former life vanished. Swallowed up by natural forces.

The slope rose on her right side, and she held onto the thick stem of a fern that grew over the edge, so she could see the water lapping the rocks below.

Gathering herself, she could feel her own emotion rising within her. This was a very personal journey, but one she had to make.

"Are you here?" she asked, speaking to the air around her.

"Are you here, John? Somewhere, listening to me?"

The sea breeze was her only reply. She sighed and shook her head.

"Truth is - you could be anywhere. Anywhere in space and anywhere in time. But it was here – *right here* – where you left me for the second time. So I suppose it is as good a place as any."

She folded her arms, embraced herself, and looked out.

"It was exactly a year ago today. I had to be here. I had to at least try to make sense of it all…"

Pausing for a moment, she collected her thoughts, swallowing hard.

"When all this…happened…the island launched an inquiry. With everything else going on… well it wasn't very thorough. They decided it was down to the hurricane and then the tsunami weakening the rocks and causing a landslide. They put your death down as an accident brought on by natural causes and closed the matter. Samuel and I did not see cause to debate that decision, under the circumstances…

"Samuel retired and moved to Miami to live with his son. And I went back to England. I needed to get away from here, from *people*. So many asking questions. So many looking at me with distrust. They did not know why, but they believed I brought the misfortune down on their island. So I did what I've always done, I secluded myself away.

"I moved back to England and lived with your mother for a while. I didn't go out and did not see anyone. Instead, I finished my thesis. But I had no desire to make it public. People don't want to hear that the world is about to end, and with Vix destroyed, I had no way of proving it. I would've faced ridicule.

"I watched the news and heard about everything going on in the world. I couldn't get enough of it. I became obsessed with every global conflict, and every natural disaster."

The weight of the moment pulled her to the edge of the cliff, and her trembling knees gave way. The cool earth felt soothing against her skin as she collapsed into a kneeling position, clutching handfuls of soil so tightly that its granules fell through her fingers like sand. She lifted her voice with fervour and intensity.

"Seeing humanity at its worst. Every gun fired, every explosion, every tragic death. Hearing reports of extinctions across the world, the oceans poisoned by the plastic we use, the sea levels rising because of our pursuit of wealth. We don't *deserve* to be part of this planet. We don't *deserve* to be part of the universe."

She took a deep breath.

"I felt shame. Shame to be born into this world of hatred and ugliness. Let humanity fail. Let the World *burn*..."

The emotion swelled within her, a mix of grief and anger, her inner turmoil spilling over. She hated the world. She hated what it had become.

"That's what I thought. That's what I *believed*..."

Her watery eyes shone in the sunshine as her feelings broiled and swayed.

But then a change came over her. The pain replaced by another emotion.

"That's what I believed," she repeated.

"...But not anymore," her eyes turned skyward.

"Not now...," she spoke between sobs.

"...I don't know if it was you who showed me the way, or universe – maybe that's the same thing – but we *have* to go on. We have to *forgive*. We have to *survive*."

The earth crumbled between her fingers as she grasped the edge of the land before her.

"That night," she began, but her words failed her for a moment, as her thoughts and feelings clashed in her mind.

The unanswered question that she needed to ask.

"That *last* night...when we were together. Did you...*fix*...me?"

Her tears flowed down her cheeks and dripped onto the Earth, absorbed and drawn away.

She rose to her feet, wiping the moisture from her face with her palms. Taking a deep, composing, breath, she stood for a moment, gazing out to sea.

Crossing back through the barrier, she approached the rear of the car, and opened the passenger door. Reaching inside the cool interior, she fiddled with the seatbelts.

Standing, she held the swaddled blankets in the crook of her arm.

The baby woke and looked up at her mother, her tiny face moving between expressions. Amy smiled down at her daughter, her hand caressing her fine jawline, and went back to the barrier.

Moving her shoulder, Amy showed off her child to sea and the sun, her face now a mask of contentment and steely-eyed resolution.

"She arrived three months ago," she said. "Samuel came over and helped deliver her. I'm going to raise her and educate her myself, keep her out of the chaos of the world. Try and keep her pure."

The little girl cooed and babbled, and Amy giggled back down at her, stroking her gentle cheeks.

"I named her Gaia, after your grandmother – do you remember us discussing?"

Amy looked out at the sea once again, allowing the rays to warm her face before she looked back down at her daughter. Her large brown eyes looked back at her.

"She's so beautiful," said Amy, focusing on her face.

"She has your eyes…"

As the light caught Gaia's irises, they glinted white.

About the Author

Many thanks for reading my debut novel, years in the making, and I hope that you have taken as much from the story as I have in imagining it to life. If you have enjoyed this story, the lifeblood of any debut writer is the review. If you can spare the time to leave me your honest opinion in support of future writing projects, I would be eternally grateful.

No doubt like most aspiring authors, I've written as a hobby my entire life, from short stories to impress my school pals, through countless false starts and scrappy bits of paper in folders, to now completing a universe-encompassing science-fiction behemoth.

Born and brought-up in Manchester, UK, I was raised on a diet of Arthur C. Clarke, Philip K. Dick, William Gibson, Tolkien (who wasn't!), and Frank Herbert. I've enjoyed a long career in the television industry, but always nurtured my storytelling desires – exercising my imagination with books and movies of every genre and artistry, feeding that mental muscle with the protein of the *tale*.

I'd like to thank family & friends for their support over the years, with special thanks to my parents, and my wife Jo, and our constant four-legged, curly-tailed, companion - little Finn.

R.T. Leader

Printed in Great Britain
by Amazon